Children and Others

Books by James Gould Cozzens

S.S. SAN PEDRO
1931

THE LAST ADAM
1933

CASTAWAY
1934

MEN AND BRETHREN
1936

ASK ME TOMORROW
1940

THE JUST AND THE UNJUST
1942

GUARD OF HONOR
1948

BY LOVE POSSESSED
1957

CHILDREN AND OTHERS
1964

James Gould Cozzens

CHILDREN AND OTHERS

HARCOURT, BRACE & WORLD, INC., NEW YORK

Library of Congress Catalog Card Number: 64-22665

LITHOGRAPHED IN THE UNITED STATES OF AMERICA
BY MAHONY & ROESE INC.

CONTENTS

I
Child's Play

II
Away at School

III
War Between the States

IV
Love and Kisses

V
Eyes to See

PART ONE

CHILD'S PLAY

King Midas Has Ass's Ears

The first time I ever saw Mr. Savage he was in a boat. I was very young. I could not have been more than seven: I may have been six. On the landing at Allen's I sat fishing in the shallow water for sunfish. While I fished I had been watching a boat which was rowed in a quick, powerful way ever since it put out from the landing over on the point. The rower proved to be unknown to me; but after he had stepped out on our landing and tied up he said hello, so I said hello. Then he asked me what my name was and I told him. He remained standing there, looking down at me a moment. He was a tall, loose-limbed man with a fine head of thick gray hair worn rather long. His big-featured face had a rugged, much tanned look. Sweat from his vigorous rowing still shone on his forehead. I saw that he was eying the three or four small fish lying dead or dying beside me on the planks. In an offhand way he said, "What are you going to do with those, John?"

"Oh, nothing," I answered, for there is nothing to do with sunfish.

"Well," he said, "why not just leave them in the lake, then?"

I stared up at him, dumfounded; but he said no more. He simply smiled cordially and walked on along the landing.

How good a composer Mr. Savage was I shall never really know. Today he seems to be little heard of or regarded; yet I can remember a time when people with pretensions to musical taste were apt to have something by Frederick Savage on the piano rack. It was the kind of music with no picture on the cover, but only some ornamental words like "In the Pine Woods," or "Lake Waters," or "To a Scarlet Tanager"; and underneath, in fancy letters, his name. Unfortunately I can hardly tell one note from another; so I know all this not because I was ever interested in music. I know it because—as I got older—eight or nine, that is—whenever I found myself in a room with a piano I looked for compositions by Mr. Savage. If I discovered any, I generally managed to remark that I knew the composer. I daresay I hoped to give the impression that Mr. Savage and I were intimate friends.

This was not quite the case. Mr. Savage had a lodge or large bungalow—it was his own, not one of Allen's—on the point. He called it, perhaps a little too appropriately, "Singing Pines." During the summer, musicians came to visit him there; and when this happened he would invite a few people from Allen's over in the evening. Once or twice I was allowed to stay up and come too. The almost painful silence in which everyone sat, hushed and reverent, while some usually odd-looking and often funny-acting person performed a long time on a piano or violin, or sang in a deafening chesty voice, impressed me a great deal. Afterward, walking home through the dark pines, my mother would tell me that I ought always to remember the occasion, for I had had the privilege of hearing so-and-so, or so-and-so, in private recital.

I remember perfectly the long low-lighted room with the polished piano. On the walls, covered with some kind of grass matting, were many frail, postured Japanese pictures. I can still see the intent listeners—my father motionless with a severe expression of patient interest; Laura Willis's aunt, old Mrs. Beazley, with closed eyes and wrinkled, be-ringed hands resting on the head of her ebony cane; Laura herself, sitting beside my mother, for whom she felt, I think, one of those sentimental schoolgirl attachments. In a rapt, pretty, perhaps slightly absurd way, Laura used to copy quickly my mother's aesthetic reactions. I remember, too, details of the walk back with lanterns through the deep, still, Maine night; but, alas, I have forgotten the artists' famous names, and of what they played or sang, I recall only that it was very tiresome.

At Allen's in those days everything was simple. You did your washing in a basin, and if you wanted more water than the pitcherful brought by the maid who appeared in the morning to clean up the bungalows you went and got it yourself. If the evening was cold and you wanted more logs than the wood basket held, you went and got these. People did these things cheerfully. They often observed what a pleasure it was not to have a lot of fuss and servants underfoot. For meals, the guests walked up from the pine grove by the lake across long meadows to the farmhouse, which had a screened and awninged dining room built on in the form of a wing. When it rained this was not very pleasant, but nobody said so. Instead they exclaimed over the excellence of the simple food. They also told each other what a nice person Mr. Allen was; and, in effect, how nice they were themselves, since the very simplicity of Allen's was said to have little attraction for undesirable people—even in the after-all-unthinkable event that Mr. Allen would ever consent to receive any.

There was not a great deal to do. There were no parties and no dancing. I don't remember seeing cards played. Though everybody knew everybody else and spoke cordially on meeting, people were intimate with only a few of their fellow guests—those they had always known at home, or those they had seen for many seasons at Allen's, and so come imperceptibly to regard as acquaintances of long standing. Most of the men, like my father, were not able to get away for the whole summer. As soon as they arrived they put on old clothes and went out and fished all day for bass; or, rowed by a guide, trolled for pickerel. Sometimes there were small picnics on an island in the lake. In the morning my mother usually took the pillow cover—afterward to be filled with dried pine needles—which she was preparing, or some embroidery, called in either case her "work," and went to sit with Mrs. Beazley, whose lameness made it hard for her to get around. I can see now that it was very prim, though in a cheerful way; and, even then, old-fashioned, like something in a book by Frank L. Stockton, or a drawing of vacation days by one of the illustrators of the *Century Magazine.*

I was not bored. There were a few other children to play with; but I had an only child's advantage of not needing playmates. In those days all the mornings were fine. By Allen's landing, the flat-bottomed boats, tied in a row, bumped and jostled each other on brisk little waves. Wind blew cool and strong off the water, up through profound shadows under the pines. Many mornings, when my mother was ready to go over to Mrs. Beazley's, I went with her, in order, as I put it, to help Laura. At the time I found nothing surprising in Laura being always there for me to help. Very likely Laura herself found it natural; but today not many attractive girls of eighteen would put up with a summer at Allen's. For entertainment, Laura could cut out and stitch together patterns of birch bark, provided in the *American Girl's Handy Book,* to make all sorts of useless little receptacles. She could collect ferns and flowers to be pressed and mounted, or she could hunt for birds. For company she had an elderly aunt, and me, a nine-year-old boy.

Laura and I would pass the time until noon. Sparkling light, now poured down vertical, broke up the shadows under the pines. Beyond the white birch trunks the cool lake spread miles away to vague forested shores. At a snail's pace, because of Mrs. Beazley, we walked to the farmhouse for luncheon. The buckboard would be just arriving with the mail. Mr. Allen, a stout, fair-haired, easygoing man, distributed it. He was fond of teasing Laura. "Miss Laura Willis," he would read. "Two, three, four —" he counted, as though appalled, the envelopes addressed to her. Laura would protest that they were just friends, but Mr. Allen insisted that the writers were all young men. "Good gracious!" he would cry, "what are the other girls going to do for beaux?"

Since some of the letters doubtless were from young men, Laura's pretty, naturally warm-colored face turned a remarkable scarlet. "John's my only beau," she would say as firmly as she could. "Aren't you, John?"

I used to think of bow, as in bow and arrow; and of bow, as in a hair ribbon or bowknot, secretly at loss; but it was plain that Laura wanted me to say yes, so I said it. "Well, you look out she doesn't jilt you," Mr. Allen would whisper to me. "She's an awful flirt."

"Why, Mr. Allen—" Laura would wail, thrown into utter, though not entirely unhappy, confusion. "Oh, aren't you terrible! I am not! Am I, John?"

I would say no.

I was, in fact, Laura's only beau; or, at least, the only one right there and able, whenever I had the notion, to monopolize her. I think of those spacious days stretching out breezy and bright, an hour as long as a morning, a morning longer than a week; and it occurs to me that Laura may have found the mornings long, too. When we had eaten, the leisurely afternoon remained. Laura and my mother sometimes walked in the woods. Many afternoons we would go bathing at a curve of coarsely pebbled beach, strewn with sodden black bits of bark and driftwood and an occasional dead perch. Eventually there would be supper. Afterward I often ran out under the summer sunset to get the mallets, so that Laura could play croquet with me on the lawn up by the flagpole. Gradually the delicate clear dusk became night. Walking to the lake you heard whippoorwills in the woods; and, sometimes, far out on the starlit peaceful water, a loon. Everybody went to bed early.

That particular morning I had been hanging around the wagon house after breakfast watching a hired man, named John, too, trying to give a horse named Marmaduke a pill. The pill was about as big as a baseball and obviously I could not leave until I found out whether Marmaduke would finally swallow it, or whether he would bite off the bare arm which this John kept shoving practically to the elbow between his jaws. Marmaduke eventually did take his medicine and was turned out in a field. Well satisfied, I started down toward the lake, and this was how I happened, from the rise behind, to see Laura walking alone on the path along the shore. She had her field glasses slung over her shoulder and I guessed at once that she was looking for birds. The best place for them was

over in a part of the woods beyond the point; and I felt sure that
she was going there. Turning, I took, pell-mell, a short cut with
which I was familiar across some upper meadows. I arrived at
what was called the glen much before she could. There I waited in
the moving shadow and sun of the birch thicket, sitting on a stump.
I got my breath. I waited a long while, idly absorbed in picking the
scab from some healed scratches on my bare leg. Finally, aware of
time passing, I had to realize that my guess was wrong. If I wanted
to find Laura, I would have to start looking.

The path from the glen went curving through the trees down to
the lake where there was an inlet over which had been built an
unnecessary rustic bridge. You came on the bridge suddenly; and,
deep perhaps in some fantasy of Marmaduke and pills, I continued
a step or two toward it before I noticed Mr. Savage standing by the
rail. He had his back to me. He was wearing white duck trousers
and a white shirt open on his tanned neck. His bushy gray head
was bent a little. I pulled up short, staring; for, holding her in his
arms, he was kissing Laura.

Encountering Mr. Savage under any circumstances I would not
have been at ease. I may have retained from the first meeting on
the landing several years before vague feelings that Mr. Savage did
not admire or approve of me. Of course I saw him only infre-
quently; but when my father, who was fond of tennis, came up Mr.
Savage regularly played with him on Allen's not very good dirt
courts. Mr. Savage played with great violence and agility. What
was more, he sometimes prevailed against my father's steady,
practiced game and won. I think this was always a surprise to my
father, who, however much he respected Mr. Savage's musical
accomplishments and reputation, undoubtedly regarded with reservation a man with nothing more serious and important to do than
devote his whole life to one of the fine arts. On these occasions, if I
were around, I was set to chasing balls. Mr. Savage thanked me
pleasantly for my efforts and addressed me by name. It made me
feel shy. Though they were cordial, Mr. Savage did not call my
father Will; and my father would say, "I make that three all. Yours,

Savage." These things, I suppose, and the solemnity of those late evenings of loud boring music, all moved incoherently in my head while I stood stupefied in the path. I looked at the water. Regaining the use of my muscles, I began to scuff a sandal back and forth, kicking at the pine needles.

Mr. Savage let Laura go instantly, turning sharp around. The two of them stood, still close together, looking at me. I began then to think of the disturbance which had arisen one afternoon last winter when a boy I knew kissed a girl at dancing class. I believe he had done it on a dare, which, like the resulting row, was proof enough that kissing somebody not related to you was no light or everyday undertaking. My impulse, for now I had recovered enough to feel one, was to go away. Before I could do this Mr. Savage said, "Hello, John. Where are you bound for?"

I flushed, balancing on one foot. "I'm not going anywhere," I said finally. I looked at the field glasses in the leather case hung by a strap on his shoulder, and added at random, "Those are Laura's."

"Yes," Mr. Savage said, smiling, "I'm carrying them for her."

"Oh," I said. "Well, I guess I'll go home now."

"We're on the way to my house to have some cocoa," he said in a friendly tone. "Why don't you come along?"

I hesitated. "Oh, all right," I answered reluctantly. A little late, I realized that I was being offered something to eat, not given an order, so I flushed again and said, "Oh. Thank you."

I had not looked directly at Laura, and she had not said anything until now. "John," she said, "why didn't you tell me you wanted to look for birds? You mustn't follow people, you know—"

"I wasn't following anyone," I said, hurt. "I just saw you with the glasses—" Not yet exactly looking at her, I looked enough toward her to see in the corner of my eye the shimmer of sunlight transforming her brown hair to a kind of diffused gold. The fluffy masses of it were bound up with a narrow red ribbon. Her dark wide eyes, generally pleasant and soft, rested on me with apparent indignation. In my injured innocence I did not know what to say.

"It's a good thing you came along," Mr. Savage said. "Mandy made a lot of gingerbread and we need somebody to help eat it up. Do you like gingerbread?"

The way into Mr. Savage's place was through a rustic gate. I had never been there in full daylight before. My ideas of it were formed from the impression of a great, low-lying bulk against the dusk with wide, palely lamp-lit windows; and, later, a vast veranda gilded by the yellow lantern light, and innumerable steep steps down. The morning sun in the clearing made it look not very different from one of Allen's bungalows. Sitting near the kitchen steps was a Negro woman peeling potatoes. Mr. Savage called to her, "Mandy, make some cocoa." He brought us up onto the veranda, which looked of course like any other veranda now. "Here we are," he said. He unslung the glasses' case and put it on a wicker table. "Mustn't forget those," he said to Laura.

The wide settee hung in an iron frame swung sharply as Laura dropped down on it. "I shouldn't be here," she said in an odd, not-clear voice. "You know what people at Allen's are like."

"But you've got a very good chaperon," Mr. Savage said. He sat on the rail, his back toward the blue lake through the trees, his distinguished face and long square musician's hands very brown in contrast to his white clothes. He had an attractive expression, partly humorous, partly serious. "Well, John," he said to me, "how's the fishing these days?"

I gave him an apprehensive look. The truth was, I did not bother to fish for sunfish any more, but my reasons were not humanitarian ones. "Oh, I don't know," I said. Mr. Savage continued to gaze at me expectantly so I said, "They gave Marmaduke a pill. I was there."

"You don't say!" said Mr. Savage. "What was wrong with Marmaduke?"

"Oh, he had worms," I answered with animation. "Shall I tell you what they did to him?"

Laura had been sitting perfectly still, her hands together. She said, "John, that isn't a very pleasant subject to talk about. Come and look at this magazine. It has some funny pictures in it."

I was an obedient child. Although crestfallen I came over and sat down beside her while she took up a magazine and began to turn the pages. "You read what it says under them to me," she said. Her voice was not very steady and after a moment she put an arm around me, holding me a little tighter than I liked to be held. I read loudly and carefully. Looking up at her for acknowledgment that I was right, I saw that she was not paying attention. She stood up suddenly and walked to the end of the veranda.

"Laura!" Mr. Savage said. He jumped off the rail, moving toward her, but he stopped before he was very close. She said in an indistinct voice, not turning around, "What's the use?" She rested her shoulder against the cedar post at the corner, looking into the woods. "I'm just a silly little —"

"Laura!" repeated Mr. Savage. He might have said something more, but the Negro woman appeared then carrying a large tray. "Thank you, Mandy," Mr. Savage said at once. "Come and have some of this, Laura." He took up the china pot and began to pour.

Mr. Savage drank a cup of cocoa, and, being urged, I drank two cups and ate two pieces of gingerbread. Laura took a cup, but she did not drink much of it, and she did not eat anything. "We'd better go along," she said to Mr. Savage when it was apparent that I had finished. She got immediately to her feet, putting her hands up to the ribbon in her hair. Her movements were quick but stiff. Her wide dark eyes glinted in a curious way which made them look even wider and darker. "Good-by," she said.

Mr. Savage had taken her hand in his and now he laid the other over it. " — could thou and I with fate conspire," he said. I gave him a startled look before I realized that he must be saying poetry. He went on, grave, shaking his head a little; " — to grasp this sorry scheme of things entire, would we not shatter it to bits, and then—"

"Good-by," repeated Laura. She pulled her hand away. She walked across the veranda and down the steps. "Good-by," I said hastily. "I enjoyed myself very much, thank you."

We walked in silence through the woods for some distance. I don't think I was a particularly insensitive child, but I had a faculty

which most children have—and which I often wish I had managed
to keep—of shrugging off things which I found difficult or perplex-
ing. Thus presently I was looking about for birds, as though that
were what we had come for. I said, "There's a cedar waxwing.
Right there."

Laura stopped, but she did not look where I pointed. "John,"
she said, "you mustn't ever tell anyone that you saw us by the
bridge this morning. You won't, will you?"

"Oh, no," I stammered, for no reason I could know, discomfited
by the refreshed memory. Laura must have been dissatisfied with
so faint-sounding an assurance. "It isn't that either of us has done
anything wrong," she said, "but you see, John, people think
things—"

Poor Laura! It seems to me now that she was naïve to an incredible degree; but I daresay in a time of more artificial ideas and
manners a well-brought-up girl had little experience with men. I
am sure, as she said, that she had done nothing wrong. I am sure
she had done everything her instinct suggested to her to get Mr.
Savage to kiss her. Remembering that curiously sweet, wide-eyed
face, I am not surprised that she was successful. Having succeeded
so far, I suppose her notion of a next step was wedding bells. Mr.
Savage must have been horrified. He must have wished with all
his heart that he had restrained that impulse. Very likely no man
could describe the numerous and cruel ways in which this wish of
Mr. Savage's, becoming apparent, had wounded not yet adult
Laura. I only know that she drew an audible breath, while I stared
at her, rather frightened, for there was a look about her eyes and
a movement of her mouth which would have made me think, except
that she was grown up, that she was going to cry. "It isn't anything,"
she said. "It doesn't matter any more, John. But it has to be a
secret. You mustn't ever tell a secret."

"Oh, no," I said, much disturbed. "Oh, no."

Laura did not come to luncheon. Mrs. Beazley told my mother
that Laura had a headache and was lying down. I think I was
relieved. My faculty for shrugging things off had really been

overtaxed. The intricate, unresolvable complication of impressions, of incompletely grasped bits of conversation, of things I badly wanted to ask questions about, oppressed me. Perhaps it affected my appetite, for my mother said suddenly, "Darling, don't you feel well?"

Emerging with difficulty from the maze of my thoughts I said, "I'm all right—" I broke it off, for the probable significance of the question jarred its way home. I took my spoon to go on with the raspberries, but not quickly enough to keep my mother from saying, "You weren't eating anything this morning, were you?"

To answer no would seem the simplest thing in the world; but telling the truth is a habit like any other. It had been drilled into me so well that, until I was eleven or twelve, I could be counted on to tell it, for I did not know what else to tell. "I had some gingerbread," I admitted.

"Why, darling," my mother said, "where on earth did you get gingerbread?"

"Mr. Savage gave it to me," I answered.

Mrs. Beazley had finished her luncheon. One hand pressed down her napkin, crumpled on the table. The other had been balanced on the head of her cane. She made a slight jerking movement and the cane went clattering. "John," my mother said. I slid off the side of my chair and picked the cane up.

"Thank you," Mrs. Beazley said. She grasped the top firmly and gave the floor a couple of taps. "I thought you and Laura were hunting birds," she said. "How did you happen to stop at Mr. Savage's?"

"Oh, he asked us," I said.

"That was very nice of him," my mother said, "but I think it would be better, another time—"

Mrs. Beazley kept her small, bright black eyes fixed amiably on me. "Was anyone else there, John?" she asked.

"There was Mandy," I said.

"I mean, any people from here?"

"No," I said.

Mrs. Beazley looked at my mother. "In view of what I spoke of this morning, that comes very patly," she said. "What would you think, Hilda?"

"It would never have crossed my mind—" my mother began. Mrs. Beazley said, "She's none too sensible a girl. It's from reading this advanced rubbish at college. I never approved of it. Ibsen and Shaw and so on. Freddy Savage is all right. He comes of quite nice people. But don't ask me to believe he's interested in her intellect, because the truth is, the girl hasn't any. I don't think other forms of interest would be suitable. Freddy's old enough to be her father; and, of course, he's really still married."

My mother said, "Oh. I didn't know that. I imagined that he might be divorced." Her constraint in mentioning the subject was not uncommon in those days.

"I can tell you that it wasn't altogether his fault," Mrs. Beazley said. "But Freddy always has been just a little bit Bohemian. I don't want any kissing in corners. We'll nip that in the bud, even if I have to pack the girl off."

At the phrase "kissing in corners" my mother colored somewhat, but she said earnestly, "I'm sure of this. People who plan to meet each other don't bring children along. Laura may be rather taken by him. It wouldn't be unnatural at her age. But I'm perfectly certain there's nothing to worry about. I know I'd trust Laura."

There was a moment's pause. I had been pleased to have the conversation move away from the subject of eating between meals, yet I think I was not altogether pleased to be dropped suddenly from the center of the stage when I was so well qualified to occupy it. I felt neglected. "We're through, aren't we?" I asked my mother.

"Don't interrupt, dear," she said; but both she and Mrs. Beazley turned as though surprised to see me still there. "Little pitchers have big ears," Mrs. Beazley said. Getting with trouble to her feet, she gave my ear a light rap with her knuckles. We went out together, across the lawn and down the meadow, waiting on, though affecting not to notice, Mrs. Beazley's laborious movement. We were about halfway to the lake when we saw Laura walking up the path toward us.

Laura's pace was listless and her manner woebegone; but, meeting us, she smiled faintly at my mother. "I thought I'd see if I could get some tea," she said.

Mrs. Beazley had come to a halt, leaning heavily on her cane. She gazed at Laura with close attention. She said abruptly, as Laura was about to go by, "I'd be much interested to know why you called on Freddy Savage this morning."

The remark stopped Laura in her tracks. The color left her face. She looked, dazed, at her aunt; and then she looked at me. "Well," said Mrs. Beazley briskly, "is there some reason why John should make a secret of it? It seems a very simple matter."

However great her shock had been, Laura must have seen from the form of the question that I had admitted nothing very damaging. She put a hand to her forehead and said wearily, but with sufficient assurance, "I'm sorry, Aunt Edith. I don't feel very well. Of course there isn't any reason. Do you mind if I go along now?"

"Go along," said Mrs. Beazley, "but don't be pert, my child."

I said, "I'll go too."

"No, dear," my mother said. "Laura has a headache. You mustn't be a nuisance."

"I wouldn't be a nuisance—" I began, but my mother was not inclined to argue. We continued on toward the lake. Mrs. Beazley was silent for a few moments. Then she said, "I'd really give a good deal to get to the bottom of this. A little bird tells me there's more to it than meets the eye."

When we were alone on the veranda of our bungalow my mother took up the hoops which held her embroidery with a preoccupied air. Mrs. Beazley's remarkable statement about the little bird still held my interest. "What was she talking about?" I asked.

"Darling, that's not polite," my mother said. "When you're speaking about a lady, say Mrs. Beazley, not 'she.' What we discussed wasn't intended for you. It isn't anything you'd understand."

"Tell me," I said. "I might."

"Well, dear, I don't think you would. And if there is anything you did hear—"

"I heard about Mr. Savage," I said.

"John—" my mother spoke very seriously "—if you did, I want you to be particularly careful never to repeat it. Not to anyone, anywhere."

"Why, what did she—Mrs. Beazley say?" I asked. I did not mean that I hadn't heard. I was accustomed to adult conversation and I could usually follow the words well enough; but I did not always grasp the sense in a way to satisfy me.

"I've just said that it was no concern of yours, dear. Now, if you don't remember—"

"Oh, I remember," I said eagerly. "It was, he was really married." Never having seen any Mrs. Savage, I paused, a little dubious, and was moved to give another example. "And he was kissing people," I said.

"John!" my mother exclaimed. She almost dropped the embroidery in her lap. "Don't think of saying such a thing! That's ridiculous, and Mrs. Beazley said nothing of the sort! Get any such silly notion out of your mind at once."

"But, she did," I insisted. "She said kissing in corners."

My mother said, "I've spoken to you before about contradicting, John. I don't want to have to speak about it again. That was simply a phrase Mrs. Beazley was using. It had no reference to Mr. Savage. Now, just forget all this foolishness. Go out and play."

"But—" I said.

"John!" said my mother.

I closed my mouth. A suffocating, if not very well warranted, sense of injustice swelled up in me so that I could not have spoken even if I had thought it advisable to. I went dragging down the steps and, slowly, toward the water. Once or twice I looked back, but my mother was busy sewing. After a while I wandered along the shore to a spot where I had what I considered a harbor. In it were four or five small planks, pointed at the ends. The hired man named John, no doubt adept at putting off work, had kindly nailed on them bits of wood, representing superstructure and funnels, to make them into steamers. As a rule I happily occupied myself for hours maneuvering this shipping in wrecks, battles, and voyages to here or there. That afternoon I could not seem to think of any very interesting trips or catastrophes. For a few minutes I watched the boats rock and roll as the onshore wind blew the little waves at them. I turned away then and wandered back to the landing where, sunk nearby, was a large box covered with wire netting in which were kept a great many small frogs used for bait. I peered in at them for a while. After that I went up to the bungalow. Though I had no particular plan, I must have appeared on the steps with an important air, for my mother, looking up, said, "Well, darling, what is it?"

"Oh, nothing," I answered. I sat down on the top step with my back against the post. My mother acted very much as though she were taking my statement at face value, so I was driven to say, "Well, it's not all foolishness."

"Darling, what are you talking about?" my mother asked.

"I mean, what Mrs. Beazley said," I answered.

"John," my mother said, "I don't want to hear any more of that. I thought I made it clear."

"You said it was a silly notion," I reminded her.

"John!"

Though that tone of hers was always good to give me pause, I had not lost my resentful feeling of being somehow ill used and put upon; at once, held too lightly and unjustly rebuked. "All right," I muttered. "But I know."

My mother, though as I have indicated a competent disciplinarian, also kept up with the times and was not uninfluenced by those then new findings in "child psychology," particularly about a child's supposed need of and right to self-expression. She must have been sorely tried, but imposing patience on herself she said, "John, what *is* this silly mystery? If there's anything you want to tell me, you may. If it's something you don't understand, I'll try to explain it to you if I can."

"Well," I said. I squirmed a little against the post. "Well, what do Laura and Mr. Savage kiss each other for?"

My mother lowered her "work" to her lap. She said, "John, look at me. That isn't something you're just saying?"

I looked at her. "I saw them," I said. "It was before they knew I
was there—" I had an abrupt recollection of that fuss in dancing
class; an instant's misgiving of second thoughts; but after all Laura
and Mr. Savage were not members of any dancing class, nor
conceivably subject to Mr. Mirabelli who conducted it. Recovering confidence, I said, "If you don't believe me—"

My mother took up her "work" again. In an unconcerned tone I
found still more reassuring, she said, "You've told me all you need
to, John. I believe you. It's nothing you have to worry about.
You'll understand when you get older. Now, I think you'd better
go and play."

My relief in being disburdened, rid of the secret I had found so
heavy, was, I'm sure, great enough to keep me from noticing that
my mother couldn't be said to have "explained" much; and even to
content me with that "when you get older" which under other
circumstances often discontented me. The afternoon had now
become like any other afternoon, so I have no exact recollection of
it. Doubtless I did go and play something with some of the other
children. When I came back to wash before supper my mother
took natural care that no mention of Laura was made; and the
out-of-sight-out-of-mind rule that governs most of a child's thinking
could keep me quite incurious. Even if I didn't see Laura at supper
(and I'm sure I didn't) I would be able to think nothing of it. Supper
at Allen's—at noon, what we ate was luncheon, but the term
"dinner," I suppose because it had undesirable overtones of dressing and formality, was avoided—used to be served from six until
almost eight. The reason was that people out fishing during the
afternoon generally brought up their catch. The kitchen, though
expecting them to, couldn't manage all at once what, many
evenings, might amount to a couple of dozen separate dishes.
Finding half the tables empty when you entered the dining room
was never a surprise; and often you'd be through before those who
would come later appeared.

The next morning I know I went to breakfast all unconcerned, to
eat with my usual appetite. Before I had finished I heard a sound of
horses coming down from the barn and the buckboard's creak and

rattle; but this did no more than remind me that I had Marmaduke to see about. John, the hired man, plainly in no hurry to get back to work, stood near the steps of the long porch when I came out. He was chewing, ruminative, on a stalk of timothy grass and gazing after the buckboard, which was all the way down the long lane, turning into the road.

To bring conversation around to horses and Marmaduke, I asked where the buckboard was going.

"Take Miss Willis to the station," he said.

I looked at him, stunned. "Laura?" I said.

"She had to go home."

Laura said the word. You mustn't ever tell a secret. No, never; not to anyone, for any reason. Even if you confide it to the unspeaking ground, reeds will grow and the wind will rustle them. I stood a moment, speechless. Then I began to run. I ran as hard as I could down the lawn. I clambered over the low rock wall and pounded away up the road. The buckboard, moving in a light haze of dust, had that fairly long start on me; but I ran frantically and for a moment I seemed to be gaining on it. I began to call, "Laura, Laura . . ." but I think I did not call very loud; for if she heard me, if the buckboard stopped, what could I find to say? The buckboard did not stop; and soon, instead of my gaining on it, it was getting farther and farther ahead. I called once or twice more; but by then nobody could possibly have heard me and nobody looked back. At last, with bursting chest, aching legs and a stitch in my side, I came to a halt. I stood in the soft dust of the road, panting. The buckboard, rounding a bend, was now out of sight. After a while I turned around and made my way back to Allen's.

Child's Play

"Why," my father said, "he's nothing but a chump!" His tone made me start. Usually, when he employed it, he was speaking to me. I looked at him apprehensively and I could see his short dark mustache drawing down in displeasure, his strong compact body stiffening in indignation. Yet he spoke without choler. As far as I know, he never in his life lost his temper. What his voice held was a dry disgusted quality. He suffered fools, not, perhaps, gladly, but with an air of experienced resignation.

My mother murmured, "Oh, Will, I don't think you ought to say that." She still held, in a distracted manner, the numerous sheets of the letter which he had tossed into her lap when he made his amazing appearance. It was only an hour or so after luncheon and I could hardly believe my eyes when I looked up — my mother had been reading aloud to me from a book called *The Wind in the Willows* — and saw him coming down the garden.

Frowning, bristling more, he said, "Read on! Read on! It's incredible. Father never had any more business sense than a child. Gentlemen's agreement! With a fellow like Ames! Of course, he's a chump. Have you come to what he did about the bonds?"

"Well, it doesn't seem quite clear," my mother said doubtfully.

"It isn't clear to him," said my father, "because he's simply incapable of thinking a thing through to its logical conclusion. It's clear to everyone else."

"Oh, Will! He was probably so upset! Think how you'd feel if you had to write to a son of yours and — "

My father gave me a brief appraising glance. "Well," he said, dismissing me, "in short, I'll have to go. I'll have to see what I can do." My mother nodded. She put the letter back in its envelope. "I'll just throw a few things in a grip," said my father. "I want to take John with me, so we'll have to get him packed too."

My mother must have been astonished as I was. "Will!" she protested. "Oh, I don't think— He has an appointment with Doctor Stiles tomorrow. And if we're going away, all that shopping! How can he go, Will?"

"Yes!" I cried at once. "I want to go! I want to go!" I was moved less by any pleasant recollection of things which I associated with the term "grandfather's"—most of them had come from snapshots: Groups picnicking on gray seaside rocks; a picture of me, as a baby in a white dress, being held up on a horse. Across the back of the print had been written: "Little John on Queenie"— than by the momentarily forgotten matter of the dentist. That had been hanging over me for a week, and my feeling about it couldn't have been very different if it had been my execution which was arranged with Doctor Stiles for eleven o'clock Wednesday.

My father considered me with a certain disfavor. Anxiety to avoid or put off doing what it was right and necessary to do was not a thing he could approve of. "I'm afraid it will have to be postponed," he said shortly. "I don't expect to be gone more than a day or two. I particularly want to take John. It's a long while since they've seen him, and—"

I can understand now what my father's real intention was. Like many men of stern nature, he showed a recurring impulse to kindness. He was severe without compunction; yet, when he could, he would often put himself to a surprising amount of trouble to do small things which he thought might make sufferers from his severity feel better. Since she said no more, I suppose my mother realized that he was doing one of them then; and, in sober truth, taking me with him on such a trip was no trifling matter. That impulse to kindness which made him face the ordeal must have been deep and strong.

. . .

For one thing, I asked questions. As much as the questions I
asked, the way I asked them must have tried my father. Trotting
along beside him, often not looking where I was going, I would
find my idle facile curiosity constantly being stirred. "Well,
why—" I would begin, as likely as not reaching and giving my
father's arm a commanding tug. "But why? But why?" I think
my mother was able to mistake this maddening habit for the
intelligent interest of a mind naturally alert and inquiring, but
every time my father saw my mouth open, he must have groaned
inwardly.

He did what he could. At moments when we were hurrying not
to miss the ferry or to get on a trolley car, he was apt to call
the question a silly one and let it go at that. When we had more
time, he girded himself with an elaborate, though not harsh or
sarcastic, patience. He would tell me that I must use my head;
that I must learn to think things out; that I was a big boy, practically eight years old, and that it ought to be what he was fond of
calling child's play for me to understand and deal sensibly with
simple everyday things.

As soon as I realized what I had let myself in for, I would start to
fidget, wishing desperately to drop the whole business. However, I
learned nothing from experience. It never took me ten minutes to
forget all the torments of being taught to think, and, idly, I would
invite them again with some needless new inquiry. Thus, though
we had hardly finished an interminable discussion of what made
the steamer go—it included a trip down to look through a hole at
the paddle wheels, which I did not mind, but it also included a lot
about a boy named James Watt and some kettle or other—I took
the first pause during supper to ask, my mouth not quite empty,
"But why do we go on this boat to Grandfather's?"

I did not particularly wonder or want to know. In fact, while I
spoke I was noticing that the Negro waiter's hands, though black
as coal on the backs, were very much lighter on the palms. Pausing
to swallow, I lost my chance to ask why this was, for my father had
taken out a pencil. Turning over the large printed menu, he began
to sketch, with the quick graphic knack he had, a map of the coast,

showing where the boat started, and where we went during the night, and where the train went from there.

Long before he was done, I had forgotten not merely my first question, but even the more interesting matter of the waiter's hands, and was anxious only to get the pencil from him and have a try at making some maps too. "All right," he said. He gave me the other menu card. "Now you draw it without looking at this."

However, I preferred to draw an island with a few flags on it and some gigantic toothy fish cruising offshore. He watched me for a while, disapproving and, I suppose, disappointed, for he must have been always hoping that just once, somehow, in some way, I would show some aptitude or sign of intelligence. We went up on the deck then and sat out under the evening sky in the stiff sea breeze. Shortly before it got dark the man called Otis, or Mr. Bogert, came along. When he saw us he stopped short and exclaimed, "Hello, Will! How are you?" He seated himself on the bench and began at once to talk, saying, "Well, I'm mighty glad you're coming down at last. I was going to write you myself. I can't tell you how worried—" He gave his soft auburn mustache a pull, looked at me with a smiling show of even white teeth and told me about his little girl, named Judith. Then he gave me the pictures from two boxes of cigarettes he had in his pocket. "Will," he said, "this is providential. There are a number of things I think you ought to know."

Long after I had been sent to bed I could hear my father's voice and Mr. Bogert's, and smell the strong drift of smoke from Mr. Bogert's cigar. At my insistence they had moved up to the top deck and were seated by the rail in the recess between the lifeboat ends, outside our stateroom window. Though my father had said only, "You see who runs our household, Otis," I could tell by his expression that my show of timidity displeased him. As well as sensible, I suppose he would have liked me to be brave and manly. Mr. Bogert laughed and said, "Will, you're just a Spartan."

The only Spartan I had ever heard of was a youth who had a fox under his cloak who ate him, and this frightening story was not exactly restful. Though I had fallen asleep before my father came in to go to bed, during the night I awoke often. I would give a start, my eyes opening in alarm as I struggled to remember where I was. The partial dark—for yellow light from the passage came through the ventilating slats above the door—was full of furtive movement and groaning noises. Sharp prolonged creaks sounded. Under me the berth would take a slight slow tilt, then very gradually swing back level. There were intermittent bumpings and throbbings; and, now stronger, now fainter, but never stopping, the wall beside me trembled to a quick tramp-tramp. Hearing that sound made me see again, as I had through the peephole before supper, the mighty paddle wheels going over and over. Immense iron spokes were coming up with a cascade of water which poured off thunderous in the electric-lighted housing. They stood erect and with no pause walked on down into a smother of foam and spray. Their size and the force of their movement agitated me and I would lie tense in drowsy anxiety.

Then I would hear the sound of my father breathing in the other berth. Once I had made sure that it was he and not (my heart took a jump and seemed to fall down leagues in my hollow chest) a strange man, or a fox, I regained some composure. Through the gap left by the partly lowered shutter of the window I saw the bright, still, pattern of stars. A dim glow fell along the white bow of the lifeboat hanging in its davit and I could spell out black letters forming the small words: PRISCILLA   FALL RIVER. Perhaps the whistle, deep, hoarse, making the whole stateroom vibrate, would break out. Perhaps there would be a few unexplained loud foot-steps somewhere above, and I would drift off, dreaming in a disturbed way of Mr. Bogert giving me packs, hundreds, of ciga-rette pictures, none of which I already had, while I tried not to notice that the white teeth under his soft mustaches were like that fox's.

It had been foggy when we came off the boat in the morning, but while we were on the train, pounding and swaying around curves, past farms and houses by the water with little piers and sheds, the sun began to come out. Beyond the rocky points of land I could

soon see the water turn from gray-green to blue. When we got off
the train the sky was perfectly clear, fine and hot. I let myself drop
from the high step onto the platform. My father put down our bags
and said to me, "Well, there's your grandfather."

I looked doubtfully at an old man, just in the act of stepping from
a cab. He was dressed in a loose suit of white material. Though I
know I must have seen him within a year or so, I would have said
I'd never seen him before. As soon as he saw us, he held up a
gold-headed cane and waved it. Then he took off his straw hat and
waved that, too, moving quickly along the platform. His head was
bald. He had bushy, partly brown, partly gray eyebrows and a
thick mustache, mostly white.

"Will, my boy," he cried in a gruff, hoarse voice, out of breath.
"Welcome home! Welcome home!"

Since home was what we had yesterday left, the term seemed to
me a strange one. I opened my mouth and then closed it again, for
he had turned and put his arms around me, cane, hat, and all—
"Well, well, little Johnny—" Plainly he had meant to lift me up,
and, I suppose, kiss me. He must have found that I was too heavy
for him, so he just gave me an awkward squeeze. I was scarlet with
shyness and discomfort, afraid he would expect me to say
something; but, letting me go, he turned to my father. "Dear boy,"
he said, still winded, "come along! Come along! I have a cab here.
The man will take your bags." His face had grown very red and
shining. My father said, "Now, now. You leave it to me. It's too
hot a day for—"

"Pooh!" my grandfather said, "why, today's a fine day! Your
mother was going to come down, too; but I told her—"

My father had shot a glance at the man who was taking the bags,
and then at the cab beyond the platform. Seeing its direction, my
grandfather paused. He gave a little cough and said, "I let Patrick
go, my boy. I'm not keeping horses. We have so little use for them.
Just eating their heads off—"

My father looked at him a moment and said, "How is Mother?"

He answered quickly, "Very well, I'm glad to say. Very well

indeed. We're all well. We ought to count our blessings. I was talking to Tom Bogert only yesterday and he said to me, 'Henry—'"

My father said, "We happened to run into Otis on the boat. He had to go up to Boston, but he'll be down tonight."

My grandfather put his hat on in an aimless, agitated way and fumbled with his cane. "Well, Otis is an opinionated boy," he said. "Very clever lawyer, I grant. But he doesn't know everything. He doesn't take into consideration—well, all that can wait. I'm sorry Hilda wasn't able to come. Another time, perhaps."

We were in the stuffy dark cab and the horses had begun to move. In the shadow, my grandfather's face, still red around the white mustache, had a heavy subdued look. My father said, "I thought she'd better not. It was short notice, and it's a tiring trip—"

My grandfather said, "I know, my boy. I know—" The stuffy silence lasted a minute or two. Then my father remarked, "Why, I see they're tearing the old Maynard house down."

"Yes," said my grandfather, "yes. The truth is, the city put it up for taxes. It was really shameful. Paul was very hard hit." He gave a loud sigh, looking at the top of his cane. "Will, if I'd known where to turn to get—"

"Well, I'm glad you didn't," my father said. "I'm sorry for the Maynards, but Mr. Maynard has been making his bed for a good many years. Now I'm afraid he'll have to lie in it."

"That's what you say," my grandfather said, "but it isn't what you'd do."

My father said, "I think a man should help his friends as far as he's able to. But I'd make sure I was able to. I couldn't see my way clear to robbing Peter to pay Paul—" He gave a short laugh. "No pun intended," he said, and we sat in silence until my grandfather, drawing a breath, broke out hoarsely, "Well, Johnny, did you bring your bathing suit? If it's a nice day, we'll all go to the beach tomorrow."

I still felt too shy to say anything, but again I did not need to, for my grandfather had put his head out the window. "Almost there,"

he said, pulling it in again. "Your mother will be tickled to
death—" He coughed and gave my father's arm a couple of pats.
"My boy," he said, "I haven't gone into detail with her much. She
hasn't any head for business, you know. I never like to worry her."

"Good," said my father. "Just say nothing to her about it. Since
I've talked to Otis, I'll go down and see Ames this afternoon:
and then we'll know where we stand. I think you'd better leave
it all to me."

"I suppose I'd better," said my grandfather, "I suppose I'd
better."

He said, "Clara, my love, Johnny and I will take a walk. You
mustn't miss your nap."

From a glass jar full of various colored pieces which she held in
her lap, my grandmother selected a bit of rock candy. She popped
it into my mouth. Her small, wonderfully wrinkled face beamed on
me, eyes bright and inquiring. "Would you like to take a walk with
Grandfather?" she asked.

She was voluminously clad—up to her chin; her wrists hidden by
bunched flounces—in rustling lavender silk. I had been sitting with
her on the sofa ever since my father had gone out after luncheon.
Perched there beside me, she did not seem a great deal taller than I
was. This gave me a certain feeling of intimacy, and I was gratified
by the candy, which was rarely offered to me—and never more
than one piece—at home; but the fact that my grandmother was
rather deaf kept me shy. If I ventured to say anything she would
put a puffed-up lavender silk sleeve around me, the thin little arm
inside it drawing me near. Then she bent her head with its rolled
mound of white hair close to mine, showing me a very small ear
with a pearl on the lobe. "Or would you like to take a little nap,
too?" she asked. That decided me, for though I was not very
enthusiastic about being alone with anyone as strange to me as my
grandfather, a nap at my age seemed an indignity.

My grandfather went through the hall to the dining room and
through that to the pantry door. I could hear him push it open, and
his voice saying, "—not a sound, now!" When he came back, he

had my hat and his, and his cane, and a big shawl. The shawl he put
over my grandmother's feet on the couch. He patted her hand and
kissed her. She looked past him to me and said, "My little John!
Kiss your old grandmother!" I did this, and we went out, down the
steps into the sun, and along the warm tree-shadowed street.

Unlike my father, who frequently walked so fast that it was hard
to keep up with him, my grandfather walked very slowly. Holding
my hand, looking about him in a brooding, vacant way, he loitered
along the sidewalk. When we came at last to the beginning of an
irregular oblong square, he stopped as though surprised to see
where he was. Then he said to me, "Old State House."

It was a rather high and narrow building, not very large. It was
whitish-gray with brown trimmings and had a squat little win-
dowed cupola on it. Some big trees crowded it in with a damp and
melancholy shade. I saw nothing attractive about it, but my grandfather straightened his shoulders. In an altered, more vigorous
voice, he said, "It ought to have a special interest for you, Johnny.
When he was governor, your great-grandfather went to his office
there. Would you like to see that?"

I had been busy with a wishful reverie centering around coming
to a store where they sold ice cream. I hung back a little and my
grandfather relieved me by saying, "We'll look at that another
time. In those days the state had two capitals. Then they gave this
one up. Do you know what the capital is now?"

The question disconcerted me, but his hoarse voice had an
easygoing quality, not like the clear exactness of my father's
questions. Besides, it was something that I thought I might know,
and I took a chance. "Boston," I said.

"My, my," he chuckled, "you must study geography! Boston is
in Massachusetts."

Though I had hoped that Boston would be right, his tone and
manner did not cause me any special chagrin. His gaze remained
indulgent and, looking up at him, I thought I might risk some direct
mention of ice cream. I began, "Grandfather, do they have any
stores here where — "

At this moment, a very fat man — old, too — appeared in front of us and started to talk in a loud voice. While my grandfather shook hands with him, he said, "Henry, I was coming to see you. . . . Why, hello, who's this?" He peered down his chest and over his vast stomach at me.

My grandfather gave me a proprietary pat. "Will's boy," he said. "Johnny, say how do do to Judge Burnham."

Uncovering a thick tangle of stiff white hair, the fat old man lifted off his hat and fanned his face with it. "Good gracious!" he roared. "Why, I thought he was a babe in arms! Why, he's a little man! . . . How old are you, Johnny?"

Appalled by his size, and his roaring and snorting, I told him faintly. "Well, that's splendid," he said, but the information did not seem to interest him much, for he took hold of my grandfather's arm, going on in the urgent voice in which he had begun — some kind of complicated expostulation. "Nobody tells me anything!" he would roar. "Now, Jeremy," my grandfather would say hoarsely, "you know I'd have come to you if — " They had both got very red, as though they were angry, but I soon saw this was not the case. "Well, Will's a good boy," the fat man puffed finally. "Will's a good boy. All right, Henry; just so you let me know if — " They lifted their hands and slowly, blowing a little, their red faces shining, they drifted apart.

My grandfather and I moved on, up a narrow street with many stores, reviving my hopes about ice cream. He had grasped my hand again. I attempted once or twice to release it, but he gave it a squeeze and held it all the tighter. "Right here," he said to me suddenly, "is where we lived when I was a boy."

I looked away from him, taken aback, for at the words "when I was a boy" I seemed to see a kind of red-faced dwarf or gnome with a thick white drooping mustache. The big bumpy-knuckled, brown-spotted hands protruded from the sleeves of a child's blouse. He wore short trousers, and his knees were bare, but on his feet were enormous elastic-sided black shoes and he had his gold-headed cane.

"In there?" I asked, swallowing. I stood, incredulous, gaping at the office of a coal company and the gate to the team yard beside it.

"The old house was right here," he said. We moved down the
hot open space with trampled cinders and spilled coal underfoot.
"Part of that building there," he said, lifting his stick at a cavernous, rusty-roofed shed with some coal wagons standing under it,
"is made out of the old stable." He moved on. "This was all lawn,"
he said, indicating the dreary waste before him. "There were big
trees there. It went down to the bay." He walked slowly and
heavily in that direction until we stood at last by the splintered
bulkhead, looking over the flat opaque green water with floating
rubbish in it, and the short pier where a barge, dark with coal dust,
was moored. "My grandfather was alive then," he said. "Your
great-great-grandfather. Think of that, Johnny."

It confused me, and I began to tug at him, hoping that we would
turn now and go. He stood immovable. "A long time," he said.
"Doesn't seem so very long. He was an old man. Older than I am.
But when he called, we jumped. We did, indeed! He was a lot like
Will. No nonsense to him." He gave a puffing sigh. "A long, long
time," he said again. "Your Great-uncle Johnny you were named
for used to have a little boat we'd go sailing in. I can remember
coming in across the bay there in the afternoon. We could see them
sitting on the lawn, and they'd wave at us."

In a way, I, too, could see a stretch of grass with people, strange
and formless, grouped on it; the boat on the water, the white sail,
the long yellow afternoon light; but it was all sad and old. In my
picture, the coalbins were there, too, standing on the lawn, and I
could see my grandfather, the aged mustached little boy, waving
and grimacing as he sailed by. His hoarse bemused voice weighed
on me. The sun shone in my eyes. The air seemed choking with the
smell of dust and coal. I decided unreasonably that we were lost,
that we would never find our way back to the house uptown. To
my own surprise, I began to cry.

My grandfather peered down at me, and, my face crumpling with
the effort, I tried to stop, for I expected him to be annoyed or
impatient. "Why, Johnny," he said. "Why, what's the matter?"

I could find no words for the sadness that his old voice and this
dejected coalyard made me feel; nor for the way in which the

things he said he remembered became something I shared, as though he and I had it in common—the sense of the long-ago afternoon on the lawn and water, the strange boys, the strange people. I sniffed and gasped, wet-eyed. He pulled out a silk handkerchief and enveloped my face in it. "That's the boy," he said. "That's right. Now, blow."

I was a little calmer, and he added, still awkwardly stooping, an arm about me, "Tell Grandfather what the trouble is."

Of course, this was not possible, but I knew one reliable reply. "I want to go to the bathroom," I said.

Though not until the end of supper in the high, dark-shadowed dining room, I finally got my ice cream. Borne triumphantly and set with great fuss and care in front of my grandmother, it proved to be in the somewhat softened but authentic and interestingly detailed shape of a locomotive. As though it were as much of a surprise to her as to me, my grandmother said, "Why, what's this, Johnny?" Amazed and pleased, I told her. My father looked at it, and then at me, with noticeable reserve. In fact, the restless night on the boat, all the candy after luncheon, our long walk, and the novelty of being present at the table with grown-up people to eat food unlike what I usually had for supper, made my appetite more mental than physical. Served with a large slice of engine, I ate the smokestack and the cowcatcher quickly. To finish what was on my plate took longer, and I did it with less assurance.

Getting up from the table, I had a premonition that all was not well. I did not associate it with my stomach, feeling instead a tired and forlorn sense of an unsatisfactory day, and now a night which I did not like either. As I went upstairs, down halls with low lights burning, into rooms unfamiliarly furnished, the dark house seemed to swell in the shadows and the pale gleam of gas jets to a kind of castle, vast and fantastic in scale, where, if the need arose, I might have to run and stumble down enormous distances before I could get back to the well-lighted places where people sat calmly talking.

This feeling of indeterminate distress probably lasted an hour or so. The feeling was much worse by then, and no longer indeterminate. Too miserable to temporize, I began to call my father, although I knew, from the way he had looked in the dining room, that I would get little sympathy. My grandmother was the one who appeared, and she was quite comforting. When it seemed finally safe, she let me come downstairs. The woman called Annie had brought a blanket, which they wrapped me in. "He doesn't want to be alone," my grandmother said, and Annie said, "Some nice hot lemonade, ma'am, is the best thing."

"You just stay here and be comfy," said my grandmother, moving, rustling, away.

The minutes passed, and though I felt better, I did not feel very well. I could hear my father's voice from somewhere beyond, and soon it occurred to me that, even if I could not count on sympathy, it would be easy to get some attention. I went tiptoeing to the door. It was not quite shut, and close to it I could hear my father say in a decided way, "Well, we won't cry over spilt milk. It's your own fault, Father, but it could be worse."

My grandfather was saying in his heavy tones, "I know, my boy. I didn't show much foresight."

Then my father was saying, "Well, we won't harp on that. Fortunately, I know where I can put my hands on the necessary amount."

I gave the door a push and let myself in. They were sitting together before a high secretary desk, the lamplight on their faces and shining up the dark mahogany. My father was writing columns of figures on a pad while he took up different papers and laid them down. I said tentatively, "Father." He turned his head. "Go back to bed at once. You know you mustn't — "

"I threw up," I answered, hesitant, but still aware of the importance of the news. As I had foreseen, my father simply said, "Well, you ought to know by this time that you can't eat all that and not be sick. It serves you right. Where did you throw up?"

Under the faded bushy eyebrows, my grandfather's eyes were on me. While my father was speaking, they visibly lightened until a twinkle came into them, as though what crossed his mind had just struck him as funny. He sat silent a moment. Then he said, "Never you mind!" He patted his knee to indicate that I was to sit on it. "When you have to throw up, you have to throw up, and it doesn't matter where, does it?"

Although the cordial observation cheered me, I still hesitated. Before I could decide whether to get on his knee or not, I heard a rustling behind me. It was my grandmother, holding a glass in her hand. She said, "He was a little upset, Will, and he can stay down until you're ready to go to bed."

"Well that will be soon," my father answered. "We're practically through here." He sat down again in front of the desk. "You mustn't spoil him, Mother."

"Now, Will," my grandmother said, "don't you try to tell me how to bring up children. He's all right, and he's going to have a good time at the beach tomorrow. . . . Aren't you, Johnny?"

"We'll see," said my father.

Judith Bogert was a plump little girl, perhaps a year older than I was. My bathing suit hung somewhat slackly on me, but she was stuffed into hers. Her damp blond hair swung in a stringy mess which she kept throwing back from her tanned face. She came sprinting along the wet sand until she reached me. I was on my knees, engaged in building a wall to keep the sea away from the central mounded mass of what I chose to regard as a castle. She swung a pair of partly blown-up water wings and gave me a smarting blow over the shoulders.

"Don't do that!" I said.

"Well come on."

"No, I can't. I have to finish this."

"Finish it tomorrow. We'll come down tomorrow."

"No," I said, "we're going home tomorrow, anyway."

"Your father's going swimming. So's my father and Mr. Judson. Don't you want to come?"

"No," I said.

"Oh, you!" She swung the water wings again, but I dodged them. "See, they're calling you."

I turned and gazed into the afternoon sun where I could see the people around the wall-less circular structure with a roof, which was called a pavilion. Mr. Bogert was walking away toward the flag flying above the bathhouse at the other cove. I could not see my father and certainly no one was calling me. I looked back in time to find Judith kicking a great breach in my sand wall. Through it a flood of water promptly swirled up and poured.

"Look what you did!" I yelled, enraged. I was a moment getting to my feet, so I did not catch up with her until she had reached the top of the rocks. I still wished to kill her, but my fury was weakened both by the fact that she was bigger than I was, and by the immediate presence of the older people. When I was close enough, I directed a weak punch at her which was half intended to miss, and did.

It served, however, to catch the eye of a little sharp-faced woman in white who was known as Cousin Amy. "Why, John!" she cried, "you mustn't do that—" Somebody asked her what, and she said, "He's hitting Judith. Judy, come over here and sit down." Judith made a face at me, and Cousin Amy added, "John, why don't you run down and help with the bake?"

"It's all covered," I answered. Earlier, while my father was directing the filling-up with what seemed to be a mixture of red-hot stones, clams, rockweed, and lobsters of a huge barrel sunk in the sand, there was plenty to do and I had been almost frantic with interest—the maneuvering of the stones from the fire, the ferocious hiss and clouds of steam, the baskets of big clams, the dark-green lobsters opening and shutting their claws, the talk and rushing back and forth, all gave a fine feeling of activity and excitement. Now there was nothing left but a part of the great fire, and the mound of sand with tarpaulin showing through it here and there. Every time I tried to investigate further a man who was taking care of the fire would say with an Irish accent, "Now, skidoo with you!"

"Well, go look for sea shells," Cousin Amy said. "Goodness me, can't a boy find anything to do at the seashore?"

I wandered, disconsolate, down the rock, and it occurred to me then that I might go out on the long, narrow-railed footway, like a sort of pier supported by metal pipes, extending some distance beyond the end of the point. I had no more than set foot on it when I heard Cousin Amy again, calling loudly, "Johnny, John! Don't go out there! You might fall off! . . . Oh, Will, look where he's going!"

My father, reappearing above in his bathing suit, said, "He'll be all right." He came down to the beach in the cove, waded into the water, breasted a breaker and began to swim. He was a powerful swimmer and I found him floating around under me almost as soon as I reached the end of the walk.

"What do they have this for?" I asked.

"Fishing," my father said. "You can cast a line into deep water. Jump in and I'll give you a swimming lesson."

"It's too high," I said, drawing back. It was about five feet.

"No, it's not," my father said. "You can't hurt yourself."

"No, it's too deep there," I said instead.

"What difference does that make?" he asked. "You don't care how deep it is. It's shallow water that's dangerous."

I held the iron piping of the rail close to the break in it where the rungs of a metal ladder went down into the water. The slight but vast and long, smooth swell, making my father's strong shoulders and extended arms and upturned face rise and fall, chilled me. I felt physically cold, and goose flesh was starting up on my arms. The too-well-known nauseating bitterness of the green water seemed to sting my mouth. Back in my nose it cut like a knife, and I imagined myself choking, suffocating on it. "I don't want to," I said.

"You'll never learn to swim if you don't try," my father told me, disgusted. "Nothing can happen to you. I'm right here."

"You won't hold me," I said, or probably whined. Though I had never ventured it under such appalling circumstances as these, once or twice, off a beach, I had gone a little over my depth with him. He would hold a hand under me to start with, but then he would keep taking it away and telling me to go on and swim. He would not put it back until, terrified and sinking, I began to bawl and clutch at him.

"Don't be a chump!" my father said. "Do you think I'm going to let you drown? Now, just jump. Just take a good breath and — "

From behind me I could hear the eager thud of bare feet on the planks. I saw that it was Judith with her water wings. The water wings gave me an idea. "If I could have those, I might—" I began.

My father answered, impatient, "They'd simply get in your way."

Judith was panting. "Are you going to jump in?" she asked. "Go ahead! I dare you! I'll jump in if your father will catch me." She hung her water wings on the rail.

"Good for you, Judy!" my father said. "Go on. I'll be right here."

"I'm not afraid," she said. She clasped her hand over her nose, glanced down to see where my father was. Then, not hesitating, she jumped out and fell with a great splash. She came up some distance away, her wet hair in her eyes, put out a hand and my father caught her arm, holding her up. "Good girl!" he said, and she laughed, spluttering. He moved with her toward the ladder. "I can swim from here," she gasped. He stopped, treading water; and, splashing and struggling, she covered the remaining four or five feet to the ladder alone. She caught a rung and hung triumphantly on it.

Seeing that she was all right, my father said, "Now, John. It's as easy as that. Just jump."

I did not answer. Instead I turned and began to walk up the footway toward the shore. "John!" my father called sharply. "Come back here!" But I merely quickened my pace, anxious to get to the rocks by the beach. My father's indignant voice carried above the gentle breaking of the swell: "—ought to be ashamed of yourself!" I ran the last few yards, but once off the footway, I stood at melancholy loss, shivering away from the gritty sand in my damp bathing suit. I felt, if not exactly the shame I ought to have felt, something no pleasanter—a familiar distracted hopelessness—for while I could see how easy it was to win favor and admiration, I knew that I would never be able to do it. Because of my considerable conceit, this was a distressing notion, and I started to sniffle. I heard steps then, and saw my grandfather coming slowly and carefully down the massive slope of the rock toward me.

"Well, Johnny," he said in his hoarse mild voice, "had enough swimming? You don't want to turn into a fish!" He took a large gold watch from his pocket. "Time to get dressed." He held the watch up. "Can you tell time?"

I nodded, sniffling, for I had learned to do so long ago. "Well, here's another way to tell it," he said. He did something to the watch, held it near my ear. To my astonishment, somewhere inside a soft bell began to ring. "Hours first," he said, "then quarters, then the minutes."

"But why do they have that?" I asked, open-mouthed.

"When it's dark and you can't see, you can tell what time it is." He held out his big loose-jointed hand and I readily put mine into it. We started together up the rocks. "Don't you mind, Johnny," he said suddenly. He coughed then and broke off. "Of course," he said, "you must always try to do what your father tells you to. He only wants what's for your own good. You know that." He did not wait for me to agree or disagree. "But you just do the best you can. And when you've done that, don't you care if other people don't think much of it." He peered down at me. "When I was your age," he said, "I couldn't swim a stroke. Then one day, just like that, I started swimming. Nobody showed me. And that's what you'll do, because you're a lot like me."

I looked up at him, amazed. Yet, meeting his brown eyes—which, for all the bush of eyebrow above them and the wrinkles around them, were familiar to me; were, in fact, exactly like mine—I had again the curious feeling I remembered from yesterday afternoon in the coalyard. I could not doubt that we did have some indescribable thing in common. This time there seemed to me to be a comfort or community of ease in it.

"A lot like me," my grandfather repeated. He shook his head. Then he gave a low, not-too-rueful chuckle. "And so, I'm sad to say, are most people, Johnny. There's this about it: You'll never have to be lonely."

Whose Broad Stripes and
Bright Stars

To my amazement, we had larks for luncheon. We had a great
many other things, too, but the larks came spitted on little silver
skewers. You took the skewer by the handle and ate off the tiny
bird. Mr. Bechtel was a big man, and for some reason his bulk
made this process all the more engrossing.

"But, Mother—" I said. Aside to me, my mother said, "Quiet."
She touched my arm to indicate that I was to take my elbow off the
table. Mr. Bechtel, through with his birds, mopped his broad chin
and wonderful rolled-up mustaches with a napkin that was several
feet square. He spoke to the waiter in German. Immediately the
man signaled with his hand and more waiters rushed up. From one
side some of them swept off everything. From the other, they put
on a kind of dark jelly with whipped cream, a cheese, crackers in
napkins, preserved oranges, a platter heaped with peaches, plums,
pears and grapes, little coffeepots, cups and small glasses. Mr.
Bechtel went right on talking to my father while all this was
distributed.

"But, Mother—" I whispered.

"Hush," she said. "What would you like? We haven't much
time."

I had already gorged myself and did not really want anything,
but Mr. Bechtel, suddenly noticing the reloaded table, gave it a
jolly, expansive smile and began to eat as though it were the first
food he had seen today. I saw that this was going to take some

time, and thought I might as well have a candied orange. "No, dear," my mother said, "I don't think it would agree with you. Have a peach. You'd like a peach, wouldn't you?"

"No," I said, "I want a—"

Mr. Bechtel had been eating and eating, but now suddenly, he mopped his mustaches again, looked squarely at me. He gave me a friendly wink. "So, John—Johnny," he said, "Hanschen! Ho, ho! That's what we'd call you! You like games? Good! Good! You'll be fine with my youngsters! You like to play in the woods?"

Stupefied, I nodded. Then, inadvertently, I giggled; for Mr. Bechtel's way of speaking brought abruptly to my mind the Katzen-jammer Kids. My father's expression showed that he was far from pleased with the impression I must be making. "Mr. Bechtel asked you a question," he said.

I nodded again, terrified; for I could feel the beginning of one of those fits of uncontrollable giggling which sometimes afflicted me at strange or solemn moments. Mr. Bechtel said kindly, "A little shy, eh? That's natural. He'll get over that when he sees the kids." He produced the last word with beaming triumph, as though it ought to make me feel at home. "Ten years old, eh? Just the age of my Harold."

I had forgotten the candied orange. I sat in anguish, almost strangling. When Mr. Bechtel said "liddle" and "dot's" and "mind Harold," and, worst of all, the fatal word, "kids," I did not know how I could stand it any longer. Luckily, he noticed that his small glass held still a few drops of white liquid. He tilted them down and wiped his mustaches again. He said to my mother: "I am using my brother-in-law's automobile. So we will not be long—"

My father's eye had caught mine. I was jolted into a sort of sobriety. Mr. Bechtel was saying, "He has a military badge." He smiled at me again. "So we will drive out the Kaiser's road. All the way to Potsdam. How will you like that?" My mother had laid her napkin down and, seeing it, Mr. Bechtel made a little bow toward her. "So, if we are—"

We all stood up. The headwaiter came with a great flourish and escorted us out of the hotel dining room. We went down a passage which was glassed in, with some sections open on a garden. My mother and I went up to get our things and she said to me: "John, what is it? What made you behave in that silly way? You're old enough to know better. What can Mr. Bechtel think of you?"

"Why, what did I do?" I asked. Any reasonable or coherent explanation would always incline my mother to excuse me, but I was not encouraged to read the funny papers and I thought I'd better not mention the Katzenjammer Kids. I took another tack. "But why does Mr. Bechtel have his nails so long?" I asked.

In fact, Mr. Bechtel's nails were all of a quarter of an inch long, so this served very well. My mother laughed. She explained that it was a custom in certain parts of Germany; that only people who had to work with their hands had short nails. "But, dearest," she said, growing grave, "you know it's ill-bred to laugh at things like that. I want you to be very careful about it when you meet the children. Just remember that from their standpoint, you're the one who's funny."

I could see that this was highly likely. It had been disturbing me a little, for I did not look forward to being thought funny. "Well," I said, "I don't see why I'm going. I couldn't even talk to them, probably. I don't see why I couldn't stay at the hotel here. I'd be perfectly all right."

My mother, who was busy pinning on her veil, said, "Now, John, please don't whine. You know that's out of the question. I think you'll find that the Bechtel children speak English." She put her gloved finger tips under my chin and added, "Now, dearest, you don't want to spoil the weekend for your father and me by being silly and disagreeable, do you?"

Made to look her in the eyes this way, I muttered, "Oh, all right. But you can't say I didn't tell you I didn't want to—" I was aggrieved. It seemed to me always bad enough to be obliged to do what I disliked, without also being expected to, myself, supply the compulsion which made me do it. I went downstairs feeling put upon.

Mr. Bechtel and my father met us and we went out to the street. It was a fine August afternoon and the street, which I knew was called Unter den Linden, had a hazy, soft glow in the sunlight, and a breeze in the small trees. I was, however, tentatively resolved not to like anything, and I gave it a scowl. I gave another to the automobile, a big high one with glass windows. I saw then that the man driving it was clearly a soldier, not a chauffeur.

This was a blow to my indifference, and immediately the soldier gave it another by his extraordinary antics. He had been standing by the door. As we appeared, he straightened up. Kicking out one boot, quite high, he snapped it in so the heel clicked hard on the other. While he did this, he saluted.

It gave me a feeling I could not analyze. It was so clearly crazy, as though he were imitating a jumping jack, that my instinct was to laugh, or, more exactly, jeer. At the same time, there was a rigid solemnity about it which I had learned, long before I was ten, never to tamper with unless I wanted a serious scolding. I gave him a couple of furtive looks. I got in and sat on the little folding seat indicated to me.

We moved off promptly, and I sat still, unsettled, not able to decide whether I felt all right or mad. I contented myself with gazing somberly out the window, and so my attention was very soon arrested by the fact that every time we passed a policeman, he, too, straightened up and appeared to salute us. Convinced that I could not be mistaken, I was letting my head turn, eyes following this phenomenon, until my mother said, "Don't sit with your mouth open, dear." I had, in fact, turned enough so that I was almost facing them in the back seat.

Mr. Bechtel said amiably, "What do you see, John?" He followed my gaze, smiled and said, "It is the military badge. You see, they must salute that. There might be officers in the car and they would be lacking in respect."

"Oh," I said. After a while I went on, "Well, but what would they do to them if they didn't?"

"John, you mustn't interrupt," my mother said. I realized then that I had interrupted Mr. Bechtel. I grew red, but he answered with indulgence, "They might go to prison. They wouldn't like that!"

"Oh," I repeated. Apprehensive, I subsided, for I could detect again the slight quiver in my stomach that threatened giggles – yet not, as at luncheon, because something irresistibly comic had occurred to me. Though Mr. Bechtel was so cheerful and friendly, there was a quality in his voice which made me feel queer, as though I might be dreaming; and rather chilly and ill at ease, as though, perhaps, I had forgotten to do something that I had been told to do, and in due time I was bound to be sorry.

My father said, in that tone he used when something he had expected little from impressed him and he felt obliged to acknowledge it, "This is certainly a remarkable piece of work. We have nothing like it in America."

What Mr. Bechtel called the Kaiser's road was really two roads. They passed in perfectly straight, parallel lines, the pavements extending ahead as far as you could see through a tall forest of endless pines, every pine straight, symmetrical, exactly like every other pine. Once in a while on the other road a car, often carrying some little flag or pennon, would go humming by.

I knew the shadings of my mother's voice well enough to recognize a certain apprehension. She said, "How fast are we going now, Mr. Bechtel?"

Mr. Bechtel took down the funnel of a speaking tube beside him, spoke into it in German, put it to his ear. He nodded then, and answered, "At the moment, one hundred and ten kilometers – that is not quite seventy miles an hour."

"Gee whillikers!" I cried, frankly delighted.

With admirable composure my mother said, "Please don't use such silly slang, dear."

I had no time for that. "Mr. Bechtel," I said intensely, "could it do seventy miles an hour?"

"To be sure."

"Well – I mean, could we, for a minute?"

My father said, "Don't be absurd, John. The driver is going as fast as he wants to."

"But it's not absurd!" I pleaded. "Then I would be able to say

I had driven—" I was not sure that I would be believed at home, but it was an announcement certain to command respect and attention. "Only for a minute!" I said, despondent; for I saw that Mr. Bechtel had noticed that my mother was not entirely happy. At that moment there was a little buzzing sound. Mr. Bechtel took the speaking tube. He nodded, said something more in German. He touched his upturned mustache end and gave me a wink. "One hundred and fifteen kilometers," he said. "That is more than seventy miles an hour." To my mother, he went on, "That is a little too fast. I have told him to slow down." Once more, to me, he said, "So you like to speed, eh, John? Well, this is the place for you. On this road you are not allowed to drive slow."

"Oh," I said, "not even if you want to?"

"Not for any reason," Mr. Bechtel said. He put out a hand and gave my knee a kindly pat. "You will see many wonderful things in Germany," he said. "Never fear!"

Not the least wonderful, I thought when I saw it, was Mr. Bechtel's house. It was fairly big, but mere size was subordinate to an architectural style which seemed to me dazzling and felicitous. We saw it first far away through the trees, and I cried, "Oh, look!" Mr. Bechtel smiled, and we went through a gate in a stone wall and up a drive; there was no doubt about it; it was where we were going. Breathless, I could observe in detail now the piled-up jumble of gables and red roofs. It had pointed turrets and a high tower on which stood a fantastic weather vane, a life-sized man blowing a trumpet in iron silhouette. The principal gable was covered with colored drawings—knights, dwarfs, giants, surrounding a sundial. On an undulating scroll above was a black-letter sentence that I could not read. There were gargoyles. There were squinches supported on gnomes' heads. There were oriel windows with dragons holding them up and little animals sitting on the corners—indeed, it had everything. The car stopped before a cavernous arch where, covered with curlicues of iron, an oak door big enough for a castle stood open.

It was necessary for me to get out first. I stood on the gravel, lost in wonder. When the others had got out, too, my mother touched my arm. I said, almost involuntarily, "I wish I lived here!"

I could see that I had embarrassed my mother, but she laughed. "That's a heartfelt tribute, Mr. Bechtel."

"Well, so!" said Mr. Bechtel, patting me. "You like Germany, eh? You ask your father if you can stay with us. Why not? We have a houseful of children. The more the better!"

I did not know whether he was joking or not. I said faintly, "I have to go to school."

"Well! Go to our schools. There are no schools so good!"

I don't think my father liked this banter much—probably because he knew no notion was too idiotic for me to embrace. He said with definite dryness: "I don't think John would do well in a German school. He's not overfond of study, I'm sorry to say."

"So?" said Mr. Bechtel. "Well, we'd soon correct that! We know how to make little boys study!"

But the subject was closed, I realized. We went under the arch. At the top of some steps a servant opened a door of plate glass, bowed while we passed, and went trotting down to take the luggage from the roof of the car. The hall was lighted in back with tall colored windows, and I saw in the gloom that, for decoration, there were several suits of Oriental armor standing upright with whiskered red-clay masks under the helmets. Then we were in a room of great size with a tremendous fireplace covered with tiles, carvings and little statues. All over the walls were game heads, trophies of arms, paintings of battle scenes.

By the fireplace stood a tall man in military uniform. He had flat blond hair, a long prominent nose and a bony little chin. There were also two women, but my eyes got no farther than the man. Except in a humorous picture, I think I had probably never seen a person wearing an eyeglass before. Certainly I had never been close enough to one to be able to see how he kept it there. In this case, the eyeglass was simply a round, rimless piece of glass not attached to anything. When the man's head moved, the glass gave a polished wink, reflecting light. I could see that he somehow squeezed it between his eyebrow and a fold of skin below. It did not even fall out when he bowed sharply, took my mother's hand and kissed it.

Mr. Bechtel said Captain von Something—I did not hear what, for an excited chattering had broken out immediately, partly in German, partly in English, while the man in uniform stood stiff, his face coloring a little. The woman I presumed was Mrs. Bechtel held out an oblong of folded paper. Mr. Bechtel roared, "So!" He clasped Captain von Something in his arms, slapping him on the back with both hands. It seemed that the paper had only just arrived. It was a congratulatory telegram signed by the Kaiser.

Scarlet with emotion, looking as though he might suddenly blow up, and with—to my astonishment—real tears in his eyes, Mr. Bechtel was speaking to my father. Stumbling all over the words, he said, "My brother-in-law is with the airships, the Zeppelins. Last week he completed an all-night flight from—"

"But how wonderful!" my mother said.

Recovering from Mr. Bechtel's bear hug, Captain von Something gave her another jerky little bow. The eyeglass never budged.

I saw then that a short fat man in a red-and-yellow-barred vest was bringing in a pail with a bottle in it. Mrs. Bechtel whispered to me suddenly, in easier English than Mr. Bechtel's, "Wouldn't you like to go upstairs a minute before you see the children? Come, I'll—"

There were five of them. They were standing aimlessly by a big tree which had a circular seat all around it. I had felt some anxiety, going out to the garden with Mrs. Bechtel, but when I saw them I knew it was going to be all right. What I had been afraid of was that they would all be playing something and I would be just left there with the necessity of making my own way into their good graces. I saw now that they had not been playing at all, but simply waiting, quite as apprehensive as I was, for me to arrive.

One of them was a girl, so I could discount her. Two of the boys were really just babies, perhaps six or seven, wearing blouses with frilled white collars. The other two seemed to be about my own age, but the shorter of them wore glasses. I looked critically at the one who didn't. He had a round face with light-blue eyes. His hair was cut very short all over his head. His manner was quiet and uneasy, but, like every child, I was an instinctive expert in such matters and I could tell that he was fairly formidable, in spite of his funny little jacket and ridiculous short trousers striped vertically blue and white.

"Come, children," said Mrs. Bechtel, and they all began to move toward us with subdued docility. To me she said, "Adolf and Reinhold really do not know any English. They will have to say how do you do in German. Now, Jette—"

The girl, who had pigtails and wore a dark-blue sailor blouse and blue skirt, grew red, but she did not say anything.

Mrs. Bechtel looked at her, astonished, waited a moment more, and then said something in German. I did not understand the words, but the tone was intelligible in any language, and the girl began to cry.

This made me extremely uncomfortable. I was not any less so when Mrs. Bechtel continued with complete calm, "Jette is a bad, silly girl, and will be punished. Now, Humfried."

The boy with the glasses drew himself up. "How do you do, John?" he said, rather like a parrot but with no particular accent. "I hope you are well."

"And now, Harold."

Harold, too, drew himself up, but he spoke without Humfried's strain: "I am very glad you have come to see us, John," he said. "I have looked forward to meeting you. Would you like to see our tree house?"

The tree house was a platform, disappointingly low, with a high rail and railed stairs going up to it, built around rather than in a tree. We trooped through the garden, solemn and silent, into some woods behind and up the stairs to this place. I was trying to be as polite as I could, so there was little to say. We stood there for a while, Jette sniffling occasionally, the two younger children staring at me. Seeing that things weren't starting very well, Harold said, "Would you like to play a game, John?"

"Yes," I said. "What game?"

"Let us see what games we know. What game would you like to play?"

"Well," I said, casting about at random, "there is a game we call Nigger Baby. Do you know that?"

Both Harold and Humfried shook their heads. Humfried said in his shrill, precise voice, "But you could teach us, maybe."

"All right," I said. "We need a tennis ball."

"A kind of ball?" said Harold.

I made a motion of bouncing a ball. Still a little tearful, Jette said suddenly to them, accenting the word somewhat differently, "Tennis, tennis, tennis ball." She darted away to the garden and up toward the house.

Relieved, I said, "Well, now we need a flat bare place. Like that. Now we make a line here." I made it with my heel. "And then, down here we make some holes, one for each of us. . . . No, push the dirt behind, see, to make a backstop. And don't make the holes too big. The ball has to be able to go into them, but you don't want it to. I mean, the one who's rolling the ball tries to roll it in one of the holes, but not his own." This was getting very complicated, so I said, "Well, I'll show you when we get the ball. Just bank it up here a little more."

Jette came running back then, and sure enough she had a tennis ball. "Thank you very much," I said. She looked more cheerful. "What should I do?" she asked, speaking English quite as easily as Harold.

"So, you found your tongue," said Humfried.

"Well," I said, brought to a sudden pause, "well I don't know. This isn't really a girl's game." I was much embarrassed. "You see, there is another part to it," I said to Harold. "If you lose three times, you are up. You have to go and bend over in front of a tree and everybody has three shots at you with the ball. I don't see how you can do that with a girl."

"Why not?" asked Harold.

"Well, if you get a good fast one, it hurts, believe me," I said.

Harold said, "What of that?" He seized Jette's arm suddenly and gave it a quick twist.

She screamed.

I was so taken by surprise that it was a minute before I was able to say anything. I said then, "Oh, quit it."

Giving her a contemptuous shove, Harold said, "She is nothing but a girl. . . . Go away, Jette, I am not going to let you play."

My opinion of girls was not any higher than Harold's, and my notions of chivalry did not go beyond the trifling, more or less meaningless conventions I had learned to use in dancing class. Had Jette stubbornly and unreasonably taken the ball and kept it, I would have considered twisting her arm a good, practical way to make her give it up. To twist her arm anyway, for no reason, seemed to me pointless, unprofitable and unduly domineering. The first two were Harold's business, but the last I viewed with antagonism and distrust. After all, it was my game, and I did not like Harold's giving orders as though he were running it. Immediately he aggravated my resentment by telling Adolf and Reinhold, in German, which I could not understand, to do this and that. Obediently they began at once to spoil the backstop.

"That's enough!" I said. "It doesn't need that. Let it alone, will you, please?" I pushed them away. Remembering that I must be polite, I refrained from saying anything more, but privately I was resolved that, as far as the game allowed, I would see that Harold got his.

Giving it to Harold proved to be no trouble at all. I discovered immediately that none of them could really throw a ball. At home I was myself regarded as little more than mediocre, but compared to Harold and Humfried, I was a wizard and the game went as I wanted it to. Harold soon grasped the principle, and he began to look at me suspiciously. "Why do you not throw at Reinhold?" he asked. "He is the closest."

"It's too easy," I said airily. "It is no fun that way. . . . No! You can duck or dodge, but you cannot move your feet." Thus I had Harold up in no time.

Although I had anticipated it with pleasure, this did not turn out to be much of a satisfaction. My three shots were well calculated to impress Harold with the painful possibilities of a tennis ball

moving fast. He could not fool me; I knew it hurt; yet he neither
flinched before I threw nor winced when the ball struck. Of course,
he was quite angry, but he prepared with alacrity to continue the
game, so it was impossible to consider him a sissy, even if he did
throw like one. I wish I could say that this show of fortitude and
good sportsmanship appeased me, but I'm afraid I was only
exasperated and all the more resolved to let Harold have it. What
would have happened if I had, I never found out, for a maid now
came down the garden with cakes and a large pitcher of lemonade.

The lemonade was good, and so were the cakes. By the time we
had disposed of the supply, my resentment was gone. Though my
temper flamed so easily, I lacked that firm purpose which can
cherish ill will for use later. I could be entirely friendly with a
person; then, fancying myself wronged or slighted, fight furiously
with him; and then, the next day at latest, be entirely friendly
again. Thus I was soon chattering away with the best will in the
world, interrupting and being interrupted. It was Humfried who
finally suggested that we might play soldiers.

This did not appeal to me much. "Is it really a game," I inquired,
"or do you just pretend you are a soldier?" If it were the last, I felt
that it was rather babyish and beneath me.

Humfried said, "Oh, we have a war."

"Well, who with?" I said.

"With the French, of course," said Harold. "We capture Paris."

"Oh," I said, disappointed, "you just make it up."

"No, we don't," Harold said. "Jette and Adolf and Reinhold are
the French, and we beat them."

"Well, that's not fair," I pointed out. "You're bigger than they
are. Of course you beat them. I'll be the French, too, and you take
Adolf."

"No, don't be the French," Humfried said. "Let them be the
French. They have to lose, you see."

"You don't know that, yet," I said. "If I'm the French too—"

"Let John be the French, if he wants to," Harold said.

"No, be German," said Humfried. "We will have a Zeppelin,
like Uncle Edi's."

"Oh, is that man your uncle?" I said. "Well, what will you use for the Zeppelin?"

"The tree house."

I shook my head. "No," I said, "you can have that and we will take it away from you." Because of their red trousers, I was always much in favor of the French anyway. "We don't need any Zeppelin."

This produced a pause. Humfried then said diplomatically, "Well, maybe we will be the Romans and Carthaginians, and not have Zeppelins."

"No, you go on and be the Germans," I answered. "We'll be the French and beat you."

"Not if we are the Germans," said Harold. "That is silly. No one can beat the Germans."

"Oh," I said, nettled. A phase of the matter which had not before occurred to me occurred to me now. "Oh, you think nobody could," I said. "Maybe you think the Americans couldn't?"

Though by this time I had entirely forgotten our previous game, I don't think Harold had. I suppose my arrogance, added to his injury, was too much for him. "I know they could not," he said harshly.

"Oh, is that so?" I said. "How about the Hessians? We beat them, I guess. I guess we could beat you now if we wanted to."

"We will be Carthaginians," began Humfried with shrill tact. "I will be Hannibal and have an elephant."

"That is silly, stupid foolishness!" said Harold. "I have seen the Kaiser maneuvers! You do not know what you are talking about!"

"We don't care for any Kaiser," I said. "I guess you know what we did to King George III. That's what we'd do to him. You and your old Kaiser, why—"

"When you speak of the Kaiser, you will not speak of him that way!" yelled Harold, quite livid.

"Oh, won't I?" I said. "He can go sit on a tack!" I am not sure that even English as fluent as Harold's could cope with this elegant idiom, but Harold easily saw I intended further offense. He gave a roar and rushed at me.

I hit him heartily, though with little skill, on the nose. My disposition and tastes, despite my moments of belligerent temper, were in general peaceful, so I was not an accomplished fighter. I had, too, the bad habit of shutting my eyes, so my second swing missed. Closing with me, Harold kicked me in the shins, scratched my neck and secured a handful of my hair. In pain and anger, I shouted, "Oh, so that's how you want to fight!" Unfortunately, I could not get a handful of his hair because it was too short. I hammered the side of his head as hard as I could and we lost our now-combined balance and went down, rolling on the ground. The fall brought Harold uppermost, but the moment's clinch had shown me that I had the advantage in both weight and strength. Confident, I got an arm around his neck and tightened it until I could see his pale, enraged face turning crimson. I was prepared to reverse our positions when fingers locked on my wrist and irresistibly removed it. Before my eyes, a white kid glove took Harold by the ear and jerked him up. Scrambling to my feet after him, I discovered that the man called Uncle Edi had somehow arrived on the scene.

He had changed his uniform. The same eyeglass was fixed immovably in his eye, but he wore now a white tunic with gold frogs and loops. At the level of my face, on his breast, he had two medals on colored ribbons. While I gaped, startled, at them, I saw him cuff Harold quite hard, but carefully, too, for Harold's nose was bleeding and I realized that Uncle Edi did not want to get blood on his white gloves. Bitingly, in short, rushing sentences, he addressed Harold in German. Then he turned and said calmly, though with a marked accent, to me: "You are hurt?"

I was outraged. "I guess not!" I said. "If he wants some more — " Looking at Harold, I felt better, for anyone could see that he did not want any more. He was almost green with obvious terror — I gladly for the moment thought, terror of me. Uncle Edi's eyeglass glinted at me and he said, "Now, why is this fighting?"

"You can ask him," I answered conventionally, winded and surly. "We were just having an argument."

He looked at Harold, speaking German again. Harold hesitated, very nervous, a narrow trickle of blood still running from his nostril. Uncle Edi gripped him by the shoulder and shook him. When the shaking stopped, Harold began, faltering, licking blood from his lip, to answer in German. I realized, shocked, that he was going to tell on me. "All right, sissy!" I cried. "Just wait till I get you."

Uncle Edi had apparently heard all he needed to. He let Harold go. He looked at me and said, "Be still, Johnny! You are not being nice." He put his arm through mine, and though I made a resistance, he turned around, still locking my arm tight in his, and walked me up the garden path. When we were some distance from the children, he said, "Why should you wish to be rude?"

"I'm not rude!" I panted defiantly. "I guess if I want to I have a right to say — All I said was what did I care about your old Kaiser."

I said no more, for Uncle Edi put his free hand over my mouth. "That is enough of that," he observed mildly. "You are undisciplined. I do not think that is your fault, but in Germany we do not have rude little boys. When you are in Germany, you must not be a rude little boy either."

I had been so dumfounded by the glove over my mouth that I remained limp, letting him walk me along. "You know nothing about our Kaiser," he continued, "so you have no right to speak of him. We care a great deal for him. Perhaps you did not know that? Common sense could tell you. No, I think you are not stupid; you are only undisciplined. You say whatever comes into your head" — he removed his hand from my mouth — "so when you say things you ought not to say to me, I have to stop you talking. You do not really mean them; I do not want to hear them. So why say them?"

I did not know. Abashed, alarmed, I had cooled down in my usual quick fashion. Unable to say anything, I looked away, and so noticed that the afternoon was almost over. It gave me that depressing sense of having to go home soon, and only hoping that news of what I had been up to wouldn't follow me. I gave an unintelligible, distressed grunt.

"So," said Uncle Edi, "you are now sorry. Harold is sorry. We will all be friends. I do not excuse Harold. He knows that he has been very bad, and what will happen to him; but that is not between you and him. You two will make up. You and I will be friends." He turned me around and we started back along the path. "So, no more of this wild-Indian business," he said, smiling, "and we will forget it. When you have been longer in Germany, when you know and understand it, I think you will learn to love it as we do."

More than abashed, I was both ashamed and sorry, for I knew perfectly well that all he said was right. Usually, acknowledging these feelings to myself, I felt a certain relief; and I had reason to feel a much greater one, since from his remark I guessed that my parents would not be told. Instead, listening to the measured, accented phrases, I continued to suffer a vague, formless apprehension. I had no idea why; for Uncle Edi was distinctly kind to me, and I liked him, and greatly admired his uniform, but that cool feeling was coming into my stomach once more.

Dimly, then, I began to see that not quite all Uncle Edi said was right. Uneasily, down in my bones, I knew that he was not right about that last. I did not mind shaking hands with Harold, or being friends with Uncle Edi, but I knew, no matter how long I stayed or how much I saw to surprise and delight me, I could never love this Germany of his—not in a thousand years.

The Animals' Fair

Miss Monk had handsome dark-brown eyes. Although she was nothing like as old as that, her hair was almost entirely white. This gave her face a curious, clean, tanned appearance. She had a light graceful figure, and though she could not have been called pretty, she was a pleasant person to look at. Moreover, she and I were old friends, for I was one of the members of the eighth grade who, five years earlier, had been in the third grade when Miss Monk was teaching that. I knew, because she had told me so, that she had to rely a lot on old academy boys like myself, and I was always glad to help her out.

On the day, a couple of weeks after school opened this fall, Hicksey first appeared at the academy, Miss Monk glanced over the class at recess and signaled to me. I stopped at her desk and she said, "John, this is Emerson Hicks. I want you to show Emerson around and help him to feel at home."

As it was meant to, this gave me a feeling of importance and responsibility which I greatly enjoyed. I said, "Yes, Miss Monk." Also, it gave me a good look at Emerson Hicks. I had been trying to get one ever since I raced in, about five seconds late, and noticed only when I was past him that somebody new had the desk in the second row heretofore empty. I had spent a good deal of time speculating on the back of the newcomer's head—which was small, and a dusty, silvery blond. His hair, I observed now, had a kind of crinkly ripple or wave in it. Emerson Hicks's nose and cheeks were covered with small pale freckles, which made his face much the same dusty tone as his head. His eyes were a very bright, arresting blue. I decided that he was all right, and, since he was rather small, that I could certainly lick him. Not that I had any intention of trying, nor that I liked fighting, but I was, as we said, eleven going on twelve, and the atavistic savage, unsubdued, wisely took notes for war in time of peace. I said, "Oh, hello." I put out my hand a little uncertainly and, bumping his, gave it as hard a grip as I could.

What Emerson Hicks thought at first glance I shall never know. I suspect, for he was a shrewd little boy, that he sized me up at once as promising material. It isn't likely that he named or clearly classified such points, but he doubtless took in the fact that I was naturally bossy and vain; that I had not been around much; that under my officious manner I was timid and uncertain. Thus reassured, he squeezed my hand back, entirely at ease. We went out of the classroom, down the wide, echoing stairs, which were lined on one side with twenty-eight large engravings of the Presidents of the United States, with their signatures in facsimile under each. I could see Emerson Hicks looking at them; not with interest, exactly, but with an automatic attention, not missing anything. Neither of us had said a word until we reached the main hall. He suddenly asked then: "What was her name?"

When I realized what he was talking about, I answered, "Oh, Miss Monk."

Emerson Hicks's blue eyes rested on me with a shining pleasure. "The elephant sneezed," he whispered in a low singsong voice, "and fell on his knees, and what became of the monk, the monk —" He giggled. Seeing me staring at him with perplexed suspicion, he added, "It's a song. I thought everybody knew that. I'll teach it to you."

"All right," I answered, though not with enthusiasm, for I didn't think the song made any sense, and the obvious jibe at Miss Monk failed to strike me as funny.

The academy was one of those advanced and enlightened schools with methods then fairly new. I suppose I was living proof of one form of their success; for, though most of their theories greatly encouraged my strong inclination to waste my time and to do only that part of my work which I could do with little or no effort, I did not hate school, and it had never crossed my mind that a teacher was my natural enemy.

Not liking Emerson Hicks very well, I said, "Well, what do you want to see? That's the fourth grade in there. And the fifth grade over there. And down here is the reception room and Mr. Apgar's office. At the end, that opens onto the gallery in the gymnasium; and—"

"I know," Emerson Hicks said. There had been a brief flicker of surprise or curiosity in his glance. He smiled in a very friendly and engaging way and dropped the subject of Miss Monk. "I saw the gymnasium," he said. "Come on. Let's go outside."

We came out on the wide sandstone steps and he stood a moment, sniffing the sharp October air, considering the groups playing in the big yard. The academy was a massive building of red brick, here and there overgrown with ivy. It stood on a sloping plot of ground, a couple of acres of banked lawn hedged with high privet in front and up on the side. Behind, it backed against a higher street, with deep areaways bridged by railed concrete entries to doors on the second floor. Emerson Hicks looked at all this carefully. Then he said, "Let's go to that store at the corner."

"No, we can't," I answered. "We aren't allowed to leave the grounds at recess."

"It would be a cinch," he said. "You could go through there and out along the hedge without them seeing you. What do they do to you if you do?"

"Oh, I don't know," I responded. "You might get sent to Mr. Apgar."

"What's he do to you?"

"Plenty," I said, though the truth was I did not know. I regarded Mr. Apgar with awe. He was a large, rather tall and stately man. His broad mild face was crowned by a dense high pompadour of well-combed black hair. His manner of speaking was slow and impressive. Monday mornings the school started the week with an

assembly, and Mr. Apgar would come into the auditorium wearing
what I later learned was a Master of Arts gown. At the time it
impressed me all the more, for I could not imagine what it was. In a
sober voice he read the part from the eighth chapter of Proverbs
about knowledge rather than choice gold. Then he coughed and
made a few solemn announcements. The only other glimpses I got
of him were accidental—momentarily, through an open door, I
might see him sitting at the extensive polished desk in his office,
looking over papers which his secretary, Miss Tyrrell, was handing
to him. Sometimes, effacing myself as much as possible, I would
pass him in the halls. I suppose I must have been shown to him
when I first came to the academy, but I couldn't remember that we
had ever exchanged a word.

Emerson Hicks said, "Listen: at one school where I went once,
the principal would wallop you with a stick so you couldn't sit
down for a week." What he had seen of the academy doubtless
satisfied him that no such barbarities were likely to be practiced
here. "Come on," he said. "We should worry!"

He had judged me very well. In the face of his airy tone and
manner, I did not see how I could refuse without, in the humiliating
presence of a person not so big as I was, reflecting injuriously on
my courage and spirit. "All right," I said, "I'm certainly not
worried if you're not."

We got back before the bell—safely, I decided, to my relief, as
we went in the side entry. However, when I was in my seat, with
the period started, I looked at Miss Monk and began to wonder. I
could very soon see that all was not well. Soon after I entered,
Miss Monk eyed me gravely a moment. After that she never
looked in my direction until the last bell rang. She beckoned to me
then. "Wait," she told me, "I want to speak to you."

I attempted an expression of innocent wonder, but it was poorly
simulated, for I could feel in my pocket the lump made by the bag
of jelly beans. Emerson Hicks had munificently bought two, one
for him and one for me.

From where I sat, I had been able to see Emerson, with a highly
accomplished technique, eating his. After Miss Monk's first disturb-

ing glance, I had decided to leave mine untouched; not only because my appetite for them had departed, but because, when I feared that I had been caught doing something I ought not to do, it was an idea of mine that I could better matters by behaving in all other respects with ostentatious virtue.

Miss Monk said, "Why did you take Emerson down to the store? It's not a bit like you, John. I've always said to myself: 'I know John is a boy I can trust.' Don't you see how it makes me feel when you deliberately—"

The outcome was that I lost my privilege of being the one to collect homework papers when they were called for, and got down to the lunchroom so late that the only dessert left was tapioca. Though my sense of self-importance was dashed by the loss of my informal office, and I was genuinely aggrieved about the tapioca, I did not feel that I had been unjustly treated. I merely repented the folly of falling in with Emerson Hicks's suggestion.

When I discovered that he had got through his own lunch without waiting, or showing any interest in my fate, I was, in addition, indignant and offended. "All right for him," I told myself somberly while I took a tray and collected my food. While I ate I was busy imagining various scenes and conversational exchanges in which I injured or tellingly humiliated him. I was too absorbed to notice when Elizabeth Jones, a large, strong girl from my class, paused in front of me on her way out. She got my attention by giving my head a shove. I started half up in anger, but she skipped heavily aside, jeering, "Well, smarty! You thought nobody saw you. Miss Monk saw you from the corner window all the time."

She gave me no time to make a response, and, indeed, I could not think of any to make. When I wandered glumly out into the hall afterward, almost the first person I saw was Emerson Hicks. I met him with a hostile look. He winked at me. "Come on," he whispered.

I said indignantly, "Like fun! I—"

From his pocket he produced an object the color of gun metal. I got only a glimpse of it, but I was able to recognize a water pistol of an expensive and desirable type.

"You'd better not shoot that around here," I said. "You'd better not take it into class. If Miss Monk spots it you'll have to hand it in. And you won't get it back either."

"Come on," he said, "we'll go down to the washroom and fill it."

I tagged along unwillingly. While he was immersing the pistol in a basin, letting it suck up water, he said, "How'd she catch you?" His tone was sympathetic but casual, as though I, too, were hardened to the fortunes of war, and it would take more than that to down me.

Enjoying this novel view of myself, I shrugged and said, "Oh, Elizabeth Jones snitched on me, I guess."

"Which one is she?" he said, lifting the water pistol from the basin and squinting down the barrel. "The big fat lummox?"

I nodded, interested in his pistol. "We'll get her for that," he said, with assurance. He held the pistol out to me. "Want to try it?" he asked generously.

As I had foretold, before school was out Miss Monk had the pistol. Aiming under his desk, Hicksey — he had already told me that he was to be called that; that only girls, sissies and teachers called him Emerson — picked a moment when Elizabeth Jones was standing to recite to drive the thin jet of water against the back of her ankle where the top of her buttoned shoe met her brown lisle stocking. It made her yell, all right, and the shot was a remarkable one, but it was obvious who did it.

Hicksey gave up his weapon with composure, and Miss Monk kept him afterward to explain that at the academy we didn't do things like that. She probably thought Emerson just didn't understand, especially after I had set him such a bad example in the morning. I was, naturally, not present at the interview, but I'm sure that Hicksey put on a good show — not of the amateur, pretending-he-hadn't-done-anything sort, but a subtler, embarrassed business of its being all just a foolish impulse, for which he was really sorry. He shouldn't have done it, and he didn't try to excuse himself, but you could see he meant no actual harm, and he was touched and much impressed by what was being said to him, for he looked you straight in the eye, like the manly little fellow he was — somewhat shamefaced, yet in brave agreement. I'm sure Miss Monk accepted it all and was pleased with his attitude. For myself, I mistook the whole matter for simple bad judgment—just throwing away a good water pistol. To Hicksey it must have been a necessary reconnaissance in force, a demonstration to make Miss Monk develop her strength and position.

I duly waited to hear how this came out, but, waiting, I got into a game, and so missed Hicksey. The next day he was cordial enough, only I soon found that he was making friends with several other boys. This left him little time for me. He had realized that though I was bigger than he was, there were boys in the class bigger than I was, or, if no bigger, none the less more than a match for me. Of course, he meant to find out if one of them would make a more useful best friend.

When he decided not, as he did suddenly about two weeks later, it must have been because whatever else he was offered, he had found no one so amenable and easily impressed. I had been offended by his neglect and was cool toward him. That made no difference. Coming up from the gymnasium period one afternoon, he got himself into line next to me, gave me one of his winks. He put his hand to his mouth and spit out a wad of gum. When the file of girls came from their locker rooms and we were moving in the constricted stairs from the basketball floor, I saw him eying Elizabeth Jones. By crowding on the way up, he got almost abreast of her. At the dark turn he made an effort to clap the wad of gum into her hair.

I wished Elizabeth Jones all possible bad luck. I appreciated the friendly gesture on Hicksey's part. Yet I would have dissuaded him if he had let me see what he was planning to do before he did it. I knew Elizabeth Jones. Girl or no girl, she was hefty, and wouldn't take it lying down.

As it proved, Elizabeth was also quick. Exactly what happened was lost in the shadow, but some intuition must have warned her. She wheeled, ducking her head aside, and caught Hicksey by the wrist. She bumped him so suddenly and hard against the wall that she was able to force his hand up before he recovered, and so to get the gum into Hicksey's own hair. With her other hand she smacked him across the cheek.

It created only an instant's disturbance. Both lines were jostled a little, but they kept moving. Not many people had really seen it, though I heard Katherine Boyd, her small pretty face wrinkled with mirth, giggle, "Serves you right!"

Hicksey was scarlet, not only at his failure but at the appalling disgrace of learning, as he must have, that Elizabeth Jones was twice as strong as he was. He could not speak for a moment. Then he muttered to me, "Gee, I can't hit a girl back, can I?" implying hopefully that all that saved her was his chivalry and forbearance. A boy named Geoffrey Allen, behind me, said eagerly, "What'd she do?"

Hicksey muttered something more, dropped out, and ran down to the washroom. We were into class then, and with much presence of mind, I went straight to Miss Monk. I said that Emerson had to be excused a moment; so no formal notice was taken when he entered. I observed, as he sat down, that he had been obliged to cut hair off the side of his head to get the gum out. Elizabeth Jones, at Miss Monk's desk with some papers, also saw it. She gave Hicksey a derisive grin, turned and started jauntily up the aisle, still grinning.

Hicksey had gazed back at her with miraculous blandness, as though he wondered what on earth she meant, so, perhaps, I ought to have realized that he had the situation well in hand. Instead, angry and indignant—for I had already forgotten Hicksey's neglect and my coolness—I saw a possible opportunity to fix Elizabeth. I didn't seriously hope for much, but, anyway, I shot my left leg out. As sometimes happens, unconsidered impulse served better than any careful plan. Still looking at Hicksey, Elizabeth Jones walked directly into the obstruction. Her other foot, which she had been lifting to complete the interrupted step, came forward fast in automatic reflex to save her balance. That bumped my leg, too, so she fell forward, flat in the aisle.

To any eighth grade, such a tripping is one of the supreme comic spectacles. No one who saw it could help laughing. I had to laugh myself, but I got out no more than a quick giggle. Scrambling up, Elizabeth turned in main fury, like an Amazon, on me. I slid from my seat with a hasty side motion, putting the desk between us, poised ready for any emergencies. Perhaps fortunately for me, none arose. Elizabeth Jones had to realize that she was hurt. Her knee and elbow had been banged hard enough to bring her up wincing. The fight went out of her and she burst abruptly into furious, painful tears.

This produced an appalled hush.

"Excuse me," I stammered, not without sincerity, for though I had intended to trip her, I hadn't planned on anything so thorough and spectacular.

As Miss Monk had told Hicksey, at the academy, tricks of this kind and roughhousing in general were not common in class. As far as she knew, they were not much in my line anyway. For an instant she may have imagined that it was really an accident; but when she heard my "Excuse me," of course, she knew it wasn't. She came down the aisle to see how badly Elizabeth was hurt. Then she motioned to Katherine Boyd, who stood up with earnest alacrity, and the three of them went into the hall.

"Gee. I never meant—" I began in abashed general defense. A sharp-eyed, dark-haired girl named Mabel Parsons, whom I deeply disliked, said contemptuously, "Oh, you! You think you're so clever!"

Abashed, I looked toward Emerson Hicks. He was sitting calmly, without expression, and for an instant I thought he had turned against me too. Then, casually, he let an eyelid drop in his unmistakable wink. Setting both elbows on the desk, he put his hands together and shook them warmly.

"Oh, tell it to Sweeney!" I said to Mabel Parsons, for I had experienced one of my mercurial lifts in spirit and now saw the episode as a good job, well done. I sat down at my desk and waited defiantly.

Miss Monk came back soon. She was alone, which meant that Elizabeth had gone down to the nurse with Katherine Boyd, but it also meant that she was not hurt seriously, or Miss Monk would have gone down with her. I had been ready to be dealt with at once, and perhaps Miss Monk saw that I was, and deliberately let me wait. She simply took up the lesson and went on with it. Elizabeth Jones duly returned with some adhesive tape around her knee under the stocking and her arm stained with arnica, but nothing was said. By three o'clock, when the last bell rang and school was over, I no longer felt very defiant. By half past three I felt about the way I deserved to.

Against one wall in Miss Tyrrell's office there was a long wooden settee. Hicksey and I sat on it. I had been surprised to see Hicksey kept after school too. Hicksey had been a good deal more than surprised. He was injured and outraged. It was easy to guess that Elizabeth — or Katherine Boyd, more likely — had told about the chewing gum as a possible reason for my act, and Hicksey might reasonably have blamed them, or even me. Instead, though he came docilely, it was obvious that he held Miss Monk responsible. I could see his blue eyes fixed, narrow and reflective, on her back as she led us downstairs.

However angry he may have felt, Hicksey had seated himself on the bench with quiet dignity. I think he had no nerves. As for me, I took no comfort from his company. My stomach, a large distressing lump, quaked and thrilled, making it hard for me to breathe the thin and tasteless air. From Mr. Apgar's office beyond kept coming the sounds of prolonged conversation. A good deal louder, a voice in my own head repeated knowingly, "Now you're going to get it. Now you're going to get it." I stared, while my sensations grew more and more intolerable, at the bookcase against the opposite wall. It had glass doors and was filled with bound volumes of some educational journal. On top was a bust marked Cicero. In despair I studied the bust until I noticed suddenly that someone had sometime given it a mustache, either in ink or crayon. The mustache had been rubbed off, but not entirely. With a kind of relief, I uttered an unplanned feeble giggle.

This brought me to Hicksey's attention. He had hitched himself along the bench until he was close to the door. He hissed now, "Shut up, will you? Can't you see I'm listening?" Apparently he misinterpreted my sickly laugh, for he added, "And look serious, you sap! Do you want to make him mad?"

Steps sounded and the door was drawn open. Hicksey had moved like magic on the bench, back toward me, composing his face into a meek, injured expression. Miss Monk came out and did not look at us. On her heels was Miss Tyrrell, who eyed us coldly and said only, "Go in now."

Hicksey stood up. His air was so solemn and guileless that he gave me a quite a shock when, reaching the door, he hit me inconspicuously in the ribs with his elbow. Under his breath, he said, "You keep your trap shut!"

Mr. Apgar had been standing by the large window behind his desk, looking out at the afternoon sunlight on the playground. He turned with impressive deliberation. I could see Hicksey looking right back at him, but my own eyes fell immediately, for his sober brown ones made me wish I could get under something. When he said in his measured voice, "John, you may close the door," I stood like an idiot, unable to move. There was an awful silence.

"The door," Mr. Apgar said, still more deeply and carefully, "behind you." I turned, bumped into it, and somehow got it shut.

"Thank you," he said, with a ponderous politeness which set me shaking worse than ever. "Now you may sit down. Both of you."

Things have happened since which frightened me badly, and with much better reason, but I don't think I was ever again frightened to the degree I reached then. Mr. Apgar had begun to speak in his Monday-morning voice. I literally did not hear a word he was saying. The light from the window behind him was in my face and made it hard to see him clearly. Outside, the declining sunlight shone reddish on some bare treetops, and I tried to look at them instead of him. It was his voice finally stopping which startled me into partial awareness. After a little while, I realized that he had asked me a question. Having no idea what it was, I moved my head in a motion meant to combine yes and no. Mr. Apgar said then, "What about you, Emerson? Have you anything you want to say?"

I looked at Hicksey with a vague remote curiosity. His face had pinkened to what looked like embarrassment. When he spoke, his voice was distressed and low. "Well, gee, Mr. Apgar, only one thing—" He stopped as though he had thought better of it. "No, sir," he said.

"Come," said Mr. Apgar, not unkindly, "if you have something to say in your defense, you owe it to yourself to say it. I want to hear it. That's the only way we can understand each other."

Hicksey seemed to be struggling with himself. Then, with an obvious brave resolve, he put his chin up as though he were facing a firing squad and intended his words to be a last statement. "Well, Mr. Apgar," he said, "it's just Miss Monk, I guess. Miss Monk always playing favorites, I mean. We don't think it's fair." He made a sound something like a gulp, but restrained himself stoically. "If she doesn't happen to like you—"

"Now, now," said Mr. Apgar gently, "when you try to put chewing gum in a girl's hair, you are not making yourself very likable. No one likes a boy who behaves that way."

On Hicksey's face spread an expression of alarm and anguish. Noting it, Mr. Apgar said, "Or haven't I understood you, Emerson? What did you mean?"

Hicksey composed himself. He started to mutter, but his voice cleared suddenly and he proved to be saying, "—wasn't trying to get out of anything. I just mean, why we did it. Sort of seeing Elizabeth Jones getting away with things all the time, I guess it made us sore. And then—well, like before we knew it—I didn't say it was any excuse or anything—"

"I see," said Mr. Apgar. He sat silent, his large sober face turned steadily on Hicksey, while Hicksey, red but resolute, met his eye. "I see," he repeated at last. "Of course, you're right. That is no valid excuse. But I am glad that you explained how you felt. All of us sometimes feel impulses of anger or jealousy. What we must do is learn to control them." He took up a paper knife from his desk and looked at it a moment. He put it down then, arose, and, ignoring us, stood gazing out the window a little while. When he turned around he said, "Now, I think we will all forget about this. I feel that you are both sorry. That is the principal thing.

Tomorrow I want each of you to go to Elizabeth Jones and apologize to her for your ungentlemanly conduct. John, I want you to apologize to Miss Monk for disturbing the class." He paused. Then he said, "I think that will be all." He reached and pressed a button on his desk. Miss Tyrrell opened the door.

"Good night, boys," he said, inclining his head.

"Good night, sir," we said, or, rather, Hicksey did. I made a kind of croak. We turned and stiffly we walked past Miss Tyrrell to the outer door. The hall was deep in late-afternoon shadows. There was no one in sight, and no sound in the big building but the bump and shuffle made by Dennis, the janitor, or one of his assistants, while they swept some classroom.

"Jimminy crickets!" whistled Hicksey softly. He gave an exultant skip, and suddenly, with a skill and ease I had to admire, turned a cartwheel down the twilit hall. "You'd better not go doing stunts," I told him, "not in the building."

A fountain pen had dropped clattering out of his pocket in the process and now he returned to pick that up.

"Oh, you kid!" he said, giving me a push.

My various emotional ups and downs had left me shaky and irritable. "Quit it!" I cried. "What's so wonderful?"

"Didn't you get it?" he asked, pausing.

"Get what?"

"Brains he has nix!" said Hicksey.

"I suppose you know a lot," I answered, sullen.

"Well, she'd better go easy, see? I can fix her, all right. At one school I went to once, I got a teacher who picked on me fired, see?"

"Yes, you did!" I said. "Just because we happened to get away with it this time, don't think—"

"We?" said Hicksey. "You didn't get away with anything. You were so scared you—"

"Oh, was I?" I said. I was suddenly impelled to punch him. No doubt it hurt, for his cheekbone stung my knuckles. "You big slob!" he cried. "Don't you hit me!" I started for him again, and he retreated. "All right," he said, his tone changing entirely, "I take it back. I'll show you whether you're scared or not. Come on."

I stood at the bottom of the stairs, looking up at him suspiciously, for already, by the invitation, he had shown me whether I was scared or not. I was. His jubilant conspiratorial friendliness, replacing so suddenly his outraged yell, made me feel approximately the way a flyer who has just crashed must feel when, crawling, by a miracle, uninjured from the wreckage, he looks at a new plane which, for his soul's good, he is advised to take up right away.

"Where are you going?" I asked feebly.

"Come on. We aren't going to let her get away with sending us to the principal. We'll fix her an ink bomb."

"A what?" I said.

"Say, don't you know anything?" said Hicksey. "You fix an ink bottle in her desk, so when she opens the drawer it shoots all over."

"She'll think right away we did it," I said gloomily, for, although I abhorred the whole idea, I knew, with a sort of sad fatality, that I was going to embark on it.

"Let her think!" said Hicksey. "When I fix something, believe me, she can think all she wants, but she can't prove anything. We'll show her she'd better leave us alone."

As I had foreseen, I went, lagging a little, upstairs after him. The still twilight of the swept and tidied classroom, the clean blackboards still damp from washing, gave me an ominous sense of being where I ought not to be. "No," I said faintly, "I'm not going to do it."

"You don't have to," Hicksey whispered, "if you'll just please give me your ink bottle. And look in my desk and get some thumbtacks and some big rubber bands, not the little ones." He watched me while I collected these things. "There's nothing to be scared of," he said impatiently. "There's no one on this floor." He opened the top drawer of Miss Monk's desk carefully. "Look," he said. "See what you do?"

"No," I said. I put the things down and moved away a little. "You go on and do it if you want to. I've done all I'm going to."

Hicksey looked pained. "Did I ask you to?" he said. "I'm not scared. I'll do it. I've done it hundreds of times. I never got caught

yet. You can bet your life I won't get caught this time." I don't
know whether his choice of pronoun was conscious or unconscious,
but, in any event, I was far too agitated for it to make an impression on me.

I was still agitated the following morning. When the weather was
good I rode my bicycle to school, and usually I liked to arrive
early, so that there would be plenty of time to fool around before
class; but that morning I put off getting there as long as I possibly
could. I think I was hoping that Miss Monk would try that drawer
of Hicksey's and get the whole thing over before I appeared. This,
it seemed to me, might somehow show that I didn't have anything
to do with it.

I wasted what time I could getting to school and when I got
there, after I had locked my bicycle in the long rack in the
basement hall, I gave it a thorough, needless tightening up until the
first bell rang. After that I washed my hands, which didn't leave
any spare time. I raced upstairs. I had gained the turn of the second
flight, still at full speed, when I saw, to my consternation, Mr.
Apgar's monumental, somberly clad figure moving with precise
dignity around the corner and into the eighth-grade classroom.

This brought me up, stumbling, and I scraped my shin on the
next step. Clasping the injury in anguish, I was not too occupied to
jump to alarming conclusions — somebody had seen us last night;
Mr. Apgar had reconsidered his decision to do nothing about
yesterday's matter; the so-called ink bomb had gone off and Miss
Monk had sent for Mr. Apgar to question the class. I climbed the
last few steps numbly, as though my feet and even my sore shin
belonged to somebody else. I came quaking into the room.

To my vast relief, everything seemed to be in order. Miss Monk
was standing by her desk with that immaculate, gracefully erect
and alert air which so became her, speaking calmly to Mr. Apgar,
who bulked over her, inclining his torso a little in elephantine
courtliness. Trying not to see Hicksey, I walked by with elaborate
casualness, went past my seat on up the aisle until I got to
Elizabeth Jones's desk. Not without a feeling of virtue, I looked

her detestable large round face almost in the eyes, and said, "Sorry I tripped you yesterday. I beg your pardon." As I was praying it would, the second bell rang then and I was able to conclude the ceremony with a conscientious dash back to my seat.

Miss Monk said, "Quiet, please. Mr. Apgar has a few words to say to you about conduct in the library." I got in a deep grateful breath and relaxed, for I had not been in the library for weeks. I looked down, but there was a pause, and so I looked up. I was in time to see Mr. Apgar apparently ask Miss Monk for something. She nodded, and, horrified, I saw her put a hand toward the desk drawer.

Though I had not dared or cared to look at Hicksey before, I did look at him now, stricken. For an instant Hicksey seemed perfectly placid, bright-faced, sitting straight in his seat, but, while I watched, the freckles started suddenly out on his cheeks. He had gone white. Looking where he looked, I saw the drawer must have stuck quite hard. Mr. Apgar, moving around to that side, said, "Allow me," in his majestic voice. He took the knob and gave it a powerful tug.

I suppose Hicksey's self-control had never been more magnificent. He, after all, knew what was going to happen. I almost yelled myself, though I had expected little more than an overturned ink bottle. Doubtless Mr. Apgar's powerful pull greatly improved the effect. The drawer yielded suddenly. Into the air, perhaps three feet above the level of the desk, the uncorked bottle sprang, spinning a wide gush of ink far and wide, over the desk, floor and Mr. Apgar.

In the room arose a sound like one tremendous drawn breath, and there was total silence. Though in itself the drenching of an unwary person with ink was certainly funny enough, we were not amused. We simply stared in horror, as though we expected a thunderclap or the heavens to fall.

On Mr. Apgar dignity's obligations rested easily. He took a handkerchief from his breast pocket and wiped away the ink dripping from his chin. In a mild and measured voice, as though nothing had happened, he said to Miss Monk, "I must ask you to excuse me for a few minutes." Without any sign of haste, he walked to the door and disappeared.

Miss Monk had been standing frozen, not, I suppose, with quite our horrified sense of lese majesty, but with shock enough. It must have been hard for her to believe that such a thing could actually happen in a class of hers. To remain, as she did, perfectly self-possessed, was a feat. The phrase I vaguely associated with her appearance and manner I had heard my elders use. It was: cool as a cucumber.

First of all, she looked at the desk and floor, and then at the empty ink bottle, which had rolled to one side. Raising her eyes, she looked at us, her gaze traveling from face to face. In the end it settled on a boy sitting in the first row just in front of Hicksey. "Carl," she said quietly, "go down and find Dennis, please. I want him to clean up." She walked around to the front of her desk. "I am going to ask if anyone knows anything about this," she said. "Before I find out for myself, whoever did it has a chance to tell me. I strongly advise him to." I saw the flicker of Hicksey's eyes shot guardedly in my direction, but no one moved and no one spoke.

"Very well," Miss Monk said. "I know of two boys who were in the building late yesterday. I wonder if either of them knows anything about it?" She gave me a long steady look and then said suddenly, "Emerson, did you come up here after you left Mr. Apgar's office?"

Hicksey's color had got a good deal better. He gave a start of surprise and said, "No, Miss Monk."

"You're quite sure about that?"

Hicksey assumed an injured look. "Yes, Miss Monk."

"You and John left the building as soon as Mr. Apgar let you go?"

Hicksey opened his mouth and then closed it. "Sure, I guess so," he stammered.

"Either you did or you didn't," said Miss Monk. "You don't have to guess."

Hicksey remained silent.

"Emerson," said Miss Monk, "you must answer my question."

"Well, all I know is, we came out, and then we had a kind of argument. And then I went home."

"What did you argue about?"

"Oh, nothing. John had something he wanted me to do, and I didn't want to. He hit me and—" Hicksey raised a hand and touched his cheek. There was, sure enough, a slight red mark below the eye.

"What were you arguing about?" Miss Monk repeated.

Hicksey had looked down at his hands, frowning. "I won't tell you," he muttered.

A kind of icy paralysis had come over me. The sense of fury and outrage, swelling in me, made me want to shriek, "You're a liar!" but I wasn't able to utter a sound. Hicksey shot me a second sidelong glance, and I suppose my imbecile appearance of stupor and guilt more than satisfied him. "I'm not going to tell you," he said in a low, defiant voice. "You can't make me."

"I don't think it will be necessary," Miss Monk said. "Let me see your ink bottle, please."

At the words, I gave myself up for lost. Even I could see that when it came my turn to produce mine, I was simply caught, that Hicksey had me hopelessly entangled. The only thing not clear to me was Miss Monk's attitude, what she was waiting for, why she didn't ask everyone to produce his ink bottle then and there. This must have puzzled Hicksey too. His expression never changed, but there was a slight tightening and flaring of his nostrils, as though he scented danger. He waited a moment, no doubt thinking, and then he said sullenly, "Why don't you ask John for his bottle?"

"I want to see yours."

Hicksey still hesitated. I have seen that hesitation since. It is the one affected by a professional magician who has allowed his audience to imagine they have seen through his trick—in fact, to be sure that they have caught him—before he dumfounds them by showing that the hat is perfectly empty. Hicksey raised his desk lid with a reluctant movement. He put his hands in. There was a moment's delay, and suddenly he raised the desk lid higher, turning over books and papers.

"Haven't you got it, Emerson?" said Miss Monk calmly.

"Gee, I don't know what happened to it," he began. He gave a wild look around, his composure dissolving. "Somebody took it!" he cried. "Somebody took it to make them think I did it!" He turned his congested face toward me. "And I know who!" he shrilled. He must have been casting about in his mind, frantic, for some clue as to how I had made the change. I suppose he could not find one, since everything had been done at his direction, under his eyes. "John was up here!" he shouted. "Ask him, why don't you? Ask him!"

Miss Monk seemed willing to take his suggestion. She turned a profound appraising glance in my direction. I can imagine what I looked like, for the next thing to a smile went across her face. "John," she said, "did you put Emerson's bottle in this drawer?"

With a great effort I managed to move my tongue. I licked my lips and said, "I was up here. But I never touched his bottle."

"So you were both here," said Miss Monk. "I thought so. . . . Now, Emerson, think carefully. Did—"

Hicksey had got hold of himself. His voice took on that old, frank, manly ring, and he interrupted quickly, "All right. I admit it too. I tried not to tell you. I didn't want to go telling on anybody. But if he thinks he can take my ink bottle when I'm not looking—"

"This much is clear," said Miss Monk. "Somebody used somebody's ink bottle. The question is who?"

Hicksey gave an admirable shrug. He scratched his head. "Gee," he said. "Well, would I use my own bottle, if I did it? That's all I can say."

Miss Monk looked toward the door. It proved to be Dennis, carrying a mop and pail. He ambled in, gave a nod to Miss Monk, and looked at the floor. He made a clicking sound with his tongue. "Fine mess!" he said cheerfully.

"Yes," said Miss Monk. She looked at me and then at Hicksey. "But we're going to clear it up." Her messenger had entered behind Dennis, and she waited until he took his seat. "Carl," she said then, "I think Emerson may want to get his school things together after he has seen Mr. Apgar. Have you anything of his?"

I have forgotten Carl's last name, but I can remember his guileless vacant face and short whitish hair perfectly. He blinked in the bewildered way he had. "Why, no, Miss Monk." The words weren't out of his mouth when he blushed, struck his knuckles against his head. "Nobody home!" he said. He reached into his desk, faced about and set an ink bottle in front of Hicksey. "Say, thanks," he stuttered. "I borrowed it before you came in. I hope you don't mind."

"Emerson," Miss Monk said, "you may go down to Mr. Apgar's office now."

Hicksey sat motionless. His expression was distraught, and I was not sorry to think how he must be feeling. Still angry, still outraged by his attempt to betray me, I looked at him with scorn and hatred, unable to imagine what I had ever seen in him. A moment passed while he continued to stare at Carl's amiable, somewhat witless face, and then I suppose Hicksey showed me — in fact, he showed us all. He got to his feet. He made a kind of bow to Carl. "Oh," he said with some elegance, "don't mention it. You're quite welcome, I'm sure."

Total Stranger

Clad in a long gray duster, wearing a soft gray cap, my father, who
was short and strong, sat bolt upright. Stiffly, he held his gauntleted
hands straight on the wheel. The car jiggled scurrying along the
narrow New England country road. Sometimes, indignant, my
father drove faster. Then, to emphasize what he was saying, and
for no other reason, he drove much slower. Though he was very
fond of driving, he drove as badly as most people who had grown
up before there were cars to drive.

"Well," I said, "I can't help it."

"Of course you can help it!" my father said, adding speed. His
severe, dark mustache seemed to bristle a little. He had on tinted
sunglasses, and he turned them on me.

"For heaven's sake, look what you're doing!" I cried. He
looked just in time, but neither his dignity nor his train of thought
was shaken. He continued: "Other boys help it, don't they?"

"If you'd just let me finish," I began elaborately. "If you'd just
give me a chance to—"

"Go on, go on," he said. "Only don't tell me you can't help it!
I'm very tired of hearing—"

"Well, it's mostly Mr. Clifford," I said. "He has it in for me. And
if you want to know why, it's because I'm not one of his gang of
bootlickers, who hang around his study to bum some tea, every
afternoon practically." As I spoke, I could really feel that I would
spurn an invitation so dangerous to my independence. The fact
that Mr. Clifford rarely spoke to me except to give me another

hour's detention became a point in my favor. "So, to get back at me, he tells the Old Man—"

"Do you mean Doctor Holt?"

"Everyone calls him that. Why shouldn't I?"

"If you were a little more respectful, perhaps you wouldn't be in trouble all the time."

"I'm not in trouble all the time. I'm perfectly respectful. This year I won't be in the dormitory any more, so Snifty can't make up a lot of lies about me."

My father drove dashing past a farmhouse in a billow of dust and flurry of panic-struck chickens. "Nonsense!" he said. "Sheer nonsense! Doctor Holt wrote that after a long discussion in faculty meeting he was satisfied that your attitude—"

"Oh, my attitude!" I groaned. "For heaven's sake, a fellow's attitude! Of course, I don't let Snifty walk all over me. What do you think I am? That's what that means. It means that I'm not one of Snifty's little pets, hanging around to bum some tea."

"You explained about the tea before," my father said. "I don't feel that it quite covers the case. How about the other masters? Do they also expect you to come around and take tea with them? When they tell the headmaster that you make no effort to do your work, does that mean that they are getting back at you?"

I drew a deep breath in an effort to feel less uncomfortable. Though I was experienced in defending myself, and with my mother could do it very successfully, there was a certain remote solemnity about my father which made me falter. From my standpoint, talking to my father was a risky business, since he was only interested in proved facts. From his standpoint, I had reason to know, my remarks would form nothing but a puerile exhibition of sorry nonsense. The result was that he avoided, as long as he could, these serious discussions; and I avoided, as long as I could, any discussions at all.

I said laboriously, "Well, I don't think they told him that. Not all of them. And I can prove it, because didn't I get promoted with my form? What did I really flunk except maybe algebra? I suppose Mr. Blackburn was the one who said it." I nodded several times, as though it confirmed my darkest suspicions.

My father said frigidly, "In view of the fact that your grade for the year was forty-four, I wouldn't expect him to be exactly delighted with you."

"Well, I can tell you something about that," I said, ill at ease, but sufficiently portentous. "You can ask anyone. He's such a bum teacher that you don't learn anything in his courses. He can't even explain the simplest thing. Why, once he was working out a problem on the board, and I had to laugh, he couldn't get it himself. Until finally one of the fellows who is pretty good in math had to show him where he made a mistake even a first former wouldn't make. And that's how good he is."

My father said, "Now, I don't want any more argument. I simply want you to understand that this fall term will be your last chance. Doctor Holt is disgusted with you. I want you to think how your mother would feel if you disgrace her by being dropped at Christmas. I want you to stop breaking rules and wasting time."

He let the car slow down for emphasis. He gave me a look, at once penetrating and baffled. He could see no sense in breaking the simple, necessary rules of any organized society; and wasting time was worse than wrong, it was mad and dissolute. Time lost, he very well knew, can never be recovered. Left to himself, my father's sensible impulse would probably have been to give me a thrashing I'd remember. But this was out of the question; for my mother had long ago persuaded him that he, too, believed in reasoning with a child.

Looking at me, he must have found the results of reasoning as unimpressive as ever. He said, with restrained grimness: "And if you're sent home, don't imagine that you can go back to the academy. You'll go straight into the public school and stay there. So just remember that."

"Oh, I'll remember all right," I nodded significantly. I had not spent the last two years without, on a number of occasions, having to think seriously about what I'd do if I were expelled. I planned to approach a relative of mine connected with a steamship company and get a job on a boat.

"See that you do!" said my father. We looked at each other with mild antagonism. Though I was still full of arguments, I knew that none of them would get me anywhere, and I was, as always, a little alarmed and depressed by my father's demonstrable rightness about everything. In my position, I supposed that he would always do his lessons, never break any rules, and probably end up a prefect, with his rowing colors and a football letter—in fact, with everything that I would like, if only the first steps toward them did not seem so dull and difficult. Since they did, I was confirmed in my impression that it was impossible to please him. Since it was impossible, I had long been resolved not to care whether I pleased him or not. Practice had made not caring fairly easy.

As for my father, surely he viewed me with much the same resentful astonishment. My mother was accustomed to tell him that he did not understand me. He must have been prepared to believe it; indeed, he must have wondered if he understood anything when he tried to reconcile such facts as my marks with such contentions as my mother's that I had a brilliant mind. At the moment he could doubtless think of nothing else to say, so he drove faster, as if he wanted to get away from the whole irksome matter; but suddenly the movement of the car was altered by a series of heavy, jolting bumps.

"Got a flat," I said with satisfaction and relief. "Didn't I tell you? Everybody knows those tires pick up nails. You can ask anybody."

My father edged the limping car to the side of the road. In those days you had to expect punctures if you drove any distance, so my father was not particularly put out. He may have been glad to get his mind off a discussion which was not proving very profitable. When we had changed the tire—we had demountable rims, which made it wonderfully easy, as though you were putting something over on a puncture—we were both in better spirits and could resume our normal, polite and distant attitudes. That is, what I said was noncommittal, but not impertinent; and what he said was perfunctory, but not hostile. We got into Sansbury at five o'clock, having covered one hundred and three miles, which passed at the time for a long, hard drive.

When my father drove me up to school, we always stopped at Sansbury. The hotel was not a good or comfortable one, but it was

the only convenient place to break the journey. Sansbury was a
fair-sized manufacturing town, and the hotel got enough business
from traveling salesmen — who, of course, traveled by train — to
operate in a shabby way something like a metropolitan hotel. It had
a gloomy little lobby with rows of huge armchairs and three or four
imitation-marble pillars. There were two surly bellboys, one about
twelve, the other about fifty. The elevator, already an antique, was
made to rise by pulling on a cable. In the dark dining room a few
sad, patient, middle-aged waitresses distributed badly cooked
food, much of it, for some reason, served in separate little dishes of
the heaviest possible china. It was all awful.

But this is in retrospect. At the time I thought the hotel more
pleasant than not. My father had the habit, half stoical, half
insensitive, of making the best of anything there was. Though he
acted with promptness and decision when it was in his power to
change circumstances, he did not grumble when it wasn't. If the
food was bad, favored by an excellent digestion, he ate it anyway.
If his surroundings were gloomy and the company either boring to
him or nonexistent, he did not fidget.

When he could find one of the novels at the moment seriously
regarded, he would read it critically. When he couldn't, he would
make notes on business affairs in a shorthand of his own invention
nobody else could read. When he had no notes to make, he would
retire, without fuss or visible regret, into whatever his thoughts
were.

I had other ideas of entertainment. At home I was never allowed
to go to the moving pictures, for my mother considered the films
themselves silly and cheap, and the theaters likely to be infested
with germs. Away from home, I could sometimes pester my father
into taking me. As we moved down the main street of Sansbury — my father serenely terrorizing all the rest of the traffic — I
was watching to see what was at the motion-picture theater. To my
chagrin, it proved to be Annette Kellerman in "A Daughter of the
Gods," and I could be sure I wouldn't be taken to that.

The hotel garage was an old stable facing the kitchen wing
across a yard of bare dirt forlornly stained with oil. My father
halted in the middle of it and honked the horn until finally the

fifty-year-old bellboy appeared, scowling. While my father had an argument with him over whether luggage left in the car would be safe, I got out. Not far away there stood another car. The hood was up and a chauffeur in his shirt sleeves had extracted and spread out on a sheet of old canvas an amazing array of parts. The car itself was a big impressive landaulet with carriage lamps at the door-posts. I moved toward it and waited until the chauffeur noticed me.

"What's the trouble?" I inquired professionally.

Busy with a wrench, he grunted, "Camshaft."

"Oh! How much'll she do?"

"Hundred miles an hour."

"Ah, go on!"

"Beat it," he said. "I got no time."

My father called me, and, aggrieved, I turned away, for I felt sure that I had been treated with so little respect because I had been compelled to save my clothes by wearing for the trip an old knickerbocker suit and a gray cloth hat with the scarlet monogram of a summer camp I used to go to on it. Following the aged bellboy through the passage toward the lobby I said to my father, "Well, I guess I'll go up and change."

My father said, "There's no necessity for that. Just see that you wash properly, and you can take a bath before you go to bed."

"I don't see how I can eat in a hotel, looking like this," I said. "I should think you'd want me to look halfway respectable. I – "

"Nonsense!" said my father. "If you wash your face and hands, you'll look perfectly all right."

The aged bellboy dumped the bags indignantly and my father went up to the imitation-marble desk to register. The clerk turned the big book around and gave him a pen. I wanted to sign for myself, so I was standing close to him, watching him write in his quick, scratchy script, when suddenly the pen paused. He held his hand, frowning a little.

"Come on," I said, "I want to – "

"Now, you can just wait until I finish," he answered. When he had finished, he let me have the pen. To the clerk he said, "Curious coincidence! I used to know someone by that name." He stopped short, gave the clerk a cold, severe look, as though he meant to indicate that the fellow would be well advised to attend to his own business, and turned away.

The elevator was upstairs. While we stood listening to its creeping, creaky descent, my father said "Hm!" and shook his head several times. The lighted cage came into view. My father gazed at it a moment. Then he said "Hm!" again. It came shaking to a halt in front of us. The door opened and a woman walked out. Her eyes went over us in a brief, impersonal glance. She took two steps, pulled up short, and looked at us again. Then, with a sort of gasp, she said, "Why, Will!"

She came right up to him. She put her hand on his arm. "Will!" she repeated. "Well, now, honestly!" She gave his arm a quick squeeze, tapped it and dropped her hand. "Will, I can't believe it! Isn't it funny! You know, I never planned to stop here. If that wretched car hadn't broken down — "

I was looking at her with blank curiosity, and I saw at once that she was pretty — though not in the sense in which you applied pretty to a girl, exactly. In a confused way, she seemed to me to look more like a picture — the sort of woman who might appear on a completed jigsaw puzzle, or on the back of a pack of cards. Her skin had a creamy, powdered tone. Her eyes had a soft, gay shine which I knew from unconscious observation was not usual in a mature face. Her hair was just so. Very faint, yet very distinct, too, a smell of roses reached me. Although she was certainly not wearing anything resembling evening dress, and, in fact, had a hat on, something about her made me think of my mother when she was ready to go to one of the dances they called assemblies, or of the mothers of my friends who came to dinner looking not at all as they usually looked. I was so absorbed in this feeling of strangeness — I neither liked it nor disliked it; it simply bewildered me — that I didn't hear anything until my father said rather sharply, "John! Say how do you do to Mrs. Prentice!"

"I can't get over it!" she was saying. She broke into a kind of bubbling laughter. "Why, he's grown up, Will! Oh, dear, doesn't it make you feel queer?"

Ordinarily, I much resented that adult trick of talking about you as if you weren't there, but the "grown up" was all right, and she looked at me without a trace of the customary patronage; as though, of course, I saw the joke too. She laughed again. I would not have had the faintest idea why, yet I was obliged to laugh in response.

She asked brightly, "Where's Hilda?"

My father answered, with slight constraint, that my mother was not with us, that he was just driving me up to school.

Mrs. Prentice said, "Oh, that's too bad. I'd so like to see her." She smiled at me again and said, "Will, I can't face that dreadful dining room. I was going to have something sent up. They've given me what must be the bridal suite." She laughed. "You should see it! Why don't we all have supper up there?"

"Capital!" my father said.

The word astonished me. I was more or less familiar with most of my father's expressions, and that certainly was not one of them. I thought it sounded funny, but Mrs. Prentice said, "Will, you haven't changed a bit! But then, you wouldn't. It comes from having such a wonderful disposition."

The aged bellboy had put our luggage in the elevator and shuffled his feet beside it, glowering at us. "Leave the supper to me," my father said. "I'll see if something fit to eat can be ordered. We'll be down in about an hour."

In our room, my father gave the aged bellboy a quarter. It was more than a bellboy in a small-town hotel would ever expect to get, and so, more than my father would normally give, for he was very exact in money matters and considered lavishness not only wasteful but rather common, and especially bad for the recipient, since it made him dissatisfied when he was given what he really deserved. He said to me, "You can go in the bathroom first, and see that you wash your neck and ears. If you can get your blue suit out without unpacking everything else, change to that."

While I was splashing around I could hear him using the telephone. It did not work very well, but he must eventually have prevailed over it, for when I came out he had unpacked his shaving kit. With the strop hung on a clothes hook, he was whacking a razor up and down. Preoccupied, he sang, or, rather, grumbled, to himself, for he was completely tone-deaf: "I am the monarch of the sea, the ruler of the Queen's — "

The room where we found Mrs. Prentice was quite a big one, with a large dark-green carpet on the floor, and much carved furniture, upholstered where possible in green velvet of the color of the carpet. Long full glass curtains and green velvet drapes shrouded the windows, so the lights — in brass wall brackets and a wonderfully coiled and twisted chandelier — were on. There was also an oil painting in a great gold frame showing a group of red-trousered French soldiers defending a farmhouse against the Prussians — the type of art I liked most. It all seemed to me tasteful and impressive, but Mrs. Prentice said, "Try not to look at it!" She and my father both laughed.

"I don't know what we'll get," my father said. "I did what I could."

"Anything will do," she said. "Will, you're a godsend! I was expiring for a cocktail, but I hated to order one by myself."

I was startled. My father was not a drinking man. At home I could tell when certain people were coming to dinner, for a tray with glasses and a decanter of sherry would appear in the living room about the time I was going upstairs, and a bottle of sauterne would be put in the icebox.

My mother usually had a rehearsal after the table was set, to make sure that the maid remembered how wine was poured.

Sometimes, when I was at the tennis club, my father would bring me into the big room with the bar and we would both have lemonades. I had never actually seen him drink anything else, so I had an impression that drinking was unusual and unnecessary. I even felt that it was reprehensible, since I knew that the man who took care of the garden sometimes had to be spoken to about it.

To my astonishment, my father said, as though it were the most natural thing in the world, "Well, we can't let you expire, May. What'll it be?"

She said, "I'd love a Clover Club, Will. Do you suppose they could make one?"

My father said, "We'll soon find out! But I think I'd better go down and superintend it myself. That bar looks the reverse of promising."

Left alone with Mrs. Prentice, still feeling that astonishment, I was uncomfortable. I studied the exciting details of the fight for the farmhouse, but I was self-conscious, for I realized that she was looking at me. When I looked at her, she was lighting a gold-tipped cigarette which she had taken from a white cardboard box on the table. She seemed to understand something of my confusion. She said, "Many years ago your father and I were great friends, John. After I was married, I went to England to live — to London. I was there until my husband died, so we didn't see each other. That's why we were both so surprised."

I could not think of anything to say. Mrs. Prentice tried again. "You two must have wonderful times together," she said. "He's lots of fun, isn't he?"

Embarrassed, I inadvertently nodded; and thinking that she had found the right subject, she went on warmly, "He was always the most wonderful swimmer and tennis player, and a fine cyclist. I don't know how many cups he took for winning the century run."

Of course, I had often seen my father play tennis. He played it earnestly, about as well as a strong but short-legged amateur who didn't have much time for it could. He was a powerful swimmer, but he did not impress me particularly, even when he swam, as he was fond of doing, several miles; for he never employed anything but a measured, monotonous breast stroke which moved him through the water with unbending dignity. It was very boring to be in the boat accompanying him across some Maine lake. I had no idea what a century run was, but I guessed it meant bicycling, so my confusion and amazement were all the greater. The fad for bicycling wasn't within my memory. I could as easily imagine my father playing tag or trading cigarette pictures as riding a bicycle.

Mrs. Prentice must have wondered what was wrong with me. She could see that I ought to be past the stage when overpowering shyness would be natural. She must have known, too, that she had a more than ordinary gift for attracting people and putting them at ease. No doubt, her failure with me mildly vexed and amused her.

She arose, saying, "Oh, I forgot! I have something." She swept into the room beyond. In a moment she came back with a box in her hands. I had stood up awkwardly when she stood up. She brought the box to me. It was very elaborate. A marvelous arrangement of candied fruits and chocolates filled it. I said, "Thank you very much." I took the smallest and plainest piece of chocolate I could see.

"You mustn't spoil your appetite, must you?" she said, her eyes twinkling. "You take what you want. We won't tell your father."

Her air of cordial conspiracy really warmed me. I tried to smile, but I didn't find myself any more articulate. I said again, "Thank you. This is really all I want."

"All right, John," she said. "We'll leave it on the desk there, in case you change your mind."

The door, which had stood ajar, swung open. In came my father, carrying a battered cocktail shaker wrapped in a napkin. He headed a procession made up of the young bellboy, with a folding table; the old bellboy, with a bunch of roses in a vase; and a worried-looking waitress, with a tray of silver and glasses and folded linen.

"Why, Will," Mrs. Prentice cried, "it's just like magic!"

My father said, "What it will be just like, I'm afraid, is the old Ocean House."

"Oh, oh!" Mrs. Prentice laughed. "The sailing parties! You know, I haven't thought of those — and those awful buffet suppers!"

"Very good," my father said, looking at the completed efforts of his procession. "Please try to see that the steak is rare, and gets here hot. That's all." He filled two glasses with pink liquid from the cocktail shaker. He brought one of them to Mrs. Prentice, and, lifting the other, said, "Well, May. Moonlight Bay!"

She looked at him, quick and intent. She began quizzically to smile. It seemed to me she blushed a little. "All right, Will," she said and drank.

They were both silent for an instant. Then, with a kind of energetic abruptness, she said, "Lottie Frazer! Oh, Will, do you know, I saw Lottie a month or two ago."

I sat quiet, recognizing adult conversation, and knowing that it would be dull. I fixed my eyes on the battle picture. I tried to imagine myself behind the mottled stone wall with the French infantrymen, but constantly I heard Mrs. Prentice laugh. My father kept responding, but with an odd, light, good-humored inflection, as though he knew that she would laugh again as soon as he finished speaking. I could not make my mind stay on the usually engrossing business of thinking myself into a picture.

". . . you were simply furious," I heard Mrs. Prentice saying. "I didn't blame you."

My father said, "I guess I was."

"You said you'd break his neck."

They had my full attention, but I had missed whatever it was, for my father only responded, "Poor old Fred!" and looked thoughtfully at his glass. "So you're going back?"

Mrs. Prentice nodded. "This isn't really home to me. Becky and I are—well, I can hardly believe we're sisters. She disapproves of me so."

"I don't remember Becky ever approving of anything," my father said. "There's frankness for you."

"Oh, but she approved of you!" Mrs. Prentice looked at him a moment.

"I never knew it," said my father. "She had a strange way of showing it. I had the impression that she thought I was rather wild, and hanging would be too good—"

"Oh, Will, the things you never knew!" Mrs. Prentice shook her head. "And of course, the person Becky really couldn't abide was Joe. They never spoke to each other. Not even at the wedding." Mrs. Prentice gazed at me, but abstractedly, without expression. She started to look back to my father, stopped herself, gave me a quick little smile, and then looked back. My father was examining his glass.

"Ah, well," he said, "there is a divinity that shapes our ends, rough-hew them—"

Mrs. Prentice smiled. "Do you still write poetry?" she asked.

My father looked at her as though taken aback. "No," he said. He chuckled, but not with composure. "And what's more, I never did."

"Oh, but I think I could say some of it to you."

"Don't," said my father. "I'm afraid I was a very pretentious young man." At that moment, dinner arrived on two trays under a number of metal covers.

I thought the dinner was good and ate all that was offered me; yet eating seemed to form no more than a pleasant, hardly noticed undercurrent to my thoughts. From time to time I looked at the empty cocktail glasses or the great box of candied fruit and chocolates. I stole glances at Mrs. Prentice's pretty, lively face. Those fragments of conversation repeated themselves to me.

Intently, vainly, I considered "century run," "Ocean House," "Moonlight Bay." I wondered about Fred, whose neck, it seemed, my father thought of breaking; about this Becky and what she approved of; and about the writing of poetry. My mother had done a good deal to acquaint me with poetry. She read things like "Adonais," and the "Ode to a Nightingale," to me; and though I did not care much for them, I knew enough about poets to know that my father had little in common with pictures of Shelley and Keats.

Thus I had already all I could handle; and though talk went on during the meal, I hardly heard what they were saying. My attention wasn't taken until Mrs. Prentice, pouring coffee from a little pot, said something about the car.

My father accepted the small cup and answered, "I don't know that it's wise."

"But I've just got to," she said. "I can't make the boat unless —"

"Well, if you've got to, you've got to," my father said. "Are you sure he knows the roads? There are one or two places where you can easily make the wrong turn. I think I'd better get a map I have and mark it for you. It will only take a moment."

"Oh, Will," she said, "that would be such a help."

My father set his cup down and arose with decision. When we were alone, Mrs. Prentice got up too. As I had been taught to, I jumped nervously to my feet. She went and took the box from the desk and brought it to me again.

"Thank you very much," I said. I found another small piece of chocolate. "I'm going to put the cover on," she said, "and you take it with you."

I made a feeble protesting sound. I was aware that I ought not to accept such a considerable present from a person I did not know, but I realized that, with it, I was bound to be very popular on my arrival—at least, until the evening school meeting, when anything left would have to be turned in.

She could see my painful indecision. She set the box down. She gave a clear warm laugh, extended a hand and touched me on the chin. "John, you're a funny boy!" she said. My mother had sometimes addressed those very words to me, but with an air of great regret; meaning that the way I had just spoken or acted, while not quite deserving punishment, saddened her. Mrs. Prentice's tone was delighted, as though the last thing she meant to do was reprove me. "You don't like strangers to bother you, do you?"

The touch of her hand so astonished me that I hadn't moved a muscle. "I didn't think you were, at first," she said, "but you are! You don't look very much like him, but you can't imagine how exactly—" She broke into that delighted little laugh again. Without warning, she bent forward and kissed my cheek.

I was frightfully embarrassed. My instant reaction was a sense of deep outrage, for I thought that I had been made to look like a child and a fool. Collecting my wits took me a minute, however; and I found then that I was not angry at all. My first fear—that she might mean to imply that I was just a baby or a little boy—was too clearly unfounded. I was not sure just what she did mean, but part of it, I realized, was that I had pleased her somehow, that she had suddenly felt a liking for me, and that people she liked, she kissed.

I stood rigid, my face red. She went on at once: "Will you do something for me, John? Run down and see if you can find my chauffeur. His name is Alex. Tell him to bring the car around as soon as he can. Would you do that?"

"Yes, Mrs. Prentice," I said.

I left the room quickly. It was only the second floor, so I found the stairs instead of waiting for the elevator. I went down slowly, gravely and bewildered, thinking of my father and how extraordinary it all was; how different he seemed, and yet I could see, too, that he really hadn't changed. What he said and did was new to me, but not new to him. Somehow it all fitted together. I could feel that.

I came into the lobby and went down the back passage and out to the yard. It was now lighted by an electric bulb in a tin shade over the stable door. A flow of thin light threw shadows upon the bare earth. The hood of the big landaulet was down in place, and the man was putting some things away. "Alex!" I said authoritatively.

He turned sharp, and I said, "Mrs. Prentice wants you to bring the car around at once." He continued to look at me a moment. Then he smiled broadly. He touched his cap and said, "Very good, sir."

When I got back upstairs, my father had returned. The old bellboy was taking out a couple of bags. After a moment Mrs. Prentice came from the other room with a coat on and a full veil pinned over her face and hat. "Thank you, John," she said to me. "Don't forget this." She nodded at the big box on the table. I blushed and took it.

"Aren't you going to thank Mrs. Prentice?" my father asked.

She said, "Oh, Will, he's thanked me already. Don't bother him."

"Bother him!" said my father. "He's not bothered. Why, I can remember my father saying to me, 'Step up here, sir, and I'll mend your manners!' And for less than not saying thank you. I'm slack, but I know my parental duties."

They both laughed, and I found myself laughing too. We all went out to the elevator.

In front of the hotel, at the bottom of the steps, the car stood. "Just see he follows the map," my father said. "You can't miss it." He looked at the sky. "Fine moonlight night! I wouldn't mind driving myself."

"Will," said Mrs. Prentice, "Will!" She took his hand in both of hers and squeezed it. "Oh, I hate to say good-by like this! Why, I've hardly seen you at all!"

"There," said my father. "It's wonderful to have seen you, May."

She turned her veiled face toward me. "Well, John! Have a grand time at school!"

I said, "Good-by, Mrs. Prentice. Thank you very much for the—"

The chauffeur held the door open and my father helped her in. There was a thick click of the latch closing. The chauffeur went around to his seat. We stood on the pavement, waiting while he started the engine. The window was down a little and I could hear Mrs. Prentice saying, "Good-by, good-by."

My father waved a hand and the car drew away with a quiet, powerful drone. It passed, the sound fading, lights glinting on it, down the almost empty street.

"Well, that's that!" said my father. He looked at me at last and said, "I think you might send a postcard to your mother to tell her we got here all right."

I was feeling strangely cheerful and obedient. I thought fleetingly of making a fuss about the movies, but I decided not to. At the newsstand inside, my father bought me a postcard showing a covered bridge near the town. I took it to one of the small writing tables by the wall.

"Dear Mother," I wrote with the bad pen, "arrived here safely." I paused. My father had bought a paper and, putting on his glasses, had settled in one of the big chairs. He read with close, critical attention, light shining on his largely bald head, his mustache drawn down sternly. I had seen him reading like that a hundred times, but tonight he did not look quite the same to me. I thought of Mrs. Prentice a moment, but when I came to phrase it, I could not think of anything to say. Instead, I wrote: "We drove over this bridge." I paused again for some time, watching my father read, while I pondered. I wrote: "Father and I had a serious talk. Mean to do better at school—"

Unfortunately, I never did do much better at school. But that year and the year following, I would occasionally try to, for I thought it would please my father.

Something about a Dollar

The new road, in three lanes of good concrete, had been straightened out so that it missed the village of Sparta altogether. As I got up into the hills I knew that Sparta was somewhere around. Soon—I have never met a person quite immune to that senseless, melancholy curiosity, and I am not—I might have begun to look for it; but the new road did not follow the old one closely, and I forgot how, driving fifty miles an hour, once-familiar distances are telescoped. As a result, I was not thinking of Sparta when I reached, without knowing it, the great bend which would have carried me past and away. What I saw was an intersection marker, and looking past it for the entering road, I looked, in amazing effect, a quarter mile down the past.

It was a fragment of the old Sparta road. It lay in ineffable, unused stillness, like a painted road in a picture, forever bending through the pines, with a drift of brown needles undisturbed on the weather-rotten macadam, forever sloping to the lichen-marked abutments of the little bridge; then, in perspective, in a marvelously done quiver of heat, it went up the hill and disappeared. What it really did, I knew, was go on to Sparta, for I had walked that road a hundred times. We used to come down the path from Camp Ponemah Saturday afternoons and straggle along there, going to Wood's store.

I was past as soon as I had seen it, but I slowed down on the impulse of surprise; for no real reason, moved. When I came presently to a second road with a single narrow pointer which said

90

SPARTA O, I turned, though I did not know what the use was or what I wanted. The short road crossed the same brook, a little wider here. It intersected Sparta's single street by a filling station. The filling station was new, but nothing else was. I turned left and stopped in front of Wood's store.

Inside there had been some changes. There was a new, larger soda fountain, though they had kept the sweetish, not-very-clean smell which had gone with the old one.

There was a long candy counter with a glass front, but the chocolates displayed in it might very well be the same ones which that greedy, milling herd — I could see the press of gray-flannel shorts, the sleeveless gray jerseys with the scarlet monogram on the breast, the violently pushing brown arms and knees — had struggled to buy so many years ago. I could even remember what they would taste like. On the rack of the magazine stand opposite, it wouldn't have surprised me to find that the ranks of bright covers hanging there were those for July and August, 1920.

I stood and looked until someone who had been reading a newspaper by a back window dropped it and walked forward through the shadows. I turned toward him, half prepared for it to be old Mr. Wood. I saw, instead, a loose-jointed lout of a man, not more than forty. I asked him for some cigarettes. While he was finding them, I mentioned Mr. Wood.

At first I could not tell whether he had heard me. He went on with his work of peering in the long pigeonholes stacked with cigarette packages. When he had found those I asked for, he said, "He's not living."

I said, "I'm sorry to hear that. I used to know him." Because the fact was interesting and vaguely important to me, I added, "I used to go to the camp up the valley. Do the boys still come down here Saturdays?"

As if it gave him positive pleasure, the man shook his head. "Nope! Camp's closed. Closed after Mr. Small died, six or seven years back. No camp there now."

Although it had happened as long ago as that, and could not make any real difference to me, since I had never even known it, I was dismayed by the news. Pete Small had certainly not been young; yet I thought of him as ageless. I had been at Camp Ponemah three seasons as one of the kids; and then, four years later, again as a counselor. Time had never seemed to touch Pete. In his youth he was supposed to have worked in a blacksmith's shop. When he ran the camp, he wore glasses and taught mathematics in a city high school, but he was still made of iron. He could take an apple between his hands and break it in half. I had never seen him tired and could not imagine him ill.

I murmured, "Oh, why, I didn't know that." The idea of Pete Small dead for years and the camp I had gone to no longer in existence made me feel, in a way I was not yet used to, how far beyond recovery was all the past. I wondered what had become of Mr. Mosher and Mr. Barrett. I thought of Hank Potter and remembered how much I had disliked him; and how much, against my will, I had admired his bulk and strength and envied the great fame we all thought he enjoyed by being named on Walter Camp's second All-American eleven. I thought of Herman's flat Virgina drawl; and Sam whatever-his-name-was—the fat fellow. And, of course, Virgil Conway—he was called Jack, because, as he explained, there was really no regular nickname for Virgil—who had tented with me that last year. We knew each other eight weeks, and for several years afterward I thought of him as an old and intimate friend.

The man behind the counter was waiting. Embarrassed, I remarked, "I was a junior counselor up here fifteen years ago."

To my surprise, he nodded. "I know," he said. "Can't say I recall your name, but soon as I seen you I knew your face."

I could hardly believe it—he seemed too old—but, with the sudden jerk of his chin, I thought I knew his face too.

I asked doubtfully, "You're not Jake Phillips, are you?"

"Oh, yes, I am." He gazed steadily at me. "You're the fellow who fixed it to catch the kid stealing things."

Astounded, I said, "You've got a good memory. I remember that. It was something about a dollar. Yes, I'm Frank Wade."

"Quite a trick, that was," he continued, not heeding the interruption. "Quite some trick." He chucked the cigarettes on the counter and picked up my coins. With the expression, I couldn't have failed

to know him anywhere; it brought everything back; and I realized
that what he said next would be something I didn't want to hear. He
said, "Well, takes all kinds to make a world." He shrugged. He
turned and ambled back toward his chair. When he got there he sat
down, took the newspaper again and began to read.

When Mr. Small rang the bell, there was a great racket of chairs
pushed back and the kids poured, yelling, out. He called the
counselors over to his table and told us that a sum of money had
been taken from Mr. Barrett's drawer. We had been having trouble
for a couple of weeks about things disappearing from the kids'
tents. Mr. Small wanted to hear any suggestions we might have for
putting a stop to it. Since there wasn't much we could do, except
somehow catch the thief, we didn't get anywhere, and Mr. Small
let us go before my idea had occurred to me. Virgil Conway
thought the idea was good and might work. By then it was pretty
late to get down to Sparta and arrange that part of it before taps.
Virgil asked why I couldn't do it just as well in the morning. He
had an orderly mind; which, perhaps, explains why, although he
wasn't two years older than I was, and I had only finished my
fourth-form year at school, he was a sophomore and an honor
student at Tech.

I knew that Virgil was giving me perfectly fair warning that if I
didn't get back to take the last inspection, which it was my turn to
take, he would take it, and I would owe him the setting-up exercises in the morning. Nobody wanted to take those when he didn't
have to, but my ideas came quickly and easily, and they always
seemed to me so brilliant, so exactly the thing, that I found any
delay in acting on them insufferable. I couldn't wait to see Mr.
Wood. "I can run it easily," I promised Virgil. I had that year
made the track squad at school. My distance was the 440. I had
placed in every meet and actually won once; and once, though
there may have been a slight error, I had run it against the watch in
fifty seconds. When there was any running to be done, I considered myself the man to do it, and I didn't mind an opportunity to
show Virgil that it was child's play for a trained runner to get to
Sparta and back in half an hour.

Running in the dark on a path and paved road is not the same thing as running with spikes on cinders, but I was going to do it or die, and I did do it. I got back up the hill just as Herman was coming out on the lodge porch with the bugle. Virgil sat in the starlight on the steps in front of our tent, ready to do his duty, but we were good friends, so he was giving me a minute. It stabbed me in the calves, but I came down fast. Not knowing what a pity it was going to be, I said, pulling up triumphant, "Well, I got here."

Virgil looked at the luminous dial of his watch and whistled. "That was nice going. . . . Did he kick?"

I patted my chest. The hill had hit me pretty hard. I got another breath and said, "Oh, I fixed that. I told him Pete would be pretty certain to put Sparta out of bounds if he wouldn't co-operate." I said it with modesty, for I thought it showed a good deal of resourcefulness on my part; but Virgil observed soberly, "I'm not sure that's so good. We'll have to hope Pete doesn't hear about it." He looked so doubtful that I was really worried myself. Though I had played my trump with great positiveness, I hadn't been able to help thinking that I would be in a funny position if, for answer, Mr. Wood just took up the telephone and called the lodge and told Pete he could do his own detective work.

"I had to do it," I said; "it was the only thing. It all depends on him and Jake Phillips. Jake seems to think he owns the place. I saw him first. Mr. Wood wasn't there. He just said no, he wouldn't; it was none of their business. Mr. Wood came in, and I saw unless I—"

I could hear the last notes of the bugle hanging on the darkness, then returning in faint echo from valley slopes. I could see the flashlights begin to move, winking, down the west and south lines. "Well, don't worry about it," Virgil said. "I certainly wouldn't worry about that little squirt Jake."

"I'd like to take a poke at him," I admitted, for I was feeling depressed and dispirited, no longer convinced that my idea was such a good one; and, though I did not realize it, very edgy. This was ordinary exhaustion. You may think you can, but you cannot run the mile like the 440, and if you try you will not only be dead-beat but last in the field.

I started down the east-line tents. They were good, big, double-fly wall tents pitched on permanent platforms. They held four cots each. All I had to do was twitch up the flaps and see that everybody was in bed. Often it took me some time, for I was a poor disciplinarian. That is, though I could be both severe and patient, nobody — least of all myself — knew which I was going to be. I took my responsibilities with exaggerated seriousness, and since, a few years before, I had been one of the kids myself, I could command a certain respect by being able to anticipate this or that little scheme and catch the offenders in the act. When I outguessed somebody this way, I was often so much mollified that I would treat the frustrated attempt as a joke. Then, belatedly, I would remember my duties. To make up, I would penalize the next offense that occurred, too severely. The result was that half the kids in our line liked but did not respect me, because I let them get away with things; and the other half, who suffered from my reaction, greatly resented my unfairness. Either state of mind was fine for making trouble and the last inspection was always a good time to make it.

However, tonight most of the camp had been up Mount Pleasant on an all-day hike. A good many kids would be asleep as soon as they touched the bed — literally, in the minute between the end of taps and my arrival with the flashlight. You could count on it after any hard trip, and that was how Starbuck put one over. In his tent he had a rear cot. My flashlight swept carelessly across what I took, relieved, to be Starbuck, sound asleep. I had no wish to wake him up, for he devoted every waking minute to what was then called getting my goat. I dropped the flap, satisfied by the simple dummy he had prepared for me, and went on to the next tent. One of the kids there, drowsy, but automatically making conversation to delay matters, said, "Say, Frank. Something was moving around behind here. It was a porcupine, I bet."

"Like fun!" I said. "They never come down here. Now go to sleep."

At that instant, from the tent beyond, went up a sudden horrible shriek. It had an intensity of terror, a timbre, a sort of fearful frenzy which, to the unprepared ear, meant nothing less than death. I dropped my flashlight. Fortunately it didn't break, and in the second needed to snatch it up again, I had time to recognize that the voice was Lefferts Price, and so to know that it was undoubtedly not murder but some trick which had been played on him.

I bounded down the platform steps. I shot my light between the tents, for I knew where to look. The shaft fell fairly on Starbuck's pajama-clad form scrambling under the guy ropes to get away along the back of the line. "All right, Starbuck!" I called. "I saw you! I'll take care of you in a minute."

I ran on to the next tent and threw the flap open. "Shut up, Price!" I snapped, for he was going to raise the whole camp at this rate. "Don't be such a baby! You aren't hurt."

The beam of light went over Price, who stood, shaking and bawling, on his cot. It reached the floor to find there a neat, narrow, beautifully blotched snake about three feet long—which is quite big; what people mean when they say the snake they saw was over five feet. The snake had hesitated in great bewilderment and terror, but the light meant to it more enemies, so it went frantically into action, whipping under the opposite cot to the edge of the flooring and away.

I knew what kind of snake it was, for in the mornings I took a nature-study group which collected and indentified the ten or eleven local species. None was venomous. In fact, as I duly taught the kids, all of them were not only harmless but useful, and should never be killed. Notwithstanding, most people suffer a turn when they come unprepared on a fair-sized snake, and I did.

My own recoil annoyed me. What with Starbuck fooling me about being in bed, and Price raising his row, I was already annoyed enough. "It's just a milk snake," I said. "It's gone. No wonder people want to play tricks on you, when you yell like a little imbecile."

This was, indeed, the case. To people like Starbuck, Lefferts Price was a standing invitation. A slight, thin boy with a nervous, shrill voice and a cropped mop of flaxen hair, Price, once he had got well tanned, looked a good deal like an incredible little albino. If you are eleven years old you cannot afford to look so funny unless you are strong and ferocious too. Price might have liked to, but he clearly couldn't hurt a fly. For offense, all he had was a quick tongue and a taste for obvious sarcasm. When somebody wanted to fight him for his remarks, Price cringed and retreated, yelling, to a counselor. Nobody admired the maneuver.

I never admired it either, but, in a way, I did condone it. I was quicker than some of the counselors to protect him when he was in danger of getting beaten up. This was my duty. But, since it was the only place where he was really safe, I let him hang around our tent a good deal, too, which wasn't my duty at all. Though it was an embarrassing thing to admit and I glossed it over to Virgil by this talk about duty, I was impressed by Lefferts Price. His father was quite a distinguished writer, a retired Unitarian minister well known to all readers of the serious monthlies for his articles on social and political reform. I found out next that Lefferts knew a surprising amount of Shakespeare by heart, had been over most of Europe, and could read music. The kids said that Price was a stinker, by which they meant a coward, a sissy and a tattletale. That is just what he was, but I liked him and I knew he liked me. I suppose he was taken aback when I turned on him.

"Are you going to stop that?" I asked. "Look at them!" I said, meaning his tent mates. "They're all laughing at you! Now get into bed and shut up!"

But Price wouldn't get into bed. Not into that bed. Feeling reasonably secure where he was, he had almost stopped crying.

He did not want to put his feet into the blankets again and feel another snake there, so he began at once to bawl, "No, no, no!"

I lost all patience. "Get down on the floor!" I said. I took him by the arm and jerked him down. He immediately yelled, as though he thought he was bound to land on the snake. I tore the blankets back and turned the flashlight into them. I shook out every fold and wrinkle. "Look at it!" I said. "There's nothing there! Now get in there, or—" I had taken him by the forearm, ready to force him to get in, but he put a stop to that. Ducking his head and twisting away, he sank his teeth suddenly into my hand.

That really hurt. In automatic reaction I slapped him so hard that he sat down involuntarily on the cot. From outside I could hear Virgil's voice, calm, reasonable and authoritative, disposing of people who wanted to see what was going on, "Come on! Back to bed!"

I said to Price, "You've got ten demerits. If you ever try to bite anyone again—"

Virgil's flashlight lit the canvas yellow. "Who's dead?" he asked.

"No one," I said. "Starbuck scared him with a snake." To Price I went on, "If I hear another yip out of you, I'll make you really sorry. Do you understand?"

I suppose he did. Still cowering and sniffling, he burrowed more or less into his blankets.

I was relieved. Though Virgil did it with tact and deftness, nothing mortified me more than to see him get in hand a situation that had been too much for me. I said quickly, "Come on. It's all over. We'll take Starbuck up to see Pete."

Starbuck had hidden himself in the shower shed, but we weren't very long finding him, for I was well acquainted with likely hiding places. Mr. Small simply turned him over his knee and spanked him, which, when you had hands and arms like Mr. Small's, was no joke. I'll say for Starbuck that he never made a sound. While Virgil got an iodine bottle and insisted on painting my hand, I thought of letting Price off without any demerits. The kid had obviously been scared to death, and ten was pretty steep for something he couldn't very well help. It was Starbuck, much as I detested him, who decided it for me. He had certainly taken his licking like a man, and though I can't pretend to follow, now, my logic in the matter, I went to the big demerit slate and wrote: "Price, 10."

Virgil and I decided to put the dollar bill between two books of mine laid carelessly at the back of the table. With the tent flap up, it was easy for anyone walking along behind to see the edge of it, and equally easy, at most hours, to reach in unobserved and take it. In fact, Virgil thought it might be a little too easy. "Whoever's doing this is no fool," he pointed out. "That looks a lot like a plant. Maybe we ought to just put it in the drawer."

I objected, "The way he got Mr. Barrett's money shows he's been looking in drawers. He's probably looked in ours and knows we don't keep money there. He might not look again, and so he'd never get it. At least, we could try it this way."

I could see that there was a good chance of Virgil's being right, but next morning, when I dismissed my reptile-study group, I got a moment to look into our tent, and the bill was gone. This certainly made Mr. Mosher's idea about it being someone in the kitchen unlikely. None of the help had any time off in the morning. Plainly it was one of the kids. Knowing the kids, I could be fairly certain that it would work after all. Barring Jake Phillips being the one to see the dollar, and being sore enough at me to say nothing, there was a good chance that Saturday we would know which kid.

At four o'clock on Saturday afternoon, while I was taking swimming for the boys who had spent all their money or were saving it and didn't want to go to Sparta, Virgil appeared and called me off the float. They had just telephoned the lodge. The dollar had turned up. Lefferts Price had tried to buy sodas for himself and the Fowler boys with it.

"Well, I don't believe it!" I said, when I could. "The old fool got the names wrong probably." I was just saying whatever came into my head, for the last person on earth I wanted it to be was Lefferts Price. The affair of the snake and the ten demerits had kept me uncomfortable all week, for, though I could justify myself perfectly, I didn't like the feeling of needing to. Price, sulking about, forlorn and sullen, was a personal reproach to me. I could and did say to myself that if he were going to bear me a grudge, that was his hard luck, for he certainly hadn't any other friends; but I would have been very much obliged to him if he managed to take it like a good sport. "It couldn't be Price," I said. "That's crazy! He wouldn't have the nerve, for one thing. Who said it was Price?"

"Hank was down."

"Say!" I said. "Doesn't that strike you as funny? Potter was saying all along he thought it was Price, and—" Potter and I weren't very cordial, and I knew he would be pleased that it was Price, whom he always described scathingly as my little pet. I had once told him that, though Price might not be good football material, he was the only intelligent kid in camp. Just the same, I saw that that was no good, even while I was saying it. A whistle was attached to an elastic cord around my wrist. I brought it up, agitated, and blew it twice, getting yells of "Have a heart, Frank!" and general protest, for the swimmers could tell that it wasn't time yet and my lack of firmness was well known. Virgil came to my rescue. He called, "When Frank blows all out, he means all out! Anyone who wants some demerits can stay where he is!" I took my towel and dried my arms and legs. I pushed my feet into a pair of broken sneakers, and got a comb from the pocket of my school blazer.

"All right," Virgil said. "Up the hill!" He looked at me, and I could see that he was no easier in mind than I was. "Pete's fit to tie," he remarked.

I answered bitterly, "I don't see what he's kicking about. He always thought Price was a little mess."

"Well, I don't think he liked the dollar business. At least, he said right away, 'Whose bright idea was that?' "

"And you said it was mine."

"Now, can that, Frank!" he said reasonably. "We're in this together, and I told him so. The only thing is, I think we should have said something to him. I know he and Mr. Mosher had some scheme of their own up their sleeves to catch whoever it was, but very likely he wanted to do it quietly and not have half the camp in on it. I think maybe they had the goods — "

"You mean on Price?" Since, a moment before, the idea of it being Price upset me, I could not think why I felt relieved. If Price really had taken the missing fountain pens and dollar watches and the money from Mr. Barrett's drawer —

"Search me," Virgil said. "Pete was in no mood for chatter. Hank's bringing Price up in Mr. Wood's car and I thought I'd better get you."

On the lodge porch Herman was busy shooing kids away: "I said beat it! It's none of your business. That means you, too, Starbuck. Now, get up to your tent, or I'll warm your little — "

Virgil and I went in, through the main hall with the fieldstone fireplace to the small room lined with book shelves which had a rustic sign over the door reading THE NATURE LIBRARY. Mr. Small sat back in a big chair by the table, his tanned, hairy forearms crossed on his chest, his solid face tinged an angry brick color. On the table in front of him were his glasses and the dollar bill. Mr. Mosher and Mr. Barrett were both looking duly troubled. Potter was leaning against the bookcase with the modest composure of the person who knew it all along.

Opposite Pete sat Price, his face much streaked with tears, his thin brown arms, like Pete's, folded across his chest; but Price clutched his skinny elbows in his hands and the effect was not the same.

"Sorry, sir," I said to Pete. "I just heard about it. I had to get the kids out of the water."

"Yes," said Pete. He put on his glasses and looked at the dollar bill.

"May I see that, sir?" I asked, for I felt impelled to keep talking. I already knew it was the bill. I had found an ingenious way to mark it. On the seal of the Treasury Department, between the key and the balance pans, there is a chevron bearing thirteen white stars. What I finally did was ink out the stars. If you knew what to look for, you couldn't mistake it; it seemed impossible to miss. You would miss it every time if you weren't looking for it, for the seal is printed in blue.

Everyone watched me while I made a needless, elaborate examination. "That's it," I said. "Jack will bear me out."

Pete said, "That's the dollar bill you put between the books on your table?"

"Yes, sir." I thought it better not to address Price directly. "Of course, I don't know that Price got it from there. Somebody else may have taken it."

Potter said, "Don't worry, Franky. He took it. He admits it."

"Oh," I said. There was a quality in the silence that I found disturbing. I noticed old Mr. Wood in the corner looking at me without much favor. I found myself saying, "For heaven's sake, Lefferts!" I could hear my own voice, and when that happened I knew that what I was saying wouldn't be a success. "Why did you swipe it? If you needed a dollar, I'd lend you one."

"Never mind, Frank," Mr. Small said. "That's aside from the point."

Mr. Barrett said mildly, "Well, I don't know that it is. In fact, quite the contrary.... Let me ask a few questions, Pete." His bony, tanned forehead bent forward a little. He looked a moment at Price. "Lefferts," he said, and I recognized the tone I had failed to get when I spoke, "you didn't take that dollar just because you wanted the money, did you?"

Potter moved impatiently. "I suppose he didn't try to spend it just because he wanted those sodas, either." Mr. Barrett gave him a look, waited a moment, and went on: "Let's get this straight, Lefferts. Now, you can't tell me the son of a man like Doctor Price is a natural thief. Of course, he isn't."

"I don't think he is either," I said uneasily. "There's something pretty funny—"

Mr. Small said, "Frank, would you just as soon subside?"

Mr. Barrett sighed. "Lefferts," he said, "I wish you'd tell us. It would make everything a lot easier. You were walking along the back, and you looked in the tent and saw a couple of books of Frank's with a dollar bill between them. Now, why did you think you'd take it? Didn't you have any money of your own?"

Lefferts gave a sort of sniff and muttered what seemed to be "... had seventy cents."

"Well, that would appear to be ample," said Mr. Barrett. "I don't believe you were thinking that if you had that dollar you could get something at Wood's. Were you?"

Lefferts let go an elbow and pushed his dirty hand up to his eye. "No," he said finally.

"But you did think something, didn't you? What did you think, Lefferts?"

There was a profound silence. I had not felt comfortable before, but as we waited I began to feel less comfortable still. I opened my mouth, but Pete made a motion and I shut it again. Lefferts had pushed his hand up over his eye altogether and began to rub it.

"Just say it," Mr. Barrett told him mildly. "Just say what it is. You'll feel much better, boy. You know that."

There was a second pause, and suddenly, muffled by his wrist, Price said, "I didn't want him to have it."

"Of course," Mr. Barrett said. "You mean you thought the dollar was Frank's, and so you'd get even — "

Price gave a jerky nod. "Just because I wouldn't — " He gulped violently and began without delay to sob.

"Now, now," said Mr. Barrett. "That's all. You see, you do feel better. Now it's all out. Everyone understands." He stood up. "Come along," he said. "You come up to my tent for a while and we'll have a talk." He brought Price to his feet. "All right, Pete?" he said. Mr. Small nodded and he took Lefferts out into the main hall.

After a moment, I said, "I'm sorry about this, Mr. Small. It's my fault. Lefferts was quite a nuisance the other night and I lighted on him. I certainly didn't know he was going to take it to heart."

Virgil said, "Do we have to do anything about this, sir? Why couldn't we — "

"Well, I think we do," said Potter. "All right; suppose the kid was simply sore at our Franky." He gave me a look and grin. "Francis, I can just barely conceive of that. All the same, he took a dollar that didn't belong to him and tried to spend it." His eyes met Mr. Small's fairly, with a resolution it was hard not to admire. "That's stealing in any language. And a person who steals is a thief. And we don't want him around. And don't forget all the other stuff that was missing. Before you send him home, you'd better look through — "

Mr. Mosher put a hand to his polished bald head and tilted back in his chair. "One thing at a time, my boy," he said. "Don't you know that practically all kids that age will steal if they get a chance? Well, I do; and there is no need to feel so bad about it."

"I didn't say a kid mightn't swipe something if you put it where he could. That's Franky's idea, remember."

"Please, please," Mr. Mosher said, "be patient with me. Pete and I just think that all this is very unfortunate and you won't let me tell you why. It's important. Now, it happens, while you were in Sparta this afternoon, we took the cook and went through the quarters up there. We now know all about it. We have everything that was missing and we no longer have the pleasure of that dishwasher Mac's company. Now, what do you think of that?"

Potter was brought up short, but he recovered more handily than I could have. He said, "What I think of that is, it's all right. Fine. I'm glad to hear it. But it doesn't change the fact of Franky's dollar."

"No," said Mr. Small, "it doesn't change that. And so we're going to send Price home." He picked up the bill, looked at it and then looked at me. "We won't miss him any," he said, "though I'm sorry about his father." He continued to look at me, and I could see his expression slowly change, the ordinary derisive, not unfriendly glint coming into his bright-blue eyes. "Here's your money, Frank," he said. "Do you know where money belongs? In your wallet." He shook his head. "Now, clear out, all of you. You've only got twenty minutes before the line-up."

We left him there saying something to old Mr. Wood. Mr. Wood made what was, as far as I know, his only remark. "Boys," he said, "will be boys."

In our tent, Virgil Conway sat down on his cot while I stripped off my still-damp bathing suit. "Well, that was some party," I said, rather spiritlessly. "It's all right for Pete, but he wanted us to do something, and we did something and—" I turned a towel about me, ready to run up to the showers.

"Don't worry about it," Virgil said. "It's just Price's tough luck. Those things happen. It's all right."

"Oh, no, it's not," I said. "Not by a long shot. In fact, it's all wrong, and I know whose fault that is, and so does Pete, and so do you."

"Forget it, Frank," Virgil said. "Forget it. And keep moving: it's late."

I forgot it. For years I never gave it a thought—not until that afternoon, going out with the cigarettes to get into the car at Sparta. I realized then that I never had forgotten it, and a good thing too.

PART TWO

AWAY AT SCHOOL

Someday You'll Be Sorry

He was known as Smith Three, or, thus they printed it on the Durham School list, Smith III. With the graduation of older namesakes, most boys, before they leave, overcome such a tacit numeral inferiority, but in his case, Smith One and Smith Two — no way related to him — happened to be members of his class. He entered the Durham School in the third form. The others had been there earlier. He was permanently Smith III.

Smith I was Han Smith, an exceptional athlete. Even to this day there are men who went to Durham, and many more who went later to Yale, who can still remember that name. Smith II was John Stuart Smith. With patronizing respect, he was known as Jo-Jo. Short, quiet and dogged; term after term his name headed the scholastic honor roll. Afterward, at college, he took numerous prizes and scholarships. At Durham, Smith III was neither an athlete nor a scholar; he was merely a difficult boy.

Perhaps there is a justice that operates about such things. Hanover Smith — somehow he was not a success at bond selling — is a football coach at a small Ohio college. Jo-Jo is in a bank. Indeed, he is already an assistant vice president, but the bank has thirty-two city branches, with a few assistant vice presidents attached to each, and Jo-Jo should have moved up several years ago if he were ever going to. Smith III is, of course, Benson Smith.

He was not any less Benson Smith when he was at Durham, but no one knew it. "Smith III" concealed completely the name

destined to be so famous. Even the headmaster, who appraised
boys very accurately, failed to recognize him. Not that recognition
would have made any difference to Doctor Holt. His evaluation of
a boy was based, correctly, on a boy's behavior, and a somewhat
subtle product of it described by Doctor Holt as "his attitude."
The raw material for that disturbing and so often unpleasant
quality called genius may have been distinct in Benson Smith, but,
as sometimes it does, it happened to look very much like laziness,
bad temper and deliberate, insolent contrariness. Such capacities
made Doctor Holt roar.

Doctor Holt was, in fact, a roaring schoolmaster, being a genius
himself. His instinct instantly rejected much of the nonsense
making up modern pedagogies. He had an inspired knowledge of
when to be patient and when to be impatient. His genius was his
uncanny gift for grasping what nine boys out of ten thought and felt
and intended to do next. He turned hundreds of them out; healthy,
honorable, quite intelligent enough to have no trouble with college-
entrance examinations. A thousand more — many of whom with
their names entered when they were born — waited perpetually
to get in. "Durham," "Doctor Holt" were great names among the
Eastern preparatory schools.

Doctor Holt had a magnificent, solid, convex profile. The type
is often small-boned, intellectual, but Doctor Holt's face was like
something outstanding and lordly cut from a cliff. His blue eyes,
keen, haughty and wise, waited, ready to leap. His tangled blond
eyebrows — these were a sandy, strong blond, and similar hairs
grew out of his massive nostrils — resembled somehow the illustra-
tions in the fourth-form Caesar, showing a cross section of the
Gallic defenses — ditch, glacis and a hedge of uprooted trees.
Rather round-shouldered, he was not tall enough to have a hollow
appearance. He was intensely solid; a considered, terrible energy.
Also, he was slightly deaf. This seemed sometimes a stratagem, for
whatever it was disastrous or inexpedient for him to hear, he
heard. Involved explanations, trembling evasions and artless false-
hoods he could not hear. He roared for their repetition — a task
beyond many a guilty conscience.

. . .

Smith III's difficulties at Durham were instant and endless. Smith III was a slight, dark boy. Although his health was actually excellent, he looked somewhat sickly — a combination which Durham could only excuse on the basis of outstanding scholarship. He had nothing approaching this, but to make Durham's trial more grievous, he was inescapably clever in a moody, reticent, rather insolent way. Most of all, he was agonizingly vain. Clearly he did not understand how third formers ought to behave. By the end of his first October, the prefects had come to Doctor Holt. They were very definite about what Smith III needed. He was a fresh brat and they had, with Doctor Holt's permission, ways of dealing with fresh brats. Doctor Holt withheld his permission until the end of November; he knew the difficulties of getting adjusted, getting settled, but by the later date he probably had a premonition that Smith III would never get adjusted or settled to anything regular or reasonable in this world without help, persuasion. There remained now only the minor detail of producing Smith III, informing him of his offenses, requesting him to bend over a table and receive ten cuts with a prefect's stick.

How these things get around it would be hard to say, but Smith III had his supper spoiled by the gratuitous information, supplied by delighted classmates, that the prefects were going to lick him. Without any proof or actual indication of the probability as yet, Smith III knew that it was so. He was not cold, calm or indifferent about it, either. He had imagination. Being condemned to death would not be much different. The terrible tastelessness, the elastic minutes, now stretched to break, now snapped short; the utter, intolerable inevitability, poisoning every thought, were his; and, in addition, the need to remain calm, indifferent, contemptuous of whisperings and gigglings.

At eight o'clock the prefects' sergeant at arms came into the quiet, bright study hall. He proceeded in silence, alert and tense, up the long side of the room, through to the center, down past dozens of passionately quiet, furtively watching heads. He dropped a hand on Smith III's shoulder.

"You're wanted outside, Smith," he said gravely.

The schoolroom breathed one great sigh—many boys hadn't been so sure as they wished that Smith III was going to be the victim, and they were exultant in this proof of their personal escape. There was a shuffle of feet, a stir of general relaxation, even a rash turning of faces, which the sergeant at arms checked by saying sharply, "Get to work!"

Smith III, however, sat still. "I'm studying," he said, in a hoarse but loud croak, widely audible. "I'll come after the period."

The gasp was more definite this time, and there was delight in it—not delight in support of Smith III, but delight that there was going to be a scene. Study periods can be indescribably long and dull.

The sergeant at arms was taken aback. "Come on, Smith," he repeated. "Snap out of it!" The sergeant at arms was invariably an athlete of stature and strength, selected for that reason. His appearance was intended to overawe, but Smith III had been waiting since supper, and he was far past any such reasonable process as being overawed.

"Can't you leave me alone?" he said. "Can't you see I'm studying?"

There was a rising murmur of cordial comment from the back of the big room. Like any social system, student self-government is solidly founded on the expectation that people will know the proper thing to do, will recognize customs in conduct. Smith III should have arisen, terrified but docile, and gone trembling to his doom. When he didn't, the whole system collapsed. There impended the embarrassment of an unseemly uproar. It is not easy, even if you are a crew man weighing a hundred and seventy pounds, mainly muscle, to remove with dignity a determined objector through a room cluttered with desks and packed with excited spectators.

Fortunately, these problems are the decent fictional products of the adult mind. The sergeant at arms' mind was destined never to be really adult, and though he afterward attained a superficial acquaintance with adult conduct, he was unhampered now. He solved the problem—how well Doctor Holt understood the advantages of having boys deal with boys!—in a natural way, regardless of appearances. One big hand, calloused from the long sweep oar, strung with relative steel from the great, winning spurts of Durham crews, locked hard on Smith III's collar, shirt included. The sergeant at arms picked him up like a sack. Smith III gave one despairing shriek. The sergeant at arms cuffed him neatly with his free hand. Then he passed, holding him aloft with cold indignation, through the breathless room, out the swinging doors into utter darkness, where Smith III's renewed lamentations grew fainter and fainter.

This was not the last occasion on which the prefects licked Smith III—the last occasion was at the end of his fourth-form year, when he had been found smoking cigarettes in the North Building furnace room, and consequently understood precisely what he was being licked for. This first one was important, for he did not really understand, even after they had informed him in detail that he was too fresh. The ecstasy of his hate and rage and terror—later to color, long after he had forgotten its exact source, his impression of Durham and his feeling for Doctor Holt—was due originally to that night. Smith III was not simply an incorrigible rebel. Smith III's intelligence was much too acute to waste its strength in a permanent and ridiculous war with his environment. Real rebels are rarely anything but second rate outside their rebellion; the drain of time and temper is ruinous to any other accomplishment. Smith III was not so much at odds with the universe as intent on bending it to his desires. He was not popular, but he had his friends. It is true that later he forgot this, seeing himself lonely, forlorn, despised and persecuted; just as he forgot that he was mainly happy, stimulated, fascinated by the unfolding world. It goes without saying that he was uncritical and many of the ideas he began to develop were not really his.

Much less were they Doctor Holt's. When, early in his fourth-form year, Smith III took occasion to inform the headmaster that he no longer believed in God, Doctor Holt sighed. Smith III's point had been that he did not see how he could honorably go to chapel when he considered the practice a superstitious farce. It is usual to hear most about the other side of these things — Shelley, at Oxford, is almost unbearably familiar — so it is worth a moment to consider Doctor Holt's position, confronted by a supercilious and impudent youth who appeared to get the only exercise he took from making trouble; who was very justly suspected of smoking without permission; whose marks were bad, and whose important comments on life, society and the school were fitted nicely to the puerile sensation they made. Doctor Holt hadn't the smallest intention of putting such a premium on atheism as excusing Smith III from chapel. He did not consider Smith III's arguments to be as novel, compelling and conclusive as Smith III did.

"Nonsense," he said, "nonsense. Certainly you'll go to chapel. I'll give you some books on the subject. When you finish them, we'll discuss it."

Smith III, as the saying goes, had read a book. It was Paine's *Age of Reason.* "I can't conscientiously do it, sir," he repeated. He never lacked what might be called courage, if courage describes that exhilarated stubbornness whose finest flower is impudence. He was afraid of Doctor Holt, but he had a temper of his own which was not contemptible, and now he was delighted to find that he stood, perhaps paradoxically, with those others who had trial of cruel mockings and scourgings — yea, moreover, of bonds and imprisonment.

Just as, long before, the prefects' sergeant at arms had been faced with a problem in unreasonable behavior, so was the head-master now, and Doctor Holt's mind was entirely adult. He was sorely tried, but, as usual, until some last insupportable development swept him away, he was patient with Smith III. He sensed easily enough a difference in the boy. Whether it was unnatural worth or unnatural worthlessness was hard to tell, but it was there. Doctor Holt raised his eyebrows, laid his hands open on the desk — a gesture indicating candidly that he was not concealing weapons in them.

"Smith," he said mildly, "I understand your problem. We're all troubled sometimes by doubts. It's only human. Work, study, prayer, have a way of solving them. I want you, as a personal favor to me, to continue to go to chapel. It is, if you like, merely a matter of school rules. Here," he said, reaching toward a bookcase behind him. "Take this book of Bishop Gore's and read it. When you finish, come and have a quiet talk with me."

But Smith III said, "No, thank you, sir. I have explained my position."

Doctor Holt should have known that what troubled Smith III was not doubt, but the need, which never left him, to be in the limelight. Perhaps he recognized it now; at any rate, instinct informed him that the moment had come for other methods, and his other methods were one.

"Get out of this room!" he roared. "I'm sick of the sight of you! Report yourself on detention for a month. If you're absent from chapel, the prefects will take care of it. Get out of my sight!"

Smith III got out, retaining a mouthful of especially insolent remarks which he had neither the time nor the presence of mind to utter until the door closed after him. He clenched his fists then and said them, firmly, with nice emphasis and hauteur—a business he was interrupted in by the opening of the door and Doctor Holt's congested face.

"What are you mumbling about?" Doctor Holt roared. "Anything you wish to say, say to me!" He made a movement which seemed certain to culminate in physical violence, and Smith III fled downstairs, slipped and fell part of the way, picked himself up and disappeared. It was apparent in the last analysis that he did not have quite the same attitude as the Hebrew martyrs.

Most young men—mercifully, they fail to realize it—reach, in the sixth form of a big school, the acme of such power and glory as their lives will provide. This was not true of Smith III. He was destined for what might, fairly enough, be called the world's sixth form; but not knowing this—even if he annoyed Doctor Holt and many other people by seeming to expect some future of the sort—he was highly gratified to be in Durham's sixth form, with all that it implied in relative position and privileges. He enjoyed himself; he even found pleasure in hating Doctor Holt — at least until the May of that final year, when he really hated him, when everything that went before crystallized in the cold determination that Doctor Holt would live to regret Smith III.

This crystallization was the result of one scene, when the atmosphere of antagonism was supersaturated at last, but there was, naturally, plenty of past material. Smith III had differed with Doctor Holt approximately once a week on every possible and impossible subject, from the time of the discussion about God to the final earth-shaking disaster of Mrs. Delancey. These differences took two forms — one, Smith III's contempt for and infraction of school rules; the other, a type of difference exemplified by such roaring moments as that when Doctor Holt personally removed from the bookcases and tossed out the window of Smith III's room several works, admittedly immortal, whose spirit and candor he none the less considered unsuited to the general circulation which Smith III was giving them. Almost constant roars reverberated from Doctor Holt's study during that exciting winter. Smith III was a thorn in Doctor Holt's paw, affording him no peace. That Doctor Holt refrained from plucking it forth was due partly to his pride — the injured pride of his genius for boys and how to handle them. The other part, you might think, resulted from an infrangible limit he set to even his worst tempers. He never, when he was enraged, allowed himself to expel a boy, and in Smith III's case he never ceased to be enraged.

Smith III was by now accustomed to living on a volcano. Eruptions might still appall him, but he knew what to do to escape real injury, and how to settle exactly where he had been before with little lost motion. If, on occasion, he had seemed to be doing something suspiciously like kicking stones into the crater, the last, most terrible eruption he never planned on, and it takes a mature mind to see justice in the belated lift of one's own petard.

Lorna Delancey was twenty-five. Two successive marriages had turned out badly for her. The second was even then being dissolved. Entirely through the chance that a friend of hers had offered Mrs. Delancey the use of a place there, she had selected the village of Durham as a quiet spot to spend several obscure months with her four-year-old daughter while the unpleasantness connected with Mr. Delancey was cleared up. Such are the ignorances of women, she had not even known that there was a school at Durham. But she soon found out, for her borrowed cottage was about a mile down the river and the four-year-old daughter had been regularly kept from a few hours' mischief by the afternoon appearance of eight-oared shells, coxswains barking, and the boom of critical comment from a megaphone decorated with a white D in the coach's launch.

Thus, when she saw the D, black this time, embellishing the white hats worn by several of a group of pleasant youths in flannels who were strolling the river road one Sunday afternoon, she felt amiable toward it and paid them a moment's attention, thinking, from the vantage point of twenty-five, how young and charming they looked. She herself was sufficiently young and charming for most tastes. She reclined in a couch on the veranda, a small, golden-headed figure in pale-blue muslin. The strollers in flannels saw considerably less of her in this position than she saw of them, but they were at an age uncannily susceptible to mere femininity, let alone something very much like beauty. They looked that way casually, one after another.

One of them said, "Not so bad. Who is she?"

No one knew. But Smith III, always an expert in the unexpected, inquired without emphasis, "Would you like to meet her?"

The suggestion received what might have been mistaken for merely bored indifference. "One of your girl friends, Smith? No, thanks."

Clark I earnestly informed him that he'd better not let the Old Man — Doctor Holt was indeed forty-five or -six — catch him playing around.

"That," said Smith III, "certainly worries me a lot."

"Mr. Smith" — they were all instructed by a boy called Frazer — "is a sensation with women. They stop him on the street and ask him how he's doing in school." The reference, producing mirth inexplicable to outsiders, concerned an old woman, harmless and half-witted, in the village, who sometimes, for no ascertainable reason, halted Durham boys and urged them to study hard.

Clark I, who felt rebuffed, as so many people did simply from some subtle perfection of Smith III's disregard, suggested, with more scorn than grace: "Trot in and give her a kiss, Smith. She'll think you've forgotten her if you walk right by."

A youth named Grant Lindsay phrased suddenly what they were all thinking. "Come on. Let's see what Smith's woman is like."

Smith III declined. "I gave you your chance. No, I'm afraid I don't know her after all."

"No," they told him, "of course not." Clark I, a little more discerning, observed, "Oh, Smith's bluffing again. Let's heave him in the river."

Grant Lindsay took his arm. "Come on, Benson," he said, turning him about, "do your stuff."

"All right," said Smith III coolly. "I don't know her. I never saw her before. But she happens to appeal to me. Suppose we see if she has any drinking water lying around handy."

"You know what the Old Man said about stopping at houses in the village," Clark I pointed out. "We'll lose our privileges and be in a rotten mess if he hears about it."

"Who's going to tell him?" asked Grant Lindsay nastily. "You?"

"This isn't the village," Smith III said. "He never said anything about stopping at places down the river."

When Lorna Delancey's sister came up to join her in the Durham retreat about the third week in May, she was pleasantly surprised to find that Lorna was not moping.

Lorna said to her presently, "Nancy, I've met some of the sweetest children you ever saw. They're boys from the school. My dear, they're simply too delicious! You must be nice to them. They'll adore your being here. They need someone else to dance with. And remember not to let them smoke when they're down, like a darling. It's against their rules and I don't let them. I don't want them to get into trouble."

It had not, you see, occurred to Mrs. Delancey that any trouble could possibly result when several of these sweetest children appeared at half past eight or nine and remained, taking advantage of the sixth-form privilege of late lights, until half past ten or even eleven. She provided an immense collection of cakes for them, and lemonade. Benson Smith, having the advantage of being the most articulate, she was most intimate with. She would have said candidly that she adored him. She meant by this that she liked his face and manners, and, even as Doctor Holt, who liked neither, she was, in addition, aware of something exceptional about Smith III.

This special feeling made her present no objection when Nancy, who had always been considered by the family better looking than Lorna, monopolized Benson Smith's companions. Lorna was accustomed to sit with him for varyingly long periods on the veranda steps while the phonograph supplied tireless fox trots inside. Out here you could smell shrubs flowering in the dark. Stars lay flat on the river and innumerable fireflies moved under the great soft shapes of the elms. She listened, her lovely and rapturous face soberly intent, her hair glinting in the shadows, to Benson Smith, who told her a great deal about himself, including much that was only partly true now, but which he meant to make true soon. Since—hers was acute instinct rather than any unusual intelligence—she did not want him to regret these rather touching confidences, afterward she told him a little about herself—enough to make her entirely tragic and almost holy in his eyes.

When he came at last to say that he loved her, she said that it made her very happy. It did. She was, despite everything, barely twenty-five herself, and the poignant innocence of the emotion that this timid worship caused her was sufficiently close to tears. Two or three evenings later he had accumulated courage enough to ask if he might kiss her. She hesitated a moment, taking his face suddenly between her cool hands and kissing him with a deliberate tenderness that he had not the experience to appreciate.

"No," she said at once, pressing her fingers hard against his lips. "Not again. I wanted you to know that I'm very fond of you, Benson. And that I believe in you, dear. You're going to be everything you want to be. Women can tell about those things."

She was deeply serious, and Benson Smith, naturally, loved her beyond speech. "When you go away next month," she continued, so he could not say anything, "you will never hear of me again. But I'll hear of you. Everyone will hear of you. And I'll be happy, Benson, to remember what a sweet boy you were."

Thus she had said, out of the kindness of her heart, out of the exquisite emotion that his simple inexperience caused her—perhaps out of that premonition about him—the words that he had been waiting all his life to hear. She did not let him explain, as he would have, that he could not possibly be anything without her. He would have asked her to marry him, not only because he was stunned by his love for her but because it seemed to him the necessary next step. She stood up.

"Now, darling, you must all go back to school. It's so late. You'll come and see me soon, won't you?"

"Tomorrow afternoon," he told her.

"Darling," she told him, "I have to go to town tomorrow, but I'll be back Wednesday. Come Wednesday evening and tell me that you've been studying hard and haven't had trouble with Doctor Holt."

Actually, a sixth former named Weston—not Smith III; certainly not Mrs. Delancey; not, directly, Doctor Holt— was responsible for all that followed. This Weston, leading greedy and dissolute companions, had found a new way to rifle the pantry closets. At nine o'clock Wednesday night the expedition, loaded with the evidence of Weston's ingenuity, encountered Doctor Holt without warning. Doctor Holt knew the value of violent discipline in minor matters. It maintained the morale which left him free to be much less arbitrary, more advised, in matters really important. It was obviously time he investigated sixth-form activities, and he walked immediately up and down, seeking whom he might devour.

In the roar of the following roundup, someone, intent only on getting the sixth form accounted for as soon as possible, mentioned that he had seen Smith III start down the river road. The moment was not one for considered speech or nice foresight. Doctor Holt had snatched some offending prefect's stick, and it switched like a lion's tail as he collected reports and explanations. Given the hint about the river road, Doctor Holt's knowing exactly where to find Smith III was not supernatural. He kept close track of people and places around Durham. Immediately he postponed his local investigation. He strode out and slammed himself into the fast motor which he was accustomed to drive like a fury over the countryside. Roaring in every sense, he swept out the school gates and down the dark river road.

Benson Smith had been sitting in the moonlight on the veranda steps, close to Lorna Delancey's satin-shod feet. He watched the moon over the great mounds of the treetops and said almost nothing. He was overwhelmed with a beauty, a peace, a radiant solemnity not to be described or defined. He might have guessed — though, naturally, he did not — that never again in his life would any woman or any moonlight be so unspoiled, so innocent, so entrancing as this. Neither May, nor music — how beautiful the fox trots seemed to him that spring! — nor the miracle of femininity like Lorna Delancey's could ever again be quite so rapturous. Now he wanted nothing except for it not to stop. He did not even look at her, for in his mind he had everything — more than there was to see — everything about her — face and form, the faintly perfumed things she wore, accumulated word and gesture of hers, even the sweet, keen pain of what he thought that she had endured.

It seemed to him that he might have sat there forever, but even thus lost to himself, sunk in the moonlight, in the scent and sense of her presence, he had other faculties, neglected but faithful. These caught the unexpected flash of headlights far off in the pacific moonlight, on the almost-never-used river road. They marked the torrential speed of the coming car, identified it and its driver, prodded Smith III instantly back to awareness. His heart contracted, his stomach turned over.

He cried out sharply: "Grant! Tom! Out the back and get to school! The Old Man's coming!"

That dreadful final phrase halted the phonograph.

"Come on!" Grant Lindsay called.

"No," said Smith III, "I'll stay." Every impulse he had was to flee, to flee far and hide deep, but even real alarm proved to be now less to him than Lorna. The hideous notion of leaving her alone, to face Doctor Holt, enraged, froze him where he was. He continued hoarsely: "He knows somebody's down here. If he finds me he won't bother about anyone else. Hurry up, and don't cross the open fields there. You have a couple of minutes, maybe."

Inhibitions against running away, deserting a comrade, develop, if they ever do, at a later stage. Grant and Tom Frazer kept clear of theories so intangible in a matter whose horror would presently be concrete and hard to exaggerate. If they had also been missed, there were ways far less disastrous to account for their absence. Nancy was kind enough to help then.

"Do run," she urged warmly. They ran.

"You go inside," Smith III said despairingly to Lorna. "Don't listen. He's going to be awful. But don't worry," he added, swallowing. "I can handle him. I'm used to it. We have much worse rows almost every day."

Lorna looked at him, aghast. "Benson," she said, "I'll explain to him. He certainly can't object to anything you've been doing here."

He shook his head. "No," he begged, "don't. Don't try to say anything. I'll make him stick to me. I'll see you don't get into any trouble, somehow."

Ordinarily, Smith III's own temper, his exhilarated impudence, his unconscious zest for conflict would have been mustering under the thin surface weakness of his apprehension, ready to break out at the first offense to his self-esteem. Now he felt his failings; he could take care of himself, but whether he could take care of Lorna or not he didn't know; whether he could keep her out of it, inviolate, as she must be; whether he could bear the shame of failing to defend her. He had, in fact, something like that fatal sickness of Antony's at Actium—danger not solely his dazed him; immemorial affections which had enslaved his heart now nicked his captainship. The sudden sweep of headlights into the little drive, the intolerable, brilliant shafts on the veranda steps, found him with no more resource or resolution than a sleeper can bring against some dreadful and incredible dream. He stood up jerkily, rubbing the palms of his hands on his white flannels, in a terrible sickness and confusion. The car door smashed shut and Doctor Holt came stockily across the dew-wet grass.

"Smith," he roared, "who gave you permission to leave the school grounds?"

"No one, sir," said Smith III faintly.

"Then why are you here?"

Smith III had a feeble idea. "I was walking, sir," he suggested. "I stopped to get a glass of water—"

"Speak up!" exploded Doctor Holt. "I can't hear you!"

"I said," Smith III repeated, even more feebly, "that I—"

"Answer me!" Doctor Holt shouted. "Don't mumble! I asked you a perfectly simple question! I want an answer!"

"I don't know, sir," responded Smith III, for that response at least he did know.

And now Lorna Delancey intervened. She had not as yet grasped Doctor Holt's well-known attitude toward anything unlucky enough to be female. His state of mind was the entirely understandable result of contact, before he had perfected the means to refuse it utterly, with that hopeless and maddening creature, the mother of a Durham boy, but Mrs. Delancey was naturally taken aback when Doctor Holt roared at her directly, "Be quiet, madam. I wish to hear nothing you have to say!"

Smith III interrupted falteringly, "Don't talk that way to Mrs. Delancey. I—"

Doctor Holt probably didn't hear him, for Mrs. Delancey,

although shaken, was proceeding. "I'm really frightfully sorry if anything has been wrong. Benson only came down here because I invited him. You must understand — "

Smith III could, after all, be dealt with any time, but so favorable an opportunity to defend his boys from small golden-headed women might not occur again.

"Madam," he roared, "I presumed that he was down here by your invitation. I do not hold callow youths entirely responsible for their reactions to the incitement of unprincipled women! Oblige me by not interfering in a matter of school discipline!" His terrible blue eyes appraised her sudden paleness in the cruel glare of the headlights. What make-up she used stood out stark; she looked frail, painted, and Doctor Holt had no taste for frailty or paint. "Madam," he roared on, "I am familiar with certain aspects of your past" — part of his ordinary information had been her divorce — "and they do not recommend you to me as a neighbor. I do not regard such proclivities or activities as they imply with moderation. I do not tolerate them in the vicinity of the Durham School!"

Smith III shouted: "You talk to me, you rotten old bully!"

This did create a pause, but it was shame, the rage of despair, that brought it out, not warlike anger; there was nothing behind it but tears when Doctor Holt awarded him his whole attention. "We'll have no more of your impudence, Smith!" He meant to tell Smith III that he was expelled, but he came, even at this awful moment, against his self-regulation regarding that act. Instantly he substituted tactics far more to his personal satisfaction. He had retained the prefect's stick that he had taken, and he applied it now with promptness, skill and a whole heart to Smith III.

Smith III retreated. He would not have believed himself capable of anything so shameful as desertion in the face of the enemy, but his outraged emotions gave him no command over himself; his nerves betrayed him to a hysterical cowardice. He winced back from those stinging cuts, and as he moved, Doctor Holt moved after him. When he ran, Doctor Holt, astonishingly, ran too, and very well. An epic chase began on the moonlit lawn. Up the river were about three hundred youths, left in a state of anxiety, who would have given anything to see it. They didn't. There was only

Mrs. Delancey and her sister, who had come out now and stood beside her, interested. The spectacle of Doctor Holt, stick in hand, pursuing Smith III was too much for Nancy; she melted in gales of laughter.

This fatal sound reached Smith III. He made no mistake; he knew it was Nancy that laughed, not Lorna, but more agonizing than any cuts from Doctor Holt's stick was the conviction he immediately had that the laughter was at him, at the unbearable shame and absurdity of the part he played.

He scrambled over the rough stone fence, tumbled into the dirt road below, frustrating Doctor Holt. Then he ran, without any sense of direction, as hard as he could. He would have liked to put the whole width of the world between himself and the irreparable ruin he left behind him.

Doctor Holt, turning back from the fence, had experienced a long-delayed ease of spirit and release. He looked at the stick between his hands, broke it and threw it away. He came quietly back to the steps where Lorna Delancey waited, horrified, and Nancy was still choking on her laughter.

"Madam," Doctor Holt said with the brusqueness which represented the height of his deference to females, "I deplore the unfortunate events just past. I will simply ask you to co-operate with me in a matter of discipline. Durham boys are forbidden to stop at or enter any house in this neighborhood. I will go so far as to say that I deeply regret any words of mine which your own conscience may convince you were unwarranted and inapplicable. Good night."

Driving more moderately on the river road, he halted when he came up with the stumbling figure of Smith III. "Get in, Smith," he said. "If I can rely on your good behavior for the remainder of the term, it will not be necessary to go on with this matter."

Smith III hesitated in the moonlight. Then he got in and sat beside the headmaster. Very quiet and white, he said, "Yes, sir." He saw that it might be a long time before a really suitable moment came to make Doctor Holt sorry. He sat cold and collected, ready to wait.

. . .

Just as it was not true, but a long-held idea of Benson Smith's, that he had been altogether miserable and unhappy at Durham, it was another of his ideas that he had worked a long time, neglected and unappreciated. As a matter of fact, though his fame was not established beyond reasonable question for ten years after that spring he had been in the sixth form, he had been appreciated almost at once. If he wanted to know how numerous his early admirers had been, he could count the considerable numbers of his present enemies. They were the ones who had discovered him, extolled him in his obscurity, and afterward, wounded and indignant, found that they had been perfectly right — Benson Smith was going far. He no longer depended on their good opinions or found the former balm in their company.

Much more constant and loyal was the Durham School, though Benson Smith never went back or paid it any attention. Benson Smith thought that he understood their attitude. Certainly they had nothing to lose by crediting themselves with having turned out yet another famous son. He confided as much to Grant Lindsay, almost the only Durham boy he remained acquainted with eleven years after his graduation. Lindsay, who had an amiable habit of neither agreeing nor disagreeing with anything, was at once impressed and amused by the conversation and company of a famous man.

"Oh, they all hate me at bottom," Benson Smith told Grant, whom everybody liked. "Everyone always has. Well, I hate everyone. I wish that made us even."

"There are plenty of people," Grant Lindsay said amiably, "who like you a lot, admire you more. And you know it."

"They're the ones who don't know me yet," Benson Smith said. "I'll show you why people hate me. I don't particularly mean to, but I just don't notice them. I haven't time for them. I have important things to do." He halted and pointed a finger at Grant. "Now, you know how it works," he said, "because it's working. You're thinking, 'He certainly takes himself hard. He doesn't need to put on so much side with me, even if he is wonderful — and by the way, I wonder if he really is.'"

Grant Lindsay grinned, recognizing that it was true. "I didn't know you cared what people thought," he said. "I suppose you like people to admire you. Well, oddly enough, so do I. That's just healthy vanity."

"I am vain," said Benson Smith. "I have to be. I couldn't do anything without a lot of admiration. It hasn't happened often, because usually I get so mad it doesn't hurt me, but I've never been able to forgive one or two"—the "two" was an exaggeration—"people who really hurt my vanity. Do you know, until I've shown those people, I'll never be satisfied. And it may not be long now."

"They've probably been shown already," said Grant Lindsay. He was thinking, good-humoredly amused at himself, how glad he was that someone like Benson Smith wasn't out for him. He detested unpleasantness. "Even Doctor Holt thinks you're quite an ornament now—and if you can remember as much as I can!"

"I can remember," Benson Smith said gravely. "But I imagine Doctor Holt's forgotten. Yes, I know he thinks very highly of me. In fact, I was even asked to speak at the endowment-drive dinner. There'll be lots of important people there, and I gather I'd be an advertisement."

"I guess maybe you would," said Grant Lindsay. "What did you do—turn him down cold for old times' sake?"

"No," said Benson Smith. "I thought I might speak, for old times' sake."

Benson Smith, although he had a gift for extemporaneous speaking, spent some time and thought on the remarks he would make at the Durham dinner. He would, after all, be talking for Doctor Holt, and Doctor Holt would understand instantly. Doctor Holt would have fifteen of the worst minutes he ever spent, waiting for the moment—and it wouldn't need to come—when Benson Smith might change his tone. He could simply extol, extravagantly, Doctor Holt's methods and manners, ignoring the wily and brutal implications which he would know best how to bring out.

When he sat down, no one could say that one word not in praise had passed his lips, but there would be a bad taste in everybody's mouth.

He had plenty of time, the night of the dinner, to think of this, as well as what more private score he might have. A former Secretary of State, who had a son now at Durham, sat on Doctor Holt's right, but Benson Smith was on his left — he had not seen Doctor Holt for eleven years, and it was pleasant to note how little he had changed. The table in the hotel ballroom numbered 1 was lined solidly with men — men of weight and importance — graduates from such antique classes as '04, '07; men nationally prominent, such as the secretary, whose sons were Durham boys.

Benson Smith had enjoyed honors more appropriate and more intelligent, but there was a certain difference here. All these grave, dignified and graying figures, persons of power and wealth and distinction in so many different fields, could not have been gathered together any other way. Their interests would not lead them naturally to see and sit with Benson Smith. They looked at him with that unique curiosity, the frank admiration such people reserve for those they do not understand but know they must esteem. In their scheme of things, they respected, of course, the Secretary of State, but they were, Benson Smith began to realize, much more interested to dine with him. Any one of them could just as logically have been the secretary, but Benson Smith, who sat there, dark, reserved, slender — actually he was getting a little plump, but he looked slender in this company — and so astonishingly young, was something none of them could ever have been.

There were four hundred other men in the room, gathered at lesser tables, and Benson Smith stood out for them in much the same way. The constrained conversation peculiar to such functions turned gratefully on him, and at a big table where a dozen members of his class had gathered to stare, astonished, at the changes in each other, there was real excitement. Everyone who had known Benson Smith felt slightly more important.

The perfection of the arrangement was unexpected. In his most optimistic moments, Benson Smith had not realized just how it would be. No gathering could ever be more impressed and less critical, for their pride in Benson Smith was pride in themselves; honor they paid to him was honor paid to Durham, and honor paid to Durham was paid to themselves; no one there would want to stint it. In many ways it was the oddest experience in Benson Smith's life to sit here, Doctor Holt at his right, the severity gone out of the solid blond profile, the bushy eyebrows eased in a warmth of good humor and satisfaction, his roar simply cordial and agreeable, while before them the table was banked with the Durham colors, as at a football dinner—Benson Smith saw a certain irony in that—and spread behind their heads was an immense oblong banner, white on black.

Benson Smith sat and waited. He had that old sense of exhilaration; the charm of the impending, spectacular and unexpected, intrigued him. It would be entirely adequate, he recognized, and dinner over, he heard out, grave and attentive, what the Secretary of State had to say about their beliefs and hopes, the importance of secondary education in the life of the nation, the meaning of great schools like Durham—which, it developed very gracefully, was Doctor Holt. There was a warm crackle of applause.

Doctor Holt moved over the amplifier disk connected with the loud-speakers in batteries of fluted trumpets at each far corner of the room. He explained what a pleasure and an honor it was to have the secretary there.

"I have now," he continued, "a pleasure—and an honor—very personal to Durham men. Durham is proud and happy in the success and distinction that have come to her graduates, and our pride and happiness is very full to be able to welcome at this dinner—so important for what we hope will be the future of the school—one of Durham's most distinguished alumni. I do not need to introduce Benson Smith to the public, to our friends, but for the benefit of that table over there, where I seem to see an inordinate number of men from his class, I will say that it gives me very great pleasure to ask Smith III to say a few words for us."

Doctor Holt moved over the microphone stand and, in a sudden fury of applause, Benson Smith stood up. He had been applauded before with better reason, and it was wine to him, but he had never been applauded like this; it was a sharp and intense violence, deliberate and purposeful. He knew it even better when he raised his hand, smiling, and the noise broke off obediently to a perfect attentive stillness. He looked about at the hundreds of turned faces reaching to the corners, to the walls where more oblong banners — class banners in their several colors — ran a rank of numerals around the great room.

He said clearly: "Doctor Holt has been good enough to remember that, for everyone in this room, and I hope especially for him, I am Smith III. I mean, that to talk about Durham one must be a Durham man. . . . Mr. Secretary" — he turned easily and addressed him — "we have all heard with the warmest appreciation the fine things you found to say about Durham and about its headmaster. To know how the school is regarded by one of your eminence is far more important to us than anything I could say. I can only tell you" — his eyes swept back to the hundreds of faces watching — "how the school is regarded by those of us she has educated — "

Grant Lindsay found him afterward, as the meeting was breaking up. "Listen, Benson, you missed your calling. I'll bet you netted him an extra hundred thousand."

"That's funny, isn't it?" Benson Smith said. "I came here to pan the whole outfit."

Grant Lindsay looked at him, dumfounded. Finally he had an idea. "Yes," he said, "the old place has sort of a hold on one, hasn't it?"

Some younger graduates, enthusiastic to the end, had persuaded the orchestra in the corner to play the Durham football songs, and they sang them. Abstracted, Benson Smith saw what Grant was talking about; just as he could see, with not-unmoving clarity, the sharp autumn afternoons, hear the roar of the big games — Hotchkiss and Kent and Choate and Somerset — but he shook his head.

"No," he said. "I wouldn't have cared about that. I meant to get even some day. I happened to find it was out of my hands."

"You mean you were carried away," said Grant, who understood that. He had been doing rather more cheering and reminiscing himself than he had intended to.

"That would be a nice way to put it," admitted Benson Smith. "Yes, I was carried away. I said what I had to. I couldn't have said anything else. Not with all those people who thought I was wonderful. I had to be wonderful, Grant."

"But what about Doctor Holt?" said Grant, perplexed. "Do you still feel the same way about him?"

Benson Smith smiled gradually. "I signed a pledge for much more than I can afford," he said.

It took a long time, but in the end the account seemed somehow to get squared.

We'll Recall It with Affection

Candidates for admission the following fall come up to Durham in June of the same year to write their preliminary examinations. The three upper forms remain only to take the college board examinations. Candidates for admission are supposed to be in bed and asleep at nine o'clock; but Walter Pickering could remember best, through the ensuing slow summer, those fine June nights in the Durham quadrangle. Like most of his fellow candidates, he had never been wider awake in his life. They were accustomed to hang out the darkened windows of the dormitory turned over to them for those three days. They watched the informal figures of upper classmen, massed on the steps of the study hall, sprawled in groups under the trees, everyone keeping his pipe proudly in evidence — they had smoking permission for an hour — while spasmodic singing arose with pleasant enthusiasm if no remarkable harmony.

Thinking of this, as he did constantly while July turned to August, Walter Pickering knew that such things could not be explained to his brother. Hugh was two years younger — only ten, in fact — and could not be expected to understand much. Hugh misunderstood matters much more simple and obvious. He had, for instance, merely giggled when he found that Walter purposed to do exercises in the morning. "My goodness," Hugh squealed, "what do you think you are?"

Walter, breathing faster, numbering his movements aloud, disdained to answer. He was, for one thing, practically a Durham man; and he meant to be an athlete. That, he had recognized quickly, was quite important; for during those three days he had made a close if inconspicuous study of Durham's great ones. Most of them were tall, massively muscular young men — revered half-backs, mighty oarsmen. Walter appreciated his own deficiencies in these lines, but he meant to begin correctly. He had, in fact, a real horror of any wrong start. To a degree this was disinterested; he meant to be a credit to Durham in a way surpassing his proud, similar hunger to be some day a great man and a credit to himself.

It was the disinterested part, the yearning to be a credit to Durham, that he could not have explained to Hugh or anyone else. That was emotional naturally; and the vividness of his emotions had years ago trained him into a concealment of them. He had a special sensitive need to conform outwardly. Inwardly, feelings beyond his control took their own course with him. He did not know how the other boys, watching with him from the dormitory windows, had felt; but if they remained there long enough — and very few failed to — the gathering below would at last prepare to break up, arising, knocking out pipes, gradually moving without plan or formality into a closer, more unified body under the shadows of the elms.

The singing had already run through the football and crew songs — and it was good to hear those arrogant rhythms; to realize that it was no use when Durham broke loose; to know that the Somerset School crew would certainly never get home tonight, having a long way to row and being already far out of sight. Now, in solemnity, conscious but, being universal, unashamed, they sang a song which Durham stands to sing. It cannot be said to have any great beauty of words or music. About its appeal to Durham's quiet river, passing placid and surely unheeding in the starlight; its proprietary mention of Durham's pleasant hills was something perhaps a shade pompous, certainly a shade or more hackneyed; but a hundred fresh voices were surer about this tune.

They turned with a strong unified sweetness on Durham, a place we'll all remember when we're scattered far and wide:

> "We'll recall it with affection,
> We'll recall it, too, with pride.
> Durham, thy sons to thee. . . ."

When they left, a residue remained; a very slowly fading echo of their simple and not altogether unreasonable mass emotion. It lived through the casual departing voices; it was there after the ten-o'clock-lights bell cut vibrant through the stillness; it was there, as far as Walter Pickering could tell, all night. The old brick seemed to have soaked it in; the trees were heavily hung with it.

In the darkened dormitory the watchers now went reluctantly to their beds. Some of them said good night to each other, but there was no general conversation. Afterward Walter lay in the darkness, listening to the breathing of the stranger who was his temporary roommate. His eyes, he found, were likely to be wet with tears; his throat was contracted with a painful, devoted joy, a sad unreasoned sweetness. He lay tense with violent resolutions, plans unlimited by any regard for possibility, hopes in no way tempered by experience, and most of them were devised to prove his passionate allegiance. Durham, thy sons to thee . . .

It was unfortunate that Walter Pickering, with intentions so high and anticipation so keen, should have begun his career at Durham by making Mr. Clifton dislike him. Mr. Clifton had charge of the old main dormitory. Here the first form lived in semiautonomous isolation, seldom subject to the direct attention either of the prefects or of the headmaster. It amounted to Mr. Clifton's kingdom.

Known irreverently as Snifty, Mr. Clifton was a short, severe man, dusty blond with inquisitive gray eyes. For all its dryness and economy in times of peace, his speech was capable of a cruel elaboration when hostilities were in order. At the first sign of trouble he unsheathed his tongue, and this edged instrument carried havoc over that psychological battlefield, the first form. An unfriendly faculty member had once remarked that Clifton could

well—as he did—afford to spare the rod. What child could spoil
when he was pickled perpetually in brine?

Mr. Clifton's study was at the south end of the dormitory. The
door opened directly on the long line of double alcoves, each with
two beds, two bureaus, one chair. Dormer windows lighted it;
sunny on one side, green with the summits of the quadrangle elms
on the other. All was ordered, clean and quiet. Mr. Clifton devoted
himself to keeping it exactly the same way, even when forty new
boys had been put there.

Pickering was not the only one, nor the first, to disturb the
dormitory's serenity that September afternoon of the school's
arrival. He did it, however, with something of the fatal enthusiasm
with which he did—and felt—everything in regard to Durham.
He had not, for instance, bothered to look at the bulletin board.
Downstairs he had thought only, in an unsteady excitement,
of taking definite possession of Durham, or at least his share of it.
Reckless with this yearning, he pushed his way through the moving
crowd in the main hall. Unluckily, he pushed no one really important. If fate had put a prefect in his way his attitude would have
been remarkably different by the time he reached Mr. Clifton's
kingdom.

As it was, he came unchastened into the dormitory, uttering for
good measure a meaningless shout. He raced from end to end, far
too rapidly to notice—it was a second chance, for the neglected
bulletin board would have told him—that cards were plainly posted
showing who slept in each bed. He had gathered such momentum
that he coasted directly into Mr. Clifton's study. Mr. Clifton,
reading in an easy chair, had already frowned a little when he
heard Pickering's initial shout.

Mr. Clifton now lifted his sharp gray gaze and saw a moderately
dark and somewhat sallow youth. This boy's face, slightly boned,
flat-cheeked, narrowed past a mouth which looked at once sensitive and too quick to speech, and ended in a frail sharp chin. The
eyes which encountered Mr. Clifton's were quick too; quick
enough to know better, but they showed no signs of doing that.
Instead they appeared to appraise Mr. Clifton's study in self-

confident curiosity, conclude that there was nothing in the room at the moment required, and return, not much impressed, to Mr. Clifton.

Mistakes, however, could happen, and Mr. Clifton reserved judgment, saying neither agreeably nor disagreeably, "How do you do?"

Fate, which had cleared Pickering's path downstairs of important people, now presented him with one; but Pickering was otherwise preoccupied. He did not recognize danger when it lifted its forbidding face and looked at him; he did not know that his whole immediate future was tottering as he opened his mouth. "I'm fine, thanks," he said, breathless. "Listen, where do I live? I'm Pickering."

Mr. Clifton's sharp eyes flickered as he unsheathed his tongue. Seven years in his present position had taught him to know a fresh brat when he heard one. "So you're Pickering, are you?" he said. "And you're fine? Well, even so, I'm afraid that you haven't altogether grasped the way we do things."

He paused, giving Pickering an opportunity to apologize. Pickering didn't take it. Comprehension very quick and complete can often result in the same appearance and the same speechless paralysis as no comprehension at all. Since Mr. Clifton's weapons were whetted for service on amazingly thick skins, they cut deep in thin ones; but experience didn't lead Mr. Clifton to flatter himself in this respect. He put his point home again with dexterity. "The most immediate thing for you to grasp is that we do not enter masters' studies without knocking. Next in importance is that in speaking to our elders we say 'sir.' You will find the prefects and the sixth form unpleasantly exacting about that. The faculty perhaps matters less; but we, too, are always grateful for any small courtesies. Another habit you should form is that of reading announcements on the bulletin board. The everyday routine will seem considerably less mystifying. Do I make myself clear?"

He did. More than from Mr. Clifton—for Pickering had known in one terrible flash all Mr. Clifton's points before Mr. Clifton so aptly summed them up—Pickering recoiled from himself. Pickering was not, in fact, accustomed to enter rooms without knocking, or show himself disrespectful to his elders. He needed no help from Mr. Clifton to be conscious, with a stunning horror, of the nasty solecisms he had committed. Mr. Clifton was not particularly surprised by fresh brats and bad manners. Twenty more years of living had taught him what Pickering did not realize and would not have believed — that at thirteen little one does has any lasting importance.

Mr. Clifton did not know the intensity with which Pickering had planned to be a credit to Durham. The matter was closed as far as he was concerned. "Go down now and look at the bulletin board," he said. "That will be all."

The Durham School arises at 6:15. During the winter months it might as well be midnight, but this Spartan custom had an honorable theory. The school's founder, an intellectual of the high-thinking and simple-living type, had pointed out in his austere day that boys no older were getting up and going to factories at that hour. Was the education of the nation's leaders — he believed that, too — a less exacting and important matter than learning to tend machines?

One could see the sun rise at the first assembly, and breakfast was electric-lighted. Classes began at eight o'clock. This routine was obviously no very real hardship; but psychologically, darkness encourages the disinclination to get out of bed. Consequently, instead of a five-minute bell customary for assemblies, they rang a one-minute bell. You could not possibly get up and dress — even if you omitted bathing — and reach the schoolroom in one minute. The prefects were remorseless in checking the first assembly for any short cuts in the toilet. It was a serious matter to be found wanting.

Pickering was absent eleven times in October, which probably broke the school record and suggested that Pickering was an outstandingly slothful and recalcitrant youth. In point of fact, Pickering was only average in those directions; but two boys named Allen and Hone helped him to his perilous distinction. They were accustomed to seize and conceal all Pickering's shoes when he went to wash. In the end Pickering attained a sort of solution. He slept with a pair of shoes under his pillow, thrusting his feet into them as soon as he got out of bed. This was rather a nuisance and normally you might have expected him to be able to borrow a pair. Unfortunately, by October, there was very little that was normal left in Pickering's existence, so he simply resigned himself. He had hoped at first that Allen and Hone would soon tire of the trick—his elders had informed him that tormentors would tire if you just paid no attention to them—but Allen and Hone never did. He added this correction to his other painfully gained wisdom.

It was a wisdom mournful and confusing, for he did not very soon understand how completely outside the rude pale he had put himself. Consequently he did not take advantage of the real, if rather dreary, privileges of such a position. He could, without arousing much comment or undue retaliation, have appealed to Mr. Clifton, who would have made short work of Allen and Hone. Mr. Clifton did not, it would have interested Pickering to hear, tolerate bullying in the dormitory.

Inside the accepted circle, of course, such an appeal couldn't have been made; but it was just what they expected of Pickering. Inside, two did not fight one; people were not hit when they were down; one shook hands and made up after fighting; one loaned readily one's belongings; and supported an ally or accomplice to the death. Outside, there was no law and no limit, nor could Pickering do himself any service by trying to observe one. Allen had definitely ruled Pickering out.

Unfortunately, Allen shared Pickering's alcove. This was no choice of Allen's, and he punished Pickering for it at least once a day. Allen was a sturdy and handsome youth, a born bully of amazing competence and fruitful invention. Pickering, who shared among his other quaint beliefs the one that bullies are cowards, had a hard disillusionment. Allen's bold and restless blue eyes sought unceasingly harder knocks, more disastrous chances, more moving accidents, more hairbreadth escapes in the imminent deadly breach. His loud voice was cheerful, rich with his unbearable energy. He was amazingly impudent, but his impudence had a courageous and sunny quality which evoked only admiring amusement. Even sixth formers called him, two weeks after his appearance, Heinie. He was not remarkable for his intelligence, but he had quite enough to recognize, when the pleasant fact was thrust in front of him, that the world was much the same everywhere to such of its natural lords as himself.

Allen began by fighting with Hone. In Hone he correctly suspected the presence of almost an equal. Hone behaved splendidly. He blacked one of Allen's eyes before Mr. Clifton's arrival ended the conversation; but Hone knew that, given time, Allen could and would have licked him. They were both satisfied, and since they both served detention every afternoon for a week, they became very friendly.

Pickering, for his part, had been somewhat shocked by the vigor and savagery of this brief battle; but he was comfortable in the sharing of Allen's alcove. He saw that he was lucky to have someone so impressive living with him. That he was safe only so long as other business occupied Allen didn't occur to him. He was taken by surprise when Allen, bored, gave him a thought.

Allen's thought came one day in the first-form classroom. He sat conveniently behind Pickering. By driving it through the upper front edge of the sole of his right shoe, Allen was entirely successful in his scheme to sink a pin well into Pickering; the whole with neatness and inconspicuous dispatch. Pickering shrieked.

If Allen had hoped that Pickering would attract some unpleasant penalty from Mr. Reeves, at the moment teaching them Latin, he underestimated Mr. Reeves. As it happened, that pin-and-shoe idea was not exactly Allen's original invention. Mr. Reeves said briefly, "Take two hours, Allen."

And that was that. Allen was free to reflect on the impropriety of Pickering's yelling like a baby. If Pickering had kept still Allen would have been able to go on jabbing the pin into Pickering from time to time for the rest of the period. Cheated of this pleasure, he considered the back of Pickering's head with indignation growing righteous.

They were released for recess after that, and Allen wasted no time. One has to act quickly to get a thorough beating up provoked and completed in fifteen minutes, so he turned promptly in the hall, laid his *Fabulae Faciles* on the ledge and said to Pickering, "Listen, you sad bird, I've got a good mind to bat you one!"

Even Pickering knew, by that seemingly meaningless term "sad bird," that Allen intended mortal offense. He was naïve enough to consider this outrageous on Allen's part. As far as he knew, he was the injured party. In the resulting confusion of mind, Pickering let his all-too-quick tongue lead him whither he would not. The response came with wholly deceptive readiness: "You call me a sad bird again and I'll bust you one."

"Is that so?" said Allen. On the basis of his frail appearance, Allen had been discounting Pickering. Not realizing that Pickering didn't remotely mean what he said, Allen gazed at him with somber satisfaction. "Look out, crybaby," he whooped, "it's coming at you!" His hand—a sense of etiquette forbade him to double his fists until fists were doubled against him—whipped out and rang on Pickering's cheek, slapping him over to the wall.

The sting of that blow restored Pickering's sanity. Pickering pardonably disliked fighting because he had never been any good at it. He knew that Allen could hit him harder than anyone enjoys being hit, and the insane idea now came to him that if he provoked Allen no further it might pass off. He said, and his alarm was perfectly obvious: "You let me alone. I didn't do anything."

Allen was outraged. For all of fifteen seconds, he had been allowing Pickering the honor of a doubt about his being a sad bird. To the previous injury of the betrayal to Mr. Reeves, Pickering now added the insult of attempting to deceive Allen. "Aw, crybaby!" he said. "Don't you want to be licked?"

"You let me alone," repeated Pickering, aghast. He could not back any farther because of the wall; but his stomach did not seem to be so hindered—it receded indefinitely. Allen advanced on him, making any other escape impractical. "You let me alone," Pickering continued, more faintly.

"How can I let you alone," inquired Allen with elaborate zest, "when maybe all the time you know what you need is a licking?"

Pickering swallowed and made a slight side movement. Allen corrected it by slapping him skillfully. "Now, now," he said. "Don't go. You shouldn't be so bashful." He put his palm against Pickering's nose and bumped Pickering's head vigorously on the wall. "There, now," he said, noting the results with pleasure, "don't you cry. Heinie's going to give you a good licking absolutely free. Oh, you don't want a licking? Well, when I ask you a question, you'd better answer it right away. Because, now, it's too late—"

His speech was tellingly interrupted. *Fabulae Faciles* is a slim volume, but thrown hard at close range it is no contemptible missile. The hard corner hit Allen full in the face with one of those sounds that make you wince. Allen stood quite stupid a moment, raising an automatic hand to his nose, from which blood now began to make an embarrassing appearance.

What little belligerent rage Pickering had mustered was immediately dissipated. He was capable of quick thought and it took him to no comforting conclusions. In an ecstasy of terror he cried: "Gosh, Heinie, I'm sorry. I didn't mean—"

Allen could take infinitely harder knocks without distress. His stupor was already past. "Oh, no," he said, "you aren't sorry yet. But, oh, boy, are you going to be?"

The answer was naturally yes; but at this moment a section of sixth-form trigonometry was released up the hall. Out, among other people, came a very great man named Kennedy. Kennedy enjoyed the distinction of being senior prefect. Seeing the disturbance, he halted with a slight frown of authority. Then he approached. "What's going on here?" he said. "Oh! Well, brat, what's your name?"

"Pickering," admitted Pickering too promptly. Kennedy was addressing them both. It was usually the one with the guilty conscience who spoke, Kennedy knew from experience. What he did not know was Pickering's sweet and unsteady relief at this postponement of Allen's actions.

"All right," said Kennedy; "tell Mr. Clifton you've been fighting and I gave you an hour."

He turned now, about to give Allen an hour, too, on general

principles; but the unfairness of the penalty rearoused in Pickering a little of that fury of despair which had caused him to throw the book. Shrill-voiced, he made two more mistakes. One of them was speaking to a prefect at all; the other was his own dreadful sort of error. "Why should I get an hour?" he cried. "He hit me first!"

There was a second's frozen silence, in which Kennedy commemorated the outrage of one of Durham's more sacred canons. Whatever happened, you did not make an effort to shift the blame.

"Oh," he observed icily, "he hit you first, did he?"

Pickering, in all literalness, would have forfeited his tongue to recall that statement. "No," he yelped, "no, no. I—"

"Sure," said Allen. "I hit him first, sir. Who wouldn't?"

"All right," said Kennedy, recognizing him agreeably; "that's an hour for you, Heinie."

"Yes, sir," said Allen. "Could I hit him again and take two hours, sir?"

Kennedy grinned. "Get out of here, brat!" he said. He twitched his stick down from under his arm. "I'll tan your hide!"

"I get an hour, too, don't I?" said Pickering.

"No," said Kennedy with complete contempt; "you don't get anything. Go on, beat it; all of you!"

At Christmas his mother was somewhat concerned about Walter Pickering. She did the Durham School the injustice of thinking, privately, that they must feed the boys badly. She was disturbed, too, by the unusually poor showing Walter made in his studies. He had always been very satisfactory that way; usually leading, or nearly leading, his class. "And another thing, darling," she said. "You really must write home more often. I know you're very busy with your work and games, but I simply must hear. You'll try to write once a week, won't you, dear?"

Walter assented to everything. The ecstasy of his relief at being home made promises easy; made it easy to display the one virtue which Durham had managed to inculcate—keeping his mouth shut. He even found it politic to agree, when his mother found to her horror that his underwear was restricted to shirts and shorts instead of woolens, that he would henceforth wear something more suitable. He was sorry that she felt it necessary to buy him more to replace the ones he had lost—their losing had been rather difficult to manage without attracting comment. Hugh said simply, "Did you play football?"

Walter answered that he did, some. The subject was a sore one, for he discovered soon enough what Allen and others had told him at once. He had no aptitude for foctball. It wasn't altogether true that he was afraid of getting hurt; but there is a certain discouragement in getting hurt constantly—a matter Allen was pleased to take into his competent charge—without ever accomplishing anything or attracting any attention aside from reproaches and sneers. On the whole, he decided that he had better give up football. If this decision pleased Allen, it displeased Mr. Clifton. Mr. Clifton, consciously or unconsciously, had paraphrased the motto of a much more venerable English school. Football, he believed, maketh men. He did his best to see that all boys in his charge who were physically sound had places on the several teams of a lower-form league which played hopeful and inefficient through a schedule of games with one another. Mr. Clifton could not compel Pickering to play, but he could be and was rather abrupt with Pickering.

Curiously enough, Pickering elected to take the morning train to Durham when he returned. His mother perhaps mistook it for zeal to be back, but Pickering had other thoughts. He felt no desire to travel with most of the school on the afternoon train, subject as he would be to the eager attentions of Hone and Allen. He had, too, the necessity of getting rid of his new underwear, about which he was taking no chances.

As a result, there were not more than ten Durham boys going up when he did, and he saw only one of those. This was no less than Carraway Dickson, a notable Olympian. To the glory of rowing No. 5 on the first crew, he added a prefectship and the honorable nuisance of being managing editor of the school paper. It was the last office which brought him up early. He had to arrange assignments and supply several editorials and get off copy which should have gone before the vacation started. He purposed to do all he could on the train.

He would not have noticed Pickering at all if he hadn't come out on the rear platform to smoke one of his last legal cigarettes and so discovered Pickering in the astonishing act of opening a vestibule door.

Carraway Dickson met the situation with athletic efficiency. He caught Pickering by the collar before Pickering knew what had happened. He jerked Pickering back to supposed safety and so prevented the disposal of a bundle roughly wrapped in newspapers. The bundle dissolved, littering the vestibule with woolen union suits.

Viewed from his own level or from above it, Carraway Dickson was a naturally amiable, scholastically somewhat obtuse but not stupid youth. He bore, in fact, no remotest resemblance to the grim, glorious and long-limbed giant which Pickering, looking up at him, saw. "Well, what do you know—" Dickson said candidly, grasping the situation.

Pickering began to weep. He pressed a fist, dirtied by the door fastenings, into his eye. He foresaw the complete ruin of any possible fresh start this term. While he knew that he was less than nothing to Dickson, he was used to a world where unpleasant things never proved improbable. He saw nothing improbable in Dickson's reporting the incident to the first form.

"Here, here," said Dickson, frowning, "cut it out!" He was embarrassed and even distressed. "Oh, I guess you're Pickering, aren't you?" He hesitated a moment. "You ought to know better than to throw good underwear away," he said.

Pickering continued to weep and Dickson looked again at the underwear, indecisive. "What's wrong with it?" he asked rather insincerely.

Pickering managed to say, "I'm not going to wear it."

"Hm," said Dickson. He bent and collected the garments. He looked at Pickering's dirty and swollen face again. Then, bunching the underwear in his big hand, he deliberately opened the door and tossed it out. "You shouldn't fool with those locks," he said to Pickering. "Suppose you fell out?"

"What would I care?" asked Pickering. He rather wished that he had fallen out, now he thought about it.

"Oh, don't be dumb," said Dickson, impatient. "What are you crying about? They're gone, aren't they?"

As anyone but Pickering might have guessed, Dickson never did mention the matter to Allen or Hone. Dickson even went further. When he noticed Pickering and was not thinking of anything else, he spoke to him. This did not seem a very important action to Dickson. He simply encountered from time to time the intense, doglike gaze of a small, dark, somewhat thin little boy. With the amiable good temper resulting from his muscular and athletic well-being, Dickson said, "Hello, brat!"; grinned slightly; and passed on. The matter was more important to Pickering, for Dickson seemed to be the only person at Durham who ever said anything civil to him. As Pickering had nothing else to do, he spent much of his time loitering about where Dickson might pass.

It might have been better if Pickering had employed some of this leisure in going out for the little boys' hockey teams, and so pleased Mr. Clifton. Unfortunately, Hone and Allen were again the bright first-form stars on the rinks, and Pickering knew better than to attract their attention needlessly. He might even have occupied himself by studying more; but studying is a dreary business anyway, and drearier when you have nothing to relieve its monotony. At the very least, he might have spent some of the spare time in writing his mother, but he avoided writing. It was a melancholy task to invent material suitable for her to read.

It was, in fact, so melancholy that she was driven finally to a system of her own. This included a stamped and addressed envelope inclosing a sheet of important questons, each followed by a blank space for the answer. Certainly Walter could not be too busy with those games and studies of his to fill this document in and return it. She was, of course, right. It was much simpler; but the actual mailing of letters Pickering still found difficult. He avoided as much as he could the unfriendly publicity of passing through the main hall where the mailbox was. Envelopes he meant to post sometimes reposed in his pockets for days, growing grimier and fraying at the corners. He chanced to carry, in this messy manner, one of his mother's questionnaires for so many days that the envelope was obviously no longer fit for the United States mails. He discovered this as he sat one afternoon in the corner of the library and regretfully he removed the inclosed sheet, planning to get a new envelope.

Arising to go to the night assembly, he left it there, unobserved.

The combination of resulting circumstances had the fateful inevitability of most of Pickering's misfortunes. As it happened, the headmaster was that week absent, and when the headmaster was away Mr. Clifton was accustomed to take over temporary direction. Mr. Clifton sat at the head table in the dining room. He said grace before the meal and gave out announcements afterward. It was to Mr. Clifton that somebody brought the sheet which Pickering had left in the library.

To say that Mr. Clifton knew as soon as he saw it to whom the sheet belonged would be unjust. Very likely Mr. Clifton didn't, and certainly the information on it would have been no clue. Pickering naturally answered his mother more as he knew she would wish to be answered than as the facts of his life might dictate.

At any rate, with supper concluded, Mr. Clifton arose, read out several general notices. "I have," he said, "also a paper here, dropped by someone. I would like to know who it is who can't write home often enough and has to be supplied with a list of questions. Perhaps the owner will recognize some of this." He began, thereon, to read aloud.

"'Are you,'" he read, "'wearing your warm underwear?' The answer is 'Yes.' 'Are you playing hockey?' The answer is again 'Yes; our team won a game yesterday!'" Mr. Clifton paused and frowned gravely. The dining room, after an amazed pause, dissolved in a roar of laughter and sardonic cheers. Mr. Clifton held up his hand. "This is a very talented young man," he continued dryly. "It appears that his weekly marks were: History, 90—"

This certainly sounded rather as though Mr. Clifton did know who it was and did not mind punishing the obviously untruthful author. It sounded too much that way for Pickering. Distracted, he did, as usual, the worst thing. He made a sudden gurgling noise. Violently he deserted his table far down at the room's end. He galloped, frantic, for the doors.

There was again the hovering pause of surprise, again the immediate rich thunder of laughter coming down. "Who was that?" said Mr. Clifton, and a prefect answered him, "Some brat, sir." But down among the lower-form tables the electric word had already been passed: "Pickering! Sure, didn't you see him? Listen, dearie, are you wearing your warm underwear?"

Pickering was eventually discovered in the trunk room on the top floor. Mr. Clifton was somewhat exasperated, for he was due at a faculty meeting that night, and the discovery had required a diligent search. He presented Pickering with an hour's detention for cutting—as indeed Pickering was by that time—night study. He also spoke to Pickering about lying, a habit of which Mr. Clifton heartily disapproved.

"What earthly use," he asked reasonably, "is there in writing your mother that your marks are all over eighty? She will see the term marks and—"

Pickering didn't explain that he was accustomed to let the future take care of itself, since he was not even capable of taking care of the present. He merely sniffled and rubbed his eye.

"Report to the study hall," said Mr. Clifton, displeased. "Make another copy of this, with a little more care about the answers, and bring it to me to see that it gets posted. Henceforth you will come to my study every Sunday afternoon and write a letter home. That's all."

But naturally it was by no means all. Allen and Hone decided— Mr. Clifton was still safely at the faculty meeting—that the only way to make really certain about Pickering's underwear was to conduct a personal investigation. They sat on him and relieved him of his outer garments. Pickering was certainly not wearing what Allen called his woolies; but the disrobing had entailed some squirming on the floor; and Allen was, to a degree, justified in reporting that Pickering was a dirty mess.

"I wondered," Allen said with cheerful lack of refinement, "what smelled so funny around here. I'll bet you he hasn't had a bath since September." The upshot of the matter was that Pickering, supervised by Allen and Hone, thereon did get a bath, which included plenty of soap, especially in his mouth. It was not a very happy evening.

Nor was it pleasant thereafter to be known as Woolies. The only person who appeared not to know that Woolies was his name was Dickson. Dickson continued to call him brat, and once, by some chance, Pickering. In the whirlpool of cruel circumstance which had surely sucked Pickering somewhere near to its fearful bottom, Pickering considered this remaining straw with prayerful hope. The delirious fancy that he might repair his prestige with Dickson's Olympian aid continued to visit him. The result was a good deal of thought; and even implausible hope is better than none. It carried him somehow through the spring vacation, while he struggled with plans to get Dickson on his side. He wanted to do something for Dickson. Short of finding that great man in a net and gnawing him free, it would be hard to guess what; but finally Pickering did have an idea.

The Durham School discourages indiscriminate feeding. One may receive two boxes of things to eat a term. The recipient and such guests as he selects may be excused from supper and are required to consume everything at one sitting; or, at least, are required to turn over to the prefects anything that remains. Pickering had not been naïve enough to imagine that he could placate his enemies with food; and since he had no friends, he had not yet asked for a box. But, he thought at last, he might have one now; save out all the best, turn the remainder over to anyone who wanted it, and dutifully convey his selected offering to Dickson. Presumably Dickson would be favorably impressed; might pay more attention to Pickering.

Heartened by this scheme, Pickering even ventured, on the box's arrival, to mention the matter to Allen. Allen considered the question briefly. He was far from having no ethical standards, and he quickly decided in the negative. He purposed, when occasion arose, to treat Pickering as Pickering deserved to be treated. Consequently, while it would be proper for him to swipe food from Pickering, it would not be suitable for him to accept it and sit down with Pickering to eat it. He said, "Keep your rotten food, Woolies."

Fortunately he was deeply engaged in baseball at the moment when Pickering transferred the box from the office to the dormitory, and Pickering was able to remove the more desirable portions, secrete them in a locked suitcase under the bed. Put off the scent by the fairly adequate remainder, Allen duly swiped a representative selection. The rest Pickering ate with the assistance of several lowly and ignoble boys who were content to reflect that food was food, and remarked only in passing on the poorness of the present offering. The melancholy feast finished, Pickering furtively got the things from his bag and went over to Dickson's study in the North Building.

Dickson happened to be alone. He had a Vergil on his desk, but he was in fact writing a letter to a young lady and he did not much like being disturbed. "Well, brat?" he barked. Pickering stammered, nervous enough, "I had a feed, sir, and I brought over the stuff that was left."

"Right," nodded Dickson. Pickering did not expect anything more. He trusted the quality of the offering would bring later reactions. He piled it on the table and turned to take his humble departure.

Dickson covered the letter to the young lady with the Vergil and scowled. "No," he said with sudden decision, "take it away."

Pickering paused, stunned. It was a second before the horrid and obvious truth struck him. Dickson, Durham's great No. 5 oar, was naturally eating at the training table, a diet rigorously supervised.

"Give it to Kennedy," Dickson said. He prepared his return to the letter. Then he turned quickly, his brows together. "What's wrong with you, brat?"

"Nothing, sir," said Pickering weakly. "Only I—" He refrained from sniffling. "I—" There seemed to be remarkably little to say. Finally he fell into rather than decided on "I saved all the good stuff I could for you. I—"

Dickson's good-natured and facile sentiments were undoubtedly touched. "That's nice of you, brat," he said with amiable sincerity. "I wish I could eat it, but they'd bounce me from the squad." He grinned slightly. "Anytime I can do something for you—"

The invitation was no doubt faintly tinged with irony, but it was friendly too; and Pickering, absorbing it, was stunned again by an inspiration so blinding that he didn't consider its probable impudence.

Dickson said: "What is it? Want something?"

Pickering sucked in air. "Yes," he blurted, "—sir. When you beat Somerset could you give me your shirt, sir?"

In the annual Somerset-Durham crew race it is indeed the custom for the losing boat to toss over its rowing shirts, reposing unused and suitable for preservation in the bottom of the shell, to the winner. Many of the nine successful heroes then passed on to favored brats, or to anyone else capable of appreciating them, the trophies thus obtained. There is no more desirable room decoration, and none so pregnant with prestige, known to younger Durham than the white, half-sleeved, low-necked garment, marked over the heart with the red crossed oars and the gold S of defeated Somerset; inscribed with the date, time and the donor's name for future inspiration.

Dickson laughed. "Listen, brat," he said, "how do you know I'm not going to lose my own shirt?"

"But if you do win," gasped Pickering—he was already unnerved by the irregularity of his request—"could I have it, sir?"

"Oh, sure," said Dickson, "if we win."

. . .

There was, of course, that faint possibility. Somerset might get home first. Such things had certainly happened in the past and Pickering tried to prepare himself for it. He said merely — and that to an unimportant youth of his own sort — "If we win, Dickson's going to give me his Somerset shirt."

This boy, called Cole, doubted him. "What would he give it to you for?" he asked, for he was sensitive to the distinction implied. "Listen, if he should, I'll give you — I'll give you ten dollars for it."

Pickering repulsed him with outraged scorn. Still, he reminded himself, it wasn't settled. Somerset might win.

It wasn't settled on the Friday of the race weekend either; but hundreds of people and scores of motors were arriving to see it settled. It wasn't settled Saturday morning, when Somerset arrived in insolent force, cheering, undismayed, their crews going down to the boathouses. Pickering, nervous and devoid of appetite, would have liked to speak to Dickson, but that proved impossible, for Dickson made his only public appearance with his mother, who had motored up, bringing with her a small and radiantly redheaded girl who was plainly to be Dickson's guest at the dances impending.

When they did come to settle it, the afternoon was almost over. A sprinkle of rain had fallen on two minor races which went duly to Durham. Now the torn clouds were opening and dull, smoke blue showed over the eastern hills. The great Durham elms at the boathouse were deep green, dripping. The river lay opaque and flawless.

At this breathless and beautiful moment, Somerset displayed unexpected prowess. Her red-and-gold blades were clocked to a clean and astounding forty at the three-quarter flag, with her frail prow half a leaping length in front of Durham's. It was a heartbreaker, for Somerset lowered the course record; but, unfortunately for them, Durham lowered it too; ten seconds more effectively. Rowing a fine unhurried thirty-four, Durham came out to a final lead of open water. Twenty strokes from home Durham got her up effortlessly, went away and left Somerset in the monstrous uproar of the lined automobiles. Somerset dumped back, lay forward; Durham, oars angling every way, drifted toward her launch, dipped hands, dabbed faces with the cool water.

Pickering, jumping up and down on the road, saw the Somerset shirts presently tossed and caught. A rabble of Durham boys trotted away for the boathouse, climbed on the running boards of loud-horned, gingerly maneuvering motors. Pickering would have started to run a hundred miles with confidence; but a fine car, long and shining, with a knot of Durham's black and white at the radiator head, paused beside him, invited him to jump on. Pickering did. He saw with awed and wordless pleasure that it was driven by Dickson's small redheaded guest and carried Dickson's mother. He would have liked to tell them that Dickson was going to give him the Somerset shirt, but they paid him no great attention beyond a kindly anxiety about the chances of his falling off, so he didn't speak, holding tight and grinning foolishly.

He said "Thank you," and dropped off at the boathouse.

Here Durham was gathering to see that great crew come home. Pickering shouted himself hoarse with the rest as they reached the float. He yelled with vicarious pleasure as they caught French, who was their coxswain, and tossed him as far as they could into the river. French swam deftly ashore and joined them as they put their heads together to cheer defeated Somerset, now arriving.

That left nothing to do but wait, and Pickering perched himself on the fence with the boy called Cole. Allen, Pickering admitted, would probably get someone's shirt, but he doubted if Hone would. He had settled the point raised by Cole, who was not so bad when you got to know him, by planning to live with him next year, and already he had in mind the arrangement of a vastly pleasant second-form room. He sat there, quite patient, engrossed in these matters, with Cole beside him, until the crew, more conventionally clad, made its gradual reappearance. The long car with Dickson's people was waiting with others, and Pickering did not know whether Dickson would have a chance to speak to him or not. He assisted in the small general shout which greeted each appearance, and made even a longer and louder noise when Dickson came out.

Dickson nodded acknowledgment in that direction, but he went, as Pickering really expected, to the car, where he stood a moment, plainly being told how wonderful he was.

Pickering, watching him hungrily, had now an abrupt choking sensation in his chest; his heart, hammering harder, appeared to be crawling up his throat and sweat started out on his forehead.

"Huh!" said Cole, getting off the fence. "A hot lot you know, Woolies!" For Dickson, though you might wonder forever what she would do with it, had beyond any doubt given the Somerset shirt to the redheaded girl.

On June eleventh the three lower forms went down. Walter's parents had driven up for him, bringing the still-casual Hugh. Hugh had several days previously finished another year of the contemptible education a day school provided for him, and Walter was glad that functions connected with this business of Hugh's had prevented his parents from coming up to Durham for Prize Day—prizes were the last thing that Walter could expect.

Hugh, presumably because he was at last approaching an age of reason, appeared slightly impressed by Durham. He made no objection when Walter said that they would have to go to the station before they left to see the morning train off. He had, he said, to say good-by to people.

He did, in fact, say good-by to Cole, who had decided finally to room with him anyway. Under Hugh's attentive eyes Walter was able to bustle about through the throng on the platform in an important fashion while people, rendered indiscriminate by approaching freedom, took no time to be unpleasant to him.

Even Allen said patronizingly: "Bye-bye, Woolies. Remember to come in when it rains."

At this point Mr. Clifton arrived and the crowded platform was boldly inspired to cheer him, describing him to his face as Snifty, which gave them all, including Pickering, a warm feeling and did not appear to annoy Mr. Clifton. Presently, too, the headmaster arrived, driving his car with Kennedy beside him; and there was a constantly growing crowd of upper formers, clad comfortably in sweaters and flannels. With these was Dickson, and Pickering was moved to overlook his faithlessness. He wormed his way toward Dickson and touched him timidly on the arm. "Good-by, sir," he ventured.

Dickson wheeled amiably about, and though perhaps nobody else noticed, in full sight of the wide-eyed Hugh in the car, he shook Pickering's hand. "Good luck, brat," he said, and resumed his former conversation with his equals.

Now the train roared in and Pickering stood watching them struggle aboard. Kennedy hopped out of the headmaster's car. "Let's have a long Durham for the brats!" he shouted.

It made a fine, shattering sound under the big trees. The train stirred, moved on with boys yelling through the windows. Walter went back to the motor.

"Gosh," said Hugh, no longer skeptical, "you have a pretty good time here, don't you?"

Walter looked at his brother. Passengers, peering curious from the train windows, smiled fleetingly, interested to see so many cheerful young men, prefects with their sticks, strapping young athletes wearing their varied insignia on felt hats and sweaters donned, carefully casual, with the letters inside out or on their backs. The fine proud sound of their cheering echoed still and Walter, on the heights, looked down compassionately at Hugh. The power and glory of his Durham broke up now, drifting away in strolling groups. He, too, got into the car.

"Listen," he said tolerantly to Hugh, "wait till you come up. You don't know the half of it."

The Guns of the Enemy

I think that the war made Doctor Holt sick. I know that he faced it with a brusque expressionlessness, curtly noncommittal, which boys who were then at Durham School remember very well. This attitude of Doctor Holt's probably perplexed many people—people like Van, who taught us French then, and had intelligence of no low order; as well as boys in the school, parents and fellow educators, who might not be expected to have any particular intelligence. Since, naturally, Doctor Holt never explained himself, it was ten years before I heard—and then from Van—what really happened that fall of 1917. I only knew at the time that Doctor Holt was quicker-tempered and that it was more terrible to come athwart him than ever before, or, I believe, since.

Doctor Holt could not be expected to take the war calmly. His work, which was his whole life and endeavor, concerned itself too closely with the necessary raw material, the one essential ingredient. War's gluttonous consumption of youth must have seemed, in its unspeakable way, a joke on Doctor Holt. It reduced all he was, all he did, to futility.

Nor could Doctor Holt see youth in so dispassionate an abstract. It takes a speechmaker to talk of raw materials and ingredients. Youth in solid flesh and active spirit had moved familiarly through his hands; his hands had shaped it somewhat in the passing. I suppose that Doctor Holt could shut his eyes and see sixth form after sixth form; not just the vague shape of marching men, but faces, every one with a name he knew; every one with peculiarities, distinctions and a history he had not forgotten. Catchwords would never seem so compelling as that long, living parade.

I was thirteen in 1917, a second former. Thirteen is too young for service, but not for war. For war, it is ideal. To carry thirty-nine pounds, one ounce of regulation fighting equipment and still be able to kill people requires more than thirteen's physical stature and strength; but inside, spiritually perhaps, no man any older ever had his heart in the equipment or his resolution in the killing. Neither can you — and I am not thinking merely of Van and the October of 1917 now — be much older than thirteen and give your brain or your belief to dogmatic protest or conscientious objection after the war is there. The fact is that a mature person has no proper place anywhere in a war. He is sure to find himself in Doctor Holt's hard position when they strike up the band.

What the band struck up was the Marseillaise, which is not so easy a piece as it may sound. The band was better at Durham football songs. Watching in the spring twilight, one could hear the occasional hasty snorts of big horns catching up, but that did not matter much; the drums were fine, and the skin of one's back crawled to the blare of the brass when it reached any sort of unison. The French officer's name was Loiseaux. Going the rounds of the Eastern preparatory schools to tell them what France was fighting for, he had certainly been well received; but I don't think he had been given a reception similar to Durham's before. He happened to reach Durham the day that President Wilson asked Congress to declare war.

Loiseaux — he was a major — had a fine brown face, with eyes plainly courageous. Everything that is admirable in an army stood with his uniformed figure against the light of the Pullman vestibule. He had stopped a moment; even he was startled, I suppose, to find the dusk alive with faces. Then he came quickly down, and boys who had climbed on the station hand truck could see that the top of his cap was scarlet, crossed with gold braid. The ragged roar of an unpremeditated cheer had gone up. Now the band began to play the Marseillaise.

Somehow, he recognized at once what it was going to be. He froze where he was and saluted the way the French do — that curiously awkward arrangement of palm and cap brim. The train went out two inches behind him, but he didn't flinch. He was left suddenly standing there, backed against nothing but April darkness, with the station lamps on his face. Everyone could see then that he was weeping; tears went shining down his stiff cheeks. Things like this probably do not happen twice in a man's lifetime. He knew, of course, that now France was going to win the war.

There was a special school meeting that night and Loiseaux sat on the platform of the study hall. He wore his medals and he looked, even so, as though he had fewer than he deserved. Beside Doctor Holt, he was short; and Doctor Holt was not a tall man. Loiseaux was beautifully neat and dark, too; which helped Doctor Holt look bigger and heavier. The reserved, ponderable threat of Doctor Holt's presence, making you leap to examine your conscience, was intensified. Doctor Holt's blue eyes were more menacing than ever, smoldering under his tangled blond eyebrows. Doctor Holt's intolerant and autocratic head tilted slightly in his customary brusque concession to his slight deafness. His strong convex profile jerked now right, to speak inaudibly to his guest, now left, in impatience, to see the prefects. The schoolroom rang with a warm, bright clamor — desk covers banged, feet shuffled, excited boys pressed in. This really didn't last very long, but Doctor Holt got up before it had finished. He strode over to the buttons which rang the big school bells and pushed them himself — you could hear the violently reiterated clangors of the one in the hall downstairs. He raised his voice sharply. "Quiet, there!" he said. "Quiet!" You might have thought that he was going to ask next who had been smoking this term without permission.

Instead, he said simply that before he invited Major Loiseaux to address them, he would read — he produced a folded paper — the

President's message to Congress. "You all know," he said, "that
the United States is entering the European war. I would like you
also to understand the reasons given." He began to read at once,
loud and fast. Frequently he interjected summaries of his own.
"He then speaks of submarine warfare," he would say, resuming
again at a lower paragraph. "He then declares that our enemy is not
the German people, but the Imperial Government." He deserted
the text a moment and, lifting his profile, barked: "I hope you'll
understand that; keep it in mind. We have no quarrel with the
German people. None whatsoever!" You could see a slight
movement of Loiseaux's eyes. He did have a quarrel with the
German people; they had killed three of his brothers, and forty-
seven years before — showing that they did not change — they had
killed his father.

This information he supplied when he came to speak. He was
not saying anything directly about the German people; merely he
mentioned that he came from a family of soldiers. He was familiar
with war and he did not want anyone to think that war was fun. He
had no words to describe the horror of it. Then, immediately, he
found words. You might wonder if his intolerable memories made
him forget why he was there. You might think that this was no way
to get America into the war, for in those days no one — certainly no
American who had not been there — knew what sort of war they
were making in France.

Doctor Holt sat heavy in his chair, the strong profile tilted,
which made him look away as he advanced his ear, listening. I
suppose he knew, for he was a great speaker himself; I suppose he
felt, for he was miraculously tuned to youthful reactions, what the
major was about, but Loiseaux took the breathless and appalled
schoolroom by surprise. His voice went up like a trumpet; he stood
suddenly even straighter, his hands dropped out, his fine impas-
sioned face lifted. "My friends" — his voice was amazing — "I can
say now, my allies — I am an old man — I will say, my sons — you
see where America is going, where your great President will lead
you, your brothers, your fathers. Not one, I think, will hold back.
There are things which can make honorable men endure to live and

glad to die." He was not making whatever regular speech he was intended to make — not tonight. He was talking as the French talk — out of his heart. One felt a little intoxicated. I can remember, too, the terrible concussion of our cheers. Remembering them, one turns cold; and that night on the platform Doctor Holt must have turned cold, but he applauded. I can see him sitting there on the platform and striking his hands together.

Most of the faculty attended that meeting, sitting informally along the side of the room. Mr. Van Artevelde didn't, but I imagine that nobody noticed it. The idea that anyone could take issue with Major Loiseaux was so incredible that even a noted absence would not have been considered significant. Similarly, facing our elementary-French section the next morning, Mr. Van Artevelde made no impression when, at least by implication, he first stated his position. It seemed that Loiseaux would make a second speech, in French, to a meeting of all the French courses in a large classroom later in the morning. Our consequent release from the usual recitation was a circumstance so pleasant that nobody paid much attention to what Mr. Van Artevelde had to say after he had said that.

Slight, rather tall, Mr. Van Artevelde had frank and unabashed artistic tastes. His head was crowned with very fine and soft reddish-brown hair. Its silky quality made it move into greater confusion every time he turned his head. The color was no doubt responsible for the seeming green of his eyes as they gazed, direct and candid, glittering a little, from either side of a thin, sensitively sharp nose. He dressed in tweeds with wide, soft-collared shirts, and neckties, thick, plain-colored and loosely knotted. He had been born in Antwerp, where his name and family were notable, though historically Dutch, not Belgian. For teaching French, this was his principal qualification. He had been brought up speaking it, though he must have been in America since he was ten or twelve, and was himself a Durham graduate. Doctor Holt was indulgently fond of him; during his first terms at Durham his parents had lived mainly abroad and Doctor Holt must have acted practically as his father. He had not been out of college quite a year. Though he looked like a man to us, he was not more than twenty-two. Doctor Holt doubtless thought of him still as one of his sixth formers. Doctor Holt called him Van, though his name was Frederick; and so, except in addressing him, did we.

That morning when the Frenchman was going to speak to us in French, Van did not appear in any way unusual. His reddish hair had tumbled down one side of his forehead; he stood a little to the left of the blackboards, tossing a piece of chalk up and down. He was accustomed to do this when he was waiting, and since he never looked at the process and yet never failed to catch the chalk easily, it gave him a curious air, at once nonchalant and impatient. His greenish eyes were no more bright and irritable than ever, but his tone was crisp.

"Now, shut up!" he said. "There won't be any recitation this morning. Monsieur le Commandant   Loiseaux"—his effortlessly perfect accent might have been a ten-foot pole with which he poked dirty and dangerous rubbish; but no one was then alert enough to see it that way— "is going to talk to you in his native tongue—to all the French courses. I presume that he is going to sell you more of the war. Fortunately, you'll only be able to understand about two words. When he finishes, shout at the top of your lungs: *'Vive la France, à bas les Boches!'* Now get back to the study hall."

What he thought was not precisely obscure. We might have foreseen everything that was going to happen, but still we didn't, nor did we even notice particularly that he alone of the French department was again absent when the major spoke. As Van foretold, we only understood about two words, but, as he sardonically suggested, several of the more literal-minded did shout, *"Vive la France!"* Afterward they wished they hadn't, for it takes more than a war to destroy Durham's scorn of any such showy demonstration. The cheers in the schoolroom had been a mass matter; no one was conscious of scrutiny or feeling like introspection, but that incident was closed. In broad daylight, at ten o'clock on a spring morning, Durham was not going to take its war in any death-glory mood. War was already enhanced by a noble solemnity and an emotional importance. Our attitude was, in fact, exactly that of America; with the special, local result that when we took things hard, less than usual was said about it. When little is said, much must be taken for granted. As you know, what people took for granted was that we were fighting for humanity and could not longer allow the Germans to infest the earth.

This may not have been entirely true, for Doctor Holt. His was a singularly pure patriotism, simply a respect for our different state which was unflinching and calmly reasoned. He had the courage — and courage it is if you value your reputation as a thoughtful man — to state: "Our country, right or wrong." Most people mistake the statement for jingoism, but it can be — and in Doctor Holt's case it was — the hard, honorable answer to an intolerable question. The question was not: "Do I believe in war?" At that moment when the republic had irrevocably committed herself, there could be only one question: "Will I work with her, or must I work against her?"

As a result, Doctor Holt did not roar out his very real detestation of militarism. Keeping his ominous guard over what he believed in, he had no time for irrelevancies of that sort. The most important thing he could do seemed to him to be preserving Durham unchanged as far as possible. Farsightedly, he could make a preliminary submission to changes of an irking sort. It would be too much to say that he did this with an easy mind, or philosophical. He must have had many bad moments. His profile was somber and dangerous as he looked at the class of 1917 — fine, long-limbed, hard-muscled boys, who had now in mind insignia more desired than Durham athletic letters. Their ambitions centered no longer on beating Somerset. Their chief anxiety concerned the preposterous apprehension that recruiting sergeants might find their hard and healthy bodies not good enough for annihilation by high explosive. Meanwhile they petitioned the headmaster to have daily drilling.

Doctor Holt did not refuse them. Here he went with the war. In the evenings he certainly stood out against it. He wanted his sixth form to go to college, not to the army. He didn't consider them fit for the army, or, at least, fit for the undreamed-of experience the war would probably offer them. Taking them for talks, one by one, as he did, he was probably educating himself too. He would see the possibility of having some time, perhaps very soon, to face the whole school in emotional opposition. He meant to hold Durham like a fort against the national extravagances of war. People who work with boys must take, automatically, a long view; what they would be like in ten years concerned Doctor Holt more than the present.

Some of that graduated sixth form probably gave way during the difficult summer, did not go to college. But his fifth form, which was the sixth now, Doctor Holt got back intact. Two young masters had gone. The new alumni directory showed page after page of names whose business or college address had changed to a camp. We began drilling again as soon as school started, and now there were wooden rifles to assist the illusion. Some patriotic person had presented us with a fine stand of colors; in addition to the national flag, a black silk one with the Durham seal in white on it.

Perhaps these small finishing details, acquired and employed with a very blatant zest, were instrumental in driving Mr. Van Artevelde to protest. Perhaps he had been spending the summer in touch with high-minded and determined semiprofessional pacifists. Van was, naturally, a socialist of some sort. In those years directly before the war, almost everyone who had the happiness to be young, intelligent and carefully educated was a socialist. This was in part simple intellectual snobbery, and the first cold wind from the world as it was blew it away, but Van was also an idealist, as well as being stubborn. To men of his temper, socialism's pathetic impracticality is not its worst argument; just as the principal charm of pacifism may be its dangerous unpopularity. I think those wooden imitation guns and the second flag—the black one with the Durham seal—touched Van off. He contented himself, to start, with the most passive protest. It was, in fact, a good deal more like surly bad manners than the frank stand of conviction. Van had a class getting out before recess. Consequently, he passed through the quadrangle while the battalion was forming up for fifteen minutes of drill. I don't know how many times he had gone by the colors without removing the beret, which he wore, I suspect, on purpose. It was on a morning well into October that some idle and aggressive sixth former did notice it, as the color guard went by Van, and shouted, with blunt disregard of our fragmentary discipline, "Take off your hat!"

The shouter undoubtedly thought that Van had simply been absent-minded, and he stole the chance to emphasize his unnecessary zeal. I dare say he didn't grasp the appalling fact even when Van gave him no heed. Some others, their attention attracted, noticed now, and they all yelped together, not unlike excited puppies, "Take off your hat!"

They were, however, in motion, and their officers intervened with indignant commands. Van continued on his way to the study hall, where his rooms were, and disappeared. Most of the marchers never understood, or promptly forgot, the disturbance; but there was one at least who knew Van's tastes and habits. This was a prefect named Kenton. Kenton was a slight, good-looking boy with intellectual tastes. He had been fairly intimate with Van. Consequently, Kenton did know something of Van's socialistic attitude. He knew, for instance, that Van received a liberal magazine, at the time—it was about to be suppressed—devoted almost entirely to vicious cartoons, mocking this capitalistic war and America's shameful part in it. Kenton knew that a long file of the publication reposed on a shelf in Van's closet. That afternoon he went there with Bunny Potts, one of the biggest and most magnificent halfbacks who ever wore Durham colors; and a third sixth former named Webster. They tore up all the magazines and littered Van's study with the pieces.

They were, naturally, in a very righteous mood, but the action was almost reflex. Van had injured something—perhaps less tangible—of theirs that morning, and they retaliated by injuring something of his. Since—in the rudiments at least—they were thinking beings, they selected something whose destruction could be explained on the then-highest grounds. Their strength reached approximately the strength of ten because their hearts were patriotic.

Van, returning to his rooms, was doubtless annoyed, but he may have been exhilarated too. He walked over to Doctor Holt's study. "Pater," he said—the term was one used by Durham men in affectionate familiarity to the headmaster— "some little rotters have ripped up a lot of magazines in my room. Sting them, will you?"

Doctor Holt went promptly into one of his disciplinary rages. At Durham, masters are sacrosanct in person and property. Outside their classrooms they have no duties or responsibilities. They do not mix in the ordinary discipline of the school. This was a fine but important point. They are, so to say, unarmed, because the notion that a master might ever have to protect himself passed the realms of the possible.

As Doctor Holt didn't ask the nature of the magazines—the offense was *ipso facto* too heinous to make that important—he did not expect the delicate situation which might be forthcoming. At the afternoon assembly he came striding, without warning, through the doors of the schoolroom, his eyebrows together. He had his chin well up, his head turning from side to side, as though he expected to determine on sight who the offenders were. He mounted the three steps to the platform.

"Attendance taken, John?" he said to the senior prefect. If anyone hadn't been sure when the doors opened what was coming, the sound of Doctor Holt's voice was self-explanatory. Almost everybody suffered an immediate cold malaise around the stomach, a slight sweaty feeling in the hands. The Old Man, in the popular phrase, was on a rampage.

"Well," he said, facing the school with a sort of roar, "I want to know at once who went into Mr. Van Artevelde's room during his absence and destroyed property of his. Stand right up!"

There was a second's quivering silence. Scores and scores of tense nerves relaxed in thanksgiving. No sensation was ever sweeter than finding that, after all, Doctor Holt wasn't looking for you. Then, deliberately, like an elephant coming, majestic, to his feet, the peerless Bunny Potts appeared above the sixth-form rows at the back. Webster, in the corner, stood up too. Doctor Holt opened his mouth to roar, but at that instant, on the platform, Kenton arose.

For another second Doctor Holt was enraged into speechlessness. He looked from one to another, and they looked back at him, dogged, serious. Then he took two violent steps on the platform and jerked the silver-banded prefect's stick out of Kenton's hands. He broke it and slammed the fragments on the floor.

"If I ever hear of anything like this again," he said, "it will mean instant expulsion for the participants. Potts, Webster, Kenton, I'll speak to you in the study at once. Dismiss, John."

I don't think that Durham had ever seen such a thing happen to a prefect before. The bells rang; the school stirred in stunned incredulity. Only in the halls did the inevitable murmur of question and passionate conjecture arise. Kenton was quite white, but the obligations of greatness kept him composed. Bunny Potts was perfectly placid, his big frame swinging easily. Webster looked nervous. Doctor Holt was walking across the quadrangle and they followed him at a formal distance. People paused to watch them as they went into the opposite doors. Then somebody said — you could never know how it had been found out — "Van had a lot of magazines against the war, and they tore them up." It was all so astonishing that there was no immediate reaction, one way or another.

Webster was the one who explained. Bunny Potts had an awkward speechlessness not uncommon in fine athletes. Kenton's pride was slashed to the quick; he would have died before he let Doctor Holt think that he was trying to save his prefectship with excuses. Though Webster's explanation would in no way be adequate, Doctor Holt's attitude must have changed instantly. Facing these three cowed but still-rebellious young men, he probably saw at once that it had come — the war had arrived. I suppose that he meant to nip it there, when he had three only to deal with. This would be why the one or two intrepid souls who secreted themselves on the stairs outside Doctor Holt's study to report the roaring heard nothing. Kenton and Webster and Potts were up some time. That night at supper they went to Mr. Van Artevelde's table, and though what they said was of course inaudible, plainly they were apologizing.

Van was not very cordial. That much could be noticed. If he

cared about peace, it was a mistake. Unformed sentiment undoubtedly crystallized against him, for the school considered that Kenton and Webster and Potts, regardless of possible pressure, were doing an essentially sporting thing.

That feeling must have been very strong the next morning. A special section of third-form French—I may as well admit that it was for people not doing well, and that I was in it—which Van taught, had assembled and we felt surly. Van's shirts and neckties, his floppy reddish hair and little mannerism with the chalk seemed somehow insolent and irritating. Several boys neglected to say "sir" when answering.

Van could not help being aware of this, but no young man wants to make a scene over whether brats called him "sir" every time they opened their mouths. This was a delicate little dilemma, since Van could sense, too, that each successful omission increased a furtive impudence in the class. Unfortunately, he postponed, as most people would, the unpleasant issue.

As it happened, the textbook that we were using was French Government propaganda, though nobody then thought of propaganda as meaning anything you believed. The war, deloused and disinfected, free from the more revolting forms of bloodshed, went on in anecdotes, each preceded by a vocabulary. They were anecdotes about the extraordinary gallantry of the French people and the chivalry of their troops. I can still remember the ridiculous little story that morning. It turned on the alleged fact that the phrase *tête de boche* had, "thanks to the German atrocities," assumed a meaning so deadly that its application by one Frenchman to another must be punished by law to keep angry people from mutual slaughter. The smirking, artificial naïveté of this story would have been hard enough for anyone to swallow any time; for Van this morning it was absolutely impossible. He said sharply: "Of course I hope you won't believe all this drivel. If we want to fight Germany, that's one thing; but people not engaged in the holy murder are under no obligation to disguise themselves as imbeciles."

He was answered, and promptly, by a sullen, semiaudible snarl.

We were restrained by our position and his, however. Military camps are not the only places where people are disciplined to stand under fire; and though this fire was especially galling, we were, most of us, starting our third year at Durham. Perhaps the similarity occurred to Van, or maybe his own age didn't separate him from us much in spirt, for he wheeled at the sound. "Well, you little fools," he snapped, "you aren't in the army yet! But you will be. You're just the sort they can stuff full of stupid lies about how you owe it to civilization to behave like muckers."

There is no particular need to mention who, at that point, was coherent enough to stand up, vibrant and heroic, and tell Van that we wouldn't stay in his classroom. "We won't be taught by a rotten pro-German!" this boy shouted, and started eagerly to leave.

Righteousness, as so often it does in such matters, here re-enforced again the natural juvenile impulse to get out of a class. Everyone arose, delighted to break the monotony of the morning for so good a cause. "Sit down!" Van said, but seeing that nobody was going to, he dropped his dignity and won the race to the door. He put his back against it and said over the uproar, "You've all got two hours' detention."

We formed an indecisive circle, a nervous pack. "You let us out!" cried several voices. Little as Van liked killing, I think that he could have killed then, had he any suitable instrument, or any inspiration as to how to begin. The boys in back started to shout, "Pro-German! Pro-German!" Somebody yelled impulsively, "He's not even an American. He's a dirty Dutchman!"

We had never, so far as I know, thought of the Dutch people as being dirty or in any way inferior before, but the idea was instantly very popular. "You nasty little muts!" said Van. I think he might have hit some of the nearer ones, had not the door at that moment opened behind him.

At the same hour, fourth-form algebra was held in the classroom next to us. Though Bunny Potts was in every respect a sixth former, he hadn't yet managed to pass his college-entrance algebra. As a result, he happened, unfortunately, to be the only person of any authority within earshot. He came into the room, belligerent.

"Shut up!" he rumbled. "Sit down!" He saw Van then, and said rather truculently, "Keep them quiet, will you? We're trying to work in the next room."

"Get out of here, Potts!" snapped Van, ungrateful for the pause instantly produced. "When I need help from a thick-headed boob like you, I'll send for it" — Van had not forgotten the magazines yesterday. He was, for all spiritual purposes, right back in the sixth form himself; with Potts merely the not-very-big and far-from-bright brat Van remembered in those days.

This division of authority gave the third-form section its chance. "We won't stay here, Bunny!" someone cried. "He isn't teaching anything! He just talks pro-German!"

"Shut up!" thundered Potts, in angry perplexity.

"If you want to have a bad attack of patriotism," said Van, icy with rage, "just sit down and I'll go on with what I have to say on the subject."

"I guess you won't," said Potts, scowling. "You say one more word against America and I'll smack you a couple." His own forthrightness shocked him a little and he attempted a sort of lumbering reason. "You weren't born in this country, Van" — so, I suppose he was going to say, Van wouldn't understand how he, Potts, and we, the third form —

"Born in it?" said Van. "Thank God for that! I wouldn't be seen dead in it, nowadays!"

Bunny Potts was in many respects a slow and troubled thinker, but he knew instantly what he was expected to do when somebody insulted the United States. He hit Van so hard that Van actually left his feet, went down in a heap in the corner. He was knocked senseless.

I think we all ran out then, and kept running, to nowhere in particular. Fourth-form algebra surged impulsively from its classroom, and, down the hall, second-form history joined them.

Bunny was very much frightened. He picked Van up and carried him over to the infirmary so fast that Van was still unconscious when they arrived. No doubt Bunny Potts imagined that he might have killed Van; but the nurse had little trouble in discovering that Van, even as he had so rashly declared, was not going to be seen dead in America — at least not this time.

I dare say that no one actually expected the fist that struck a member of the faculty to wither, but the school certainly suffered a reaction not unlike the one which results always and everywhere from the sudden discovery that the gods are impotent and filled with dust. Bells ending the period had rung. More boys, coming out of the study hall with books under their arms and the intention of going to their scheduled classes, found the whole routine in a perfectly plain state of collapse. They paused, asking what had happened. Then they joined the indecisive groups around the quadrangle. It would be hard for an outsider to understand the difference made by the absence of the handful of young men who served as prefects; but the prefects were the thin, strong skeleton of authority on whose articulation the school's movement and morale had been trained to depend. The sixth form had thought it necessary to have a meeting, and the prefects were attending it.

To an expert like Doctor Holt, the demoralization in the atmosphere must have been instantly apparent, but since his trusted lieutenants avoided him, he was some minutes in getting the facts, and those minutes were fatal as far as the application of ordinary measures was concerned.

Potts was the one who reported, and Doctor Holt rewarded him, Draconically, by informing Potts that he was no longer a member of the school. This was done without a scene, for Doctor Holt's rages were in a way instruments at his disposal — that is, they were sincere and unpremeditated, but he did not have them if he did not want them; and there would certainly be no use in one now. With Potts dismissed from the study, he must have sat a few minutes in thought, for some time passed before he appeared in the quadrangle. He proceeded to the infirmary, unhasty, looking neither to the right nor left, ignoring the slight, automatic consternation the sight of him had produced.

Van was sitting in the dispensary. He had a cold compress on the side of his face and the nurse had administered some brandy. Physically he was none the worse, but Bunny's heavy fist had not stopped at bruising Van's jaw. That socket-spraining impact was a thrust of reality, and it shook down the whole fantastic structure of his self-esteem. Strictly speaking, this had nothing to do with the school, or the war, or Bunny's highly correct patriotism. Van had read the right books and learned the right principles for a liberal intellectual; but from their initial urge to resist and resent Major Loiseaux's too eloquent and artful emotionalizing, Van had been taken step by fatal step to a point he hadn't planned on reaching. Every gesture had required a further gesture to justify it; and here he stood, or, rather, sat, in the infirmary, entirely alone and entirely friendless — Kenton's defection had been yesterday a scratch in a hot battle, but now, cold, it was deeper than he thought. He had liked Kenton.

Loneliness and hostility can be, of course, the price one pays for self-respect; and the historic blood in his veins had never shown any signs of lacking the old, intrepid stubbornness and valor in defense which had made the Netherlands too hard a nut for kings to crack. That strength, however, was in conviction; and Van had long since himself gone past his own conviction. Now he might be sure only of one thing — that he had pressed a bad course to the shameful spectacle of its worse end. If the land, in a wordless and immemorial way, seemed to bid him tread no more upon it, he himself was angered to some kind of sickness at his own actions.

Even the nurse, he thought, looked at him with a sort of contempt; similar impatient contempt had animated the very children in his French section, he could believe — not quite correctly — now. Even the slow-witted and amiable Potts had been able, despite the probably great cost, to endure it no longer.

This might have amounted to one of the worst half hours he ever spent in his life, and the results of it undoubtedly surprised Doctor Holt, who would have been ready for Van to be enraged. Doctor Holt came into the dispensary quietly.

"Well, Van?" he said.

Van got up. "I'm all right," he said. "I'm going."

"Oh, no," said Doctor Holt. "Sit down." He waved the nurse out and closed the door. "This is a disagreeable business, Van," he said. "I'm sorry it happened. I've had to fire Potts."

"I don't see why," Van said. "It was entirely my fault, Pater. If you thought it would be a good idea, I guess I might enlist. At any rate, I'll leave this afternoon. I can't stay around here, Pater, and I guess you don't want me anyway."

"Is that all?" said Doctor Holt.

"No, sir," said Van. "I'm sorry I've made so much trouble."

"I'm glad you're sorry," Doctor Holt nodded, "because you ought to be, Van. You've put me in a very hard position. As I told you, Potts is leaving the school."

"Could he stay if I went, sir?" said Van. He had a slight nervous reaction toward his ordinary manner. "He'll be missed in the Somerset game."

"Somerset may be missing men, too," said Doctor Holt. "Well, we'll do the best we can without him. I haven't had to give my talk on too much emphasis on athletics this year. No, you'll stay."

"Everyone's going to resent it," said Van. "I doubt if I'm worth a good halfback, Pater. I —"

"I know," nodded Doctor Holt. "Ordinarily you might not be. I don't object to your leaving; in fact, I think it would be a decent thing for you to enlist. We'll arrange about your papers and you can leave the school at Christmas. But not now; just now I need you here."

"You wouldn't have any trouble about third-form French," said Van. "You could —"

"It's the sixth form that needs instruction," said Doctor Holt, "and French isn't the subject."

The result of the sixth-form meeting was, besides a good deal of excitement, the decision of five young men to vindicate Bunny Potts by resigning. I suppose that they were rather intoxicated by the nobility of their decision. For the rest of us, feeling was running imitatively high, but little could be done about it. Doctor Holt appeared to have gone somewhere in his car, and the school seemed, strangely enough, to have ceased to exist. At least, there were no more bells, and though bells are a nuisance when you hear them, it is astonishing how disturbed you feel when suddenly you don't. Nobody knew what time anything was to be done. Nobody seemed to be in charge.

Technically we were having what amounted to an unexpected holiday, but it was spoiled by a certain confused solemnity. Outside it was breezy and bright under a fine October sky, but no one felt like going out. For hours on end one expected that at any moment something important might happen.

There was luncheon, all right; but since there were no bells, many boys didn't notice the time and so got nothing to eat. The sixth formers who felt that they had to go had finished their packing in the first burst of indignation, but the next train left after five o'clock. Meanwhile there was little to do. The objectors had fallen into two groups in two rooms, and they read magazines.

At three o'clock a notice appeared on the bulletin board announcing general town permission. This seemed, I remember, much the most dismaying thing that happened. Town permission was restricted to two afternoons a week, and was distinctly a privilege. Subconsciously the school felt that it was behaving rather badly and didn't expect to be rewarded for it.

All of an hour was required for the general consternation and suspicion—of who knew what?—to subside, but by half past four, boys were beginning to cross the bridge in small, pioneering groups. Many of them were hungry and headed for the village stores; many were going because word had somehow passed around that we ought to see Bunny Potts and his supporters off.

I don't think that the latter feeling was very decisive however. Bunny Potts, with the passing hours, seemed certainly less of a hero and martyr. He was talked out as a subject. You couldn't go on forever saying, "Gosh, I don't blame him!" The fact that remained was the fact of his expulsion. It is not considered exactly an honor to be expelled from Durham; indeed, for members of the school it is the ultimate catastrophe. This accepted, uneasy flavor of the catastrophic was coming back; we were a little shy about Bunny Potts. I remember that I did not in the least want to go in town; what I wanted was for someone to ring a bell and have an assembly to explain how matters stood and what we were going to do next. I went in town because everybody else seemed to be going.

When I got to the station with several companions, it was astonishing to see how many boys felt the same or some similar way. There must have been as many of us as on that evening when Major Loiseaux arrived the spring before. Only we had no band and no impulse to cheer; no one struck the emotional keynote which would make up our minds for us. Those who might possibly have done it—the five sixth formers with suitcases and hats, or Bunny Potts—probably felt too much the same way themselves. They had come in earlier still. Bunny Potts, I remember, sat on his suitcases, looking at his hands and saying nothing, even when his supporters addressed him. The dusk was pleasant-colored and you could smell the sad sharp smoke of the inevitable October leaf fires on the lawns. The wind was down; the air was gaining a clean chill in the shadows of the hills.

We had stood that way, shifting and restless, hands in pockets against the cold, murmuring to one another and waiting for something to happen for perhaps fifteen minutes more, when something did happen. The barely needed headlights of a motorcar came fast up the thinned tree arch of the long single street. This car turned in to the station, made its way quietly through the parting crowds, slid almost to the platform and halted. Doctor Holt sat in it, his gloved hands on the wheel. Van, his beret aslant, the collar of a tan topcoat turned up, sat beside him.

We didn't, naturally, know anything that had passed between Doctor Holt and Van. Van was simply there, and he looked as he always did; as always, he was the recipient of Doctor Holt's indulgent favor. You might think that nothing had happened, and

I'm sure we resented it, but resentment, in the twilight and the cold and the aftermath of a hard, emotional day, was curiously mute and even halfhearted. We had fallen instantly silent, as though we expected Doctor Holt to say something; and the silence continued, deepening, while Doctor Holt lit his pipe and sat puffing deliberately, looking at no one in particular, unless it was Bunny Potts on his suitcases. Bunny had placed himself apart from the others, and the fact that he was not with them made them appear confused, rather aimless. They continued to talk in whispers to one another, but Bunny Potts was still looking at his hands, and Doctor Holt was still, contemplative, looking at him. Just then, faint but hoarsely clear and traveling fast, came the full roar of a locomotive whistle.

Bunny Potts undoubtedly jumped. Then he stood up, ponderous but swift. One could recognize anywhere that curious bearlike gesture of his with which he sized up the field and came to a decision as he lumbered into an end run. He left his bags and went right over to Doctor Holt in the car.

He looked across Doctor Holt and said to Van: "I'm sorry I lost my temper, sir."

"It's all right," Van nodded. "We all do. Sorry for what I said. Good luck, Bunny."

"Good-by, Pater," Potts said, finally looking at Doctor Holt.

The bell at the railroad crossing above began to ring with mechanical fury. Far-reaching, the radiant sweep of the locomotive's great headlight fled past us down the track. Doctor Holt held out his hand. "Try to behave yourself in the army," he said. "I'd like you to be a credit to Durham."

Speech was drowned for a moment in the uproar of the locomotive's passage; dark-sided baggage cars, succeeding rows of bright windows, slid more slowly, jerked to a halt. Bunny turned and got his bags. Beside Van, Doctor Holt came quickly to his feet. He raised his voice, a clear roar, much louder than the locomotive.

"The regular evening assembly will be in fifteen minutes!" he thundered. "All Durham boys are, as always, expected to attend!"

He sat down, and you could see the movement of his hand. The car trembled on the roused engine, began to back. Now a lantern swung from the train vestibule; the yellow windows started to slide again. Abruptly we were looking at the retreating red lamps ending it. The five boys with hats and suitcases still stood just where they were before.

There came a general stir, a sigh and sound of voices. Turning, we could see the taillight, and the swift-shafted glow leaping ahead of Doctor Holt's motor. It had reached the very end of the fine leafless tunnel of trees. Boys who had suitcases picked them up and we all began to move; quickly, for we had only fifteen minutes to get back to school.

Candida by Bernard Shaw

Mr. Naylor gave me permission for late lights, but of course you are expected to go to the schoolroom and do your work there, unless you are a member of the sixth form and so have lights until ten anyway and may study or not study where you please. Naturally, on the other hand, there is no law against a sixth former and a prefect studying in the schoolroom, if he wants to; and the first thing I saw when I came over from reporting to Mr. Naylor was that Paul Lanford wanted to. Technically I suppose that Paul is a friend of mine; but his own exaggerated idea of his duty to the school would make it impossible for him to refrain from giving me detention if he should notice that I was reading instead of studying. I do not know where he got such a high idea of himself, but it seems to me that it has been particularly pronounced ever since Mr. Pollard spent a week at the Lanfords' house in town during Christmas vacation and took Paul with him to hear Wagner or other great music about every day. This you might think was a personal matter, between Paul and a master who happened to like him, and why it has led Paul to regard himself as about the most wonderful thing Durham ever saw, I cannot say.

At any rate, Paul's being in the schoolroom was the primary reason for my thinking that it would be simpler to go downstairs to classroom C. I know from experience that if the lower hall light is on and the door closed, nobody can tell you are there unless he happens to be walking around behind the building. You just have to take a chance on that; and I had about half an argument—that is, I could say I had got permission to be up, and in the schoolroom everyone was so restless that it prevented me from concentrating.

Having decided on this, I brought a cushion from our room (which was a mistake, since that worm Ellicott naturally knew I wasn't going to try to take a cushion into the schoolroom), and a copy of *Candida* by Bernard Shaw; which I got from Mr. Pollard's study, he having said that I might take anything I wanted while he was away, and that Shaw ought to be read. *Candida* is fairly good; but I expect that it is dated; and certainly there are modern writers considerably better. However, it compares more than favorably with the Manilian Law. I really asked for late lights because I meant to try and finish the Cicero; but when I thought more about it, I remembered that I was stuck in the eighth section around the cities of Pontus and Cappadocia—*uno aditu adventuque*—and not likely to get anywhere without breaking my head until Harris II gave me my trot back. I could then do an hour's work in about two minutes; and so I might as well read *Candida.*

I suppose it was half past nine, and I had *Candida,* which was bound in green cardboard, open on the Cicero, which was open too, in case there was any reason to change them around. I will say for *Candida* that it holds your attention; and of course I had no way of knowing that some egg (probably Lanford) had seen the hall lights on from upstairs and decided to switch them off and thus save the school a half a cent's worth of electricity. I did not know either that Doctor Holt would have to pick out tonight to go on a rampage; but he had found that several fourth formers had been cutting chapel regularly and so we were off. When he settled with them, he was feeling in the mood, so he started to go the rounds and see what else he could find.

Now while I do not think Ellicott did it on purpose, it is merely an additional proof of his slovenly habits and inability to foresee anything that he should have left our door open when he went down to the washroom. This was a great convenience for Doctor Holt, who happened to pass through our hall in quest of trouble, because he could of course see into the room and that no one was there, although lights were long ago. Ellicott came back with his toothbrush at this point, and Doctor Holt asked him where I was. I suppose because Ellicott remembered the cushion, as well as being one of the world's saddest birds, he became confused and said, "I guess he is down in a classroom studying, sir."

As I have pointed out, you are not allowed to study anywhere except in the schoolroom, and Doctor Holt would be unlikely to make an exception for me, as he had it in for me anyway. Lanford, or some prefect of the same sort, had undoubtedly been showing his zeal by saying that he suspected I might have been smoking with Horatio Browne on the river road — which I admit was true, but I would like to see anyone prove it. However, the Doctor and I were on our customary hostile terms and barely speaking to each other except when he thought of some new penalty for me. Although he may have been disappointed that I did not happen to have gone into the village to a dance or something he could automatically fire me for, he could still catch me out, and he did not waste any time about doing it.

As I say, *Candida* holds your attention; and since the hall light was out, Doctor Holt could readily see the light I had on showing under the door; so he knew where to go without needing to look in the other classrooms first, which I might have heard him doing and so prepared myself a little. As it was I had not heard a sound beyond suddenly about three steps outside and the door opening. I just gave one look and personally I could not think of anything except how a couple of days ago in English 5 we were reading *Macbeth* by William Shakspere in parts, and how Macbeth explained in act three scene four that he would rather see the rugged Russian bear, the arm'd rhinoceros, or the Hyrcan tiger.

This was by no means the first time that Doctor Holt and I had enjoyed a run-in; and if I had been given any sort of warning, I might have taken steps. Unfortunately I had my feet on the master's desk and the chair tilted back with the cushion where it would do the most good. I would also have got the Cicero over the *Candida* and been able to sit there absorbed in my work.

Doctor Holt came right down to the desk, his chin tilted up and his eyebrows looking somewhat heavy. I had known better than to try to alter my arrangements in any way while he was looking on, so I remained as I was. He said, "Take your feet off there!" So I did; and while I was doing that, he reached and picked up the Cicero from my lap and saw the play inside it. He laid the Cicero down then and looked at the cover of the play, on which Mr. Pollard had written, *Evan Pollard.*

"Who gave you permission to take books out of Mr. Pollard's study?" he asked. And I said, "He did, sir, before he went away."

"How did you get in there?" he inquired; and I saw I should have made it clear that Evan gave the book to me before his departure; because I had been forced to climb through the window, as they had locked the door; and while Evan would certainly not mind, climbing on the roofs would be one more rule I had broken. I thought about it a second and decided that I would not be contradicting myself; so I added, "He gave me several books he wanted me to read before he left, sir." Which, you will notice, while giving the required impression, did not involve a direct falsehood.

I had stood up then, and Doctor Holt was thus enabled to see the cushion. I sort of had a premonition that it would make him mad; I mean, if I were going to do what is called defy the school regulations, I needn't be quite so comfortable about it; but I would also be disrespectful if I remained sitting down much longer. "Well," he said, "you lose your fifth-form privileges and will remain on close bounds until the end of term."

I thought I might as well make no comment, because I suddenly remembered that I happened to have a package of cigarettes in my pocket which I intended to give to Horatio; and though Doctor Holt would not be likely to go through your pockets, the package began to feel about as big as a trunk, and I would not be surprised if he noticed it. In that event, I would not have a prayer; for yesterday or the day before they had had a grand spring roundup, and the Old Man had announced in assembly that anyone in whose possession tobacco was found would be summarily expelled; and when it is put that way, he means it, even if it happened to be some great credit to the school, like Lanford.

Of course, you might imagine that, considering Mr. Pollard was away and I did not know when he would be well enough to come back; and my rooming with a mess like Ellicott, instead of Horatio, with whom I would have roomed except it made what Doctor Holt called an unsatisfactory combination; and the Old Man being daily so down on me that I could hardly breathe; and now, not having my fifth-form privileges (they do not amount to anything; but on May 1st the fifth form takes over the school and becomes in effect the sixth form with privileges that are quite a different matter); and being unable to get out of the schoolyard without risking my life at every step; I mean, considering all those things, you might imagine I would enjoy being fired. But, as it happens, you wouldn't; and, in fact, except for having Doctor Holt on my neck, and getting one kind of pain or another every time I looked at people like Ellicott and Lanford, I love Durham; and after all I have spent five years of my life here; and furthermore, I would never meet anyone like Mr. Pollard again. Also, though I stand no chance of being a prefect, I will at least be a sixth former next year, and be editor of the *Durham Review,* which I intend to try to make into a magazine with less stuff about My Summer in the Rocky Mountains, and A Good Book: Silas Marner.

"Go on, go to bed!" Doctor Holt roared suddenly, while I was reflecting on some of these things. "You don't do your work, you won't behave yourself. You do nothing but break rules and make trouble. I ought to expel you!"

"Yes, sir," I said, and got out as quickly as I could; for on the whole I do not want to be expelled; and probably the longer he looks at me, the more the idea appeals to him.

When I got to our room, I hoped that Ellicott would be asleep; but of course he was not. He turned over in his bed and said, "Say, did the Old Man catch you?"

"What did you do in the Great War?" I asked. I felt, in fact, pretty rotten about the world in general, and anyway, I cannot endure Ellicott. I don't know whether it is because of the way he talks, or because he is always trying to pretend he is a friend of mine or because he walks as if he had flat feet and you can hear him miles away shuffling down the hall like a half-wit. Another thing about Ellicott that you can't stand is when you snap his head off, he takes it. Instead of snapping back at you, he just gets sort of meek. "I hoped you wouldn't get caught," he said, doing it. "The Old Man was up here and I knew he was looking for you. I was afraid he might catch you reading because I knew you weren't doing your Latin. Harris II brought your trot in just before lights."

Of course that was a pretty good crack. In fact it was the only good one I ever heard Ellicott get off; and I was so surprised it took me a minute to see that he had only said it by a mistake and did not intend to be insulting. I had thought at first that the worm might be in the process of turning and we'd have a scrap, which would be more of a relief than I can tell you. Instead Ellicott said, going right on, "Were you reading *Candida?* Lend it to me when you finish, will you?"

"Certainly not," I said. "It is not mine. I've got to put it back."

"I know," he said. "It's Mr. Pollard's. Mr. Pollard told me I could read any books of his."

"He never told you any such thing," I said. Mr. Pollard hadn't, either; and I cannot see any use in telling untruths except perhaps in a matter of life and death. Of course, I will admit that, had Ellicott ever got up nerve enough to ask Mr. Pollard, Mr. Pollard would unquestionably say yes; but I knew that Ellicott had never asked him, because he is rather unpopular with most people and I suppose he has an inferiority complex. Furthermore, I will say for Paul Lanford that one of his pet aversions is Ellicott, and when he has a genuine aversion, he can be so nasty about it that Ellicott knew better than to try to enter a room, even if it happened to be Mr. Pollard's study, into which Paul was likely to come at any moment.

Of course this merely goes to show that if you insist on behaving like a worm, you will probably get stepped on; and a fear of feet no doubt makes Ellicott seem even more of a fool than he naturally is, if possible. Of course, on this point, I suppose I am inclined to act like a fool myself. In fact, in moments of introspection, I would not be surprised if all I have against Paul Lanford is that Mr. Pollard pays more attention to him and is more friendly with him than he is with me. Besides, being a sixth former and a prefect, Paul can go up to Evan's study with a couple of other sixth formers practically every night and sit around and talk or listen to Evan play the piano, while fifth formers must be in bed at nine o'clock; or are supposed to be.

Of course, as you can see, this is a sort of natural accident and I do not mean to imply that Evan gets anything like the little gang of saps collected by some masters I could name, to whom tea is given every afternoon in their studies and a general playing of favorites goes on, which I am prepared to suspect extends even into their mark cards, though I am unable to prove this, and it is nothing to me anyway. In Evan's case, if you have come only for food you will be dead of Wagner and Brahms before you get any; and if you are not interested in what Evan chooses to talk about, you will look somewhat foolish sitting in a silent state of suspended appetite. Thus Evan simply gets together without any effort on his part the fifth and sixth formers who show some signs of intelligence, and to them he talks and lends his books and so on, not so much as persons he chances to like, as the raw material for what you might call educated men.

However, he has such a great charm of personality that you can't, or I can't, help wanting Evan to like me — that is, to think that I am fairly clever and interesting; and when you feel that way, you can pretty easily imagine, every time you miss a trick in his English history course, which I occasionally do; or he's too busy correcting papers or something to have a discussion with you when you drop into his study; that he has concluded you are a fool; and maybe has as much trouble standing you as I have in standing Ellicott. This leads to what I expect is nothing but a sort of jealousy; as for instance, I know that it makes me for some reason mad that, since he has been home, ill, and I have been writing him every week, spending most of the study periods for the previous four days making up a letter which might sound intelligent, he has written Paul at least twice and me only once. Now in Ellicott's case, I suppose too that I like to think it is a sign of his esteem to be allowed to borrow Mr. Pollard's books, and I did not want Ellicott calmly taking part in it. As a result, I said, "He would not lend you the contents of his wastepaper basket. Probably the real reason he had to go home was because you bored him to death by trying to attract his attention all the time and sounding like wah-wah, the idiot boy, whenever you opened your mouth in history."

That is the sort of thing it is hard to bear yourself for saying, at least to a worm; and why I said it — at any rate, that got home, all right. He shut up and turned over in bed again and I certainly wished he were dead for making me feel rottener than I felt already. "Listen," I said, "you can have it if the Old Man ever gives it back. And I haven't any idea what Mr. Pollard thought of you or thinks of you. . . ."

Ellicott for once did not have anything to say.

"Well, are you deaf or dead?" I snapped. "Did you hear what I said?"

He might have been either; and knowing that probably like everyone else he admired Mr. Pollard very much and wished to be on friendly terms with him, I could imagine that I had given him a swift kick in the finer sensibilities; which was a pretty rotten thing to do; and made me madder. So I added, "Gosh, but you're the most unspeakable mess ever invented. . . ."

However, we were not getting anywhere. There was nothing to do but hurry up and get to bed and go to sleep. I took a towel and a toothbrush, and Ellicott's toothpaste, and went down to the washroom.

It was such a beautiful spring morning that I might have known something would have to ruin it. Every time I am simple enough to be glad I am alive, Doctor Holt can be counted on to land the marines, so to say, and get the situation in hand. Horatio moved over to my table after the bell rang to let people leave breakfast who had finished; and since the Old Man went out then, I sent a brat to get a couple of cups of coffee. This is an idea I thought up myself. There is no way of telling whether a brat is getting it for sixth formers or fifth formers; and I must have done it a thousand times with no trouble. Of course, this morning, just as I was explaining all about last night's fuss to Horatio, Lanford had to come down, and you could see him bristle up when he noticed that we had coffee in those cups and not cocoa. "Listen," said Horatio, "be your age! What is it to you?" Paul said, "You know darn well what it is to me. You can both take an hour's detention."

"Well, now the good news has reached Aix," Horatio observed, "farewell."

"What I came down to tell you" — he was addressing me — "was that Doctor Holt wants you in the study right away."

"He would!" I told Horatio. "See you afterward, if I live."

Paul walked out with me. In the quadrangle there was dew on the grass and the leaves of the elms seemed to have made a lot of progress since last night. The sun was into the colonnade of the dining hall; the sky was washed-off, with no clouds at all and a good deep blue. I wished I were about a thousand miles away and had never heard of school. Paul said, "I don't think he's nailed you for anything." Which was decent of him, because if I knew the Old Man hadn't got anything on me, I need not lose a year's growth trying to guess what and not give myself away on something else before he told me. "As a matter of fact, I think it's about the *Review*," he said.

I supposed that the Old Man was going to caution me against letting any sense creep into it. As I have explained, the fifth form takes over the school on May 1st — that is, next year's prefects are appointed and the publications board and so on get their new officers, and things like that. "The board elected you editor-in-chief last night," Paul said. I had, as you may have gathered, known that that would happen, so I could not get very excited about it. "Thanks for telling me," I said. "Listen, Paul; Horatio shouldn't get an hour for that coffee. I sent a brat for both cups, and since it was there, Horatio thought he might as well drink it."

"That's what he gets an hour for," said Paul, "drinking it. I am not going to sting the brat."

I hoped that he might feel less official; but if he didn't there was no use fighting about it, so I said, changing the subject, "Listen, give me something for the June *Review,* will you? If you start to think about it now, you might actually get it done. What I want to begin running is a set of articles under a sort of general heading; like: If I Were Teaching Latin, or Geometry, or Tiddlywinks, or anything. I know in many respects it is a lot of rot, and probably will leave the world substantially unaltered; but at least you get at fairly original material, and you can at least say what you think would make this or that course not so deadly dull; d'you follow?"

"Yes," said Paul; and as I was going to walk by the door, having forgotten, he added, "You go up and see the Old Man."

I could tell from the way he said it that he knew that Doctor Holt and I would probably differ somewhat on policy; but I felt a good deal more cheerful, because after all I hadn't really been sure I would get the *Review;* and I had been thinking up a lot of things I wanted to do with it; such as getting one or two alumni who are quite well-known writers to give me something for old times' sake, since there would be no cash in it. That would not be upsetting any policy, and would put a couple of names into the *Review* that a person ever heard of, and some writing you could read without having an acute pain.

The study door was open so I knocked on it and said, "Good morning, sir. Lanford said you wanted to see me."

Doctor Holt was sitting in the easy chair by his desk and while he was not looking cheerful, he did not appear outstandingly ferocious. "Close the door," he said; so I did, and then came down the room. He took one of the eight-by-ten faculty record cards off his desk and looked at it a moment while I stood there. Then he said, "Forty-five in geometry," so I knew that it was my card. However, I made no comment, as I do not expect ever to pass my mathematics except by going to a tutoring school and getting my college credits that way. Probably I was not at the time passing my French or Latin, either; because I hadn't had an opportunity to do more than open a book in either for about three months. "Your scholastic standing is altogether unsatisfactory," he said.

"I think I will get by my board exams, sir," I responded quietly.

"I just did not happen to have my work prepared on some days when I was called on." I was thinking that I could do a piece for the *Review* on the marking system. I could call it, The Great Mark Mystery; that is, the mystery would be what on earth they proved.

Doctor Holt said to me, "Well, under the circumstances, you can see that I am unable to confirm the publication board's election. I wished you to understand, as you appear to, the reasons. If you are unable to find time to satisfy your scholastic requirements now, it would obviously be that much more impossible with the *Review* on your hands."

I looked at him a couple of seconds and then I said, "Yes, sir. I was telling Lanford that I did not feel I had time to waste on a magazine so entirely hidebound and whose policy is so subject to interference from above." I turned around then because I thought I would be shouting at him in a minute, and walked down the room and out the door.

Horatio was strolling up and down the side path of the quadrangle, with a book under his arm, waiting to view the remains. "Listen," I said, "this is a darn nice morning. Let's cut the second period and go down the river."

"Right," said Horatio, "I was going to do that anyway; but I hope you remember that you are on close bounds."

"Would I forget it?" I said. "I've got some cigarettes for you. I'll bring them along. Meet you below the boathouse, and for heaven's sake, be there!"

I went over to our room then and for once Ellicott was not mooning around waiting for a chance to butt into my business, so I calmed myself somewhat by reading some more of *Jean Christophe* by Romaine Rolland, which I like very much except that it is so long, until assembly. Fortunately I have geometry the first period, so I was able to finish the second volume and more or less get my mind off my own troubles.

When I got down to the boathouse, which I did by walking right out as though I had an errand and trusting that nobody who knew I was on close bounds, and could do anything about it, noticed me, I found Horatio leaning inconspicuously against the south wall, and we were safe for the minute. As far as the study period went, I was not worried, for it is very hard to check up on who ought to be in the schoolroom and who has a class at any given time; and barring bad luck, you are not in any grave danger.

The place where we go is across a quite wide field at the bend of the river, where the bank is rather high, and the top of it hidden from the road by bushes and a lot of small white birches. In that way no one can see you unless he is in a boat; and you can see anyone who leaves the road and starts across the field in plenty of time not to be there when he arrives, if that matters.

We sat as usual on an old plank we had moved over there and lit cigarettes and looked at the sun on the water, which was pretty nice seen through the birch leaves with the slight wind moving them. "The Old Man did me out of the *Review*," I said. "He told me my scholastic standing was unsatisfactory."

"That's rotten," said Horatio, "but what do you care?"

"I don't," I said. "Only it makes me mad. Let's talk about something else."

"Would you be interested to know that Mr. Pollard is coming back tomorrow?" Horatio observed.

"Rot," I said. "He probably won't be back this term."

"Listen," said Horatio, "yesterday I had an hour's detention, if you can credit it; and I was told to report to the Old Man. So I did. He wasn't in the study, but there was a heap of mail on the desk, so I just looked it over while I was waiting—"

"You've certainly got plenty of brass!" I said.

"That is the secret of my great success at Durham," Horatio said. "At any rate, Mr. Pollard wrote that his doctors agreed he might come back; and so he was coming back, either this afternoon or tomorrow."

"Well, that's fine," I said. "I am certainly fed up with having not one literate, let alone civilized, person in the school." On the other hand, I remembered suddenly that Doctor Holt had taken Mr. Pollard's *Candida* and Mr. Pollard might not be particularly pleased that one of his books was the means for my getting in my weekly disagreement with Doctor Holt. Also I thought it would be typical of Ellicott to do something wormlike, such as going to Mr. Pollard and saying that if it were true that Mr. Pollard was pained by his presence in English history, he would not mind being dropped from the course rather than continue to give pain. Mr. Pollard might easily think that I had something to do with the offer. Of course, with Mr. Pollard coming back, I also felt rather more simple in regard to the *Review,* as I had discussed it with Mr. Pollard on the supposition that I would get it, and Mr. Pollard would think that I was undoubtedly a fool. While he does not regard our educational system as by any means ideal, and would change almost everything in it, if he could; none the less, it is not changed yet, and an intelligent human being ought to be able, in his opinion, to pass more than a couple of subjects. Consequently, if I did not get the *Review,* I would owe it to my own idleness and stupidity. I saw that I had better do something about at least some of this, so I threw my cigarette through the leaves and it fell ten or twelve feet into the water, making a circle where it hit.

"Give me some chewing gum," I requested, for you cannot very well go up to school smelling to high heaven of tobacco smoke. "I have somehow got to swipe a book from the Old Man's study. It was the one he confiscated last night, and it belongs to Mr. Pollard."

"What," said Horatio, "is a book more or less to him?"

"Yes, I know," I said, "but I need this one to lend to Ellicott."

Horatio merely looked at me. He said at last, "Do you mean to tell me you plan to risk your neck to provide Ellicott with reading matter?"

It did sound rather foolish put that way. "Why don't you get him to swipe it for you," Horatio asked, "and then lend it to him?"

However, I did not take that suggestion, because while I could have told Ellicott exactly where it was, having noticed before Doctor Holt distracted my attention in regard to the *Review*, I knew that if you wanted a thing done wrong, Ellicott was the man to do it; and there was no bad matter of any delicacy which he could not instantly make worse. Consequently I cut luncheon and got it myself. As it was just thrown with some papers on top of a bookcase I doubted if the Old Man would remember about it, for I am glad to say that much of the time he is concerned with things other than me and my misdemeanors.

After luncheon, which, as I have mentioned, I did not attend, eating a box of crackers belonging to Ellicott in our room instead, Ellicott came over and I could hear him shuffling up the hall, but I resolved not to let it infuriate me. "Where were you?" he said, so I answered, "Swiping *Candida* from Doctor Holt for you. There it is, and see that you read it."

As I had expected, he brightened up wonderfully, and I saw that hope certainly does spring eternal, for he was plainly thinking he was not such a worm after all. "The Old Man just announced that Mr. Pollard was returning this evening," he said. "I thought you'd like to know."

"I have known it for weeks," I informed him. "Thanks for the crackers. I may buy you another box if I ever get off close bounds and can go into the village." I then went downstairs to attend what is known as Special Study, bringing with me the third volume of *Jean Christophe* by Romaine Rolland, and afterward I was able to oblige Mr. Naylor by serving the hour Lanford gave me, and another hour I happened to have from geometry, which I forgot to mention; Mr. Lewis having given it to me for inattention, or failure to hear him when he was asking me about the perpendicular from any point on a circle to a diameter; which, as a matter of fact, is the mean proportional to something, but who could care what? As a result I did not finish in time to play tennis with Horatio, but I certainly got a lot of healthful exercise rolling courts five and six, while everyone else played for miles around, except some of the fourth formers who had cut chapel yesterday and so were helping me.

While we were doing this (it was pretty late by now), I saw the school car come back from the afternoon train, and Evan was in it; so I pointed out to the fourth formers that there was no reason why they should not finish up easily by themselves, which made them mad but what could they do about it? Getting my shirt, and keeping an eye out not to meet Mr. Naylor, I went up to school, where I found that Mr. Pollard had naturally gone to see Doctor Holt, so I got a shower and dressed. By the time I was ready and went over to his study, it was open and he was there. He said right away, while he was shaking hands with me, "What makes you such an infernal ass?" but I could see he was feeling quite cheerful and looking very well, not so irritable as before he went away, and I answered, "How can I help it if Doctor Holt is down on me, sir? As a matter of fact, we have had relatively few scraps." I could not imagine what he had found out in so short a time. He just shook his head and went on unpacking his bags in his bedroom, presently turning around and throwing me a copy of *Evelyn Innes* by George Moore. "Take that along," he said, "and get out of my sight. And what did you do with my copy of *Candida*?"

"I lent it to Ellicott, sir," I said. "I thought it would do him good."

"I hope it will," said Evan, "because I would like some good to come out of it, and what Doctor Holt will do to you for swiping it from his study, you can adequately imagine for yourself."

I could see then that what had happened was that Doctor Holt, while he was talking to Evan, remembered it; and when he looked for it, he could not find it, and so he made the obvious conjecture. "Sir," I said to Evan, for I did not want him to think I was entirely foolish, "there is nothing left he can do to me, because I am already on close bounds and have no privileges, and the Doctor has done me out of the *Review* for certain reasons. I suppose he can give me detention every afternoon, forever; but I often have that anyway, so it will not be a great shock."

I could hear Evan putting away his shirts with a sort of groan. "Go on," he said, "get out. I'll have to think it over. I'll talk to you after supper."

I thanked him for the book and left then, and read it until assembly, when I brought it down to put in my desk so it would be there for night study. As a result I had forgotten about Doctor Holt and the *Candida*; but into the assembly Doctor Holt came suddenly, meaning no good, and went up on the platform. "I want to

know who has a copy of *Candida* by Bernard Shaw, the property
of Mr. Pollard, and taken from my desk sometime today. Stand
right up, please," he remarked.

Of course he was incorrect, because it had been on his bookcase,
and I wondered whether it would be worth while making a point
out of the error, but I guessed not, and nerving myself for the fray,
I was about to get to my feet when I saw to my astonishment that
Ellicott had already jumped up. Doctor Holt seemed slightly
surprised, but he recovered himself and said, "Take an hour's
detention every afternoon for a week, and return that to me
immediately after supper." He then went on to make a few general
remarks about entering the study during his absence and we were
dismissed to go over to chapel. In the hall I said to Ellicott, "You
sad bird, what did you do that for? Now I shall have to go up and
explain that I did it; and he will ask me why I am such a sneak as to
let another person be punished for what I did."

"He did not ask who took it," said Ellicott, "he asked who had
it. His exact words were — "

"Yes," I said, "and I would just as soon see you get a little
detention, but not for something I did; so kindly keep your feet out
of the ice cream, before I smack you a couple."

"Let's see you do it," he said, to my surprise, so I let him see me
all right, pasting him one in the eye. Unfortunately we had been
walking along and by now we had almost reached chapel; but
without regard for that fact, Ellicott hauled off and smacked me
back; so it was necessary to hit him again. This, of course, made a
sort of uproar on the chapel steps, and Lanford and a couple of
other prefects who were loitering about the door came wading in
and broke it up; and I knew that our unseemly attitude would
result in plenty more trouble. Paul said to me, "What do you think
this is, anyway?" And feeling somewhat enraged, I said, "It may
be nothing right this minute, but after supper it will be the sudden
death of an Ellicott." That irritated Paul, so he answered, "All
right, you can both report to Doctor Holt. And you had better not
forget about it, because I will be reporting myself."

I looked at Ellicott in an unfriendly way then, and saw to my surprise that though his eye was going to be quite a sight before prayers were over, he seemed to be having the time of his life. That made it clear to me that he was extremely pleased because he had at last attracted some attention; what with making people think in assembly that he read Mr. Pollard's books; and, now, that he was such a desperate character that he would start a fight on the chapel steps, which many people would think twice about doing. As for me, I saw that I was undoubtedly going to get fired, since to everything else I had added fighting, and (Doctor Holt would insist) trying to evade a penalty by letting somebody else stand up for me; and in addition, of course, having done what the penalty I was evading was for.

After supper Lanford said to me, "Go on over to night study. I'll send for you when I want you," which did not cheer me any, because it meant Ellicott would have his side of it heard first, and since you can never tell what he would say, I would probably make some mistakes in detail and have the crime of deliberate falsehood imputed to me. I thought I might as well start a rough draft of a letter home, but I had only got about as far as *Dear Dad, I fear that I am proving somewhat of a disappointment to you in being, as you probably have heard* — when Lanford came into night study, so I turned the sheet over and started to do a geometry original on the back. He came up to my desk and said: "Let's go," so I got up and went out with him. "Listen," I said in the hall, "you are not the Lord High Executioner. Just relax and tell me what Ellicott had to say."

I thought for a minute he was going to be one hundred per cent prefect; but finally he said, "Ellicott told the Doctor he started that scrap. I know darn well I saw you hit him first. The Doctor didn't do anything but tell him not to do it again."

I thought of several possible wisecracks; but I was not as a matter of fact feeling very humorous, being nervous, so I said nothing.

When we got into the study, I saw to my astonishment that Mr. Pollard was up there, and was sorry that he had been dragged into it, but I got myself in hand and said, "Good evening, sir," to Doctor Holt, and he said, "You can go, Lanford."

Evan got up and lit a cigarette somewhat impatiently. "We could suppose the facts were essentially as stated, couldn't we, sir?" he asked. Doctor Holt looked at him very pleasantly and said, "Yes, unless you would like to hear how different the events can sometimes appear to different people."

"I can imagine, sir," said Evan, yawning.

Doctor Holt looked at me suddenly and said, without so much warmth: "Mr. Pollard has asked me not to expel you. What improvement he expects to effect in your incurable laziness and insufferable impudence, I am at loss to imagine. He says, however, that he will undertake to see that you behave yourself for the rest of the term."

"Yes, sir," I said, greatly cheered.

"He has also asked me to reconsider my decision in regard to the editorship of the *Review*. He made the point that it might keep you out of mischief."

I had always known that Mr. Pollard had a great deal of influence with the Old Man, because Doctor Holt is very fond of him, and thinks quite correctly that he is a fine teacher; and consequently I saw that it was very lucky for me that Evan had returned and thus induced Doctor Holt to release a few malefactors, as they were accustomed to do in ancient times to celebrate this or that.

"Thank you very much, sir," I said, when I had taken it in. "I will try to make the magazine more of a credit to the school." I did not by that mean anything against Tate, who was this year's editor and doing the best he could; but whether I have learned any Latin or geometry or not, I have at least picked up some of the fundamentals of English prose composition, and as a result enjoy a considerable advantage over Tate.

"You will have your hands full," said Doctor Holt briefly to Evan. "That will be all."

"Thank you, sir," said Evan. "Good night." We went out

together and when the door was closed, he said, "I shall ask Mr.
Lewis tomorrow if you have your geometry prepared, and I advise
you to have it prepared."

We had not got to the head of the stairs yet, and before we could,
Doctor Holt called out, "Evan! Come and take this book!"

"What book?" wondered Evan, turning; so I said, "I expect it is
Candida by Bernard Shaw, which Ellicott must have brought up. I
am relieved to have you get it back safe." I did not wait for him,
because I thought I would just go over and let Ellicott know that I
had got the *Review* before I did any geometry, which might take
some time.

PART THREE

WAR BETWEEN THE STATES

Men Running

Insistently, prodding him awake, George Holcombe heard, unreal, then harsh, more urgent, "Captain! Say, Captain!"

He made himself stir. Straws poked his cheek and, recoiling, he lifted his head from the saddlebags. "What the devil!" he grunted. At once he was wholly aware; tense, remembering where he was.

To all appearances it was night still. A play of firelight entered the open doors of the barn, showed him dimly the thick cross-beams high above. Sitting up on the straw in the wagon, he groped for his boots in the dark. "What is it?" he asked quickly. "Are we going to be attacked?" He climbed stiffly over the side, landing on his sore stockinged feet.

"The colonel ain't back," said his awakener. It was Carl Hurd, bulking big and aimless against the firelight. "So I—"

"Well, what are you doing here? How dare you leave your post? Don't you know yet what picket duty means?"

"Sure I do, George; but there's a cavalry fellow or something here looking for the colonel. You better talk to him. I stopped him all right and he didn't have any countersign; but I figured how could anybody have it except us? He said he's from General Runyon with orders, so I—"

"Tell him I'm coming." George Holcombe found his boots, forced his feet into them. He came out into the firelight past the short picket line of the officers' horses. Several groups of men by the fires were still playing cards—making a night of it, apparently.

They ought to be getting some rest, but probably they found they couldn't sleep on the ground. The ones who could were rolled in blankets here and there off in the shadows beyond the irregular stacks of muskets. A few of them, not wrapped in anything, might be drunk as well as asleep.

A uniformed man was sitting his horse, looking from right to left slowly. It was possible to recognize in no more than the silhouette of his carriage that he must be from the regular army. What he thought of this encampment wouldn't be hard to guess. He watched George Holcombe approach a minute and said, "What troops are these?" Plainly it cost him an effort to call them troops at all. George Holcombe could see the insignia and shoulder bars of a first lieutenant, U.S.A.

"Second New Jersey Volunteers; First and Sixth Companies, First Battalion. I'm Captain Holcombe."

The rider saluted him with a kind of negligent precision. Obviously he did not consider George Holcombe's years and general appearance adequate for a captain. "These orders are directed to Lieutenant Colonel Tucker. He's not here?"

"He heard there was to be a conference somewhere up the line. He went up. He said he'd be back, but he may have lost his way."

"He'll be lucky if the Secesh cavalry don't find it for him," the lieutenant said. Wearily he allowed himself to relax a little in the saddle. "You haven't a major?"

"He was left sick at Roach's Mills. I think I'm in command. I'm First Company captain. We lost track of the Second Battalion. Maybe Colonel Tucker's with them."

The lieutenant unbent more. He swung painfully out of the saddle. "Well, Captain," he said, "you haven't a drink on you, have you?"

"I have a pint of brandy, sir."

"It would be a favor if you'd give me a drink. I'm about in. Have you any kind of map? Do you know where you are now?"

"No, sir. Not very well. Colonel Tucker had a map, but he took it with him."

The lieutenant groaned slightly. George Holcombe had unbuttoned the flap of his deep blouse pocket and produced the glass flask. The lieutenant tilted it up, took a remarkable swallow, and handed it back. "Well, I have a map," he said, wiping his mouth. "Find a bit of paper if you can and try to copy some of it." He produced and spread out a frail, soiled sheet. "The Warrenton Turnpike runs directly west from Fairfax to Centerville to Gainesville Station, up there. The first three divisions started moving just after midnight. The engineers found them an unfortified ford over the Bull Run several miles north of the turnpike bridge. As we understand it, there's to be a feint at the bridge to cover a flanking movement by the ford which is expected to take in reverse the whole enemy line along the run. Colonel Miles's Fifth Division is at Centerville. General Runyon would like to get the Fourth Division up to where it would be available to re-enforce Miles. Better have your men get breakfast, and as soon as it's perfectly light march them east on any paths or roads you can find — you're bound to come on the Fairfax Court House road. You're about three miles south of Vienna Station." He shivered a little and yawned. "Listen," he said. "Hear the locomotive whistle?"

"Yes, sir."

There had been a general stir around the fires and more fuel had been thrown on the nearest one. In the brighter light the lieutenant's puffed eyes and drawn cheeks were gilded. The young sandy mustache drooped its ends. Removing his hat a moment, he showed the wisps of his light hair matted damply with sweat. He looked about him, shivered again, and said, "You may as well keep the map. It's dawn already. I'll have to report back. Get toward Fairfax the best way you can. One thing: the Rebels are probably as bad off as we are."

George Holcombe was moved to say, "We don't look a great deal, sir; we bivouacked here after dark and we aren't used to it, but these boys are all right. We haven't done any marching, much; but if they can find any Rebels, they'll fight all you want."

The lieutenant laid a hand on his saddle. "Captain," he said, "I hope they will. I know they'll try to. But you can't win a battle without an army. The Rebels could lose it, but we can't possibly win it. You don't know where your other battalion is—you shouldn't be formed in battalions, anyway; there's no sense in it. You have no brigade headquarters because nobody has seen fit to brigade the division. Where are your trains?"

"Captain Kingsinger of the Sixth Company went back for them, sir. He knew where they were to be."

"He won't find them there. They broke some wheels; they missed the road; they were held up by artillery. Now you're short another officer. What became of the adjutant?"

"He went with Colonel Tucker, sir."

"The roster went with him, probably. How are you going to have roll call?"

"Well, sir" —George Holcombe found himself flushing— "I think the first sergeants keep rolls for their companies."

"Good for you! Have your men anything for breakfast?"

"Most of them probably have a little something in their haversacks, sir."

"If I were you I'd see that it was shared where necessary—so everyone gets some. It's going to be a hard, hot day." George Holcombe saw that it was, in fact, day. In the east, early summer light had paled all the stars. It was Sunday, July 21, 1861.

With Hurd's help, George Holcombe found Lieutenants Joe Matthews and Harry Vanzant burrowed in a haystack. The regimental color sergeant and three corporals of his guard were also in the haystack at a point marked by the cased colors leaning casually against the side. Nathan Wright, the First Company bugler, and his nephew Pete, who was drummer, put in their appearance. The boy had shed the drum jacket, and yawning, flexing his wrists, began to coax out subdued, fragmentary periods of the long roll.

George Holcombe said, "We might as well have Wright sound assembly. We're ordered to report at Fairfax. A battle is going to be fought beyond Centerville. We're simply joining the reserve, though. I'm afraid we won't get anywhere near it."

Harry Vanzant said, "Maybe we will, if we get started. We're going to look pretty silly if we come home without ever even seeing a battle. Where's the colonel?"

"He may be with the other battalion. We ought to see if we can find where it is before we start. They won't have had any orders, maybe."

"I move we let them find us. If we don't start, they'll run the Rebs all the way to Richmond without giving us a shot at them."

"Well, we'll get lined up, anyway, and have roll call. Sound off, will you, Nathan? We can form across the field there."

Wright spat, licked his lips, and brought the bugle up. "Let 'er go, Sonny!" he said to Pete.

George Holcombe buttoned his blouse and straightened his sword belt. The eastern sky was a fine, gleaming, lucent white above the shadowed treetops. Dew was visibly gray on the short rough tufts of pasture grass stretched away to the second-growth oak woods. The bugle, clear and fresh as the early air, went ringing over the barnyard, down the lane and orchard, the drum after it, roll on roll.

Probably hardly anyone was asleep, for at once in the dusk of dawn under the trees, around the wide ruddy splotches of the fading fires, there was a swarming movement; the musket stacks were plucked apart; sergeants came running. Now, from somewhere, Lieutenants Hart and Moore of the Sixth Company came up. George Holcombe said quietly, "Maybe they're going to raise a row. They'll want to wait for Kingsinger, probably."

Hart said, "What's up, Holcombe? Colonel get back?"

"No; but orders came from General Runyon to move at daylight. We'll have to go."

"We can't go. How about Colonel and Kingsinger? How'll they know where to find us?"

"We'll have to chance it. We'll have to obey General Runyon's orders."

"I don't think so. We haven't anyone in command. We'd better wait."

"I'm in command. I'm the ranking captain."

"Who said so?"

"I'm captain of the First Company. That makes me senior captain."

"What do you mean? Any company could have happened to be first. What's senior about that?"

"Well, that's the way it is in the army. Tell your men to fall in."

"Not until the colonel comes, Holcombe. I'm not taking orders from you."

"D'you want a bang on the snout?" asked Harry Vanzant. "Because that's something you'll take, all right."

"Not from you."

"Oh, so you think not!"

"Stop it, Harry!" George Holcombe snatched his arm. "We won't get anywhere that way. Listen to a little common sense, Hart. There's going to be a battle somewhere around Centerville. General Runyon is trying to get his division together, in case it's needed." He had one eye apprehensively on the lines forming in the brightening light across the pasture. "Do you want it to be said the Second New Jersey Volunteers lay around camp all morning because they were afraid to fight?"

"Who'll say it?"

"Well, the militia regiments certainly will."

"Who cares what the militia says?" asked Hart. "Their ninety days are about up, and all they want to do is get home. The volunteers could lick them any day."

"No," Lieutenant Moore said. "Come on, Jake. He's right, there. If there's going to be any fighting, we want to help."

"All right." Hart nodded, sulky. "But look here, don't think you're commanding the Sixth Company. Until Captain Kingsinger comes back, Moore and I are commanding it."

"You mean," said Harry Vanzant, "until a gun goes off. After that you'll be so far away—"

"See here, Vanzant—"

"Shut up, you fools," Moore said. "Let's get to our places. We're just wasting time."

George Holcombe wiped his forehead.

"Battalion, attention!" he shouted. "Sergeants, to the front—march! Call the rolls."

Rations were ordinarily prepared by the company cooks, to whom the orderly sergeants issued them. Preparing their own food seemed more than many of the men could manage. There was a good deal of grumbling and quarreling around the badly built small fires while the morning grew brighter and the sun came up level across the orchard.

Hurd, who had been acting as George Holcombe's orderly, made some bad coffee which the officers drank, sitting in a circle, eating old bread and half-cooked bacon strips. Harry was still belligerent. Lieutenant Hart, who was no match for him and probably knew it, covered his sense of inferiority by being huffy and sarcastic. Joe Matthews wanted only to keep the peace and Moore was a quiet chap, not at all inclined to back up Hart. George Holcombe spread out the map for them and indicated as well as he could where they were going—supposing the men got themselves fed and they ever started. The sun was riding high, the freshness gone from the air before Wright was able to blow assembly. There was some delay in lining up. "That spring's dry," the first sergeant told George Holcombe. "They've been hunting around, but there isn't any other water. I don't think more than four or five of them got their canteens filled."

"We'll find some water," George Holcombe said. "We've wasted hours now. Get them in line. Make sure they have all their equipment."

"A lot of them say they won't carry it, George. It's quite a load for a hot day."

"Well, they'll be sorry." He noticed that several men in the first rank had removed their boots and stockings and stood barefoot. "We may have to march fifteen or twenty miles," he said, exasperated. "Tell those fellows to put their shoes on!"

"They say it hurts them too much, Captain. They've got pretty good calluses." It would be hopeless to try to correct these matters unless he wished to spend the morning arguing. "They'll be sorry,"

he repeated, futilely. He walked down the line and said to Lieutenant Moore, "We'll march them in column of companies by the
right flank—"

He broke off, turning his head. Moore turned too. The ranks,
fairly quiet before, were instantly completely quiet. After a
moment it came again, at a great distance, but distinct on the hot
morning air: a deep dull sound like something heavy—the earth
itself, perhaps—being moved in the southwest. "That's cannon," a
surprised voice remarked.

"Battalion, attention!" George Holcombe called. "By the right
flank—"

Sergeants' voices went up in chorus. Harry Vanzant roared,
"Right face, you blockhead! Don't you know how to march by the
flank?"

"Forward," George Holcombe continued, giving them time
enough to correct any initial errors. They had evolved themselves
moderately well into ranks of four. "Route step, march!" He
swung a leg over his horse. Lieutenant Hart's sharp voice reached
him above the tramping: "Arms at will, simpleton, but keep your
muzzle up! Do you want to shoot Luke's head off?" A gruffer
voice guffawed, "Luke'd never miss it." Riding to the front,
George Holcombe half turned in his saddle, looking back at the
column, now altogether into the shadowed woods closing down on
the lane. This view of them was more encouraging. Their uniforms,
seen not too closely, looked well, clean and new.

Gazing at the faces—some bearded, some brown, some reddened under the variously tipped and tilted forage caps—he could
name most of those in the First Company, remember things about
them, where they lived, who their people were. They were a good
sort, in the main—farm boys used to a hard day's work. There was
no reason to suppose that, to a Monmouth County man, the Sixth
Company wouldn't seem as good. The three companies which had
been detached Friday were largely from Ewing and Trenton—
store clerks and mechanics. George Holcombe doubted if they
would stand up to marching so well. Their arms were poorer,
too—long, heavy, altered muskets instead of the fine new Minié

rifles these men had been given. On the other hand, there wasn't much ammunition available for the rifles. On an average, they probably didn't have twenty rounds.

The Vienna–Fairfax Court House road lay full in the sun. George Holcombe called out, "Column right!" and saw the dried reddish dust puff up under his horse's hoofs. It rose at once in a haze about the first platoon. Looking back an instant later, he saw it lifting to the treetops. The Sixth Company was entirely invisible.

In a few minutes, riding his horse through the roadside brush, Lieutenant Hart appeared. "Listen, Holcombe," he said, "you can't breathe back there"—he was indeed coated with dust from boots to hat brim. "I'll halt our company and let you get a half a mile or so ahead. We can't miss the road, and if you run into anything, all you have to do is stop and we'd be up with you in a couple of minutes."

Harry Vanzant was riding forward from the haze now, and, foreseeing a new altercation, George Holcombe nodded. "All right. I think we ought to reach Fairfax in an hour, so don't halt to rest before that."

"That's the last you'll see of him," Harry said. "Well, he's no loss. Hear the guns?"

"Yes."

"It certainly must be the real thing. If it goes on at that rate, I'll bet you a half dollar it'll be over before we get anywhere near it."

"We haven't orders to get anywhere near it. I'd just as soon we didn't get into an engagement—I mean until everyone has had more practice with the rifles. Half of them would probably take an hour to reload."

"They might hurry a little more if they saw some Rebels. When you can hear them having a battle, I guess you don't need any orders about where to go."

"Well, we may find the colonel, or division headquarters at Fairfax." He looked at Harry's dust-coated face. "Ride here," he said. "I'll fall back a while."

In the deep dust, Joe Matthews's horse plodded patiently along. Joe had tied a handkerchief over his mouth and nose. He saluted

George Holcombe. "That Hart fellow ordered the Sixth Company
to halt," he observed, muffled by the handkerchief. "He was
getting his nice uniform all dirty. I couldn't blame them much, but I
think some of us ought to stay together. A fine battalion this is!
First they detach three companies; then Hart thinks he's General
Scott and holds another; and here we are with one company to the
regimental colors. A couple of troops of Rebel cavalry scouting
around could take them right away from us."

George Holcombe, coughing, looked at the sun, a firm-edged,
fierce copper disk in the dust cloud above. "Cheer up, Joe," he
said.

From the front came suddenly Harry Vanzant's voice: "Company, halt!" The sergeants in position as file closers passed it back:
"Halt!—Halt!—Halt!" George Holcombe put his horse violently
ahead, his heart jumping to a suspended beat. "Harry!" he shouted. "Harry, what is it?"

"Dust ahead there. I could hear horses."

"Joe, come up! Company, attention! Ready, arms!"

"Maybe it's just a team," Harry said, apologetic. "But I thought
we'd better see if we're running into anything."

Joe Matthews said, "I knew it. It's Rebel cavalry. They're all
over the place. Wait and see. What do you think we'd better do,
George?"

"Harry and I will ride forward. You take command. Get the
company into platoon front and fix bayonets. If you hear any
shooting, prepare to fire by volley. If it's cavalry, shoot low, at the
horses; they'd only miss the men. And have somebody ready to
send back to warn Hart."

"Now?"

"No. Give someone your horse. At the first shot, let him ride for
it. And, wait a minute—I have another idea. Get the men
re-formed, and then move forward slowly, kicking up as much dust
as you can. That way, anyone attacking might not be able to tell
how many lines there were."

"Well, it's nothing but a carriage," Harry said. "Look at that!"

Through the trees at the bend of the road appeared a pair of horses trotting laboriously. A Negro driver immediately pulled them up. "We'd better see about it," Harry said. "It may be spies, or some big Secesh fellow trying to get away." George Holcombe rode forward.

From the carriage an enormously fat, red-faced man, with curved gray mustaches thick as sausages, squeaked vehemently, "Who the devil are you?"

A younger, spryer fellow with checked trousers and a dust-powdered bowler hat laughed. "It's all right, Senator," he said. "These are our boys. Good morning, Captain."

"Good morning," George Holcombe said, at a loss.

"I'm the correspondent from the New York *Globe*, Captain. The senator and I are trying to get to Centerville. We seem to have missed the road. Perhaps you could direct us. The senator thought you were Rebels." He laughed. "You're not, are you?"

"We're the Second New Jersey Volunteers. You couldn't get to Centerville this way. But I wouldn't go if I were you. That firing you hear now is down there. There was expected to be a battle this morning."

"As a matter of fact, Captain, we came out to see the battle, but I guess it's too late. It's about over. McDowell seems to have done it. The Rebels are reported in full retreat. We thought we could see the field, however."

"You definitely know that?" The depth of his disappointment surprised George Holcombe. He hadn't, he reminded himself, really expected that they would see any fighting today, but there had been a chance—if General Runyon were getting his division together it must be wanted for something. "Are you sure it's really all over?" he asked. "We can still hear firing."

"I know how you feel, Captain. But it's as much credit to a man to have been ready to fight. There was word direct from the field at Fairfax. Burnside and Sherman had cleared the Warrenton Pike; the stone bridge was open. The artillery you hear is probably shelling Manassas Junction and the railroad stock. I should say that the rebellion—in Virginia, at least—is finished."

"Have some champagne, New Jersey," said the senator.

"Whole hamper of it here. It's no man's drink, but it takes the dust out of your mouth."

"I think we'd better get through to Fairfax, sir. I'd be glad of a drink then."

"Right about face, Sambo!" cried the senator. "Captain, you're welcome to all you can hold of it, whenever you want it. This is a great day for America." Man's drink or none, it occurred to George Holcombe that the senator was making the best of it. The newspaper fellow gave him a quick, friendly wink. With difficulty the Negro got the carriage around in the road.

Over the white cupola of Fairfax Court House, over the massed treetops and few roofs of the village, dust hung too, an immense vague cloudy pillar visible on the hot blue sky. Not far behind the senator's carriage, George Holcombe marched the First Company up the rise past the old church. Oppressed still to reflect that it was all over — they might even be back in Trenton in a week or so, and where they went or what they did was of no pressing importance — he could at least hope that orders of some sort would be found here, for at Fairfax the army seemed to be in force. Before the church at least a score of smiths worked over traveling forges, reshoeing strings of horses to a great clangor of hammers on anvils, scorching stench of red iron laid to horn. The churchyard was full of teamsters and commissary orderlies reclining to rest or play cards among the graves. The roadside was lined solidly with canvas-hooded commissary wagons. Jamming the country streets moved carts and carriages, troops of cavalry, groups of mounted officers, ambulances. Most of the Court House grounds were occupied by an artillery park of brass Napoleons. Horses crowded the hitching rails and blocked half the road before two taverns.

Reaching finally the short arched arcade of the red brick Court House, George Holcombe wiped his dust-thickened lips and croaked, "Company, halt. At ease." He dismounted, trying to slap the dust from his uniform and make himself a little more presentable.

"Stay in ranks!" shouted Harry Vanzant; but vainly, for the men had noticed the Court House well around the side.

"All right," George Holcombe said. "Let them fill their canteens. You can't stop them. Carl, hold my horse a minute, will you?"

Stepping into the arcade, he saluted a very tall man with colonel's eagles pinned to a brilliant red-and-pale-blue uniform. "Could you tell me where General Runyon's headquarters are, sir?"

"Runyon?" said the Colonel. "Never heard of him. Miles's headquarters are in Centerville, but if you're looking for him, he's over the road there, drunk as an owl. What he's doing here, nobody knows. I hear McDowell's won. Did you just come down?"

"No, sir. We came from Vienna Station way."

"Humph! Well, excuse me, I must get on."

Two artillery officers, presumably attached to the parked battery, came out the doors and George Holcombe saluted again.

In answer to his question, one of them shook his head. The other said, "Hold on! Runyon. Fourth Division. Why he never left Roach's Mills, that I heard of. He wasn't ordered forward. Who are you?"

"New Jersey, eh?" said the first officer. "Well, maybe I can help you there. I don't know anything about General Runyon, but quite a number of your boys went through toward Centerville — about an hour ago, I'd think. A Colonel Montgomery commanding. He your colonel?"

"He commands the First New Jersey," George Holcombe said, despondent.

"Well, is that in your division?"

"Yes, sir, I think so."

"Then, young man, I'd say the best thing for you to do would be to report to him, if you can find him."

George Holcombe stepped out with them from the shadow of the arches into the sun. The First Company had surrounded the roofed, lattice-walled well under the trees. One of the artillery officers said, "If those are your men, it won't do them any good. That well was drunk dry three hours ago."

"Where could we get water, sir?"

"I wish I could tell you. If you move out the pike, you'll

probably find a brook somewhere." He considered George Holcombe a moment. "I suppose you have nothing to eat, either."

"I'm afraid we haven't, sir."

"Well, I'll give you a tip. Those commissary wagons are full of
cases of biscuit. It's better than nothing. Send one of your lieutenants down with a few men. There are no guards and no drivers.
It's simply bedlam around here. Fortunate for us that McDowell
whipped the Rebels so quickly. One more day like this and we'd be
in full retreat."

At one o'clock there had been no sign of Hart and the Sixth
Company. George Holcombe could see that this might be his own
fault. Fairfax grew more and more crowded. Hart might have
found it impossible to get into the village at all.

In any event, they would have to get some water, and there was
no use waiting. George Holcombe lined the company up. As he
had expected, the men without their shoes could not possibly
go on. Their feet were caked over with bloody dust. The rest
had resulted in such swelling that they could scarcely stand.
He wrote slips of permission to be out of ranks and signed them.
They could wait for the Sixth Company.

To get out of town in column would be impossible. They broke
ranks and worked their way through. Once out on the Centerville
road, this meant a long delay in re-forming. Then they came on a
small stream at the bottom of the slope. A flimsy wooden bridge
over it had broken down, damming up a wide shallow pool. At least
a hundred men were already there, bathing their feet and faces;
despite the filthiness of the water, drinking it. The approach of the
company was watched with open hostility and George Holcombe
guessed that a column coming in reasonable military order made
many of them afraid they were about to be rounded up and
returned to their commands.

Ranks were broken again to let those who could stomach it
drink. Harry Vanzant rode up beside him and said, "What do you
think all that firing's about, George? It hasn't stopped any."

The first sergeant made his way up from the throng on the

muddy trampled bank, wiped the water from his beard, and, saluting, said, "George, a lot of those fellows say they've come down from the field and that it's all a lie about there being any victory. They say the Rebels captured a couple of batteries and are drumming the daylight out of—"

"All right, all right," George Holcombe said, agitated. "Don't believe everything you hear. Let's get formed up. We may find some better water farther along."

At the fork a faded sign, pointing left, read CENTERVILLE 5; but there would have been no doubt about it anyway. A constant slow stream of passers-by straggled down. A few appeared to be wounded. Many of them, seeing at a distance the dust-hazed shape of the tramping column, got quickly off the road altogether. Occasionally wagons or carriages came up, pulled over a little, and waited while they passed.

His sharp pointed face somber, Joe Matthews rode alongside after a while. "George," he said, "nobody seems to be going our way but us. Do you think maybe we'd better—"

"Centerville can't be more than two or three more miles. I think we'd better go on to there."

"The boys are pretty well fagged out."

"We'll give them ten minutes' rest. That looks like a little brook, there. Maybe they can fill their canteens."

For several hours now heavy white-crested thunderclouds had been gathering on the horizon. They massed up, quietly ominous, well over the roadside skirts of pine and the dense low groves of blackjack and pin oak. Looking down from them, George Holcombe was astonished to see the senator with the heavy mustaches. He sat at the edge of the woods on a log, fanning himself with his huge straw hat, with the other hand gesturing toward the great clouds. "On the just and on the unjust," he observed. "Mark my words, New Jersey."

The senator's carriage, minus a wheel, reposed helplessly in the ditch. There was no sign of horses, driver, or the newspaper correspondent. The senator had turned his attention to the men released from ranks crowding the little brook. "Every one," he boomed, "that lappeth of the water with his tongue, as a dog lappeth, him shalt thou set by himself—the Midianites are given into thy hand, New Jersey. Take some champagne. That newspaper fellow rode to Centerville on one horse. He ought to be back. Sambo rode to Fairfax to fetch another carriage. So here I am, so here I am! What's all this mob doing?" On the wicker wine hamper beside him lay a short four-barreled New Elliott revolver. "Band of thieves, most of them," he said. "Hi, there!" he cried.

The horse, lathered, had coated with dust, lathered through that and coated again. Mud clung in flat cakes all over him. The newspaper fellow had lost his hat; his dark hair was as dirty as the horse. His checked pants and narrow pointed shoes were red with clay. He wiped the mud off his lips, swung down, and tied his horse to the young oak where George had fastened his. "Where's your company, Captain?"

George Holcombe indicated them.

"You'd better get them back. It's all up—it's a rout. They're pouring into Centerville. They're—"

"You mean our men?"

"Naturally. Heaven knows what happened, but they're licked. It's nothing but a panic now. They're running so hard—"

"They couldn't be! Run from a lot of miserable Rebels! Why—"

"Don't worry, you'll see it in a minute. These are just stragglers, but a mile or so back they're coming down like a river. They'll run all the way to Washington probably."

"You mean the army's retreating?"

"What there is left of it. We'll wait for the rush to go by. Then we'll get you on this horse, Senator—what are you going to do, Captain?"

"Try to rally them, you fool. Harry! Joe! Company, fall in! Sergeant, on the right there, to guide. By platoon front across the road. That's it. Get them up, Harry. Out of that water, you men!"

"Captain," said the newspaperman, "I may be a fool, but I'm not so much of a fool as you are. There are probably ten thousand men and a thousand horses who are going to come down this road. They'll go right over you."

"That's the only way they will get by." Facing the partly formed lines, he said, "No one is to pass by this road. If those approaching do not halt on order, I shall give the command: 'Fire by files.' The first rank will then fire a volley. It will at once face about, pass through the succeeding ranks to the rear, re-form and reload. The second rank will then fire—"

"Good God, Captain!" The newspaperman seized his shoulder. "You can't do that! It's nothing but murder. You might kill a few wretches, but that won't stop them. They can't stop—too many behind."

"It will never be said that the Second New Jersey Volunteers ran away."

"Men just as good are running now, Captain. Listen! There it comes. The ones who could get horses will be first. They won't even hear you if you try to tell them to halt."

Over the low rise, down toward the brook, lifted a great cloud of dust, a tumult of hoofbeats. George Holcombe opened his mouth to say, "Get off the road, if you're afraid," but, seeing now the dust like an impending cyclone, he recognized suddenly, with a kind of amazement, that he was afraid himself. No one in his right senses stood in front of a herd of galloping horses.

There were sudden slight wavering breaks in the solid rank of the front line; bayonets shook here and there. "Hey!" roared Harry Vanzant. "Stand to the colors, you cursed cowards!" But his voice was without volume, without any warmth or conviction, for, like George Holcombe, he must have found, looking at what was coming, that he was a coward himself. He just stood lumpishly with his nerveless sword out, not certain whether he was more afraid of admitting that he was afraid than of being trampled to death. He turned his fixed eyes and blank dusty face furtively toward George Holcombe. George Holcombe yelled faintly, "Break ranks! Jump for it! Clear out!"

The newspaper fellow, putting his head down, charged straight at him. They both went over and over, bringing up in the ditch. From this angle, dazed, George Holcombe could see the swinging, bayoneted rifles, the flying boots of men leaping above him. There was a solitary shriek of someone ridden down. Groups of swaying, pounding horses loomed in the dust whirl; the ground shook under them. They were by. Immediately more succeeded them; and then more.

The newspaper fellow sat up slowly, a hand to the side of his head, where a slight shallow abrasion was beading the dust with blood. "Well," he panted, "that was a near thing, if I do say it. They were right on top of us, Captain. Pretty soon you'll see the mob on foot. After a while, when they thin out a little, if I were you I'd just take your colors, form up as many of the men as you can find, and go back. The Rebels won't be coming. There's nothing you can do here."

George Holcombe got painfully to his feet. "You saved my life," he said. "I suppose I should be grateful."

The senator had not budged from his log. His big straw hat was tilted back on the great dome of his forehead, and to this expanse he applied a silk handkerchief. Through the dust haze he said gently, "There, there, Sonny; don't take it too much to heart. We all did a little misjudging today."

George Holcombe looked at him, stony-eyed. "I take it to heart, sir, when my country's whipped. You came out here expecting a sort of picnic or something, but we—" He stopped.

"Have some champagne, Sonny," said the senator. "It's the last in the hamper. Next time we start for Richmond we won't be bringing anything fancy, maybe."

One Hundred Ladies

Elation was the proper word for what he felt. Owen Fulton felt it with an urgent, unreasonable completeness as soon as he got into the depot at Washington and saw the special train for Fredericksburg. Every car was elaborately swathed in fresh, vivid, red-white-and-blue bunting. The bunting made long formal festoons gathered at the center under plaques of painted and gilded wood. The plaques bore alternately from car to car the old First Corps disk, and the combined First and Fifth Corps badges of the last Virginia campaign.

Owen Fulton's simple pleasure assured him that, after all, he had been right to come. Hattie was wrong for once. It would do him good, just as Alfred promised. In the great crowd he looked around, not recognizing anyone, but glad to see that something was left of the army, that many people still remembered. As a rule he disliked and avoided crowds — that was what Hattie knew and meant when she told him he was foolish — but he liked this one. He had avoided it, if anything, too long. He had been letting himself forget that, whatever might be said about the present, he had once been a soldier.

The May day was very warm. A rumor that President Arthur was to join the group of guests from the Senate and House probably kept people out of the cars. Anticipating inconvenience with his leg in the last-minute rush sure to result, Owen Fulton clutched his bag tight and pushed on cheerfully. It would hardly be possible to find Alfred Bostwick before the train started.

Choosing steps at random, Owen displayed his Society of the First Corps card. He lifted his bag and threw it onto the car platform, preparing with complicated agility to follow it. On level ground his injured leg gave him practically no trouble. He knew how to manage it. But stairs he had to take sideways, keeping the knee straight while he stepped patiently up with his right foot. After all these years he could do it so expertly that, unless the stairs were long, he would be up before anyone could help him — supposing there was anyone who would think of troubling.

One of those who would have troubled was the conductor who had asked to see his card. Like everyone else, the conductor was watching for President Arthur, but he turned belatedly and cried, "Here, Captain! Wait. I'll — "

Panting on top, Owen answered, "Thank you, but I'm handy at it."

The conductor, perhaps conscious of his railroad uniform, said, "I'm an old First Corps man, myself, Captain. Eighth Pennsylvania Reserves. Magilton's brigade."

Owen looked down, surprised, at the full mild face. Those, he remembered, were Meade's Third Division men who broke Jackson's line, almost won the battle before it began. When no one was ordered to their support, they had in turn been broken. Remembering that bad December morning well enough, Owen could recall vividly the Pennsylvanians' alarming, unexpected reappearance about noon. They were falling back from the railroad through the brush and smoke in little groups — one or two behind stopping to fire, though surely at nothing visible. Others, showing the rough spite of defeat, herded ahead varying small numbers of ragged Rebel prisoners.

With that liberty of opinion which distinguished the volunteers, they felt that they had been senselessly sacrificed. They greeted the line with jeers and curses. "What were you waiting for, Dummy? Carriages to take you up?" some small-respecter of shoulder straps had roared in Owen Fulton's face.

Not knowing for what he was waiting, nor what was coming next, Owen Fulton, a second lieutenant at the time, let the company left in his charge get out of hand several times during the next half hour. Their panicky bursts of firing must have killed some men of Meade's, who had missed the first order to fall back, or been hampered by wounds. Down on one knee, staring in agony of attention, Owen would shout to stop it as soon as he could be sure. Even, rising, he would race down the line, flailing backs and buttocks of absorbed shooters with his sword flat —

This enlivening of memories, complete with all small sights and sounds, with tensions and anxieties as fresh as ever, certified the past to him, and Owen valued it as a foretaste of what he might expect when he saw Fredericksburg, saw the positions of the Left Grand Division. He found himself shaken by the mingling of regret and joy and pride. Holding the rail, he answered, "I was in the Ninety-seventh New York, the Second Division. It's twenty years since I've seen Fredericksburg — "

With a quick, overwhelming crash, a band which Owen had not noticed before broke into "Dixie" — *old times there are not forgotten*. . . . Paralysed by the fine blare and bray of horns and bugles, the matchless roll of military drums in expert hands, Owen Fulton could feel the blood come up in his face, tightening his cheeks, tingling at the roots of his mustache. The locomotive blew its whistle. Plainly President Arthur was not, and probably never had been, coming. Owen raised his hand in a quick wave to the conductor. Limping in his haste to get out of the way, he entered the car, dropped down in the nearest seat.

A few people were in uniform. Owen noticed a hardy little old man with a forage cap set on the back of his head. He noticed him because the crown of the cap still carried a Corps badge in the faded color of Owen's own division. Sergeant's stripes had turned almost white on the ancient sleeve. Down the aisle went also a distinct perfume of whiskey, and Owen hoped that there would not be too much of that, especially by men who had elected to wear a uniform which would unmistakably identify them with the First

Corps. Alfred had told him that the committee and the officers of the Society had suggested civilian clothes. You would not expect Fredericksburg to be exactly delighted by the old associations. Furthermore, General Longstreet was to be present as a speaker. He would not be likely to appear in a Confederate uniform.

Though the car, in rapid shaking motion now, was greatly overcrowded, no one had made a move to take the seat by Owen. The aisle was full of men standing. Forming boisterous circles, others perched on the arms, hung over the backs of seats. Left alone, Owen did not feel out of it. He could not really expect anyone to pick him out and greet him. The truth was that during the first years after the war he had been unable to find either the time or the money to attend army reunions. Later it had seemed to him too late. Some of the soldiers' organizations had begun to take on a pension-seeking political aspect with which he would have been ashamed to associate himself. Then, too, his wife exercised an adverse influence. Hattie's disapproval was certainly not based on unpleasant political aspects. To the best of Owen's knowledge, it was not even based on any appropriately feminine abhorrence of war and slaughter. Once or twice he had marched in Memorial Day parades in Brooklyn. He might even, Owen admitted, have liked to march in more, to talk about old days over a glass or two in some uniform-crowded saloon after the speeches. Like most women, Hattie was instinctively against this. She did not oppose him in words, or show bad temper; but she could adeptly make him realize, at first, that she would be left alone for most of one of his few holidays; and then, the desirability of taking the chance for a quiet outing with the children. She had even expressed anxiety over his joining, as this year, at Alfred Bostwick's insistence, he had, the Society of the First Corps.

"Mr. Bostwick," she said—it was perhaps significant that in fifteen years' acquaintance she had never thought of calling him Alfred— "I do hope that this won't be something with long conventions Owen has to attend. I'm sure it would be very tiring for him. It wears him out so when he has to travel on business."

Alfred, who arrogated to himself the brusque privileges of a long bachelorhood, grunted, "You should have seen Owen in the old days, Mrs. Fulton. He's pretty well domesticated now, but he used to march the farthest traveling company in the division."

Hattie didn't miss obvious opportunities. "Yes," she said. "It might be different if it weren't for his wound. You aren't likely to forget the army, are you, Owen?" She went out then, for Alfred liked a glass of bourbon with his cigar and wouldn't hesitate an instant to drink the one and smoke the other regardless of her presence. He considered her place to be in the parlor.

"Hattie just hates to have you where she can't run you," he said, grasping resentfully at his bushy, still-handsome auburn side whiskers. "That's all right. Or at any rate, it's a woman's nature. Only you oughtn't to let yourself get to like it—" He went on blowing and grunting for some time, doubtless appalled by the narrowness of certain of his own escapes from matrimony.

In co-operation with a Sixth Corps man named Hunter, who had settled in Fredericksburg after the war and done well in the foundry business, Colonel Bostwick was even then scheming about this visit to the battlefield. His friend Hunter had just financed the building of an opera house, perhaps only moderately grand, but suitable for a big banquet. Alfred had interested General Doubleday. He had written to General Longstreet and received an agreeable reply, which he showed to Owen.

Alfred had assumed right along that Owen was going; but, up to this point, Owen hadn't planned to. He was reasonably certain that Hattie would find the trip unwise, or inconvenient, or both. By not mentioning it to Hattie, he had left, he found, a loophole. Unaware of the matter, Hattie had not been given the opportunity to settle it once and for all in the negative. When he saw Longstreet's letter accepting the First Corps' invitation, Owen Fulton was curiously stirred. It was astonishing to hold in your hand a note with conventional salutation and subscription, amblingly courteous, the ordinary cordial phrases scrawled in an even, unnotable hand-writing—and this was Longstreet! A name at once remote and thunderous; the formidable direction behind battle lines which, too often impregnable to assault, were always impregnable to the imagination. Owen discovered that he had a desire to see Longstreet—perhaps, shake hands with him. None of this could very well be explained to Hattie. She could not be expected to see why a glimpse of General Longstreet in the flesh would be worth something to him, or what would be gained if he saw again the actual spot where he had stood that December day, on the left, at Hamilton's Crossing. It would be very impolitic and ill-advised if he told her that he would like somehow to get in touch again with a time of his life when he was more important—yes, more noble; a man playing a man's part in the trying and dangerous realities of the fighting which had ended by preserving the Union. She would certainly presume that he meant to criticize her, to imply that she was not of any importance or interest to him—

Least of all would Hattie think it natural for him to wish to visit Fredericksburg again. He ought to remember it painfully. A hostile town, overflowing in heat and dust; one vast hospital, to which the wounded came up by the thousand from the lines of Spottsylvania to join those thousands from the Wilderness not yet evacuated. Owen Fulton had spent the whole month of June there in '64, expected, and expecting, to die. They told him he could not possibly live unless his leg was taken off. Perfectly pictured in his mind still was the face gleaming with sweat, the big red beard (his apron often bloody from beard to knees) of some regimental surgeon appearing about every ten minutes (or so it seemed) day and night saying: "Now, Captain, you're going to be reasonable about this, aren't you? You ought to think of me. Do I want your death on my conscience? You're committing suicide as wantonly as if you put a pistol to your head—"

Owen Fulton, raving, yelled: "Just give me a pistol and see what I use it for, you damned butcher!"

Afterward, when it became apparent that he was going to live, and that his leg, which they had wasted not a minute on, was finding some slow and incredible way of repairing itself, Owen was moved out to a tent in the garden. The tent stood close to a brick building which had been the slave quarters of the big house. Here the ladies of the family had established themselves. Lying on his back under the partly lifted canvas flies, Owen saw them frequently, frequently overheard their conversation. By degrees (it was all he had to do) he could identify them by voice; then, by sight. Mama was easy enough. So was Olivia, with her distinctively young tones. Sarah Ann and Lou he was less sure of—which was which he couldn't say, for he was never given a chance to assign the voice directly to the face. They spoke only when, imagining they could not be heard, they were indoors. When they came out, they passed down the path frigidly silent, looking neither right nor left. The part Mama had chosen for them to play was the preposterous, necessarily self-conscious one of being unaware of the tent in the garden, of their house from which they had been expelled to make room for Yankee wounded, of the wagons and artillery often passing on Princess Anne Street—even, of the sentries who, amused, were accustomed to present arms when they went through the gate.

The conversation indoors, usually quite clear, troubled Owen at first. Not only because it sometimes concerned intimate matters unsuitable for him to hear, but because listening at all was ungentlemanly and could not be defended. However, he did listen and he came to mind these aspects of it less. His leg was almost constantly painful and he could find a certain distraction in adding bit by bit to his acquaintance with the speakers. He corrected his impressions of them. He engaged silently his sympathy in their private concerns. He waited with interest to hear the outcome of the trivial plans or projects discussed.

In the end he knew them very well. Perhaps sometime he would marry some girl; but it was strange to think he would know far less about any girl he married than he knew about Olivia, who was engaged to a Rebel major in Ewell's Corps. Olivia, despite some charms of manner and speech, was selfish and irritable—like everyone else. Seeing these bad qualities in their right relation to her private life, Owen believed that he could condone and understand them better, and so perhaps evoke them less often. Less often than her major ever would be able to, when their appearance in a character presented to him as only amiable surprised and irritated him.

Able to see in Olivia's impersonal good looks the humanizing traces of her weaknesses and shortcomings, Owen was filled with a deep compassion and tenderness for her. Love, he knew, was reputed to overcome all obstacles. If not at the time, at least through the years since, an understanding between a Yankee officer and a southern girl had been shown in many books and plays to be the completest commonplace of romance. In his case it did not work like that. The uselessness of attempting to make Olivia notice him, or of hoping to exchange even a word with her, kept Owen from so much as considering it. When they came to move him to be sent north, she certainly did not feel sad to see him go, for she had never known that he was there. That would be twenty years ago, next month; but, very likely, if he cared to, Owen Fulton could today look at that house and garden again, find them little changed.

"I guess you wouldn't remember me, Captain."

The statement, close to him, broke through Owen Fulton's pre-occupation. With it came again the scent of whiskey and he turned his head, startled. The little man with the forage cap and sergeant's stripes had wandered back from wherever he had been going. On the corner of the seat he put a shocking hand. The very old injury was smoothly healed, but he had only two fingers. Jolted, Owen Fulton looked from it to the face. This was familiar enough. Everyone knew it. It had the thick bending nose and knobby chin of a ruddy, aged little Punch; but Owen could not connect it with any person of his acquaintance. Embarrassed, he said, "I hope you'll excuse me, Sergeant. I've a poor memory for faces."

The little man said, "That's all right, Captain. I guess we've all changed some. I just saw your head there by the window turned a certain way, and I said, 'Lord, that's Captain Fulton!' " He grinned and nodded a few times, plainly hoping that Owen might suddenly remember him. Finally he said, "My name's Mintern."

"Mintern," said Owen, perplexed; for he had certainly heard the name before.

The little man laughed. "That's what it all comes to in the end," he said. "Lord, Captain, once I spent three whole days trying to get up nerve enough to shoot you. You had me reduced to the ranks going on to Mine Run. Me and Corporal Howard. We were out skirmishing with a keg of corn and we happened to find a horse belonging to General Warren's staff. Only trouble was, a man was sitting on the horse, so we took the man off. I remember Howard saying three was too many for one horse; it wasn't right to the horse. We borrowed his sword and pistol, and Howard happened to sell them to a sutler. I can still remember riding in, the two of us on the horse, staff blanket and all. Then the fireworks began."

They certainly had begun. In the rush of recollection, Owen Fulton saw it all again. General Warren himself came blazing over to brigade headquarters with his abused officer to have the regiment paraded. Corporal Howard had been sent to military prison for larceny.

"I remember," Owen said. He found himself laughing, glad to remember. "It made us a lot of trouble. But I don't know what you wanted to shoot me for. It was all I could do to keep you from going with Howard."

Sergeant Mintern cackled cheerfully. "Captain, I wouldn't know myself, now. It just seemed pretty hard. Just a little joke like that, with nobody hurt and Howard offering to pay the officer the money he got for the sidearms. Well, they gave me back my stripes at Petersburg, where I lost my fingers. Of course, I know now I really owed you a lot. If it hadn't been for what you called my distinguished services at Gettysburg—Lord, do you remember getting the boys back through town that first day?"

Owen remembered. It was one of those things you don't forget. "You were a good man in an engagement," he said. "By Mine Run, we were beginning to get the scum and I hated to lose a good man." He was silent a moment, recalling the consternation, really the despair, which a line officer had to feel when he saw the consignments of human rubbish sent down by the fantastic state bounties and the draft to replace the volunteers, the veterans of the Peninsula.

Mintern said at once, "You were another good man, Captain. Everybody knew that. Even when I was thinking of gunning for you, I never thought different." He shook his head sadly. "Well, there was a lot of good men in the original First Corps. I've never seen or heard of better men than crossed the river down here in 'sixty-two." He made a melancholy sucking sound. "The ones we left here were like teeth pulled. No more coming. I thought when I read how old Burny died a year or so ago, he'd been here like a young fellow running through a fortune. And not his fortune, at that. Ever after, we kept losing tricks because those that would have taken them were stopped for good at Fredericksburg—" He cocked his eye upward and got to his feet. "Why, hello, Colonel Bostwick. How are you?"

Alfred Bostwick said, "I'm well enough, Mintern. Don't you let yourself get too high, this trip. Captain Fulton will have you on the chines. Come along, Owen, I want you to meet General Doubleday."

"See you again, Captain," Sergeant Mintern said.

Proceeding down the aisle with a hand under Owen's elbow, Alfred Bostwick grunted: "He'll see you again all right when he runs out of cash and has to touch someone for a drink. Regular pest. Never been to an army meeting of any kind yet where he didn't turn up in that uniform. He's got a pension for his hand, so he can get around. Makes a business of it. I'm told he was even seen out west somewhere at a Fifteenth Corps reunion, passing himself off as an old Army of the Tennessee man. He did so well, they say he managed to borrow five dollars from General Sherman. You have to admire his confounded impudence."

"He was the best sergeant Company D ever had," Owen answered uncomfortably, raising his voice above the noise of the train. "I suppose he hasn't known what to do with himself since the war—"

"Humph!" said Alfred. "You'd better look and see if you've still got your watch and wallet. Those are the sort of things he does know what to do with."

From the high bridge across the Rappahannock, Owen could see the shimmer of sun, gold on the water, a finer gold in the hazy air around the same church steeples. There was, naturally, a new

Hanover Street bridge; but in the brief glimpse it seemed to him he could see the long repaired scars of shellfire on the riverside buildings.

Pouched eyes screwing up, still-curly, coarse gray mustache drawing down in an amiable grimace, General Doubleday said, "Here it is, Slocum. Little less trouble getting over this time."

Major General Slocum agreed. "Why, I understand from Alfred here that a hundred ladies have kindly consented to greet us at the banquet. It seems to me it was Barksdale's Mississippi boys in the cellars on the bank there who did the greeting when Burnside came to town." Their laughter, the hoarse perfunctory laughter of old men, reached Owen. He had been introduced to both of them. They were both, they said, very pleased to meet any friend of Alfred's; but they soon saw that Owen was of little interest and no importance, and took up their previous conversation. Owen did not blame them and certainly expected no attention from them. It meant much more to him to meet someone like Mintern.

The train had run past the station, for they were to go down to Hamilton's without stopping. Looking sharp through the window to his right, Owen marked the gradual fall away of ground, the abrupt tree-covered rise of hill. At the top, three parts hidden, he could see the wink of white columns of the portico of a house—Marye's, of course! Here, then, was the scene of Summer's and Hooker's repulse on the right. Owen's eyes, going lower, stopped suddenly on a distant, hardly noticeable section of overgrown stone wall. Up his back went a kind of quiver as the train, with a prolonged sad whistle, began to veer away. Bushes, trees, houses intervened, left him the sharp brief picture of the neglected back lots, the gardens and outhouses, the obscure low line of stones in the sunlight. He heard Sergeant Mintern saying, *like a young fellow running through a fortune.*

On December 13, 1862, at one o'clock the Second Corps moved out from the streets of Fredericksburg across the old canal —brigade front, intervals of two hundred paces! Owen supposed that, had it been the First Corps on this wing, instead of the Second, he would somehow have managed to make himself do it.

With the aid of good men like Mintern, the company could doubtless have been made to do it with him. Hancock's division lost more than two thousand, a hundred and fifty-six of them officers. French, succeeding him, lost twelve hundred; Howard, almost nine hundred. After an hour and a half, the Second Corps, ruined, gave way to divisions of the Fifth Corps—it hurt Owen even to think of it; but, shaken, he was very proud, too. It might be horrible, it might even be stupid; but it was an honor to belong to the same race, the same army as those men—

He realized that the train had stopped. Alfred was standing up with his customary agreeable assurance and he called out, "Gentlemen! If I may have your attention a moment!"

Conversation fell away, and Alfred continued, "We are now at Hamilton's, on the old First Corps battlefield. It is half past eleven o'clock. Remember that General Longstreet is to make an address which I am sure you all want to hear, in front of the Marye mansion at two o'clock. Those who care to, may easily walk back, following the lines. The distance is about four miles. Those who do not care to may take the train back. Assembly will be blown when it is to leave. At half past three o'clock, the mayor and city council, assisted by many ladies of Fredericksburg, will receive us at the new opera house. The banquet begins promptly at four. Members of the Society, and our distinguished guests, will spare the committee sorrow and confusion if they will please be punctual—"

The woods, the field, the road down from the Crossing toward the hidden river were full of men straggling here and there, moving in groups in the clear hot sunshine. Forced to limp by this uneven ground, Owen paused to rest his leg, breathe, and wipe his hot face. Looking back, he could see the massed bunting of the long train, the crowd by the big refreshment tent at the road. Once or twice he had thought that his surroundings looked vaguely familiar, but he saw now that he was not yet nearly far enough from the railroad. Men were too plainly visible on the higher ground behind the tracks, moving through the trees along what had been Jackson's line.

Coming at last upon a large log, Owen sat down and fanned

himself with his hat. Many men were making the effort—he could hear their loud argumentative voices across the fields—but he knew that no regiment's position would ever really be found. The growth of twenty summers changed all small features of bush and tree and field. There were new fences, probably new roads.

Owen sat still, discouraged, gazing at the low rain-worn rise of bare earth to his right. He might have been in any open, sparsely brush-covered field, anywhere. Then, curious, he got up, walked a few steps and managed to stoop awkwardly. From the red gravel he picked up a thin oval of metal. Brushing it off, he made out the big faint lettering U.S.—a belt buckle. The heat of the sun impressed itself on him now. Owen replaced his hat and, pocketing his little trophy, limped slowly back toward the train.

Sergeant Mintern said, "I was looking for you, Captain. It don't take long to see all there is left, does it?" He had, however, seen a bottle or two in the refreshment tent. That was apparent.

Owen, sitting alone in the shadows of the hot, empty car, realized that he must have been drowsing. A bad night in the Washington hotel, the early start, the heat and exertion of his vain little journey over the fields had exhausted him. It was just as Hattie said; he ought to conserve his energy. He wasn't fitted for Alfred's easy bustle and cheerful activity—Alfred, he supposed, would be in the refreshment tent having a drink with people of importance. Out of the pleasant meeting would come more meetings, more honors and benefits for Alfred in an ever-expanding future. Owen must see that his own life was the antithesis of that. He survived, like a sort of stump, blighted at Spottsylvania. He had only the past. Like Mintern, all he had to his credit was in the past.

Probably able to feel in the short silence Owen's sympathy for him, Mintern said, "Come and take a drink, Captain. What they have at the tent isn't bad."

Owen thanked him and said that he was sorry. "I never drink spirits during the day. It upsets my stomach. I had to give it up." That was quite true. Except for a glass with Alfred on evenings when Alfred dropped in, Owen had practically ceased to drink. As Hattie pointed out, he felt better for it.

That was too bad, Mintern told him. "But come and have a good cold glass of lemonade," he urged. "They have it."

"Thanks, I'm not thirsty," Owen said. Long unaccustomed to such throngs of talking, expansively cheerful men, he knew that he would only be ill at ease—a conscious specter at their feast; the very man they talked and laughed and drank to keep from being.

Owen saw now that he had unconsciously forestalled Mintern in Mintern's ordinary method of approach. Checked, Mintern was not routed, however. He was not even abashed by the exposure of a real intention behind the roundabout tactic. "Captain," he said, "I wonder if you'd care to do me a favor? Could you lend me a V note until we get back to Washington? I went into a little game with some of the boys, and—"

"Certainly, Sergeant." Owen unbuttoned his back pocket and took out his wallet. At least, he reflected, he was in General Sherman's distinguished company.

Mintern took the bill, beaming, the little Punch's face rosier still. "I surely appreciate that, Captain," he said. Heat of triumph seemed to rouse the fumes of alcohol, for he became instantly much drunker. "I always said you're a good man, Captain. I always said Company D was the best company and had the best Captain—"

With Mintern so far past shame, Owen had to be ashamed for him. He was also ashamed for himself, and angry. Alfred, if for any contemptuously tolerant reason Alfred decided to give Mintern the money, would have done it in such a way that Mintern could not consider him a simpleton. Catching Owen still wordless in vexation the sudden clear notes of a bugle sounding assembly somewhere ahead stiffened him in automatic response. Mintern, taken unawares, started, too. Caught thus in so eloquent a demonstration of their common past, Owen said, "Get along, Mintern! You have what you came for."

"Lord, Captain," Sergeant Mintern said with amiable reproach, "you wouldn't be sore at me, would you?"

. . .

Owen delayed, as usual, to let those who moved more quickly go first. The train had dropped them at the curve of the railroad, and it was necessary to pass along the narrow dirt road behind the fatal stone wall before turning up the slope to the Marye house. Dust still hung in the air from the passage of the crowd before him. Countless footprints flattened the whole soft surface. It was like trying to overtake his regiment in a marching brigade column — Owen could almost expect to hear around the bend of the road the monotonous harsh calls through a thicker dust haze: "Close up, men; close up!"

Reaching finally the top of the low rise, and turning in under the trees toward the house, Owen found the crowd so extensive that he stopped. There was a good chance that Alfred would be holding a seat for him in the few rows of folding chairs arranged directly before the portico, but he felt too tired and out of breath to attempt to push his way through. Peering between the nearer heads and over the ranks of farther ones, he supported himself against a tree trunk, trying to catch what the speaker under the big white pillars was saying.

It was not possible to hear well. The men around him had discovered that and ceased to pay attention, conversing among themselves. Owen caught several ringing, but remote and incomplete, references to a united nation, the healing of old wounds. He did not know the speaker — probably some politician introducing General Longstreet, but unable to let pass an opportunity for extensive remarks of his own. Prolonged applause broke out, partly because the sentiments expressed were proper and popular, partly because what must be Longstreet showed himself. He stood erect, his full, neat beard moving on his linen and cravat, as he inclined his broad, finely formed forehead repeatedly in acknowledgment of his reception.

Owen had wished to see Longstreet, and now he could see him well enough — a handsome, elderly gentleman with humorous eloquent eyes and a straight nose. It was not possible to be disappointed in him, for he had a face and manner which would be liked everywhere on sight. One look told you why Longstreet, of all the former Confederate generals, had been most successful in obtaining posts and honors in the government against which he had rebelled. Not disappointed, Owen could still feel let down, dissatisfied, for he had expected — he did not know what; maybe, something grimmer; something more like a soldier. A more formidable face; a presence which would command respect rather than invite cordiality.

What he had come for was eluding Owen once more. The others, even those who could hear no better than he could, seemed to be getting what they came for. They were obviously content, glad they had come. They were satisfied with the present, with their holiday. Owen reflected that it would be necessary to walk into Fredericksburg when this was over, and it occurred to him that he might as well start now. If he got there much before the others, he could go along Princess Anne Street and try to find the house and garden where he had spent that month wounded.

It was not really a great distance, but Owen's leg was throbbing before he reached the outskirts of the town. He dragged slowly down Princess Anne Street, not, for a moment, sure about the big house. Undoubtedly the brick had been red when he was there. Now it was a pale yellow, or cream. A long veranda in modern style had been added to the side, relieving somewhat the plainness common to houses built long ago, as likely as not before the Revolution. Moving along the shoulder-high brick wall, alternately in the midafternoon sun and the shadows cast by the trees across the street, Owen saw the old slave quarters. Those, too, were changed. The lower part had been given double doors and made into a carriage house. The little back gate at which the sentries had solemnly presented arms for Mama and the girls was gone. Instead there was the necessary wide opening for the drive, with an iron lamppost on each side.

Resting his elbows on the wall top, Owen looked at the old Negro in frock coat and worn silk hat who was absorbed in adjusting some buckle, ducking about an indifferent pair of bay geldings hitched to a sort of surrey with an oblong fringed canopy. Right behind there would be the spot where he had lain in the tent. The Negro finished whatever he was doing, straightened up, and turned. Owen Fulton found himself saying, "Would you be able to tell me if Mrs. Ferris lives here?"

The Negro gazed at him a moment and said, "There ain't no Mr. Ferris, sir. Unless you mean Colonel Ferris. The colonel visits here sometimes, but this is Mrs. Baylor's house. Mrs. Baylor and Miss Lou live here. Colonel Ferris ain't here now."

"I see," Owen answered, embarrassed by the difficulties of proceeding further. Obviously Olivia had married her major and sometimes came to visit. "I was inquiring about Mrs. Ferris, the colonel's wife."

The Negro looked at him with a reticent, not disrespectful suspicion. "The colonel never had no wife, sir. He's an unmarried gentleman."

Finally Owen said, "I was here, wounded, during the war. I remember that then Miss Olivia Baylor was to marry a Major Ferris."

"She surely was, sir," said the Negro, astonished. "You wouldn't know, then, Miss Olivia died the year the war was over?"

"No, I didn't know," Owen said.

After a moment he realized that the Negro was speaking to him. He said, "Excuse me, I didn't hear you."

"I say, would you like I should take your name in to Miss Lou, sir?"

Owen shook his head. "She wouldn't know me. I was a Yankee."

The old Negro smiled. "Oh, I know you was a Yankee, all right, sir. Mrs. Baylor wouldn't have dealings with you; but Miss Lou don't feel that way. I have this team out here now to take her to the big entertainment. She'd be happy to see any friend of Miss Olivia's."

"Thank you," Owen said, "I wasn't a friend of Miss Olivia's." He turned quickly, limping away, leaving the Negro staring after him.

Owen passed slowly back up the street. A distant band must have begun playing some time ago. Becoming aware of it, Owen was also aware of torpor and silence in the dusty, sunny street.

Leaves moved in the wind. An odor of wisteria reached him. Out a gate ahead stepped three ladies with parasols and, not wishing to overtake them, Owen limped still slower.

Soon the ladies were gone around a corner and Owen could hear the band again, gay and brave, but remote, as though it played back across the years. Sadly, sentimentally, he could think of it attempting to muster in, not this handful of First Corps veterans, but all the innumerable dead of the Army of the Potomac who lay not far beyond earshot, west and north and south, from Wilderness Run to Spottsylvania, to the Massaponax, scattered who knew where in one great uncared-for, unmarked, unordered cemetery.

Thinking of that, Owen thought suddenly that he could probably find Olivia's grave if he liked, and read her name on the stone. Yet he knew he would not bother. The fine melancholy afternoon light made everything seem long over, of little importance. Several carriages had passed him, and wondering how late it was, Owen began feeling for his watch. Finally he stood still, felt in other pockets.

How Mintern, tipsy as he was, had managed it, you couldn't guess; but Mintern had, all right—doubtless while Owen was dozing. Alfred was, as always, right.

Two more carriages filled with the light colors of ladies' dresses went by. The watch was a gold hunter, an expensive one. It had, too, a sentimental value. Hattie, on the occasion of a legacy from an aunt of hers, had given it to him. In the back cover under a small oval of glass, it contained an ingeniously plaited lock of Hattie's hair. Mintern might have found a way to dispose of it here in Fredericksburg; but, on the other hand, drinking more, he might have neglected to.

Being always right, Alfred in these circumstances, wouldn't wait a minute. He would denounce Mintern, have him arrested and searched. If it were not on Mintern's person, Alfred would shrewdly follow up every possible avenue of disposal until the watch was recovered and Mintern's guilt established. In his own case, Owen had even more reason to take these steps. Hattie, displeased about the trip anyway, would find the loss of his fine watch the last straw.

It would be just what she had expected and he would be a long time hearing the last of it. She would say that it seemed a high price to pay for a silly and expensive trip which had worn him out. If he had listened to her, or cared at all for her opinion, he would have stayed home and still had his watch.

Distressed and doubtful, Owen turned the corner. Before the opera house were many carriages, a crowd of people, and the band whose music he had heard. A big, red-faced, cheery man with a paper in his hand was calling out something. It proved to be: "Now, Baxter's brigade, gentlemen! Anyone from Baxter's brigade? Any members of the Twelfth Massachusetts Regiment? Table number five, please. Anyone from the Eighty-third and Ninety-seventh New York Regiments—"

Owen started to answer, to raise his hand; but the words did not come. He let his hand fall. In the foyer he caught a glimpse of Alfred with General Doubleday and General Longstreet. They were being introduced to some ladies. Jostled, he looked the other way in time to see the old Negro, the bay geldings, and the surrey which had been in the Baylors' yard come to the curb. Someone pushed through the press and very courteously assisted two flustered but smiling old women to alight. One of them must be Miss Lou, Owen realized, suddenly reminded of her and Sarah Ann, of Mama and Olivia, prim and frigid, going down the garden path. Both of these women were now older than Mama had been then. Who could doubt the war was all over; and, as the speaker on the hill had said, how glorious, how inspiring to see North and South one again!

Anxiously, the man on the steps was still calling, "Now, please, gentlemen! The Eighty-third New York Regiment! The Ninety-seventh New York Regiment! Isn't there anyone from—"

"No, no," thought Owen, "no one—" A movement in the crowd gave him a last sight of the simpering old faces of the two ladies. It was wrong, it was even wicked of him to think it, but in indignation, he had to think of three hundred and fifty thousand Union dead; of Longstreet reduced in the end to speeches and funny stories; of the First Corps persisting only as a crowd of fatuous jolly banqueters; in the place of the Army of Northern Virginia, one hundred ladies of Fredericksburg—

Owen turned away. The man on the steps had given up the Ninety-seventh New York. As he limped down the street, Owen could hear him, fainter and fainter, as though in parody of the Army of the Potomac's roll, calling the names of other regiments. At the station he learned that there would be a train, though not a fast one, for Washington in an hour.

Recovering his bag from the guard in charge of them, Owen carried it painfully back along the siding where the bright cars of the morning stood deserted. The platform of the station was empty. Owen sat down on a bench to wait and the wonderful comfort of being off his feet, able to rest, filled him slowly with a kind of content. The shadows lengthened. Musing, yawning, he reflected that things might be worse. By leaving this way, without waiting for the tour of the Spottsylvania and Chancellorsville battlefields, he would be home a day, perhaps two days, early. This would please Hattie so much that he felt sure she wouldn't make too great a fuss about the lost watch.

PART FOUR

LOVE AND KISSES

My Love to Marcia

The day that Curtis Bard was appointed an assistant vice president in the Personal Trust Department, Mr. Fitzmorris produced the photostats and portfolios of the Iddings trust agreements. He looked at them with dignified satisfaction. He touched the several flat strands of whitened hair on his clean, shapely skull and said: "Curtis, eventually you'll be taking these over altogether. You might do an analysis of the holdings to give us a basis on which to discuss them. And I'd like you to start signing the routine correspondence." Mr. Fitzmorris glanced needlessly at the photostats. "Ah—young John Clayton Iddings went to school with you, didn't he?"

"I haven't seen him for several years," Curtis Bard answered. This was not of any importance to Mr. Fitzmorris. From the Premier Union Bank & Trust Company's standpoint, what could best be called acceptability was the important thing. Without special planning, it would usually so happen that the executives of the company and most of the important clients had been at schools and universities together.

Soon enough, regarding his finger tips, Curtis Bard was saying to Miss Ames: "Now, to Mr. Iddings. John Clayton, junior, that is. Er—Dear Johnny . . ."

It couldn't be called a good letter. It jerked stiffly from paragraph to paragraph, but it had all the facts. Relieved, he recited, making a sharp gesture: "Hope to see you if you come to town

— er; my love to Marcia. Yours — just 'yours' that is. That'll be all, thanks."

Miss Ames, however, said: "Oh, Mr. Bard, may I have that name again?"

"Iddings, Iddings," Curtis told her.

She looked at him with mild reproach. "I mean" — she inspected her notes — "my love to — "

"Marcia," he said. He spelled it for her.

Curtis Bard was not only at liberty, but in duty bound, to examine the trust agreements. Five years back they had been completely redrawn. It must have been just before the old man died. " — to Marcia Hoyt Kerwin Iddings, so long as she shall remain his wife or widow." However, he read next that the severe-sounding provision was inoperative already, because of the child, here only a hypothesis. In the event of Johnny's death the funds were entailed past Marcia to the child or children, who were required as long as she should live to support her "suitably." Suitably in the Premier Union's opinion, he was glad to see.

In the portfolio was a memorandum three years old — Claire Kerwin Iddings; and — trust Fitzmorris! — a copy of the birth certificate clipped to it. Curtis spread out the sheaf of sheets listing holdings as of the end of the past month and ran down them expertly. There was nothing outside the usual Premier Union run of picked securities. Their past, present and, he could not too rashly hope, future were perfectly familiar to him. He could have dictated his analysis right off to Miss Ames. Except that Mr. Fitzmorris would have been shocked by such promptness, so he might better wait a week or two and then dictate it right off.

"Well," he found himself thinking, and he was aware that his philosophic attitude was self-conscious, for he was really saying the words in his mind instead of simply thinking the thought, "that's that! It's a good thing for everyone."

And so it was. Everything was good about it, except, perhaps, that there could never be another Marcia. He had not thought about Marcia for months. For literally years he had not only got on without her, but got on very well and comfortably, charmed and amused by other young women; indeed, engaged to Mary; yet he sat still, looking at the pale-white letters on the stiff gray-black photostat sheets, and thought: "I wouldn't be such a fool if it were all to do over again!"

There had been a time, shortly after her marriage to Johnny, when Curtis Bard thought of Marcia a great deal. He had stopped seeing her many months before, and naturally he had not attended the wedding. After she and Johnny returned from Europe he had been careful to go nowhere — to dinner, to any entertainment — where she might be.

He never did meet her; but once or twice, on the street, he thought he saw her approaching, and looked away, suddenly shaky, to collect himself. His relief had been uppermost, but he was oppressed, too, with a conflicting disappointment, ill at ease. He would like to think, sadly, but with some dignity, that Johnny, who had wanted her without hope even when they were at college, had got her because Marcia's mature choice was finally and wisely Johnny; that Marcia had refused Curtis, not that he — how ugly and ignoble the simple truth sounded! — had reluctantly refused Marcia.

At the time the simple truth couldn't have seemed quite that. Curtis did not view himself when young with indulgence, but obviously, had the truth been plain, no degree of callowness could have made him see his behavior as anything but contemptible. In a way, it was probably Marcia who kept him from seeing it. If Marcia abased herself, if she did the next thing to kneeling in the dust, she did it gracefully. "Darling," she said, "why be such a fool? What earthly difference does it make if we're poor?"

"All the difference in the world," Curtis declared heavily. He had been strongly fortified by the decorum, the conventional propriety, of his position. "I'm not going to let you in for anything like that. Not you — " Ah, but what he meant, you could see now, was: Not me! Not me!

Marcia had managed to laugh. "Beloved," she said, "you just

can't be going to tell me that you're unable to support me in the style to which I am accustomed!" Marcia came from what could be called a professional family, a long succession of college professors and clergymen who had contented themselves with learning and piety. There was no money in either. She had washed dishes and made beds before.

"For God's sake, don't joke about it," he begged her. "We mustn't go on like this. Good night."

She continued to gaze at him, just not smiling. "Aren't you going to kiss me?"

He said yes, and did moodily. She said: "Curtis, you're so sweet. Don't take on so. We'll get by."

But it takes two to get by. What he was getting was away. Somberly; not with relief, nor impatience to be gone, nor any passage from the old love to the new. If it had been one of those things, Marcia, or her pride, would have let him go quickly enough. At the train she wept, probably aware that it was all over, though neither of them suggested such an idea. Indeed, Curtis said vehemently: "Marcia, you're not going. We're going to get married."

It was then that she had begun to weep, regardless of porters and conductors and other passengers trailing their luggage past into the car vestibule. "Don't, don't, don't," she sobbed. "You know I can't now. I telegraphed Mother — "

Curtis Bard was abruptly conscious that they had attracted attention. In great pain he said: "I know, I'm sorry. I just thought — "

He did not know what he had just thought, except that she was overwhelmingly sweet and so all else was of little consequence. He would have married her if she had said yes; so, in one sense, she had refused him. He bent and kissed her wet face. He said, "Write me," and walked away.

That was the last time he saw her. A few letters saying things they had already said were written; and then he heard nothing until, about a year later, he got the wedding invitation.

Not seeing Marcia, he did eventually see Johnny again. He was living at the club and Johnny came there to play squash. Stepping from a residential floor into the elevator rising from the dressing rooms to the courts, Curtis Bard walked fairly into Johnny — sweat shirt over his shoulders, a pair of rackets under his arm. Johnny put a hand hard into his and exclaimed cordially: "Well, I'm damned! Hello, Curtis. How are you?"

"Fine, thanks," Curtis answered in confusion. He must say at once, if he meant to, "Congratulations. Give Marcia my love." Unable to say anything for a moment, it was then subtly too late — for that matter, had it ever been early enough? Why hadn't he been at the wedding to say it? "Got a game?" Johnny asked.

"I was going to pick one up, or just bat a ball."

"My man couldn't make it. Have you got too good for me, living here?"

"Probably," Curtis said, grinning.

As it proved, he was not in form and Johnny beat him. Shining with sweat, flushed with exercise, they were almost on natural terms going down to the showers. "Let's try it again, Friday," Johnny said.

"Like to."

"That's a date." He paused. "You've got to come up and see us."

Curtis realized that Johnny, and surely Johnny was, after all, right, regarded him with the greatest delicacy as a defeated rival who might feel — he found himself warming toward Johnny with a sort of impulsive surprise. He said, "I'd like to, thanks." He repeated: "Give Marcia my love."

Johnny was peeling the sweat shirt over his head. "Always a bunch in Sundays," he said, muffled. "Come any time. And don't forget."

Under his shower Curtis decided that he ought to do it. He ought to see Marcia, accept her in his mind as Johnny's wife; what they called in smaller communities, where it was constantly necessary to deal with such a situation, an old flame of his; a kind of quiet, friendly joke between them.

One or two Sunday afternoons Curtis went out, meaning to walk up to Johnny's and drop in. Quite resolved on it while he was dressing carefully, he was less resolved when he nodded to the fat club doorman. On the chill autumn street, heels and stick clicking, the closer he came to the Iddings' address, the more his mind changed, and presently he had walked by, at loss, casting about for somewhere else he could or should call. He and Johnny played squash a few more times, uneasily, and not with much pleasure. This couldn't have been kept up very long, but old Mr. Iddings died before it became entirely impossible. Johnny and Marcia went out to live in the Iddings place, somewhere near Cleveland.

Since she had nothing to reproach herself with, Marcia would long ago have forgotten; but Curtis might reflect, so uselessly late, how much better it would have been if, instead of insulting her with all those disgraceful lies, he had said: "I want to marry you, but not enough. As it is, I have no money, but I can stay at the club. If I made any change, I would have to give up (because I would not be able to live suitably to entertain them, nor dress my wife properly to present them to her) acquaintances who will be important to me in my plan for becoming, sooner than Mr. Fitzmorris or any of them expect, a vice president of the Premier Union Bank & Trust Company. I cannot tell you how dearly I love you, yet, after all, I seem to love myself a little better."

Given the Iddings' trusts, Curtis Bard had been able to foresee a chance, though surely a remote one — say, if Johnny should die — of finally meeting Marcia again. He did not specially consider it. Certainly it did not move him. In that distant future nothing had reality. They would probably both be amazed to think that they could ever have meant anything to each other. So much would have happened between — he found himself thinking specifically of Mary — that they would be complete strangers. Marcia was gone already; she was practically forgotten.

He had come downstairs one December day about three o'clock and was passing, intent on some errand, under the great marble arches of the main banking floor when a guard intercepted him.

"Excuse me, Mr. Bard, I think Mr. Duffy is trying to get you to identify a signature."

Curtis turned and saw the chief teller signaling him behind the breast-high, very wide marble counter. Duffy held a check in his hand. He slapped it across the polished stone to Curtis. "Just telephoned up for you, Mr. Bard," he said. "You handle these trusts now, don't you? I thought you might be able to identify — "

The check was for three thousand dollars on Johnny Iddings' signature. Curtis turned it and, stunned, saw a script he had not forgotten: Marcia Kerwin Iddings.

"Yes," he nodded, automatically, "that's all right. I know the writing."

"Well, you could identify Mrs. Iddings, couldn't you? We don't know her. Just tip Faulkner off if it's all right."

Curtis said, since there was nothing else to say, "Yes."

Carrying the check, he walked composedly down the long counter, turned into the deep oblong recess of the women's alcove, furnished with good reproduction Sheraton chairs, sofas and writing desks. There was a silver vase full of white roses on the table and, looking past, he saw Marcia seated on the far sofa. Voluminous folds of mink fur, shaken back a little, surrounded her. She had one hand ungloved and was holding a lighted cigarette. On one finger was the dark-green square of an obviously fine emerald. Curtis Bard let his eyes slide toward the watching teller and gave the slightest nod. Then he said, "Marcia."

She must, of course, be greatly astonished to hear herself called by name; but she was more than astonished, she was shocked. So it was plain that she had instantly known his voice; recognized, in the second of turning, those intonations. She was on her feet by the time she had really faced him. The cigarette slipped from between her fingers and she managed to step it out awkwardly into the heavy plum-colored carpet.

"Curtis," she murmured. "But, my dear, how you startled me." She was extremely pale. She took his hand in her bare one, laid the gloved hand over it. "Curtis, how are you? I'm trying to get a check cashed."

"Sit down," he said. "We'll bring it to you. How do you want it?"

"Some tens and hundreds, I guess." She sat down and obediently fumbled for another cigarette in the case he held out to her. Over his shoulder, Curtis called, "Twenty-nine hundreds; ten tens please." He lit the cigarette for her.

"Curtis," she said, "how long it's been! You've hardly changed."

"Six years. When are you sailing?"

"How do you know I'm sailing?" she asked amazed.

"Why would you come way downtown here to draw the money unless, when you got it, you were going to buy steamship tickets?"

"How marvelous of you. But you always were. I'm going to Paris. I'm in town. I want to see you. Johnny would like to see you. Come up this afternoon and have a cocktail."

"I'll try, thanks."

"No, no. Don't try. Come. My dear, I seem to sound half-witted. I knew something was wrong. I forgot to get any lunch. Please come."

"I'll come," Curtis said. "Thanks, Faulkner." He took her bag from her, snapped the catches and slid the heavy envelope into it. "Run and find some lunch now, before you collapse on us."

The door of ten-fourteen stood half open. Curtis Bard pushed it farther and stepped into a sort of vestibule with no light on, but he could see a mirror, a settee piled with coats and hats. To his right a door opened, letting out a young woman in a nursemaid's uniform so suddenly that she bumped against him. Abashed, she apologized in French and went instantly back again. He heard a child's voice raised. In the room beyond sat or stood quite a number of people, all talking, some laughing.

He laid his coat and hat with the others on the settee. Behind him sounded a rap on the door and a bellboy said: "Telegram for Mrs. Iddings." As though she spent all her time just behind her door, the nursemaid popped out and took it. Curtis saw Marcia now, making her way through the people in the sitting room.

Without a hat, her face looked thinner. She wore green and that probably made her look still paler. It was the telegram she had come for, he saw, not him; but, noticing him, a quick slight color showed on her cheekbones. She laid a hand on his arm. "Curtis, how sweet of you!" she said. "I was afraid you wouldn't. Go in. There are some people you know, I expect. They all came in a bunch. No, wait—you must see Claire." She tore the top off the envelope and drew out the telegram, glanced at it, crumpled it in her hand.

In the room to the right the child was sitting on the rug amid a litter of toys. "Claire," Marcia said, "I want you to say how do you do to Mr. Bard."

The child got reluctantly to her feet, advanced a step or so, performed a minute, perfunctory curtsy, wordless.

"Don't you say anything, darling?"

She shook her head, picked up a wool-covered dog and began to examine it.

"Of course I ought to fight it out on this line if it takes all summer," Marcia sighed, "but it would be frightful. Say good-by to Mr. Bard, darling."

"Au revoir, M'sieu."

"That's something," Marcia said. She closed the door. "She's just like Johnny. Hair, face, eyes, everything. Johnny won't be here, by the way." She raised her hand with the crumpled yellow sheet. "He had to stay in Boston."

"I'm sorry. I hope I'll see him before you sail."

"Johnny's not sailing. Curtis, can you take me to dinner?"

He looked at her a moment and answered, "Of course, if I may use your telephone."

"The one in the bedroom, there," she said. "Hello, Paul. You know Curtis Bard, don't you?"

"I don't believe so. How do you do?"

Curtis had never seen him before. Indeed, he did not see anyone here he had ever seen before. Yet, obviously, they all knew Johnny and Marcia better, in a way, than he did. The man addressed as Paul said, "How's the infant?"

"Do go in and speak to her," Marcia said. "She just adores that dog. She's worn all the wool off it."

"Oh, Marcia! What have you done with Johnny?"

"He's stuck in Boston, poor dear."

"Well, come and have dinner with us."

"Couldn't possibly, darling. I'm being taken."

Curtis Bard closed the bedroom door and, sitting on the edge of the nearer bed, laid his hand on the telephone. It seemed to him that the number was being rung an inordinately long time. He looked at his watch and found that it had somehow become half past six. If he couldn't reach — he said: "Mary."

"Oh, darling; yes."

"My dear, this is unspeakable, but I'm not going to be able to make it. The Iddings, the Cleveland people, are in town. Mrs. Iddings is sailing. Those are the trusts I took over last summer."

"Curtis, how heartbreaking! I really am sick about it. But do your duty."

"I didn't discover I was expected to have dinner until a minute ago. Can you bear it?"

"Only just. But I know how it is. Ring me tomorrow."

Curtis Bard replaced the telephone, but he sat motionless. At last he felt for a cigarette. That hadn't taken two minutes, and he was aghast; for, being all through with lying to people, he had forgotten the instantaneous comforts of deceit, its usefulness and simplicity, the wonderful way in which it let you have your cake and eat it too. After all, when Marcia asked him, what could he say? "You could have said," he answered himself, "that you had another engagement. It's a good thing you lied, for you would never be able to explain to Mary why you didn't say that."

Morose, he stood up slowly; for he did not like any of this and, since he was doing it, it was necessary to despise himself. He was facing the door, and now it opened. "Oh, sorry, my dear," Marcia said. "I —"

"It's all fixed," Curtis answered. "I'd better run along and dress."

"Curtis."

She stood still, the hand with the emerald against the doorjamb, looking at him clearly and intently. As, long ago, he had been so often, he was again filled with a sense of her sweetness. She had never really been very pretty, and, six or seven years older, she had altogether lost the intrinsic attractiveness of mere youth; yet she had kept the fine, silken quality of her hair; the appealing candor of her eyes; a gentle directness of speech and movement. She said: "You're not married to her, are you?"

"I'm not married to anyone," he answered. Looking back at her, he was exercised with a forgotten pain—the inarticulate emotions; desire too complex for speech, regrets too general and indefinite for expression, overpowered him. "You ought to know that," he said.

She dropped her hand from the doorjamb, coming forward. "Curtis, why did you—darling, how could you be—I mean, it was so silly of you."

She still used the same scent. Kissed, her face was wet, as though that night at the station had been not even yesterday, but a moment ago. "Darling, why did you write me all those things. Why did you—"

There could have been no answer anyway, but he would not need one, for the young woman in the nursemaid's uniform slipped around the door, murmured, surprised, "Oh, pardon, Madame—" and would have retired, abashed again.

"No, go on, Adele," Marcia said. "We're going out. I got rid of them," she told Curtis. "We aren't going to dress. Just give me a minute."

Buttoned in his coat, his hat in his hand, his stick under his elbow, Curtis Bard waited. "If anyone had told me this morning," he thought inanely, "that I'd be taking Marcia to dinner tonight—and since you are," he interrupted himself, "what of it? All you can do is say you're sorry. That's all she wants to hear." But he did not believe that that was all he could say, or all she wanted to hear.

The latch clicked behind them. She took his arm and they walked in silence down the hall, stood silently, not looking at each other in the elevator. A taxi crawled under the blaze of light at the door. Remembering they were to have dinner, Curtis gave an address at random. Shut within, he said: "Marcia, will you chuck it all and marry me?"

The taxi, out into the heavy traffic, had come promptly to a halt. The street light at the corner fell fully in the window on her hands. She tightened one over the other and said: "Do you want me to? Give me a cigarette, darling."

They moved on a dozen feet into shadow and he lit a match. "I thought I'd go to Paris and think about some things," she remarked. "Nothing much, except what I am getting out of this. We aren't happy — I'm not. Johnny may think he is, but he isn't really. If I left him, he'd be shocked at first, but it would be a relief. There are others Johnny would like better."

"Others?"

"Oh, no. I don't think so. There wouldn't be any now. You know Johnny. As it is, he'd grin and bear it. And so, in the end, he never would have had anything either; except a wife he never agreed with, and who was bored to death by everything he said and everything he wanted to do. Or maybe that's all you're supposed to get — " She stopped short. "I'm just talking. There's no one I can talk to. I should have stayed and married you that night at the train. I'm just a fool — " She began quietly to cry. The taxi pulled up and the driver turned his head.

Curtis shoved the glass open an inch. "Drive on," he said. "Anywhere. In the park." He put his arm about Marcia. Before that night at the train he could never remember having seen her cry. If he saw tears twice now in an hour, they meant more than anything else her exhaustion — the thinness and tiredness, most moving of the changes in her, most eloquent of some need for him. "It's such a mess," she whispered. "Do you care? Johnny, Claire — who was it you had to telephone?"

"Her name is Mary Fitzmorris. Not anyone you know. That doesn't matter. What matters is you." He frowned at the window.

In his mind the phrases began automatically to arrange themselves: Mary, my dearest, this is a letter I have to write and I wish I could write it in some way that . . . He repeated: "What matters is you, and what we are going to do."

He was right, he saw. What they were going to do could not lightly be dismissed, nor left to work itself out once they were married. He had an absurd picture of himself saying to Mr. Fitzmorris: "Oh, by the way, I meant to tell you that I've decided not to marry Mary after all. Mrs. John Clayton Iddings was thinking of getting a divorce and I'd prefer to wait and marry her. Now about those Metropolitan Savings debentures — "

"What sort of life we can make for you," he continued, more intent; for, incredibly enough, he had recovered Marcia. Thinking farther at last, he felt that confusion of other things begin again to crowd his head, making the words he was speaking vague, distant. "Do you really know what you're giving up?" he asked slowly. "It may be just about everything. Six years ago you might not have missed them much. Now — " ("Perhaps," he thought, "Welby would give me a job. I guess he would. I'd better get hold of him for lunch tomorrow.") " — well, it may be hard." He touched the folds of mink fur. "It would be years before you saw anything like that again. How about Claire? Or would you want to let Johnny have her? And where do you think she'd like it best if she spent part of the time — "

She put out a hand and laid it over his.

"Darling, don't worry about it. Don't take on so. Do you really want to marry me?"

"More than anything," he said, "but — "

She was looking at him, just not smiling, in a way with which he was perfectly familiar. Frowning deeper, jabbing the point of his stick slowly in the matting, Curtis Bard was silent, sinking under a heaviness of heart, for he knew suddenly where he was. In the gloom of the moving lights he could remember, ashamed and unhappy, what he ought to say, what came after "but — "

Finally looking at Marcia, he found her still looking back at him, clear and direct. "No, no," she said abruptly. "Don't tell me."

Sweet and sad, she smiled at him. "Let me tell you. It wouldn't be fair to Claire, would it? I suppose it wouldn't be fair to me. It wouldn't even be fair to Johnny. Oh, darling, darling — "

Wincing, for now Marcia would really be gone, gone forever, Curtis Bard answered carefully: "I've loved you a long time. I'll go on loving you, very likely, always — "

"Yes, you will, won't you, Curtis." She spoke with a kind of tired compassion, rather than anger or irony. "This way we won't ever have anything to be sorry about, will we? So we won't ever see each other again. Wouldn't that be better?"

She put a hand out, touched his cheek and, leaning forward, kissed him.

"I want you to get out here," she said. "Please do. Just tell him to take me back; we changed our minds."

The Way to Go Home

Meade Pons allowed always half an hour to drive himself from Calle H in Vedado to downtown Havana, to the offices and showrooms of the agency on Calle San Ignacio. It took him so long because the car he drove was, as a matter of advertisement, invariably brand-new. Resplendent in scratchless light enamel and glittering glass and metal, it passed, impressive and unhurried, along the Maleçon, turned out of its way, up the Prado, around the Park, and through the difficult press of Obispo Street. Meade Pons did it as nearly as possible at the same hour every morning. It was a method of taking space more arresting to the contemplative Latin consciousness than any sold in newspapers. Meade Pons knew this business; and, indeed, he ought to, for he had been sixteen years in it. The general agency for Cuba was worth having, even in times of ruinous sugar prices and depression very widespread.

The latest, and surely the showiest, car of a long, distinguished line stood in the drive now, and Meade Pons was fifteen minutes late, still at the breakfast table, listening. It seemed to him that Luis took an inordinate time leaving. Ten minutes of nine. He thought, irritated, that Richard and Judith would, must, be late for school. Confirming him, he heard Judith's voice, penetrating, passing up the steps, through the shadowed, marble-floored hall, informing Luis of the fact. Meade was startled, as he always was, to hear her speak Spanish so naturally, like a native. She was eleven years old, and Spanish seemed something of an accomplishment. Richard, who was nine, shared it, but that never surprised Meade so much.

Even at nine, Richard showed traits of reasonableness; Richard was earnest, thorough, somewhat conservative. Richard was, in truth, boring, Meade admitted; without thereby declaring any preference for Judith. He found them always, as he found them now, a mild annoyance — unnecessary. They were making him wait, for he wished to be sure that they were gone before he went up to speak to Alice. Alice could use their presence, without compunction, as a kind of club. They were entitled to an endless consideration and homage; because, presumably, they had neither the sense nor the strength to get on without it.

He heard the rising sound of a motor, then its fading, and the needless hoot of Luis's horn. He arose immediately, went out and upstairs. The door of his wife's room was open. She was still in bed, her breakfast tray on her lap; opened mail making a litter to one side. She said, "Take this away, Meade." Her appearance, considering her position, the hour, and the dominant fact of her forty-one years, was adequate. She did what she called "tidy" herself to say good morning and good-by to the children. Meade supposed that it was a point in her favor, since many women, especially when relaxed by this alien climate, would not bother. He came and took the tray, putting it on her dressing table. "No, not there," she said; "on the bureau. And ring for Pepita to take it away."

If Pepita were to be rung for, it surely mattered very little where he put it in the brief interval. Automatically he made the change, almost rang, when he remembered that Pepita's appearance would be undesirable for the moment.

He turned and said, "Johnny Cowden is getting in this morning."

He saw her face shutting up instantly; there was no pause for reflection. Her memory was often inefficient, but not here. She jumped eight years without the slightest effort.

She said, "Are you going to see him?"

"Naturally," said Meade. "I'm having luncheon with him." His voice was sufficiently casual. He looked at her directly and steadily. He meant to wait, perfectly calm, for her to say whatever she might have to say. Consequently, it was a sort of defeat when he added mildly, "Why? Do you mind?"

The question was idiotic. Alice had an infinite capacity for "minding," in that sense. You didn't catch her napping. Her elaborate and far-flung watch and ward missed nothing. The remotest threat to the state of things as she wanted them brought her to arms. Since no defense compares in effectiveness with an attack, she said at once, her eyes narrowing, the line of her chin aging instantly in its new tautness, "I suppose that means I needn't expect you home for a week."

Aiming at some cold irony of disinterested contempt, she went wide. She achieved a venomous irritation, but for the moment she saw herself, ludicrously, in the role of her intention—cold, superior. "I hope you'll try to keep out of jail," she said. It was terrible, Meade Pons recognized, for two people to know each other so well. Even were Alice suddenly to face a mirror, she could survive, cherish still the illusion of freezing dignity—a great lady. There are no defenses when two people know each what the other imagines himself to be. He thought, deliberately, removing his mind from the meaning of her words: "She wants her way; so do I. Only, her way includes me. I must suit her. On the other hand, I don't want her to do, or not do, anything."

She interrupted him, reaching for the club that Luis had taken off to school. "And don't you dare turn up here until you're fit to be seen. I won't have the children—"

"Aren't you getting rather worked up?" he asked. He meant to be calm, but his anger jumped through. Before he could catch it, shut it up again, he had added: "Or are you trying to give me ideas? Honestly, Alice—" he said, speaking quick, intent on covering it; but that was too late. He had no right to irony; irony was hers. He would be punished for attempting it, and submission would be better than evoking the clamor of contradicted righteousness. Not yet angered beyond thinking himself, he was resigned; but he was aghast, too, as no man in his simplicity can ever help being, to see the claws, the sharp-toothed worm in every woman's heart.

"Do you expect me," she said, "to be pleased to hear that you're planning a week's debauch with that drunken bum?"

"You seem to be planning for me," he protested. "I merely said I was having luncheon with him."

"Do you think I don't know what that means?"

"That's exactly what I think," said Meade. "I don't say I won't go out with him. I certainly intend to. But—" It was, after all, impossible to appeal to reason. Reason was the faculty which assured her that what she wanted could not help being right. It had, for the feminine mind, no other uses. If he were to say, "There's a difference between going on a party, and going on what you call a week's debauch," she would consider it irrelevant. Either went against her wishes, was equally damned. He might just as well turn and go now, but he wasn't angry enough. He was still looking at her with his incurable male incredulity, unable to believe that he couldn't still explain, make her understand. Understand what?

He was at an additional disadvantage, for he saw that he didn't know. He said, instead, "Johnny's pretty far from a drunken bum. He likes a good time, but that doesn't mean he's a fool. He's a pretty important man, as a matter of fact." He was, he realized, still laboring to be reasonable, judicial.

Alice, naturally, understood nothing but superlatives. "Nonsense!" she answered flatly. "You just think he is. He never was any good. I'm sure he's no good now. And what's more, Meade" —she paused, not because she was conscious of striking at a tangent, but for emphasis, her eyes deadly— "this time it may be pretty serious. I'm about through. I advise you to be careful. I'm not dependent on you."

She always produced that fact as though it were something new, something he didn't know about. She had, as it happened, a comfortable income of her own. She could perfectly well take the children and do what she pleased. The difficulty, he saw at once, was that she didn't want to. She was, he thought suddenly, like the monkey in the fable who thrust his paw into the nut jar. When he had grabbed all he could, he found that his paw wouldn't come out. Neither could he bring himself to drop anything he held. Distressed, the monkey would sit there a long while. Struck by the image, he laughed, incautious. At once he saw the worm's face in hers, contorted like a mask, and white; heard the sound of her intaken breath. That did it. He could have killed it; he wouldn't have it around.

"Johnny Cowden is the best friend I ever had," he said, "and to hell with you!"

He was tingling a little with hard, warm rage as he got into the car, started it. "This," he said, "is a hot way to live." He almost rammed Luis, bringing home the other car, and made a few appropriate remarks in Spanish. "Just for that," he said, turning along the road in from Marianao, "we will have a party! We'll take the roof off!" It amazed him to think how much Alice did get her way. As long as Johnny Cowden had been in Havana, things had broken somewhat more evenly. That is, he had occasionally done what he pleased. Johnny had actually been an object lesson. Johnny was living proof that it was possible to do what you pleased, that you did not have to go home, that revelry was within your reach. Johnny had lived in a small hotel which he as good as owned; nobody would question his right to song and laughter at dawn. People went out on incredible errands; people came in humorously woebegone with hang-overs. You could hear cocktails being shaken at almost any hour. Scattered through Johnny's whole floor of connecting rooms, everyone you ever knew could probably be found. There were two China boys who tried to clear up, broke ice, eased people incapable of movement philosophically onto beds. They never, apparently, slept themselves. Alice, of course, knew about it. She had even been there on several occasions, tried consciously to be what she called a good sport. Those were afternoon cocktail parties, and perfectly orderly, but she sensed, as one did, an atmosphere. Her expression, at once interested and resentful, betrayed her conviction that evening parties were not so orderly, but she never made any comment. Johnny was too well established an evil. She said nothing against him until he was gone.

The car went fast by the prone guns ruined by sea water, the looped chains and the white shaft of the Maine Memorial. Meade Pons couldn't, he must confess, blame Alice. He attempted, intent on his driving, to calculate, to compute the sum. What it meant to her. Of course it annoyed her. The ordinary routine could not go on. She was legitimately offended when he didn't arrive as expected. He was, too, her husband. Rumors of behavior, outrageous, irresponsible, drifting quickly over the Vedado, could sting her pride. It reflected at once on her attractiveness—since he did not come when she called—and on her good judgment—why had she ever married such a creature? Around him the Latins ordered such things better—not, he insisted, merely better for the men. Well, that was aside from the point. The point, he decided—he was so late that he went past the end of the Prado, past the Palace of Justice, along the Avenida de Las Palmas—was that he didn't want to be sober, responsible, privileged to please Alice and be an example to what the *Times of Cuba* had just last month photographed and titled "her two charming children"—both of them stared, self-engrossed and petulant, at the camera; while Alice, her face considerably retouched with no protest from her, looked on them in a way Meade supposed was loving. He wished, in fact, that it was eight, ten, twelve years ago instead of now, in his forty-fifth year; that none of it—Alice, children, the place on Calle H, even the general agency for Cuba—had ever happened.

A policeman's raised glove halted him. He kept his foot on the clutch, remembering not to change gears—this year's model picked up in high from a halt, according to its literature. He was at the corner where he could see, cool across the heat of the green square, the façade of what had been Johnny's place. It would never be exactly like that again, perhaps, but Johnny was back, at least—must this minute be ashore. The hand fell, the motor picked up as advertised, and Meade swept around the double corner, his horn throwing out a musical note. He twisted expertly into San Ignacio. He ran the car with gingerly precision across the pavement into the cool cavern of the service garage.

"Lino!" he called through the door, open into the offices. "Get the Granada and ask if Mr. Cowden is registered yet."

As he came in, Lino, putting his hand over the mouthpiece of the telephone on his desk, said, "No, Mr. Pons. Not there."

"Ask when he's expected," said Meade. His secretary had stacked opened mail on his desk. He could see it through the door of his private office. There would be nothing of the slightest importance.

"He isn't expected, sir," said Lino; "they haven't a reservation."

"Say, that's funny." Meade frowned. He paused and out of him ran some sustaining warmth and cheerfulness. He felt the heat suddenly; he saw in prospect an intolerable day, beginning there in the letters on his desk and stretched out lifeless to improbably distant sundown.

"They think, sir," said Lino, "it might be the Alhambra." He made a conventional, elaborately courteous acknowledgment in Spanish, hung up.

"Get the Alhambra," said Meade.

"Mr. Cowden checked in an hour ago," Lino announced a moment later.

"Right!" said Meade. He jerked a hand toward his office door. "Take care of that stuff. I'll try to get around this afternoon or telephone you. If Camaguey calls, tell them — well, tell them they can have a couple of stock cars; or else they can keep their shirts on. We can't send what we haven't got."

"The shipment got in last night, Mr. Pons. The brokers have it. If you could get a moment to go down, we might make tonight's train."

"Send Max down."

"They want you, sir," said Lino.

"Let 'em stew a while," said Meade. "I've got to run."

The taxi dropped him in the shadowed side street at the wide doors of the Alhambra. He trotted up the steps. Once, when it was first built, he used to come here a lot. He had even taken Alice dancing on the roof — that couldn't have been more than seven or eight years ago. Johnny was either still in town, or had recently left, and Alice felt less secure in the saddle. She gave him a little rein, valorously feigning a taste for gayety herself. It hadn't been very convincing, he remembered; and she would not be long in thinking of the children. The fault, he saw, was probably his. What must have made a deep impression on him — for the atmosphere of the pale-colored, wicker-furnished lobby here brought it back complete — was that everyone else was either talking or drinking. Alice never drank much, and, naturally, there was little left to talk about. The essence of agreeable conversation is describing the many fascinating things about oneself to a person ignorant of them — a person who may, indeed, be able to credit statements which are little more than exhilarating wishes as facts.

Alice knew everything that was true about him, and could tell instantly what wasn't. Their comment must be mainly scraps elicited by people around them, with silences. Soon enough Alice would become restive, calculating with mute protest how much he was drinking. Her trained eye was alert for the inevitable signs of its effect. "We don't want another bottle," she would say; and he was pressed by her anxious assumption to agreement. Only he did want another bottle; he had no desire to get home.

The foregone futility of attempting to increase, or even to preserve, the moment's radiant content seemed to him aside from the point. He was perfectly prepared to exchange a bad head tomorrow for more of now. Now was what he wanted. It was not what Alice wanted. She was jumpy with irritation and distaste. She was at mortal war with the entrancing liberty which he gave signs of attaining. She must get hold of him quickly, make him do what she wanted; or, presently, he would be beyond her reach, doing what he wanted.

At the desk he said, "Mr. Cowden?"

"Room 1017," said the clerk promptly. "Oh! One moment, sir. Mr. Cowden just went out. He'll return shortly. Are you Mr. Durland?"

"No," said Meade.

The clerk had started to reach for an envelope in a mailbox. "Sorry, sir," he nodded. "Mr. Cowden left a message for Mr. Durland."

That was dumb, thought Meade. He should have had Lino put the call through, instead of dropping it and running over. Durland; he thought. No one he knew in Havana. An idea came to him, and he grinned, going around to a telephone booth, but he was wrong, he found. "Well, I think maybe he will," Meade told Lino. "If he does come in, tell him I'm up here at the Alhambra."

"Yes, sir," said Lino. "Oh, Mr. Pons. Camaguey has called. They are rather upset, but I told them. And a man has been up from the brokers. He wanted you to come down. He says your supervision is necessary if the shipments are to be delivered today."

"He can go to hell," said Meade, recognizing with impotent annoyance the conventional form of a threat, a promise of what he would find if he did not show a little more alacrity. He was not going to devote half this day to that dirty wrangle. Lino's pause of anxiety came to him — a subservient, phraseless exhortation not to neglect the firm's interests. It made him angrier. No real interest of his was remotely concerned with automobile shipments, the red tape of customs brokers, the qualms of a subordinate, the problems of the Camaguey branch over filling an order or two, probably on time payments and to be defaulted anyway. He added, sharp with this resentment, "That's all?" and hung up. Passing the desk, he said, "If you see Mr. Cowden and I don't, tell him Mr. Pons is in the bar."

He crossed the lobby, went through the door. Two elderly men in tight white flannels striped with black — obvious tourists — were sitting over bottles of Tropical in the corner. Otherwise that side of the room held only morning shadows. Against the mirrors leaned a patient barkeep, his few thin brown hairs laid level on his shining skull.

"Hello, Paul," Meade nodded.

The man's eyes went over to him, flickered an instant. "Why, Mr. Pons!" he said. "Haven't seen you for a long time! Just get back?"

Meade overlooked the implications. "You'll see a lot of me," he said. "You remember Mr. Cowden?"

"Yes, indeed, sir!"

"Well, he's stopping upstairs here. You better take on a couple of extra hands." He slid onto a stool and selected a potato chip.

"What'll it be, Mr. Pons?" said Paul.

"I'm waiting for Mr. Cowden," Meade said, "but since you mention it, it will be a daiquiri. Have something?"

Paul lifted his eyebrows slightly toward the old men in the

corner. "If they get out," he murmured. "It's fine to see you back, Mr. Pons."

The daiquiri stood presently in front of him and Meade moistened his lips with it. Paul said, "I heard Mr. Cowden inherited quite a little money when his father died."

"I guess he did," Meade said, "and he's been doing mighty well on his own, by all accounts. He's about as smart as they make 'em." He raised the glass and returned it half empty to the dark wood.

"Mr. Cowden certainly used to give wonderful parties," said Paul. "I can remember one or two when he had me down to mix the drinks."

That was a fact that Meade had forgotten. Paul would be in a white coat behind an improvised bar. Often there would also be three or four men with homely stringed instruments, the pebble-filled gourds which marked out the sweet, melancholy measures of the *danzón,* not then revised for the elaborate orchestras nurtured to jazz. He saw faces, heard voices, long out of mind.

"It's not the same," Paul said, shaking his head. "Nothing like it any more. I never see any of those people. Not since I don't know when. Remember Mr. Delano? I heard he's dead."

"No!" said Meade, shocked, though he hadn't thought of Freddy Delano for years. "He was a fine fellow."

"People settle down or go away," said Paul. "There'll be a mob in here at noon, but I doubt if you'd see anyone you used to know."

"Fix me another of these," said Meade; "I want to see if Mr. Cowden came in."

The process of that general change absorbed him. If he wondered what had become of this man or that, some of them had no doubt wondered what had become of Meade Pons. Since he knew that, he knew what became of them all. You reached a point where peace seemed more important than gayety; there was nothing more to celebrate, only things to fear. Most of those good fellows had finally to see that they would never be rich, nor greatly successful, nor the free masters of their happy lives. Their aspirations, going out unfounded, came home empty; they must learn to be satisfied with the monotony of mere existence. They must keep their money, guard their health, employ their time to please the people who let them live at all. Apprehensive; with ambitions small enough to be plausible; with pleasures kept small, quiet, unexceptionable; they were said to have settled down. It was spoken of as a virtue, with an approving inflection, but the word, he saw, did not more than give a shoddy gilding to necessity. He had, for instance, in his own experience to get rid of his Cienfuegos manager. That man didn't settle down. He was a good fellow; he had very little time for business. The figures were eloquent, and Meade, in self-defense, had to fire him, get somebody who thought that selling automobiles was joy enough; somebody born to plod, or soundly scared into acquiescence. Burke had been that man's name. Meade never knew whether he learned wisdom, got virtue, or not. At any rate, Burke had roistered himself out of a position whose level he would be a long time regaining.

No, they said at the desk, Mr. Cowden hadn't come in.

Meade was still thinking of this Burke as he went back to the bar. Burke had been very much of his own sort, he knew; they had always got on well together. It might easily, in the realm of probabilities, have been himself who was fired at Cienfuegos, instead of Burke. That it wasn't, could, in one way, be laid precisely to Alice's credit. Her money had made it possible for him to stay on in Havana, refusing the deceptive advance of a branch managership. The ceaseless pressure of her opposition had made him seem sober, careful, hard-working—the sort of man who satisfied his lords in Detroit with the promise he gave of making money for them. He owed a lot to Alice—all the things about him which she liked, which they liked in Detroit. Perhaps he ought not to grumble because no one of those things happened to be what he himself liked.

The old gentlemen in the corner had gone; Paul had stepped out a moment. Meade slid onto the stool, sitting alone, his solitary drink before him. It seemed unpleasantly symbolic; everyone was gone, everyone was engaged in whatever way circumstances had taught him he would better be; Meade, startled, recognized the sensation. Infinitely long ago he had felt that same dismay, that growing loneliness; and he grinned a little, for he placed it on one bright morning of his childhood. He had left for school, but, unexpectedly moved, had not gone; he simply went his own way, amazed at the simplicity of thus obtaining freedom. The morning grew less bright; his own pleasure had faded with it before an hour ended. It was no good without companions. He had been, he recalled, spanked; promised more spanking if it happened again. And he remembered, it hadn't happened again, though he had always been ready to risk punishment in a good cause. He raised the glass, drinking slowly, and as he drank, his eye caught a movement at the door. Turning, he saw Johnny Cowden.

"Meade!" said Johnny, and his voice was just as Meade remembered it. "You old rounder! What are you up to now?"

His happiness was so sudden and so strong that Meade Pons found he literally could not speak. He got off the stool and, still trying to find words, took Johnny's hand.

The wrinkles were deeper around Johnny's eyes. Johnny's hair was thinned, definitely gray at the sides, but in his linen suit he looked as big, as red-brown-faced as ever. Meade saw then that he was not alone.

"Mr. Durland," he said, "meet Mr. Pons." His hand fell affectionately on Meade's shoulder. "Pete and I are going down to Oriente to look at some mines," he said, "but I guess we could have a drink." Paul had come through a door behind the bar. "Hello, Paul," nodded Johnny.

"Why, Mr. Cowden!" said Paul. "Haven't seen you for a long time!"

"Take a good look," said Johnny. "I'm going down the island tonight."

"What'll it be, sir?"

"Make it a bottle of Tropical," said Johnny. "How about you, Pete?"

"Not for me," said Mr. Durland. "Fix me up a lemonade."

"You don't want beer, Johnny," protested Meade. "Have a daiquiri. I'm going to."

"Wish I could," said Johnny, "but they won't let me drink cocktails. Sit down, Meade. Let's hear about everything. How are Alice and the kids?"

"All right," said Meade.

"Johnny tells me you're in the automobile business," said Mr. Durland. "How is it here?"

"So-so," answered Meade. "It could be worse, though I don't know how."

"What line do you handle?"

Meade told him. "I guess they're having pretty hard sledding," said Mr. Durland. "One of my best friends is connected with an automobile concern, and he told me —"

Meade waited until he had finished, and then he said, "Listen, Johnny; what do you have to go away tonight for? Boy, you just got here —"

"Johnny and I have got to be in Santiago tomorrow," said Mr. Durland. "A lot may depend on it."

Johnny said regretfully, "I hate to have to do it, but it's a chance we can't miss. I'd certainly like to look around here again, but not this trip, I'm afraid." He put out a hand and grasped Meade's shoulder. "It's good to see you," he said. "Believe me, I've thought of you a lot! We used to have pretty good times here eight or nine years back," he told Mr. Durland. "You'd be surprised. Wouldn't he, Meade?"

"Best time I ever had was in Paris," said Mr. Durland. "I was over on business, and I guess I'd have better sense now, but it was some show while it lasted."

"I guess that's when I first met you," said Johnny.

"That's right," agreed Mr. Durland. "Do you remember the night —"

Meade sat silent. The drinks had been brought and he took the daiquiri, tasted it, and set it down. He didn't want to hear what they did in Paris, but he couldn't very well help it, and it was, he saw, pretty stupid.

"I guess we could eat after this," said Johnny. "Where'll we go?"

Meade spoke suddenly:

"Johnny, it can't be done. I didn't know you were going out. I wanted to come over and fix up something for tonight. Got a man I simply have to see at lunch."

"Say, isn't that rotten?" Johnny said. "I certainly wanted to have a good talk. What about this afternoon? Got any time?"

"I haven't, Johnny," Meade said. "Got a shipment, and those lazy devils who do our customs brokerage want me to do all the work for them." Meade managed a bleak smile. "So I've got to run," he said. "Johnny, it's fine to have seen you. Next time—" He left it. "Pleased to meet you, Mr. Durland."

"Gosh, it's a shame!" said Johnny. They shook hands. "Well, take care of yourself, boy. Don't let water get in the gin."

Meade stopped at the bar, dropping money on it. "Say, this is on me!" called Johnny.

"Thanks, Paul," Meade said. "Not much," he called back. "It's on me."

Lino and Max went down at five o'clock to see that the cars for Camaguey got off. The porter was shutting up, and Meade, easing the brilliant car across the curblike sidewalk of San Ignacio, said good night to him. He worked his way up Obispo Street, slid around the Park and down the Prado. Along the Maleçon the sea was marvelous, immeasurable deep blue. He turned west, the rich sun flashing off his windshield. He drove at ease. He had made the customs brokers play ball.

He turned into his own drive finally, ran the car straight back to its place in the garage. Now that the direct sun was gone, Luis, in his gardening capacity, was sprinkling a flower bed. Alice, he saw, was standing in the path, watching the operation, and he walked down. She had, of course, seen him come in, but she ignored his approach until he was within a couple of yards. She turned then, looked at him in acute appraisal.

She said, "Oh, I didn't expect you." She looked at him again. "What's the trouble? Didn't Johnny get here?"

"Yes, I saw him," Meade answered. "He's on his way to Santiago."

"Well, I suppose you expect me to thank you for managing to stay sober."

"Now," he said placatingly, "it's a long time since I've been on a bat."

"Oh, I know you," she answered.

Though she kept it in hand, spoke with grudging scorn, she was gratified; crediting herself with an accomplishment. This morning it would have been true; she knew him then. He was different now. At the end of the path Judith and Richard appeared, quarreling about something. He had those, and Alice, to see that he behaved himself, and today he had saved the company five hundred dollars at least. Many men at forty-five had less, could not do so well. He was lucky, he guessed, that he had anyone or anything, for this road was one way—not back—and had one end. In spite of everything, he liked now, the present, better than he would like that end; it was a progression, hopeless and natural. He would never meet the bunch at Johnny's again, nor Johnny himself, probably; but he had still a roof over his head, and he would better be careful, for soon enough he'd have only earth there.

Every Day's a Holiday

From the front veranda Mr. Jamison called angrily, "Emily! You, Emily!"

"Oh, God!" she said. She slung the can opener into the sink, dumped the contents of the can of peas into a saucepan. "Howard! Get that liquor out of your car and make Father a drink. Make yourself one. Take them out and talk to him. He's going to run me crazy." She looked toward the door, noticing her father's chauffeur standing idle with a cigarette. "Mike, chop some ice."

Howard Hoyt had been sitting on the kitchen table, lax, in a sort of sad, dumb absorption. He stirred and stood up, removing his eyes from the stretched yellow linen of Emily's frock, the taut lines of her legs under it. Her feet were planted apart, stockingless, in ruined satin slippers which had once been gold-colored.

Mike said, "Where is the ice, Mrs. Brennan?"

"What would you think of looking in the icebox?" she asked. "And don't call me Mrs. Brennan. If you can't call me Emily, call me You. Do you think I like to be reminded of that bum?" She struck back her curly, dark-red hair, glancing the other way over her shoulder. "Howard, did you hear me?" Seeing his face, she turned quickly about. "Now, look here," she said, "if you're going to act like that, you can go home. Right this minute. Go on, get out of here! I won't stand for it. Those Peters people were down last night, and I forget who the night before, and they drank every drop of that other liquor. Now go and get what you brought and shut up!"

The screen door slammed gently after him. "Honestly," she said, "sometimes that man makes me want to scream. If he thinks he can be like that after we're married — put the ice there, Mike. Listen, is Father going to send you to the inn in the village? You can't sleep anywhere here unless you want to try the hammock on the porch. I told him Howard was coming. You didn't hear him say how long he was planning to stay?"

"No, I didn't, Mrs. Brennan."

"Listen, you aren't my chauffeur. I told you not to call me that. It kills me. If I liked to hear it, all I had to do was stay married to Brennan." She went to the door and yelled, "Phyl!" Her sister's muffled response came down to her. "Lord, she's still giving little Emily her bath. Do you know how to lay a table? Well, go and lay it. We'll never get supper."

Mike moved away with a creak of his black leather leggings, wiping his wet hands on his whipcord breeches. The screen door swung, admitting Howard, who lugged a case of bottles.

"Open one," Emily said, "open one! Father will be howling again in a minute." She whipped about and cried, "Phyl! Phyl! Look at little Emily! That child's down here without a stitch on! Honey, don't you know you can't walk around with a lot of men that way? Get upstairs and let Aunt Phyl put some clothes on you —" She dissolved in laughter. "She's just a slut at heart, like her mother. That's right, Howard. There's the ice. There are the glasses. Wait a minute. How about me?" She picked up a coffee cup. "Give me half an inch. And don't be such a lemon. I'm warning you."

In a few minutes her sister appeared calmly. "Your daughter is dressed, Emily. You're welcome."

"Where's Keith?"

"I was going to tell you. I think he's upset. I told him to go to bed."

"And I told him if he ate any more cake at Mrs. Miller's I'd tan the hide off him. She just gets the little simpleton up there to try to pump him. God, these farmers!"

"He was there, all right."

"I know it. You can't do anything with him. He's just like Brennan."

"Emily, you jackass! If Father ever heard you say that—"

"Well, what's he want? I was married to the rat for three years, wasn't I? I should think that would fix it up."

"It'll never fix up the fact you weren't married to him when Keith was born; you were still married to Sheldrick. Or have you forgotten that?"

"It's one of the things you don't forget. Lord, I'll be crazy if I try it again with Howard."

"Well, why do you?"

"I have to live. Brennan will never pay any more alimony. He hasn't sense enough to make any money. He's probably pie-eyed from morning to night. What can I do? Put him in jail? That doesn't pay any bills."

"I'll speak to Father. That's what I mean about Keith, you little fool. He'd simply disown you."

"Lord, Phyl, how dumb is dumb?"

"He isn't so dumb. But you don't have to prove it to him. And you be careful about Howard."

"Don't you worry. Howard started to go funny on all that liquor the Peters drank and what else. He's going to lie down and play dead this weekend. I've given him too darn much of a break. Father can have my bed and I'll sleep with you. We'll put Howard down on the couch in the living room. Maybe Mike can sleep on the porch. There's a dumb boy."

"I don't doubt it."

"Where did Father get him?"

"How do I know? Probably from an agency. Is there any reason why he should be brilliant? And listen, I heard you tell him to call you Emily. I suppose you think Father would love that?"

"He can't call me Mrs. Brennan and get away with it. I'll have to stay and watch the steaks. Or, you stay and watch them. I'd better look at Keith a minute. Where's little Emily?"

"On the porch with Father and Howard."

"That must be quite a party. See you in a minute."

After a while there was a sound at the door and Phyllis glanced that way.

"I finished laying the table, Miss Jamison," Mike said. "What should I do now?"

"Nothing. Take a rest. If you want a drink, help yourself."

"Thank you, ma'am."

"I see what Emily means," Phyllis nodded. "Listen, my lad, you're going to have to eat with us. Mrs. Brennan and I do what little serving is done. Don't feel you have to be fresh; but we can't stand on too much ceremony. Adapt yourself. Relax. We're all one happy family on a holiday."

"All right."

"That's better. If you've got a real shirt on under that coat, you can take the coat off. It's a pretty warm evening."

"All right." In his shirt sleeves, he sat on the edge of the chair. "Pretty country up here," he ventured.

"Nice for the kiddies," she said briefly. "We're living here this summer because we're good and poor. Or Mrs. Brennan is, and you can see how devoted I am to her. Does that explain everything?"

"I hope Mrs. Brennan isn't mad at me, Miss Jamison."

"You hope, do you? O.K., Irish. Just keep hoping."

His stout form was sunk morosely in the sagging wicker chair on the veranda. Mr. Jamison raised the glass to his cropped white mustache, tilted it shortly, drinking, set it on the wicker table by the rail. He made a sound half a snort, half a cough. From the pocket of his tweed jacket he drew a huge silk handkerchief and wiped the knee of his white flannel trousers. Then he wiped his mustache and thrust the handkerchief back. Without more warning he addressed Howard, who had been sitting silent on the top step clasping his glass and gazing out across the meadow and river.

"Where does all this liquor come from?" Mr. Jamison said.

Recovering, Howard said, "Why, I brought it up from town, sir. It ought to be —"

"Well, now, I wish you wouldn't do it," Mr. Jamison said.

"There's too much drinking going on around here. If you didn't bring it up, they'd probably never miss it."

Howard looked at him, confused; but apparently no answer was expected, for Mr. Jamison continued more sharply. "Where's Emily?"

"She's getting supper, sir."

"Humph. I called her."

"She'll come as soon as she can, sir. Is there anything I can do?"

"No, no." He turned his heavy head abruptly. "Emily! Where are you going?"

"Upstairs," she called back.

"What for?"

"You'd only be embarrassed if I told you."

"Emily!"

"Oh, keep still, Father. Everything's all right. Keith isn't feeling well."

"What's wrong with the child?" Mr. Jamison asked Howard.

"I don't know, sir. I saw him running around half an hour ago."

"I don't think he gets proper food."

"Emily takes wonderful care of the children, Mr. Jamison. They couldn't get any better care."

"Well, I suppose she has nowhere to gad about to up here. In town, she behaved like a hooligan. What business are you in, Mr. Boyd?"

"My name is Hoyt, sir," Howard said, awkward. "Why, I'm in real estate."

Keith, flushed and bright-eyed in the early shadows, was not very sick, Emily saw. "Well, just for that you don't get any supper," she said, and laughed. "That's a break for you," she added. "You don't want any, anyway, do you?"

"No, Mummy. I don't want any."

"How much of that Miller garbage did you eat? Two pieces, I'll bet. Tell Mother what Mrs. Miller asked you."

"She asked me where my Daddy was."

"What did you say?"

"I said he was away."

"That's all right. What else?"

"She asked me what he was. I said he was a bum."

"Oh, my God! You would! What else?"

"I don't remember, Mummy."

"Yes, you do. Now, think hard."

"Well, she said didn't a lot of men come to stay at night here—"

"I knew it. The snooping old—Keith, honey, Mother's simply going to wale the life out of you if you ever go up there again. Honestly, I'd do it right this minute if you weren't sick."

"I feel like I wanted to throw up—"

"You and me both!" she groaned. "Get up! Get up! Get in the bathroom. Don't you dare throw up in here!"

"I thought so," said Phyllis. "This shack is wonderful that way. You don't miss a thing. Does he feel better?"

"He'll be all right. More ice, Mike, more ice. How about those steaks?"

"About five minutes. You stay here. I heard you telling Father to shut up. I'd better go out and smooth him down."

"Call little Emily, will you? She isn't out there. Father was riding Howard about bringing liquor up. You tell him to mind his own business. I notice he drinks it, all right. Lord, I meant to get a bath and put some clothes on. This is sticking to me."

She picked up the glass, tipped her head back and drank half of it without pausing, set it aside, and took a bread knife and a loaf of bread.

While she sliced swift and even, Mike, leaning against the far wall, his empty glass tilting forgotten in his large hand, looked at her. He said nothing and Emily sliced in silence until the whole loaf had been divided. Knocking off the ends of crust, she set up the pile of slices, cut it in half from top to bottom, shifted the result to a plate. She took the nearby glass and drained it, gave her hair a quick toss. Mike was still looking at her and, turning, she easily surprised his absorbed gaze. "Ah, there!" she said. "Thinking about your best girl, I'll bet!"

Starting, he reddened; began to smile sheepishly.

"Bring your glass here, Good-looking. We'll have another drink. One more stiff one and I may be tight enough to stand supper with Father." She looked toward the door. "Come on, Howard," she said. "You need another drink, too."

"Father, please don't be silly," Phyllis said. "Emily has supper to get for seven people. In this madhouse anyone else would collapse completely. I don't know how she stands it. Howard, get Father and you another drink."

"No, no. I don't care for another drink. There's too much—"

"Get them, Howard."

When he had gone, Mr. Jamison said, "Who is that fellow, anyway? When did Emily meet him?"

"Oh, he's the one who sold the Larchmont house for her. He's a nice boy."

"What's he come up here for?"

"He comes up here because he's trying to get Emily to marry him."

"What's he want to do that for? Who wants to marry a woman with two children who's been divorced twice?"

"Now, Father, don't be childish. He's been divorced himself and he's old enough to know his own mind."

"I won't have Emily marrying another drunken wastrel. I told him not to bring any more liquor." He pulled his mustache. "If he had any regard for her reputation he'd know better than to be staying here every weekend."

"Howard is the soberest man alive, Father. You needn't worry about him. Furthermore, I don't think you have any right to interfere with Emily."

"You don't, don't you!"

"My very words. You treat her like a dog. You always have. If Mother hadn't died, do you think Emily ever would have run off from school with Sheldrick that way? Maybe you've forgotten how you used to roar around the house."

"You leave your mother out of this! I can only be thankful, truly thankful, that she isn't here. The disgrace of it would kill her."

"Father, are you trying to fight with me, too?"

"I'm not going to have you being impertinent and speaking disrespectfully of your mother."

"You heard exactly what I said about Mother. Now, aren't you ashamed of yourself?"

Tugging his mustache again, he glared at her a moment. Grunting a little, he looked away then. "As soon as Emily can show me she's ready to live a quiet, sober life and bring up her children properly and decently, I'll see she has the means. That's what I've always stood ready to do. Meanwhile, she can live on that Brennan pup's alimony."

"He hasn't paid her any for months. As a matter of fact, we've been living, and are right this minute, on what money I can spare."

"Well, you shouldn't do it. She made her bed. Let her lie in it. She had no business to get herself into a mess like this. How old is she? Twenty-seven! Think of it! At twenty-seven she's been divorced twice. Like a lot of Broadway riffraff! I'm not going to make her an allowance. Not a cent. I don't want to hear any more about it."

"You won't. We'll get along. But don't you let me hear any more about what Emily ought to do, or ought not to. And if she wants to marry Howard, that's her business."

He had begun to grumble restlessly before she finished, and, pouting under his mustache, he could be heard saying now: " — thinks of nothing but pleasure. Other people have to work for a living. Decent and responsible attitude. Too much to ask, I suppose. Well, I won't make her any allowance. I'll give you a check before I go. Do what you want with it. But don't ask me to — " She reached out and patted his hand. "There's your grandchild," she said, indicating little Emily, who had appeared silently at the bottom of the steps. "You might ask her where she's been and generally make yourself agreeable. I'd better see what I can do in the kitchen."

In the shadows of the hall she encountered Howard, who had a glass in each hand. Nodding back toward the porch, she said, "The dust's settled a little out there. He's a trial; but if you talk to him nicely he'll mellow down. Do your best."

He nodded, looking at her. Then he said hesitantly, "Phyl, I don't think Emily ought to drink any more. She's pretty tight. I mean, I don't think your father would like it — "

"All right. I'll get her in hand."

In the kitchen there was a haze of grease smoke and a fierce crackle and hiss of broiling steaks. Mike was sitting in the broken chair by the table. Emily was on her knees before the oven, jabbing the steaks with a fork. The intense jets of blue flame in the broiler shone on her flushed face. She was singing, with a certain husky sweetness which showed Phyllis that Howard was not wrong:

> "Why do I love you?
> Why do you love me — "

Glancing up at her sister, she said, "They're about done." She steadied herself with her palm on Phyllis's hip. "I'm woozy. Give me a hand up, darling. I'll never make it alone. Want another drink, Mike?"

"But not for you," Phyllis said, bringing her to her feet. "I've just finished repairing the damage and I want you to behave. I can keep these hot a while. You haven't time for a bath, but beat it up and get under a cold shower for a couple of minutes. Hurry!"

"I'm all right, darling. Honestly — "

"You are not. Hurry up. And come down decently dressed. I mean, with something on under it. You know Father."

Mike put his glass on the table. "I guess I'd better not have any more, Miss Jamison," he said. "Mrs. Brennan told me I should drive her in to the village afterwards and get some groceries for breakfast. That's pretty strong stuff. I wouldn't want to be driving a car if I had any more."

"Well, now, maybe we'd better have Howard drive her in."

"Why, Miss Jamison," he said reproachfully, "I'm sober as a judge. Honest, I know where to stop."

"That's a wonderful thing to know," she said. "You might go out on the porch and tell Father and Howard that supper will be ready in five minutes."

Emily had on a frock much like the yellow one, but clean; a pale-green linen. "I certainly threw away a wonderful edge then," she sighed. "Thanks, darling. Do I look refined? I swiped a brassière of yours." She slid her narrow tanned hand under Phyllis's arm, drew her close, their cheeks touching. Turning her head sharply she kissed her.

"O.K, brat," Phyllis said. "Get going. They're all in there."

From the dining room she could hear Emily asking presently, "Won't you say grace, Father?"

"Don't be blasphemous!" Mr. Jamison roared.

Catching up the steak platter, Phyllis came to the rescue. "That'll do from you, Red," she said. "Go and get little Emily's cereal. There's a carving knife, Father."

Later, when she came out to the kitchen to help Emily with the raspberries, Phyllis said, "If you've got to go up to the village, let Howard drive you. You've been treating him pretty rough."

"And it's only the beginning," Emily said. She filled a pitcher with cream. "He makes me sick. He sticks to me. He sits around, like a dog who wants something, looking sorrowful. I know he told you in the hall I was tight. The rat! My being tight has given him a lot of damn good breaks. He wouldn't be any treat to a sober girl, I can tell you that."

"All right, all right! Don't yell, darling. Father can hear too."

"He shouldn't mind. He didn't seem exactly glad to see Howard. He's so afraid I might have a good time, he wouldn't even let Howard by."

"He'll learn to like Howard better."

From the dining room Mr. Jamison roared suddenly, "What are you two whispering about in there? Come out! Get on with supper!"

There was a continuous wink of fireflies in the dusk across the meadow to the river. Beyond the river, the white fence of the valley highway rounded the bend. Preceded by their pale shafted lights, occasional cars appeared swift, small and silent in the distance. Resuming his seat on the veranda, Mr. Jamison offered a cigar to Howard. When they had them lighted, Phyllis said, "Father, let Mike drive Emily up to the village. We need some stuff for breakfast."

"All right. Don't get any liquor. She was drunk at supper."

"Oh, no, she wasn't, Father. She can't get any liquor in the village anyway."

"She can get it anywhere, and does."

Howard, turning his face quickly in the dusk, said, "I can drive her up, Phyl. I'll—"

"No, no," Mr. Jamison said. "Let this fellow of mine do something. He never gets half enough work."

Embarrassed, Howard looked wretchedly at him. Mr. Jamison drew on the cigar, regarded the end of it a moment and said, "I'm sorry to sound short. I don't mean it that way, I simply don't want Emily to get herself a reputation—humph! I mean people in a small community like this misunderstand. Would you care to tell me a little about yourself, Mr. Hoyt?"

"There isn't much to tell, sir."

"Well, what I meant, frankly—humph! That is, I had been given to understand that you entertained—I mean, in regard to Emily—"

"Yes, sir. I hope you wouldn't have any objections, if she were willing, to our being married."

"Yes. I see." He puffed a moment at the cigar. "Perhaps you'd care to tell me something about your financial—qualifications—" He turned his head. "Phyl gone?"

"She went out to the kitchen, sir. Did you want her?"

"No, no. I don't think the matter is one we need to discuss in her hearing, that's all. I mean, are you in a position to—"

In the kitchen Phyllis said, "Now, take that slow and easy."

"Caught again," Emily nodded. She set the glass down. "Come on, Mike. You don't have to put the coat on."

"Listen, Red."

"Yes, darling."

"Don't you be too long."

"Quick as a flash," Emily said. "I'll do all tomorrow's dishes, Phyl. Get little Emily to help you. She won't have to go to bed for half an hour."

"See you get back to put her to bed."

In the dusky sky over the eastern hills appeared the great edge of the rising moon.

"Beautiful night," said Mr. Jamison.

It was, in fact, practically night. Only a last radiance of sunset or twilight remained on the pale dusty surface of the dirt road at the bottom of the short lawn. There was no wind, but the river and meadow and massing of big treetops about the wooden bridge across the small brook breathed a distinct coolness in the dark, now coming alive with the many sounds of summer evening.

Mr. Jamison said, "Are you a college man, Mr. Hoyt?"

Rousing himself, Howard answered. "Well, sir, I was at Lafayette for a little over a year. I didn't graduate. I couldn't afford it. I had to come home and work."

"I'm not a college man, myself," Mr. Jamison said. "They seem to make more of it nowadays, but I often think it's just a waste of a boy's time. More to your credit to have been able and ready to pitch in and help your family. You seem to have done well. I'm glad."

"Yes, sir."

Mr. Jamison removed the cigar from his mouth and looked first at it and then at Howard. He coughed and said, "I think Emily will settle down. She's not been in a good environment. Those fellows she was married to weren't any good. If she could get away from all that into a wholesome atmosphere, she'd be different. I hope so for both your sakes."

"I wouldn't want to make Emily do anything she didn't want to do, sir. I'd want her to be happy. To have a good time."

"Of course. Of course. But that isn't all of life. Every day's not a holiday. Emily thinks it is."

Howard moved a little on the top step. Turning his wrist inconspicuously he managed to bring into view the luminous dial of his wrist watch.

From the door behind, Phyllis asked, "Are you all right, Father? I'm going to put little Emily to bed."

"Yes. It's high time. The child shouldn't be up as late as this. Emily should have seen to it before she went."

Left alone, Howard and Mr. Jamison were both silent. The sound of a motor reached them after a minute and they both turned to look. Headlights were descending the slope through the trees to the little bridge.

"That ought to be Emily and the car," Mr. Jamison said. "She had no right to go off like that and leave Phyllis with all the work to do. She could just as well have given that fellow of mine a list to take up."

There was a rumble of the coming car on the bridge. The headlights mounted the slope on this side. After a moment it was apparent that the car was a Ford. It went on past toward the Millers' farmhouse.

The moon, whiter, well clear of the low wooded hilltops, shone exactly mirrored, swaying a little with the slow current but unbroken, on the river. Howard had long ago finished his cigar. He lighted another cigarette. Finally Phyllis came downstairs and out into the shadows quietly. She dropped into the chair behind Howard. "Peace at last," she sighed. "Let me have one of those."

"What's keeping Emily?" Mr. Jamison said. "She ought to have been back long ago."

Howard had got up to give Phyllis the cigarette. He lit it now for her. She could see his disturbed face in the small glow and putting out a hand patted his arm twice. "Thanks," she said. "Emily had a lot of things to get, Father."

"Call up that store and see if they know anything about her."

"Father, don't be absurd. They'll be back in a minute."

"There's nothing absurd about it. She's been gone an hour and a half. It shouldn't take her twenty minutes. I want to know if she's been there, or if she's running around looking for liquor."

"Well, I'm not going to call up."

"If she isn't back in ten minutes, I'll call myself."

"That wouldn't do you any good. The store closes at nine."

"Humph! Exactly as I thought! She's trying to find a bootlegger. You don't expect me to believe she's riding around looking at the moonlight."

"Why not?" said Phyllis. "She's been cooped up here all day."

"She has no business to stay away. She has a child sick upstairs, and—"

"Keith's been asleep for hours. He's perfectly all right."

"She doesn't know it."

"Lord," said Phyl, "let's have a drink."

"No. I don't care for one."

"Well, I do. How about you, Howard?"

"I guess so." Belatedly he added, "Could I help you, Phyl?"

"No, sit still."

Busy with ice and glasses in the kitchen, Phyllis heard presently the fast hollow rumble of a heavy car on the bridge down in the trees. A moment later headlights wheeled, flashed along the side of the house. A motor was shut off. From in front Mr. Jamison called loudly, "Emily! You, Emily! Come here."

Phyllis held the whiskey bottle motionless, listening. Emily laughed clearly. "In a minute," she said. "I want to put these things in the kitchen."

"Emily!" Apparently it was a failure, for he roared, "Mike! I want to speak to you."

"Yes, Mr. Jamison. Be right there."

Phyllis set down the bottle, went and pushed the screen door open. "Hurry up," she said.

Emily, her arms full of packages, slid in. She dumped them on the table. "Darling," she said, breathless. "Am I all right?" She smoothed the dress, fluffed back her hair with both hands.

"Yes," said Phyllis. "You're all right. Go on out there."

"We weren't long, were we?"

"Hours. I ought to kill you, Red. Go on, before I do."

"Phyl."

"Yes, you bum!"

"Father?"

"No. He thinks you were trying to get some liquor."

"Thanks, darling."

On the porch Emily said, "I'm sorry, Father. We had to wait around for the proprietor at the Inn so we could get a room for Mike. He can't sleep down here. He can go back now."

"Is that true, Mike?"

"Yes, Mr. Jamison."

"Is there any liquor in the car?"

"No, sir."

"Well, all right. I'll telephone when I want you tomorrow."

"Yes, sir. Good night, sir." He looked at Emily and said, diffident, "Good night, Mrs. Brennan." He turned quickly toward the car.

"O.K., Irish," she said.

Mr. Jamison looked at her. He said: "What do you mean by talking to him that way?"

Phyllis had come out.

"Well, now," she said, "don't start a war. He is Irish, isn't he?"

Farewell to Cuba

From the Calle Lamparilla the voices of the newsdealers crying late-afternoon papers mounted at last to Martin Gibbs. In lengthening shadows, in sunlight diluted by a preparatory stir of evening air, these regularly changed calls joined with the continuous hoot of taxi horns and the hard squeal of applied brakes where the traffic came together three reckless ways under the soft weather-marked masses of the Christo Church. To Martin Gibbs it seemed a sound peculiarly Havana's. Surely nowhere else did they drive so impetuously, or raise a wail so drowsy and so sad over final editions. Similarly, you could not smell anywhere else the Havana smell, the blend of air-slaked lime, roasting coffee and spilled anisette; reinforced now with a perfume of flowers, now with the breath of butcher shops where the meat has been too warm all day. Although so many things had altered, things like that hadn't. Long, long ago Havana smelt and—though cars must have been few—managed to sound the same. Afternoon ended then as now, in sunlight limpid without being dim, clear and sad in its own way on ancient stone, on faded tints of colored plaster, and ribs of hoary tiles, red dulled to gray. The sky displayed a fine satin blue which it might be pleasant to touch. Martin Gibbs pushed back the tall shutters on the constricted hotel balcony and the familiar noises came a little louder.

On one of the beds Celia stirred and said without opening her eyes: "Martin."

"It's half past five, honey," he told her. "How do you feel?"

She murmured: "All right." Her tawny hair was soaked with per-spiration. Moisture shone unmistakable on her face, catching in ugly, artificial pallor the light twice reflected; up from the street, down from the pale-blue walls. Her body lay awkwardly, inert; wrapped in a damp and wrinkled dressing gown of white silk. A vital energy which made her look always less than her age had ebbed very far; she looked more, now; over forty, certainly. Under the cool simplicity of her regular features and clear moderate coloring appeared a sharpness, a wasting of tissue which was drained of blood, and gray. Her arms were less slender than gaunt. Perhaps he felt some dismayed concern, for she protested suddenly, her eyes still closed: "Don't look at me. It must be awful."

Martin Gibbs said: "Never mind, honey. We'll be out of this tomorrow morning." His eyes had moved obediently away and he saw his own reflection in the shadowed pool of the mirror above the dressing table. The heaviness of his big plain face was always a surprise to him. Except the bold, slightly bent nose, no feature of it looked like Martin Gibbs. The nose had always been that way, but not the lines slanting past the end of his mouth. The southern sun, relentless, had formed the wrinkles at the corners of his calm eyes. His hair had receded so far that the central point, where he parted it, formed a lonely, isolated projection on his sun-browned skull. He was reminded at once of the fact that he was getting old — fifty-two, in fact.

He said aloud: "We should have done this ten years ago." It was an appeal to what might have been and it was a mistake, he realized. It prodded up in him an impotent and puerile rage; he would like without any warning to break things, but he steadied himself, consciously restrained and temperate. Leaving Cuba at his time of life, he was in a way staking everything on his capacity for exact judgment, his competence and coolness when situations new and unavoidably difficult would face him. As for leaving before, he knew that was nonsense, not to be argued about. He was leaving now, getting Celia away. He had done it just as soon as he was able to see how things really stood. Being young prevented any such view, up to a certain point. You could stand anything easily while you believed a lot lay ahead. When you saw that nothing remained, it was different. No rubbish about the country or the climate getting you. Age was the same everywhere, getting everyone, everywhere. A decade more, and age would have had him, fairly. Had him empty-handed. He had a positive, reassuring sense of his rightness in throwing it all up. There were thousands of careers and positions but only one life, and not much time left to be happy in it. He did look back at Celia now, and—for he himself had felt slowly safer and happier—he was jolted to see that her eyes were wet. While he watched, tears pushed slowly up through the closed lashes.

"Honey," he said, "what's the trouble?"

It was, of course, a silly thing to ask and it took her a minute by the distinct ticking of his watch to find any answer. Her lips, looking almost blue in the thin queer light, worked a little, finally tightened, stiff over her teeth, and she said huskily: "Martin, what are we going to do? We don't know anyone in the North. We—"

She stopped. Her courage was amazing; and Martin thought about such special qualities in her character with a wondering affection, a sort of harassed reverence. He wiped his forehead. "We've got some money," he said. "We're not poor. That's what matters."

Celia had none of most women's acute concern and sober practicality in such things. She was acquiescent, incurious; and for this he was grateful. There were difficulties which could only be made worse by explanations. "We have some money," he repeated. "There isn't a thing to worry about. Except getting away from here as soon as we can." He didn't, he told himself, actually believe that. He saw no limit to the things he must worry about; but they didn't dismay him. The platitudinous truth was so strong that he stated it: "As long as I have you they can't lick me. I won't have to; but I could start from the bottom, and in ten years—"

She moved her head in a minute gesture, as though of thanks or acknowledgment, rather than assent. She was nervous, and she

was tired, but it wasn't in her to be difficult. A flood of tenderness
and a moving gratitude heartened him. "Celia," he said, "why
don't you have something to eat now? What would you like?"
Practical questions helped him. Just in time they stopped a
renewal, now helplessly on her behalf, of that congested feeling
which rose with the sting of ridiculous tears to his eyes. The
familiar useless anger, at what Cuba allied with the ruinous years
had done to them, went down. He breathed again and repeated the
question.

"Nothing," she said. "You go on. You mustn't be late." She did
open her eyes now, clear and sad in her unhappy face. "I'll be all
right. The heat and traveling. It's better for me not to eat anything."

He started to object, but the protest got not so far as words.
Even in a matter like that he wanted her suddenly to have her way,
to find things easy, to see him always at her side. "Can you sleep?"
he said.

She nodded. "There's that medicine I could take if I didn't," she
told him. "I hate to wake up and find it's not morning. . . ."

"You've got some?" he said. She nodded. "Enough. I won't
need it in the North." That was true, Martin told himself. Her
health would unquestionably be better in another climate.

"I'll stay until you get to sleep," he said; but she shook her head,
settling back. "No. If you stay it will take longer." She moistened
her lips and smiled. "Lock the door, darling, and don't let them
bother me."

He came and kissed her damp forehead. Her arms seemed so
thin, her face so taut, that he said: "I love you, Celia. More than
anything."

She put a hand on his arm with a sort of nod. "I love you,
Martin, too. I wanted to leave Cuba, darling. It's all right. I'll be
asleep in a minute. Have a good time."

He was startled by the phrase, the idea of leaving her there and
"having a good time." Rejecting that, he was startled again to
wonder what, if not a good time, he was going to have. Carriker,
George Biehl, Homer Loren—he never had anything but a good

time with them. If he did not expect a last pleasant evening, why should he see them at all? Locking the door from the outside, he stood a moment in the corridor with its windows on the small dingy patio.

It might be a mistake; when he was leaving it all it was silly to bother to see people without future significance, whatever the past had been. Probably, he thought (scoffing at his overmastering desire, since he did not seem to be able to struggle with it), it would be a bore for them, too. Only he knew better. Down here one kept friends. Even a man like Homer Loren, who had thousands of acquaintances, felt the fundamental loneliness. They drew together in defense. They fought off the underlying isolation of an atmosphere which no familiarity with the people, the language, the life and climate could change from the permanently alien.

This sentimental, almost silly aspect of it troubled him, Martin knew. He might have been making a furtive escape to personal safety from a sorely besieged and dangerous fort where every man's presence counted. Counted a great deal, for never had he himself seemed to want so much the comfort of shared memories, the security of long acquaintance. Though a deserter, though he didn't deserve to, going finally away; he must see their faces, hear their voices. He could not help looking a last time on what he had to show for the vanished years and the outworn youth, the Cuba of their common past.

Martin Gibbs walked down two flights of stairs paved with stained, cracked marble, tossed his key onto the narrow desk. His wife, he said, was sleeping; on no account to be disturbed. Outside the street was bright still with the level slant of the setting sun. He glanced at his watch and walked slowly.

"This is something like it!" Joe Carriker said. "Martin, you old son of a gun!"

Carriker was enormously heavy, with a face broad and brick-colored. His hair, of which he retained plenty, stood up over his shining forehead in a short gray ruff. Martin Gibbs shook hands with him, and then with Homer Loren, across the table. Homer was lean-faced, deeply brown from mornings on the Marianao sands. He owned and edited an English-language daily. The *Evening Mail* was famous for its warm defense of the Cuban administration, and everyone suspected that the government subsidized it, at least indirectly. The President's nephew was widely believed to be the author of the lead editorials on local affairs. Some of its competitors were bitter, but Homer remained unmoved. He was rich now, for whatever reason; he was the only really prominent and influential man that Martin knew well in Cuba. "I see the Wail is worse than ever," Martin told him, happy.

"Ah," said Homer, "but did you see it tonight? You'd better buy a copy and frame it. I had them run a quarter inch on the front page lower right with a small head: 'Leading Santa Clara Banker Visits Havana.' No wonder the sheet is rotten."

Martin Gibbs nodded to him. "Much obliged for the buggy ride," he said. It would be just as well, he saw, to get this matter over at once. "Only you're wrong as always. I'm leaving Cuba for good."

"It would certainly be for good, if true," Homer said. His oblong brown face cracked in a smile. "What did you do? Ask for a raise and get turned down? Or are you running off with someone else's wife? Tell Uncle Homer so he can have a beat for Life in American Circles."

"I'm through," said Martin. "That's all. Homer, are you too poor to buy a drink? If the worst came to the worst, I'd treat you."

"Made your fortune?" asked Homer agreeably. "Listen, Martin, do you mean it about going?"

"You heard me," Martin said. He took a cocktail glass from the waiter's approaching tray. "Never mind such elegant service, chico," he told the man; "just run back and throw the stuff together again. Mud in your eye," he said to Homer and Carriker, "and I hope you rot to a ripe old age down here."

"Well, can you tie that!" said Carriker. "I'll bet he really is going!"

"Why don't you stick on in Havana, Martin?" asked Homer Loren. Homer made a practice of avoiding surprise. His long brown face with the patches of wiry gray hair lying close on his oblong skull above his ears, far behind his temples, showed a certain alertness. "One would presume you understood figures," he said; "I'd risk it to the extent of a position in the Cuba-American Publishing Company. I expect to need a treasurer about next week. I can't say it has a future, but the present would be made about twice as good as anything your bank ever had."

"Thanks," said Martin, indifferent. Homer had the reputation for being singularly gifted in the choice of his executives. Homer would like to have Martin, and the generosity of his offer was flavored a little with his intelligent self-interest. "Thanks," repeated Martin, displeased by this realization, "that's nice of you, Homer. But I'm through with Cuba." He felt the gradual warmth of the cocktails in his stomach and it helped him over a natural moment of doubt, a fear that he might be a fool to face the unfriendly North after all these years. "Stay and rot," he said. "Lots of good men are doing it."

"You must have made money," said Carriker, who sold automobiles and knew ways of spending what he made faster than he made it. "If I could get a dollar ahead, I'll bet I'd leave myself. Everything's going to go bust. Every sugar mill in the Island."

"What do you know about it?" Homer said. He was suddenly aggressive, as though a button marked "Future of Cuba" had been pushed, switching on power.

"Homer believes all that drivel he prints in the *Mail*," Carriker said, recognizing it. "If people don't make money, they can't spend it. How you made yours, I'd like to know."

"You're crazy to go North if you haven't money, Martin," Homer said seriously. "When you've been away as long as you have it's no joke to break in."

"If the liquor doesn't kill you up there, the climate will," Carriker said. "When you've been in the tropics over fifteen years your blood gets thin. Fact. Scientific fact. You'll get pneumonia the first winter and that's the end of you."

"Bunk," said Homer. "Never mind what you will get. What have you got now, in cash? If you're bound you're going, I'd lend you five or ten thousand. So don't high-hat me. How much cash have you got?"

"I've got some,"said Martin. "I have enough for another drink, anyway."

"What you need is about a hundred thousand," said Homer, almost malicious. He was a little hurt, Martin saw. He was used to arranging other people's business for them. Here, however, was one business Martin couldn't possibly hand to him. It was a matter strictly between Celia and himself. If she didn't mind the prospects of the future—

"You're a fool not to stay with the bank, at least," said Homer. "Wouldn't Spofford let you transfer? I'll bet you if I went and had a talk with him, he'd—"

"No, he wouldn't," snapped Martin. It would be like Homer to have, as he said, a talk with the General Manager for Cuba. "Spofford's a good friend of mine. I can get anything out of him he has to give. I tell you, I'm sick of it. I've just been a sucker! They'd keep me down the island the rest of my life if they could. They know what I'm good for. I don't mind saying, and you know it's true, that I was the best man they ever had. Every branch they gave me I made a business of. I'll bet you I've been worth a million dollars to them in my day—" He stopped, surprised at the note of anger in this unbecoming boasting of his. "What do you suppose these glasses are for?"

"Let 'er go!" sighed Homer. "The least I can do is get pie-eyed over your departure. George isn't even here yet. We'll have to swim to dinner."

"Where is George?" asked Martin, conscious abruptly of this important absence.

"Believe his outfit dropped a peseta in the Calle Compostela. All hands helping to find it. No wonder bankers go loony. He's coming. He'll be here."

"There he is," said Carriker. "I'm glad I'm not a big money man, much as I like money. You never get to have a drink. All right, George, we're ready to start."

George Biehl was short, rather than heavy. His face was some-what full, but firm and well-shaped. "Good to see you, Martin," he said. His brown eyes were frankly affectionate. He shook hands hard. "Start?" he echoed Carriker. "Joe looks pretty near finished to me."

"Find your money?" said Homer.

"I expect I shouldn't answer that," said George, "but I will. Your rag will have it Tuesday anyway. We've had a horrible jolt, to be candid. A teller who left us about a month ago had been taking us along—slickest system I've seen yet. They're in a panic, let me tell you. The auditors have out a hurry call to all branches to see how many other people thought up the same game. Sit still, Homer; I told you Tuesday would be time enough."

"That's tough," said Martin. He knew George's position so perfectly that he found himself already at mental work, his own long experience in exigencies of local banking automatically operating. "It won't do you much good, will it? With tomorrow Sunday, and the next day a holiday, you'll have a job rounding your branches up."

"Don't I know it?" groaned George Biehl. "When I left your outfit, Martin, I said that you people had the only system. Did these saps listen to me? They thought I'd better mind my own business. They—"

George, Martin told himself, never should have gone over. You could pass a tractor through those accounts. He—it was, thank Heaven, George's business. He was through.

"You look surprised," said Homer dryly, "and I'll bet you between your two organizations I could name twenty men I've known personally who've walked out with the cash. Must be the climate, or do you suppose bankers are just naturally a little slow?"

"We aren't so slow," said George Biehl, plainly stung into exaggeration. "Every one of those twenty got caught, too. They only do it because they're sort of crazy, and when you're crazy you don't see things. They always do something so dumb you can't believe it."

"How much did he take along?" Homer asked.

"You may think you're pumping me," said George, "but you're not. How much he took is none of your business. It's the crazy system we use—"

"Ours wouldn't be any better if a really shrewd hand had a whack at it," said Martin soothingly. The system, he recalled, was, whatever its points, no longer his. "Yes," said George, "but you can watch really shrewd hands. They're big enough to watch usually. This boy got more than he's bonded for, I'll admit; but I'm surprised he didn't take the office furniture too. We never would have known. Pretty nice for him, if we don't catch him. Wouldn't mind being young with a big pile like that for a start up North myself."

"So you think you have to be young and have a big pile," said Martin. He found himself facing with increased reluctance any mention of his own plans. "Well," he said, "better late than never seems plausible to me. I'm leaving Cuba, George."

"You're what?" said George.

It was a fact, Homer told him. "Martin's got the willies."

"Say, are you joking?" said George. He was blank with amazement and a dismay which made Martin wince a little. "Listen, did you have a scrap with Spofford? I can tell you right here and now that you can have — well, you can have Santiago right this minute, if you'll — "

"Wouldn't that be wonderful?" said Martin.

"I don't know what's come over him," said Homer. "He hasn't any money and he hasn't any sense and he's fifty if he's a day."

"What I have got's quite a thirst," said Martin, impatient.

"Well," said Homer, "at least you haven't any family to worry about. If you invested your life savings nicely, in about five thousand years — "

"That's right," said Carriker; "that makes a lot of difference."

Carriker did have a family. A wife and quite a number of children in a Vedado bungalow. He never mentioned them; and, tacitly, neither did anyone else.

"All right," said George. He hadn't finished his objections, that was plain; he merely postponed them. "Martin can stand another drink. He can stand anything. Often wish I had his stomach." Martin wondered fleetingly if George thought anything would be gained by getting Martin drunk. He decided that George wasn't so simple. That would be the sort of thing Carriker might think of.

Homer Loren was showing what he had drunk already. He often did before dinner. "You shouldn't drink so much," Homer observed generally. "You can't stand it in this climate. Half Martin's willies are just those cocktails they make in the cane. No ice and who knows where the rum comes from?"

"It comes from Santiago," said Martin, "and every *bohio* has an electric refrigerator these days. It's called raising the standard of living, and it's what you yap about in the Wail every Thursday afternoon. Don't run it down now; people will think you aren't sincere."

"Matter of fact," said Homer, "I'm not. I wouldn't be found dead that way."

George Biehl groaned slightly. "This is going to be philosophy. We'll have to get some food into him." Carriker leaned back in his chair and shouted through the open arches into the street, "Taxi!"

"Do you good to walk," said George.

"Something tells me this is going to be a hard evening."

"I've got to get in early," Martin told him. "Got a boat to catch early tomorrow."

"No, no," said Homer, "that's nonsense! Tomorrow's Easter. Don't you know that? Monday's a holiday. Tuesday you might leave, or a week from Tuesday."

"Can't be done," said Martin.

"What do you mean, it can't be done?"

"There are reasons," said Martin.

"He's got the willies," Homer repeated. "The tropics have ruined him. He was like to throw away his shoes and go native. He thinks this is the South Seas. This, let me tell you, is the Paris of America, and has the lowest death rate in—"

Sitting in the restaurant's electric-lighted cavern they could see the dusk deepening on the green trees and gardens of the Parque Central. The lights of the Plaza roof were clear against the sky and advertising signs about beer and chocolate had been turned on.

Carriker said that the trouble with Havana was that you couldn't do anything until twelve o'clock.

"We could get a carriage and drive down along the Malecon a

ways," said Martin. "The water's nice. Or it used to be." He felt
very comfortable, torpid perhaps; but a certain sadness constantly
crept up in his mind. He even thought of Sancti Spiritus without
impatience now. Its serenity of night coming down; the peace of
the paved roof on his former house—he could sit and watch the
moon, when there was a moon, in an amazing stillness over the
stream and the three ancient humps of the Spanish bridge. There
would be nothing like that in the North, nothing but trouble,
doubts, and difficulties.

Homer said: "Who wants to drive in a carriage? Let's go down
to the Sevilla bar."

Martin regretted the suggestion only a moment. It would be
better, he saw, to get a little drunk. As soon as that happened, he
could trust an old instinct of his to nag at him until he broke away
and went home. That was the bank still, he saw; as though it were
in his blood. He had always had responsibilities and he had learned
to a hair's breadth where responsibility wavered. Carriker said,
pleasantly resigned: "You must want to make it a bat."

Moving down the Prado, it was George who put an arm through
his, walking a little behind Homer and Carriker. "What's on your
mind, Martin?" he said suddenly.

"I may tell you," Martin answered. It was unexpected even to
himself. He was surprised to realize that he wanted to talk to
anyone, that he felt any need to get anything off his chest. They
turned off, into the Sevilla, and in the bar they sat under a potted
orange tree in the corner.

"Well," said Martin at once, "I might as well explain why I'm
leaving tomorrow morning. This isn't any of your business, but I
dare say I do owe you an explanation. As it happens, I'm not
alone. That's all."

Now it was out, in unmistakable words, Martin at once wished
that it wasn't. It was immediately tainted, as though their three
minds got hands on it, leaving smears of the sordid and scandalous.
Homer said with a vast, somber satisfaction: "Martin, I knew
something was up. A woman, eh?"

Martin said: "I'll tell you what you need to know. Don't ask me." They all thought, he saw, that he meant a Cuban woman; some girl who might have been his mistress. George said finally: "Martin, you know how I feel about you, so you'll listen to me. You're crazy. I'm not going to let you do anything like that. I'll take care of it. I'll put you up at my place tonight and see that she gets sent back. Now—"

"You haven't got it right," Martin said. "I wasn't asking for help. Everything is all arranged. I just wanted to tell you why I can't stay in Cuba."

George looked at him with intent concern. "Then it's that McLaughlin chap's wife," he said abruptly. "I had an idea when I was up there a couple of years ago—"

"Never mind your ideas," Martin said. "You'll have to think what you like, George, but don't say any of it."

Carriker ruminated: "McLaughlin." He concluded: "Federated Sugar. Jacinto. It's going to make a stink, isn't it?"

George Biehl was drinking Fundador. The brandy looked almost black in the small glass, twisting steadily in his fingers. Martin found himself imagining the hot and heartening taste of it. He said: "I'll have some of that, and then let's go out of here. I don't want to meet a lot of people."

"Right," said George. George could see well enough why he didn't want to meet a lot of people. "Where would you like to go, Martin?" George's voice was always gentler when he was troubled or dismayed. Turning a critical eye on these three friends, Martin realized that George was the only one who mattered to him—he started to say, the only decent one; but he checked himself. Joe Carriker and Homer were fine fellows. They didn't come finer. He had, in fact, owed them an explanation, and he ought to be glad that he had made it.

Carriker had changed the subject elaborately. He was suggesting, with a delicate indirection, to Homer that he himself might consider the job Homer had offered Martin. Carriker managed it with his usual loud and cheerful humor. Only now that he was older, his hair gray, the geniality seemed hollow. Close to pan-handling in fact. Carriker was probably in a tight place. His big

hands were nervous on the table. Heaven only knew how much
money he owed or how bad he was finding business in an era which
had discarded the boisterous familiarities, the slipshod personal
approaches of his youth.

Homer Loren was again a little drunk, but he was not unwary.
He knew that Carriker was trying to get something out of him and
he had—plainly to everyone but Carriker—no intention of allowing it to happen. His dark face was lopsided, with a chill small
smile; his eyes were tightened in cynical slant. Looking at him, it
seemed to Martin that Homer had always been a trifle too astute.
The faint evil miasma one sensed while reading the *Evening Mail*
clung to him. He was tainted with the callous corruption, the
unabashed bribes and shameless subsidies of the government.
Martin felt a chill, a cold malaise; for he seemed to have now
Cuba, his past, his cherished friends spread before him. He saw
their decay, the ruin of the years. Next, he knew, he would begin
to think about himself, about Celia, about life and the future.

George said: "Let's take a motor out to Wirth's."

The others had drunk enough to go anywhere, anywhere rather
than home. It was, indeed, the decisive moment. You had to
choose now between departure—accepting the sad silence and
depression of the night, satisfied to know that tomorrow things
might look better—or staying, recklessly forcing things to look
better right now, heedless of the certain miseries of the morning.
George, he saw, had made up his mind. George was not going to
desert him. George would be there when dawn came; Martin could
count on this companionship to get him through until it was
tomorrow and he left Cuba forever.

At midnight Homer was very drunk. Carriker, oddly enough,
was considerably less so. He seemed to entertain some only
half-tipsy notion that Homer might get drunk enough to promise
him what he wanted. The party had been augmented by two slight,
dark-eyed, tan-colored girls who sipped grenadine and water,
submitting to Homer's attentions. Carriker's problem made him
sweat. He didn't want to annoy Homer by interruptions, but

neither did he want Homer to pass out altogether without giving him a chance to get a word in. When the latter occured, about half past two, Carriker, in despair, defeated the girls' intention of taking this rich man in charge. Martin was cold with disgust and weariness but George remained complaisant. He said: "Go on, Joe, take him home."

Carriker agreed. He'd see that no harm came to Homer. Homer was his dear old pal. They were the next thing to brothers. "So long, Martin, old scout," he said. "Better not leave. Stay around and have a wonderful time. Wonderful time every night." There was nothing to be done about this.

"Good-by," said Martin. "Good luck, Joe."

George said that they might as well go back to town, but he didn't purpose going to bed. "Neither do I," Martin said. "I'd like to see how Celia is. We can get some coffee."

In the taxi George said: "I don't get on so well with those two any more. I'm sort of sorry for Joe, but he's getting to be an awful nuisance. Homer's all right as long as you don't want him to do anything for you."

"He offered to lend me ten thousand dollars," Martin told him. "I think he really meant it."

"He did," admitted George. "He really respects you. You're one of the few people he knows who isn't a shyster of some sort. That's why I sort of hate to see you quitting, myself, Martin." He became suddenly voluble, faintly impatient. "I don't like this business about the lady. You know what you're doing, only I sort of wish it hadn't happened. I have an idea that you both got worked up. Just got bored and kicked the works over the mill. Either that—now don't get mad—or it was her idea. She sold it to you."

"That's not true," said Martin.

George looked at him in the dim moving light. "I guess maybe it is," he said. "If she hadn't been there, you wouldn't have done it. You'd have hung on. I don't say she asked you, but I'll bet she just worked on you and —"

Martin sat with his legs thrust out, swaying to the jolt of the taxi.

In his nervous, half-nauseated wakefulness he could understand George's point. There was, in a way, a perverted truth in it, he supposed. "Listen," he said, "it's true I couldn't do anything else, if that's what you mean. I simply couldn't stand it. Celia doesn't get on with McLaughlin and—"

George grunted with a sort of resignation. What he saw was perfectly plain. Another good man gone wrong would describe it well enough. One more irregular exit after many decent and devoted years. There was a miserable, even frightening, monotony about men leaving Cuba that way. He said now: "How did Spofford take it?"

"I doubt if he knows yet," said Martin. "I wrote in. I didn't want him to get it until Tuesday, when I'd be gone. I've got a good assistant out there. He can carry on perfectly well."

George was plainly shocked. "You shouldn't have done that, Martin," he protested. "That's a rotten trick on Spofford."

Martin said wearily: "Maybe I shouldn't have technically. You don't seem to get the idea yet. I tell you I couldn't go it. And if I was going to leave, I had to leave like that; not after three weeks of chatter with Spofford and waiting around until he found someone else, with everyone knowing that I was going—"

"I'm not dumb," said George gloomily. "That's the lady, just as I said. You had to get off when you got the chance. Well, I guess you care a lot about her and that's your business. Only I don't mind saying that I hate to think of you getting out sort of secretly that way, leaving the bank in the lurch and taking along someone else's wife."

He said it without scorn or active accusation. He was simply depressed. Martin felt sorry, not resentful. George had still his own troubles to face; a scandal of his own, you might say, breaking on the front pages Tuesday. He glanced out and saw that they were passing the Christo Church. The doors were open and lights on; early Easter masses had begun and he watched a moment, curious, while dark muffled figures went in.

"Well," he said to George, "happy Easter. Here we are. We can probably get some coffee. I'll just run upstairs and see if Celia's all right."

George nodded. A sleepy clerk slouched in a chair behind the desk and George asked him about coffee. The clerk thought that there was a pot on the stove. He would see. Did the señor wish to use the elevator?

"I'll walk," Martin said.

His legs were tired and he couldn't think why he said it; he might have been trying to put off the moment when he would have to consider Celia as a concrete fact, not merely a theory of which George disapproved. He paused a moment in the shadows of the first floor. His stomach felt unpleasant and his head swam slightly.

It was about four o'clock, he guessed, and he ought to feel all right. Well, he was getting old! You mustn't expect to carry on the way you could once. He mounted the second flight and moved slowly down the hall, still breathing thickly. He waited a moment until this had quieted and then he inserted the key.

Street light from the corner reached part of the wall, printing a slim column of radiance near the shutters. Celia lay much as he had left her, and he was obscurely reassured. He would not like to think that she had awakened and been worried. He sat down a moment on the edge of the other bed, looking at her in the shadows, trying halfheartedly to take some sort of stock of the situation. He could make out the lax, inert line of her hip; her hair, dark in this gloom, stood out against the pillow into which her face was half sunk.

He could not think of anything in particular. He was very tired and only a disjoined series of recollections came to him: little informal dances at his house; small dinner parties at Jacinto; the American engineers from the sugar mills; Celia and the color of the dresses she had worn. George's remark remained with him — taking along someone else's wife — and it annoyed him. It carried a kind of contempt, which George had managed to expunge in the saying, but which was back now. He couldn't, somehow, think of Celia in such a position — open in any way to contempt. He might

almost have left Celia behind. Here in this hot room he sat with
somebody else. Despite everything, Celia might remain
grave-eyed, without reproach, in the gardens at Jacinto.

This sense of change or error was so acute that he got up
sharply. George might, then, be right. Kicked the works over the
mill! Something like that would have to happen before he could
persuade her. Now, at this truer point, he didn't think he would
have tried; he wouldn't surely have been able to make her do
anything so alien to her even if he had tried. Aloud, he said:
"What's done is done." It sounded rather silly, strained, in the
darkness, and he looked back quickly, for fear that he might have
awakened her. She made no move, however, and he turned to the
door. His attention was taken a moment by something on the
bureau.

His fingers found it to be an envelope and he was immediately
angered, thinking that after all they had disobeyed his instructions
downstairs. He was about to take it out with him when, standing
still, he had another idea.

Without moving, barely breathing, he ripped the flap. He
pressed a hand into his pocket and brought out a cigarette lighter.
The wheel rasped his thumb twice and a flame jumped up, yellow
on the enclosed sheet.

He looked at it quietly. He had never, it seemed to him, heard a
silence so tremendous as Havana's at this hour before dawn. Not a
sound, not a sound. No breathing but his own, and he looked
slowly where the radiance extended onto the bureau, and saw that
the veronal bottle was empty.

His solitary breath came hoarser now, quite loud, but he moved
silently. He pushed the paper into his pocket, stepped out. The
door caused a slight click, closing; and he locked it. He stood there
a moment with the little flame of the lighter still burning in his
hand, the small light shaking on his face. Then, starting, he
snapped the cap down and went deliberately to the stairs.

George Biehl was sitting in the corner with coffee in front of
him. He looked bad, Martin saw. His face was thickened, discol-
ored under the damp skin. Shadows from the bare bulbs of the

lamps clung to his chin like cobwebs. His eyes, dark, sunken a little, were bloodshot. "Hello," he said, "this will do you good." His cheerfulness was brittle. "Do you feel as rotten as I do?" he asked. "It's pretty near five o'clock."

Martin drew up a chair and set himself on it. "Well," he said, and his voice sounded remote to him, "this is a funny way for it to end. When did we first come down here, George? Twenty-two years ago. And here we are."

"Take some coffee," said George, "and have a heart. I'm not going to say anything more. If I could get out of here, I would. Go to it."

"Look," said Martin. He took a wallet from his pocket and removed a thick packet of American bills.

"All right," said George, "all right. I hope you have more."

"I have," said Martin. "It's no good to me. I'd give it to you if I could."

George Biehl stared at him. "What are you, crazy? Have a fight with the lady? Have—"

"Ninety thousand dollars in the brown suitcase," said Martin. "Here's the key. She knew. She couldn't go it."

George Biehl's thickened face, the wide eyes that looked bruised, remained on him, stupid.

"You could have figured it out," said Martin. "You said it yourself. We all do something so dumb you can't believe it. I had four days clear and everything clicked—it was good, George; not like a teller. Only I should have stayed in last night. Turn it over to Spofford. Oh, Celia's dead, of course. I'll want about five minutes before you call the police."

George Biehl sat perfectly still. His throat made a sort of croak but he didn't say anything. His hands with the swollen veins starting out of their backs lay in a paralysis on the round table top, palms to the marble. He could hear Martin's steps on the stairs for some time, receding. There followed at last a deep silence while he remained stiff, motionless. His heart seemed likely to stop if this lasted much longer.

His heart didn't stop, though; it beat on thickly, shaking him. He needn't have listened so hard, for the sound, breaking clean without a warning and no echo, was muffled very little. His heart had jumped then; it seemed to hit his gullet and fall back; but it beat right on. The clerk had come to his feet, chair clattering, his head poking out blank and wide-eyed across the desk.

George Biehl made his hands lie quiet.

"All right. That's all right," he said mildly. "Go on, boy. Go on. Telephone the police."

PART FIVE

EYES TO SEE

I was fifteen when my mother unexpectedly died. Doctor Charles Maitland, my father, was forty-seven. Because of a then prevailing social convention, women's ages were never mentioned so I know only that my mother was considerably younger than my father. Her health had always been excellent; and since women as a rule live longer than men, the thought that she would die before he did had probably never crossed their minds.

It happened this way. One autumn morning she awoke with a slight earache, which she ascribed to having "caught cold" in her ear during a drive in an open automobile the night before. Though my father had a regular medical degree, he did no general practice. Today he would be called a psychiatrist. The term was known then —the *Journal of Nervous & Mental Disease,* one of the publications to which my father often contributed, described itself as devoted to "Neurology and Psychiatry"; but medical directories listed my father as a neurologist or neuropathologist. He served on the staffs of several hospitals and institutions; and there his usual title was: Consultant in Abnormal Psychology. When he came before a court to testify on mental competence in sanity hearings he was referred to as an alienist.

Still, he was qualified to practice ordinary medicine; and for trifles like this the custom of not treating members of one's own family wouldn't obtain. He dropped in a little hot sweet oil and plugged the ear with cotton. My mother said she didn't feel feverish; but, toward night, my father's physician's eye apparently told him he'd better take her temperature, notwithstanding. He did so; and what he read made him at once call a friend, a local general practitioner, who tentatively diagnosed (as doubtless my father already had) a developing infection of the middle ear, probably streptococcal.

Today, most such infections are easily and promptly controlled. At that time, the matter was much graver. Few medical men cared to so state the case; but, actually, treatment amounted to little more than waiting with the hope that this would clear up by itself. Meanwhile my mother was given a quarter-grain morphine sulfate injection to make her more comfortable; and my father continued such injections as required over the next couple of days. Whatever their hopes, her temperature did not drop; and my father and his general-practitioner friend were obliged to see that, far from clearing up by itself, the condition was worsening. There remained nothing for it but the risky course of surgical intervention.

On short notice, the fraternal bond of the profession brought together in the operating room the three most eminent otolaryngologists of the day. Alas, to no avail. Ready there for the using, the whole sum of their skill and experience became useless when the one of them who had undertaken to operate, delicately chipping away the mastoid process, exposed the site. The operator put down his instruments. Nothing said, the three of them looked at each other. It was evident that the cranial cavity had been entered by oozing pus. However, good might be said to have resulted from their work. They had greatly aggravated the condition. With no exploratory operation, my mother might have survived for a bad week. As it was, she went into coma soon after she came down from the operating room. Never recovering consciousness, she died ten hours later.

*

I was up at school. I knew nothing of my mother's illness until the day of the operation. The decision to attempt it had been reached late in the morning; and my father, the first chance he got, tried to telephone, so I could come down on the afternoon train. Long-distance calls were not common then, and seldom got through quickly. Moreover, that day there was to be special difficulty in completing a connection. It was the late October Saturday afternoon of one of our more important football games. The school took its football with such seriousness that not only the entire student body, but absolutely everyone, down to the kitchen help, was at the field for the kickoff. Telephones might ring in the Administration Building or the headmaster's study; but no one would be answering them before the last whistle blew.

The game was a most exciting one. The first quarter had hardly opened when, horrified, we saw our quarterback fumble, the ball bounding, to be snatched by one of our opponents who, with nobody in a position to block him, ran it half the length of the field for a touchdown. The kick for the extra point, however, failed. This solitary score would seem to have been just what it looked like, a piece of luck; for, after that, the teams, well-matched (as in "important" games they usually were), proceeded to play each other to a standstill. With only minutes left of the last quarter, the score was the same six to nothing against us. We had the ball; third down; ten to go. In those days, signals were called aloud; so we learned with muted groans that a kick formation, meaning we purposed to relinquish the ball, was coming up.

Our left halfback, our best kicker, moved into position to punt; but actually what was coming up was something then known as a Trick Play. Plays of this kind had been solemnly worked out in secret drills. They were never used in less important games, nor indeed in any game unless the situation became desperate enough for the coach to make a special sign to the quarterback. The idea was that as the season drew on, scouts of our various opponents would have learned all our team's usual plays, and prepared their teams for them. But for what would happen now, they might not be prepared. They weren't. Seeing the kick formation, our opponents had disposed themselves according to the book; ends out, ready to try to get through and block that kick; backfield dispersed, ready to receive the ball wherever it might go.

Our center duly put the ball in play; but it did not go to the left halfback. It went at an angle, to right-half. He retired a dozen feet, turned; and pegged a ten-yard forward pass to our quarterback, who had run out straight left and stood waiting. As he closed his hands on the ball, our fullback (misleadingly stationed as though to keep the kick from being blocked) raced across in front of him, and was now ready, with our left end, to run a two-man interference.

The elaborately arranged timing was all good. Interference efficiently took out the two of our opponents' tacklers whose positions made them most dangerous. We could have had our touchdown, except that our opponents' farthest back defensive man managed, by an amazing dash, to get across the field, and nail our runner. Still, first down was now on their two-yard line; and, as often happens, surprise had so shattered them that the next play, nothing but an ordinary center line buck, scored. Cheering from our side, though fervid, quickly died. That best kicker of ours, the left-half, was setting himself with a show of calm he could hardly have felt, to make his place kick. Amid a fallen agonized hush, both stands watched him. Moving with deliberation, nervous or not, he took a couple of steps and booted the ball fair and square over the bar between the goal posts. Time had run out; so at the completion of this play, the whistle blew.

With an enormous erupting roar, our side rose up, the stands emptying onto the field. Members of the school band, running helter-skelter out, blowing brass and pounding drums, headed what soon became a disorganized snake dance and general roughhouse. Working his way through this pandemonium, a prefect who had been sent to find me finally located me. He had to yell "Maitland!" several times before I realized I was being called. I stopped my wrestling with another fellow, and out of breath, and wondering what I had done now, I answered, "Yes, sir?" I was told I was to report to the headmaster in the Field House at once. Winning the game made everyone feel good, so he condescended kindly to add: "I think it's just someone's trying to telephone you."

Relieved, but also puzzled—members of the student body then practically never got telephone calls—I started toward the Field

House. Many of the big maple trees on the slope beyond still held a few colored leaves which some last shafts of level sunlight touched to bright orange and bright gold. On the keen chill mostly hill-shadowed clear air the continued shouts and cheers, the boom of drums and blare of horns carried after me. Under the pillars of the long Field House porch, groups of older people, alumni and guests were talking and laughing. On my best behavior, I made my way, apologizing, through them. Inside, in the main hall, players of both teams were beginning to come up from the locker rooms, showered and dressed, hair slicked with water, bearing their mostly big frames with an air of modest worth as they moved toward the Trophy Room where open fires gave off a smell of wood smoke, and several masters' wives were pouring tea.

Someone must have been watching for me. I had no more than got into the hall when the headmaster appeared. Drawing me aside, he said in sober tones that he was sorry to tell me that there'd been word from my father. My mother was ill. I was to go right up to school. I had his permission to use the telephone in his study. I was to call my father at a number written on a piece of paper, which he gave me. By then, calling my father was all I could do, for the afternoon train had gone an hour ago. The next day, Sunday, there would be no train until almost noon.

Alone in the dusk-filled study, seated with some diffidence at the headmaster's desk, I finally got my father. The number I had been given was that of a hospital, so I couldn't doubt the matter was serious. For his part, my father, coming to the telephone, by then knew there was no hope. While he was left waiting in the hospital director's room; while, up here, that exciting football game proceeded quarter by quarter and long-distance operators rang the deserted school without result, the side of my mother's head was shaved and painted with iodine, she was sent up in the elevator; and an anesthetist, chatting pleasantly as long as she could hear him, administered ether; the gowned eminent specialists entered; the operation commenced; and they were not long in finding what they found.

However, of his certain knowledge that my mother was dying,

my father said nothing. Of how she was, he said no more than that
a serious operation had been necessary. Agitated, I explained
about the gone train. Composed enough, my father said: "All right,
Dick. Take the train tomorrow. I'll meet you if I can; but if you
don't see me, get a taxi and come up to the hospital. I've arranged
with the school office for you to have money."

I said: "All right, Father. I'm awfully worried." Perhaps to
prove I was, I said: "If Mother should be better in the morning, I
mean, before I leave, could you — "

My father said: "There'd be no point in calling again, Dick. We
wouldn't then know any more than we know now. Just be on the
train." He was quite right. I didn't need to worry about how my
mother would be in the morning. In the morning she would be
dead; and I would find that what I had come down from school for
was her funeral.

*

Funeral services for my mother were held the following Wednesday, and many people attended — so many, they packed the
church. What number I would have expected to come I don't
know; but the sight of this crowd amazed me. Blinking, I stared
down the dim-lit long nave to the radiant candle glow at the
chancel steps where a bank of flowers hid my mother's casket; and
the evident multitude filled me with dismay, with an agitated
uncertainty of mind. What kept coming to me was the absurd,
disturbed idea that there was some mistake, that all these people,
or many of them at any rate, might have set out for some other
funeral, not my mother's, and come to the wrong church. A
guarded glance or two was showing me numbers of ill-seen faces I
didn't know, men and women I could not name. Who were they?
Why were they here? When and where did they know my mother?
Or had they never known her; and if so —

I can see now the factors that worked to throw me into dismay.
Though differently brought on by this incomprehensible press
of strange people arranged in hushed rows, no one speaking,
all watchful, while the organ muted to a murmur played somber

music, my feeling was simply that recurring feeling of the unreal, the fantastic, the outright incredible, which had been breaking over me every little while since, getting down from school Sunday afternoon, I found out what had happened. The feeling's meaning seems plain enough now: but of course it wasn't plain to me then. The situation confronting me was one I wasn't able to, hadn't the experience to—actually, wasn't old enough to—understand. Naturally, I would then have rejected any such explanation. To itself, each human mind's understanding always seems adequate; and this will be still truer if the mind is a child's mind. Moreover, I saw myself as quite old enough to understand anything—not a child. (Children were boys of ten or eight or younger.) About that, I wasn't wholly wrong; I had come to a stage where satisfaction with my capacity to understand could not prevent or relieve me from certain misgivings, new to me, about the extent of my knowledge. What I did not know might not hurt me; but beginning to know I did not know could now oppress me with vague unnamable forebodings. That which was to be demonstrated lay beyond the then-grasp of my awareness; but only a little beyond.

What began Sunday afternoon had been an apprehending of the world not mine, that world I never made. My thoughts, anxious and ill at ease, moved restless about this habitation where they kept—the safe house of infancy; the child's walled garden— troubled now with presentiments of what might be the true situation. Just outside the garden wall, could there lie savage wasteland, blasted heath, darkling plain; whence, on rising winds of night and storm, were wafted confused alarms, now first heard, of struggle and of flight? Life in the garden might not be real life. It must follow that much of what I believed true could be untrue; that many opinions of mine could be mistaken; and if I wanted to know what I actually knew: why, I knew nothing at all.

In short, the idea of the "mistake" had power to disturb me not because it was an absurd idea; but because, in some ways, it wasn't. I came, in fact, near the mark. I wasn't ready, but I was getting ready, to be able to understand that this multitude did, indeed, set out to attend another funeral, not my mother's. Only I

could attend *that*. These others were attending the funeral of a
woman I never knew; and one (though living most of my life in her
house with her) I never had eyes to see. These others came to bury
a young Mrs. Maitland, wife of Doctor Charles Maitland. Mrs.
Maitland's energetic activity in club work and social service made
many people well acquainted with her. She was the Society for the
Prevention of Cruelty to Children's president. She was a trustee of
Mercy Hospital. She was on the national committee of the
movement, about to be successful, for Woman Suffrage. She was
vice president of her college's alumnae association. She was the
local garden club's secretary. She did a good deal of church work
in connection with the Altar Guild and the Girls Friendly Society.

This woman, Doctor Maitland's wife, used to be a girl named
Katherine Brownell. She had been known as a child, and at school
and college, as Kay. She was apparently a well-liked girl, or, as
they then said, "popular." She seems to have been held "good
looking" by her circle of friends; which would be to say that
nobody considered her a "raving beauty"; yet, by chance of
fashion, the male eye probably found her appearance very
pleasing. She was young at a time when norms of female attractiveness were set by the Gibson girl drawings. They prescribed a firm,
almost preternaturally clean-cut profile; a spirited lift of chin; a
grave, brave gaze; and a carriage in which frankness and modesty
balanced nicely to set off a costume, say, of shirtwaist and straw
boater.

Photographs of Kay at college show these requirements well
met. As natural result, a normal number of young men, considering
themselves captivated, began to pay her attentions more or less
serious. More or less seriously, Kay would receive the attentions.
No doubt she weighed and pondered—first perhaps, her emotional
reactions, her feelings toward this one or that one; but, second,
certainly, practical or material advantages or disadvantages likely
to go with making herself the helpmate of that one or this one. Her
deliberations seem to have been deliberate. Good-looking Kay
may have liked several young men enough to find choice difficult.
On the other hand, though expected and expecting to marry, she

may have felt no immediate desire or need to be married; and so, hardly noticing, let time go by. As Kay delayed or dallied, she got no younger. If choice among boys she liked was the real problem, earlier beaux of hers, put off, could be counted on to simplify it for her by marrying someone else. Kay might be finding new beaux less easy to come by. The consideration could explain her seemingly quick and sudden acceptance of an engagement ring from an older brother of her closest college friend, Dorothy Maitland. The brother was Charles Maitland, who had recently taken his medical degree.

Kay's family may have felt it time, and high time, that Kay married; but apparently they were not altogether pleased with her choice of husband. The doctor was older, five or six years older. As best friends, Kay and Dorothy Maitland might know each other well; and, because Charles was Dorothy's brother, Kay must also have known him—but not well, surely. Even if Charles happened to be home from medical school when Kay was visiting Dorothy, it was unlikely that he would spend much time with Dorothy's friends, the younger set that entertained Kay. This wasn't to say that his sister's house guest mightn't have taken his fancy (and he taken hers) on earlier visits; but the surprise caused by the announcement did suggest that neither Kay nor the doctor, when Kay arrived for her usual two summer weeks with Dorothy, expected any such thing. Kay's parents, unprepared for Kay's coming back engaged, might reasonably wonder if Kay had given this important matter enough thought. Shouldn't she be warned: Marry in haste and repent at leisure?

In probably exasperating fact, the objections, though valid to the Brownells, may have been hard to state. The difference in age could not be much of an objection. Men tended to be older than girls they married; and in a physician's case this must be almost the rule. Medical education was long; and few students could be in a position to marry before they were licensed and in practice. Still, that brought up a point of its own, not less real for being less than rational. Most girls (if for no other reason than that the number of doctors is limited) don't marry doctors. Why must Kay marry one?

To make this point still more troublesome was her young doctor's clearly eccentric election to shun general practice and devote himself to pathoneurology—in short, to work only with patients potentially or actually insane. Then, though Charles Maitland and his immediate family could not be called socially unacceptable, those with Kay's best interest at heart (her own family) did not quite forget that the name Maitland, borne by an aunt of the doctor's, had been attached to a scandal that, a couple of decades ago, got newspaper space, and much of it, in newspapers throughout the country. They had no desire to rake up a past for which nobody now living could fairly be held responsible; but—

But Kay had made her choice and was not to be moved. The objections no doubt remained objections; but persistence in them, such as public indication that Kay was marrying against her family's wishes, must threaten its own kind of scandal. Her parents had to give way; and indeed the threat was only to be obviated by giving way with ostentatious good grace. As a result the objecting Brownells were at pains to provide their daughter with a wedding so elaborate that the (you could be sure) much offended Maitlands were mollified or more than mollified and the happy day ended all smiles and civility.

Pronounced man and wife, Kay and the doctor left on a wedding trip. They went to Niagara Falls, for some reason then regarded (even by people of cultivation) as an ideal place to initiate women in sexual intercourse. Put up at a good hotel where, as always in June, most of the guests were other couples similarly occupied, Kay took her fortnight of instruction. Whether with the possible transports of physical pleasure, whether with the dismay and disrelish that the then-proper upbringing of girls seems planned to ensure, she was shown the vital mechanics of the male; and the way brides are to accommodate them was inculcated. Disembarrassed of her virginity in this setting of scenic wonder, she then returned with the doctor to begin everyday married life.

The average young woman, if her wedded luck is proving anything less than awful in that matter of the marriage of true minds, is bound to have positive satisfactions—her dignified new status as matron; the novel interests and prides of homemaking, of running her own house. Pleased and busied by them, she is unlikely to admit impediment from the routine of the marriage bed. Even if *that* still seems to her one of her new life's drawbacks, custom must make it one of no great moment. Not necessarily with passion, but with instinctive affection and feelings of tenderness, Kay, complying, would before long find herself very little constrained in acting her part of woman as regularly as she and the night and the double bed gave rise to fresh urgence in the doctor to act the man.

However, the normal consequences when the male is freely permitted in his lawful pleasure were slow to follow. On the chance that the difficulty might be physiological, Kay at length consulted a gynecologist rated high by medical associates of my father's. He seems to have suspected a degree of malposition in the uterus and showed Kay exercises supposed to be corrective. Today their efficacy would be doubted; and indeed, though she performed them faithfully, many more months passed before Kay finally did become pregnant. In defense of the outdated gynecologist it might be said that no difficulties of a kind to prove his diagnosis wrong developed in parturition. Kay was safely and quite easily delivered of a healthy male infant—me.

*

I have summed up here as well as I can what would seem to have been the actual facts about my mother. They are almost altogether facts which I was to learn later, facts not available to me at the time of my mother's death. Some of them, as I've said, I couldn't then have grasped because I hadn't quite grasped the nature of things; some, I simply didn't grasp; some, I actively refused to grasp. Few or none of them had part in shaping the image I denominated Mother—my view of her. In that view, the child's customary view, her *real* reality, like the *real* reality of everything else, depended in simple Berkeleian terms on the presence, to perceive it, of the child's consciousness. As far as I was concerned, before my time she simply wasn't; and in the same way she would cease to exist whenever she went places or did things without me. The image itself was static in a vacuum where no laws of life or time operated; immanent in that everlasting now of beginning consciousness, that solipsistic world where the younger child lives. Unchangeable, the image could not be imagined in any sequence of becoming—as a baby, a schoolgirl, or as the "popular" unwed Kay of college days (who might so very well have married some other man, not Dorothy Maitland's brother; with its consequence, inescapable but inconceivable, that I would have been some other boy, not I).

The refused facts, the facts I balked at grasping, were of course those forbidden my mind for what amounted to moral cause. At fifteen I had been long aware of what a man did with a woman to have children; but, for much longer, factors of environment, of precept and example had been conditioning me to regard with almost awful reverence the image I had made. In reason, imagined images must go down before known facts; but, resenting and resisting fact, human thinking, even when adult, seeks out many inventions—not least useful of them, that sleight of mind by which reason, found an incorrigible disturber of the peace, is bound over to be debarred and disregarded. Reason might reason: All children are a result of sexual commerce. A child was begotten on my mother. Therefore . . . But reason got no further. The conclusion was unthinkable; sacrilegious, even. And, moreover, absurd; since the image, never given any sexual parts, must be incapable of sexual commerce.

It followed that "Mother" could bear small recognizable relationship to the mortal Kay Maitland. Mother was never the virgin bride who abided, probably more or less nerve-wracked, a first knowing of her by man at Niagara Falls; nor the beginning housewife for whom the bedtime prelude to the night's rest had been more or less routine. Neither could she, in any fully grasped way, be that Mrs. Maitland in the minds of most of the other mourners, the energetic, well-regarded committee and club woman, whose businesses were none of mine, nothing about them really known to me except that she would often spend a long while at the desk in her sitting room; and, some mornings, and many afternoons, she would be out of the house. Still, like or unlike Kay, the image was indubitably dead, just as done-for as the Mrs. Maitland reposing calm and cold, her mortality now proved to the hilt, in the darkness of her closed casket. My consciousness was present to perceive, ready for her to come into being as usual; but she was not coming. The unchangeable had changed; and I must see that henceforth anything could happen to anyone. I could be shown fear in a handful of dust; and fear insinuated itself in the candle glow, in the great sheaves of outsized flowers, in the breathing hush of the full church; and now, the muted organ stilled, in the voice of Doctor Canfield, the rector, sudden and clear, almost ringing; like an alarm sounded: *I am the resurrection and the life . . .*

To steady myself I looked at my father, who looked straight ahead, expressionless. Our pew was full; for down the aisle after us had come relatives of ours. I let myself glance sidelong at them. The distraction could do little to restore any sense of reality; for never, I numbly thought, had I seen six odder-assorted human beings. Beside me was my Aunt Dorothy, my father's sister. She was a big muscular woman, buxom rather than fat. Her large face was quite handsome; but disconcertingly it bore on its upper lip distinct faint hairs of a mustache. Her husband, my Uncle George Adsitt, was a clergyman. Both his frame and his face were angular. His forehead, because of his near total baldness, appeared inordinately high. The clerical clothes he was wearing, while not exactly shabby, looked somewhat unkempt, as though indeed he took no thought for raiment; and his clerical collar seemed a size too big for his almost scrawny neck.

Beyond Uncle George, I could see my Aunt Sarah, a small dark, prim-looking yet pleasant-faced woman, tidily well-dressed; and next to her, her husband, my Uncle Dwight Brownell, my mother's brother. Uncle Dwight was a very short man, only an inch or so over five feet; and you couldn't but wonder if Aunt Sarah's being smaller still, an inch or so shorter, might not have had much to do with his courting, and (a kind of wedding of General Tom Thumb) marrying her. I suppose Uncle Dwight's private awareness that, to most men, he was a little fellow brought him to make up (and more than make up) for unimpressive stature by a stiff consequential manner, severely careful dress, and an incisive way of speaking. His usual expression was one of chilly disdain, which was perhaps the expression expected of a banker whose bank was a Boston bank. Right then, that expression was at its chilliest, seeming to say that Uncle Dwight neither knew nor wished to know the Maitland cousins of ours who completed the line.

Cousin Eben, at the end, must arrest any eye. He was tall with broad powerful shoulders; and, seen past little Uncle Dwight, he looked like a giant. He was, I can now realize, what would be meant by the term "strikingly handsome"; but at the time I think I hardly realized this, for Cousin Eben wore a full beard and that was all I could seem to see. In those days, many men, including my father, wore mustaches; but beards had become uncommon, almost the embarrassing eccentricity they are today. The one or two beards I could bring to mind were white; the wearers of them, old men. Cousin Eben's beard was black, of vigorously thick, curly growth. Quite as startling to me were Cousin Eben's clothes. His coat of excellent black cloth was a so-called Prince Albert, a garment then seen as seldom as a beard; and on the pew seat beside him he had placed a glossy high silk hat. That these articles of apparel were rare and strange, that their effect was what might be called rich, wasn't, I knew, just my idea; for when Cousin Eben had appeared in them, Uncle Dwight's brief disapprobatory stare said as well as words could: *Not* in good taste. By a tight pinched look around Uncle Dwight's nose, I could tell he was even now pronouncing a similar wordless opinion about the (to me) delicious whiff of violets that I detected accompanying everywhere Cousin Eben's wife, next to Uncle Dwight.

I had been told to call her Cousin Lois. She had fine, very fair blond hair; and fine, very fair skin. Her figure was slender; the word for it might have been: willowy; and she was of medium height—that is, taller than Uncle Dwight; though her head did not come above Cousin Eben's shoulder. About her features was something a little doll-like. Her well-placed eyes were deep blue with long eyelashes, which, like her arched eyebrows, were a shade or two darker than her fair hair. Her nicely made nose was rather snub; her lips were wide and somewhat pouted. Though I did not then realize it, supposing them naturally warm-colored, they were without doubt rouged. This, like her perfume (at that time ladies were not supposed to scent themselves so you noticed), would of course be held exceptionable, not only by Uncle Dwight; but by almost everybody. You might grant that she was quite pretty; but could she be quite "nice"?

I wasn't accustomed to consider whether or not adult women — my mother's friends, for instance; or the wives of masters at school — were pretty. Grown-up women just looked like grown-up women to me. In the same way, I ordinarily paid little attention to clothes women wore. In the case of Cousin Lois, I probably noticed only because I saw my aunts noticing; and whatever they might think of her rouge and scent, a certain reluctant respect in their faces let me see that they were impressed by Cousin Lois's clothes; that her coat of black Persian lamb was not merely unexceptionable, but quite beyond criticism; that it must have come from a good shop and cost a lot; and that neither Aunt Dorothy nor Aunt Sarah would mind having one like it. The crowded church was warm; and Cousin Eben had soon helped Cousin Lois out of her splendid coat. It lay now at the end of the pew next to his shining black hat. My look down the line had been sidelong, even furtive, meant not to be noticed; the hat and luxurious folds of the coat detained me. I let myself study them, while, absently, I pondered mysteries that seemed to surround perfumed Cousin Lois and bearded Cousin Eben.

*

The first of the relatives to arrive had been Aunt Dorothy; and from the moment of her arrival she took charge. The church of which Uncle George was rector was in suburban Philadelphia; so, receiving my father's wire about nine o'clock Sunday morning — my father had waited until what seemed a reasonable hour to send his wires — Aunt Dorothy was able to be, and was, in New

York even before I got there. No arrangement for someone to take Uncle George's Sunday service could be made on such short notice; but both he and Aunt Dorothy must have felt my father ought not to be alone. Their decision that Aunt Dorothy would leave at once, with Uncle George to follow Monday, may have been the measure of the real shock they'd had. None of the immediate family, now to be informed at a "reasonable" hour, would have heard anything about my mother's slight indisposition. They could have no reason to think she wasn't (as, not a week earlier, in fact she was) perfectly well. I happened to see the wire to Aunt Dorothy. In what must have been the moment's distraction, she tucked it into her pocketbook and brought it up with her. No doubt each of the wires was the same; and of those to whom it came, not one could have been prepared, the envelope opened, the form unfolded, to read: FOLLOWING EMERGENCY SURGERY KATHERINE PASSED AWAY 1:15 AM CHARLES.

Aunt Dorothy was with my father at the station to meet my train. When I saw him and a woman standing together in the small waiting group as I came out the gate into the concourse at Grand Central, I thought for a moment the man, though looking so much like him, couldn't be my father. The next moment, I recognized Aunt Dorothy; and a moment after that, the explanation, the certain truth was clear to me. I put my suitcase down; but before I could speak, Aunt Dorothy had her arm around me, kissed me; and then without pause, turned me about, walking me off. My father was left standing by the suitcase.

Being Sunday afternoon, there were few people in the concourse. Once away from the gate, and the straggle of passengers leaving the train I had come in on, we seemed quite alone, crossing the great expanse of polished paving under the vault's immense arches. Ordinarily I would have disliked my aunt's arm around me, uncomfortable in the idea that I was made to look like a little boy; but, as I say, I knew already what I was to hear, and the knowledge filled me with a sensation half stunned, half like falling through space. The pressure of an arm was helpful, was steadying.

My aunt said: "Dicky—" Most people called me Dick and even

in my shaken state I found myself taken aback (a beginning, a first swelling, of that wave of the unreal) by the notion that somebody else, not I, must be being spoken to.

With a feeling of standing at a distance, my voice sounding remote to me, seeming indeed to come from somebody else, I said: "Mother's dead."

I don't know how Aunt Dorothy had planned to break the news; but I think she was in turn taken aback. She said: "Dicky darling, I didn't want your father to have to tell you. I suppose you knew the minute you saw us?"

That somebody-else-speaking-for-me considered the question an instant. Sounding as though this were important, a vital point, he surprised me by saying: "No. Well, not the first thing. But then I knew."

My aunt said: "We're going to be very brave, aren't we, Dicky? I don't want your father—do you want to ask any questions?"

"No," I said.

She said: "It's that we mustn't make things harder for each other, must we?" She paused, squeezing me gently. "It's all right to cry if you want to," she said. "People won't see." She looked to the empty passage arch by the Vanderbilt Avenue stairs. "Shall we walk over there?"

I shook my head.

"Good," she said. "Dicky, you *are* being a brave boy." She turned me about, while, with a handkerchief clenched in her gloved hand, she dabbed her own eyes.

My father stood beside the suitcase, perhaps fifty yards from us. By some freak of chance, his straight and silent figure had become, for that moment, the only one in sight. Under the sky-high vaults, the whole pavement lay vacant; on the great stone expanse, no other human being passed or stood. A qualm, like fear's, stabbed me; as though my aunt and I were travelers in an antique land who now descried, across the lone and level sands (nothing beside remains), one solitary last inhabitant, unmoving as a rock.

My aunt said: "We'll get your bag. We'll take the subway to the ferry."

My father's practice, private patients he saw, apart from institutional work, was carried on in offices in a building full of medical men in Manhattan; but our home was in West New Brighton, on Staten Island.

*

Indefatigable, Aunt Dorothy continued during the next days competently and kindly to manage everything. Having the funeral Wednesday, as soon as possible, was her suggestion. What day to set presented a problem of some delicacy. A number of years earlier, my mother's parents, my Brownell grandparents, had retired to Arizona because of my grandfather's health. To come east in those days required most of a week. The long trip would be difficult, not good for old Mr. Brownell, and expensive. Aunt Dorothy said: "I know they aren't too well off. Kay told me their income was from the same trust hers came from; and she had a larger share. Of course, paying their expenses would be nothing to Dwight; but you know how close he is. If we gave them time to come, they might feel they had to."

As a simple acceptable way to explain their not being given time, Aunt Dorothy made adept use of me. She drafted a long night letter for my father to sign in which it was said that I must be sent back to school without delay. At school, I would be kept busy, too busy to feel my mother's loss the way I would if I were idle at home for a week. Moreover, my mother would have wished this. I must not miss more classes, get further behind in my work. The point, I think, was good; for my mother often said if I wanted to make her truly happy I had only to study harder, get better marks. Her wishes, if she still had wishes, wouldn't have changed. And, of course, Dwight and Sarah would be at the funeral.

As the case usually was with arrangements Aunt Dorothy made, all went as planned. My grandparents gave no sign of feeling hurt and contented themselves with telegraphing to have a large floral piece delivered at the church. My grandmother wrote me an affectionately phrased letter of several pages in which I was assured I hadn't actually lost my mother; she would be watching

over me always in spirit; and that Grandmother and Gra.
knew I would never disappoint her by failing to be good or to stud,
hard.

One of the tasks Aunt Dorothy set herself was keeping track of
the many letters and telegrams that should later be acknowledged.
She received them as they came and opened them, noting the
addresses of the senders. My father and I were given them to read;
but most of the names didn't mean anything to me; and comment
by my father and Aunt Dorothy on people I never heard of and
circumstances I knew nothing about was not only uninteresting but
in a curious small way irksome, somehow making me feel left out,
disregarded. Thus, while Aunt Dorothy was opening more telegrams which a boy had delivered as we were having breakfast
Tuesday, I paid no attention. Emma, our maid, had just brought me
scrambled eggs, and I was making myself busy eating them when
Aunt Dorothy, her voice lifted in surprise, said: "Well, of all
things! Cousin Eben."

She looked at the telegram again. "Charles, what do you think
of that? He and his wife are coming to the funeral. How on earth
did they hear?"

"They must have seen it in the papers," my father said. He
emptied his coffee cup. "Well, perhaps we'd better plan to put
them up. It wouldn't be easy for them to get back the same day."

To my Uncle George, who was also eating scrambled eggs,
chewing them solemnly and thoroughly, Aunt Dorothy said:
"Cousin Eben's our Aunt Margaret's son, if you remember about
that. Personally, I always thought it was extremely romantic of
her. I think she was the only really beautiful Maitland woman there
ever was."

"Indeed?" my Uncle George said. After a moment's thought, he
added: "I suppose that fellow's dead?"

"Yes," my father said, "but it was quite recent. He lived to be a
good deal over ninety. The community, in any active form, died
out years ago. I suppose there may be a few of the older people still
around. There was a good deal of money, I think." He smiled.
"Including, you might say, some of Aunt Margaret's."

Though my curiosity was no more than idle, it checked those faintly resentful feelings of mine enough for me to say: "Who's she?"

My Aunt Dorothy said: "A great-aunt of yours, Dicky. She left home to join a religious sect. Her parents tried to stop her; but she went on what I guess you'd call a hunger strike—"

"Like suffragettes?" I said.

"Yes; like the English ones. So they had to let her go. I still think it was very romantic."

"I'd hardly call it that," my father said. "Compulsive behavior. Influence exerted on her. Plainly she wasn't a free agent. Explosions of religious fervor of the kind aren't uncommon. Theophilus Pell would make quite an interesting study in the aberrational."

"Well, anyway; I think their deciding to come is extraordinary. I thought nobody ever saw or heard anything of them."

My father said: "As a matter of fact, I had a letter from Eben last year. He'd read a piece of mine on mentally retarded children. He thought I might be interested in coming to Mount Zion and seeing the work he and Edward Boyd were doing at their school."

Aunt Dorothy said: "You went?"

"No," my father said. "That wasn't possible at the time. But I answered the letter."

"Well, then perhaps this isn't so surprising. What can you do for mentally retarded children?"

By this time, feeling left out again, I was sorry that I had spoken; but my father said promptly and with some earnestness: "That depends on the child. Just what his mental capacity is. If he tests in the high moronic range, you can train him, if you're patient. Habits of behavior would be the thing to work on. The basic condition wouldn't be affected; but a child could be brought in standards of performance to appear and act much like any normal child. At least, that's what I'd try for. That's what I said in the piece."

Aunt Dorothy said: "Who is this Edward Boyd?"

"Another of Pell's sons," my father said. "He's called doctor; and I believe he does have a degree of sorts from some mental-therapy institute in Vienna. The Medical Association doesn't recognize it."

Aunt Dorothy said: "Oh, I begin to see."

Uncle George said: "And what do you see, my dear?"

"Their coming to the funeral's an attention that couldn't exactly offend Charles. I'd say Cousin Eben wants something."

"Well, unless it's my professional opinion, I haven't anything," my father said. "The other of the twin beds can be brought down to Dick's room. When that was a guest room, they were both there. Dick can sleep in the dressing room."

Aunt Dorothy said: "Yes. That would take care of beds. I must check sheets and pillowcases." She scribbled a note on the pad where she was listing things to be done. "Dicky won't mind using the cot; will you, dear?"

"I don't mind," I said, recovering. This particular strangeness of difference — the house full of people — I found for some reason, instead of disturbing, agreeably stimulating. Having to move out of my room seemed to make me party to important goings-on.

Aunt Dorothy opened another telegram. With a blink of perplexity, she said: "It's signed Mary Lutz. Now, who in the world — oh, good heavens!" She laughed. "Of course. Really, after all these years! She was supposed to be a countess. She chaperoned the tour that summer Kay and I went to Europe." My aunt smiled. "We almost drove her to distraction. We were always getting away from the others — that was the most fun; and she was always telling us we mustn't."

Faced with more of that reminiscence to me so meaningless, I finished my breakfast quickly and asked to be excused. I couldn't be said to have learned much about the "Cousin Eben" who (with wife) was ousting me from my room; and the fact that I wasn't interested perhaps indicated the stage of my mind's development. Younger, I think I might have felt the need to ask all kinds of other questions. Older, I might have wanted to get this newly discovered relationship straight; for instance, to find out why, if these cousins lived near enough to attend the funeral, I hadn't ever heard of them. At its stage of the moment, my mind must have been occupied almost entirely with its subjective growing experience — that is, with itself. It was insensible to what, earlier or later, might be the arresting challenge of stories half told, of extraordi-

nary circumstances left quite unexplained. Pressures of momen-
tary business now left no time for abstractions of the unseen and
the unknown. I had never met Cousin Eben, so the name called up
no picture. He was simply unreal to me; just as the formless and
faceless "Mary Lutz," supposed to be a countess, was; and just as
were those unimaginable college girls, Dorothy Maitland and
Katherine Brownell, whose mischievous though no doubt always
proper maidenhood my aunt paused to view in fond recollection.

Moving off in the hall, I heard Aunt Dorothy say: "About *them,*
Charles. Just one thing. Will Dwight Brownell like it? I mean;
having them here when he and Sarah are here?"

My father answered: "To tell you the truth, Dot, I don't feel
obliged to submit such matters to Dwight for his approval."

My Uncle George said gravely: "And a very proper feeling, if I
understand what Dorothy means. Censoriousness would be most
uncharitable."

My interest was so limited I may not even have realized who
was meant by "them." It was only the next day that these remarks,
coming back to me, assumed significance.

*

Uncle Dwight and Aunt Sarah had taken the Tuesday-night
train from Boston and reached our house Wednesday morning a
little before ten o'clock. Cousin Eben and Cousin Lois hadn't
come yet; but soon after the Brownells arrived my father must
have mentioned that they were coming. I didn't hear whatever was
said; for I had been sent over to the rectory on Davis Avenue with
some message for Doctor Canfield. He kept me a long time,
evidently thinking the moment a good one to exhort me (using
terms suited to my fifteen-year-old intelligence) in the faith. Since I
had decided as much as a year before that there was no God, an
awkward moment came when he suggested that we kneel together
in his study and say a silent prayer; but I made haste to comply.
After a while Doctor Canfield spoke, reciting with earnestness:
From henceforth blessed are the dead that die in the Lord,
and so on. He arose with difficulty from what I realize now were
his arthritic knees, allowing me to arise too, and go.

I got home about half past eleven. Coming in the back way, I was approaching the open library door when I heard Uncle Dwight's voice. I suppose he had only then found a chance to speak to Aunt Sarah alone. His tone was guarded; but his habit of precise articulation made his words carry. Any show of open, heated anger would no doubt have been beneath his dignity; so his voice was calm enough, but the words came with controlled incensement, biting. He was saying: "Sarah, do you understand who he is? He's the child of that Maitland woman. I marvel at his impudence in showing his face. And for Charles deliberately to ask them to stay in what was Katherine's home I consider nothing short of outrageous. 'Cousin Eben,' indeed!"

My Aunt Sarah answered no less calmly; but an acerb note suggested that from time to time she found Uncle Dwight trying. She said: "As far as I know, the son of one's aunt is bound to be one's cousin. I don't see it as any concern of ours. I'll ask you, as a favor to me, to make no difficulties."

*

While I now pondered these exchanges, wishing I had paid more attention at the breakfast table yesterday, thinking of my Uncle George's reference to charitableness and my Uncle Dwight's marveling at impudence, the rector's voice, hypnotic, continued to fill my ears with loud somber Elizabethan English. The candle glow and flower scent of the warm church bemused me. As a result, I was slow to notice that my absent stare had been seen by Cousin Eben. The high head was turned enough to let him look at me directly.

Surprised like this, I felt a jolt of alarm. Abashment moved me to look away at once; yet when I tried to, I found I couldn't. Cousin Eben's eyes, dark and large, seemed to act on my own eyes with a holding power, an actual magnetic pull of attraction; and all at once I was made aware that, deep in the black beard's luxuriant bush, a smile, grave and sympathetic, had formed. I got a second jolt. Was this a time or place to smile?

Doctor Canfield proclaimed, his intonation liturgical: *For I am a stranger with thee, and a sojourner; as all my fathers were. . . .*

The cadenced solemn syllables somehow added to the compulsion
of Cousin Eben's gaze. The developed effect came like a calming
touch of hand. All my agitations were, in an instant, eased; I
breathed in grateful, quieted relief; while I was obliged, even as I
was enabled, to answer Cousin Eben's smile.

I distinctly remember one more moment of my mother's funeral.
At a point prearranged by Doctor Canfield as convenient or
appropriate, the prayer book's order of service was interrupted.
Among my mother's college friends was a woman who had become
an opera singer. I forget her name. She was then a minor contralto
at the Metropolitan. She was seated in the chancel, wearing a
square black choir cap. At a nod from the organist, she arose to
sing the hymn: *The strife is o'er: the battle done.*

Breaking suddenly out, surging to tower over the low organ
accompaniment, the power of that professional voice fairly stag-
gered me. Sung full-throated, full-lunged, the triple alleluia coming
after the last verse seemed to set the very fabric of the stone
church trembling. However, on that thunderous last note of
singing, and on the instant of deep silence that followed, my
recollection fails. I can't remember the service ending; nor my
mother's casket being removed; nor our leaving the church.

*

There are psychologists who contend that such memory lapses,
far from being adventitious or reasonless, are calculated devices of
the mind. (My father did not agree. He professed to doubt the
existence of any such entity as "mind." The term was nothing but a
hypothetical assumption, he said.) Those who so contend argue
that the conscious personality has needs, secret or not statable,
that must be met; or feelings that must be protected. I can only say
the theory would do much to explain my retained memories of that
Monday, Tuesday and Wednesday I spent at home—episodic
scenes abruptly begun and suddenly interrupted; the next picture
presented after an interval, like the lantern slides of a lecturer of
those days. Intimations that disquieted me, implications of strangeness, frightening or painful, might be seen as the setting of distress

signals that did not go unanswered. Why the scene in church was cut where I find it cut would become plain.

Monday or Tuesday, I forget (significantly again?) just how, I had a chance to look at my mother's will. Probably my father, having taken it from a safe-deposit box, left it lying on the desk in the library. My mother's will and my father's had been drawn at the same time, some years before. Both were unusually comprehensive and long. This might suggest large affairs or complicated estates; which was not the case. The documents were one of the first professional jobs of a young lawyer. Just admitted to the bar, he paraded innocently his law learning. He was impressing on you the importance of utilizing in these matters the foresight and sagacity of a trained legal mind. The lawyer was my father's younger brother, Theodore; and this demonstrated capacity for taking pains perhaps gave promise of a distinguished career. Unfortunately, toward the end of September 1918, he was gassed in the Argonne forest, and died of it.

The young lawyer's handiwork survived him. Among many and specific detailed provisions in my mother's will appeared a direction that her body be cremated. On this subject my father held vigorous views. Embalming corpses, dressing them in finery, boxing them up expensively and then arranging them in cemeteries under monuments as pretentious as the means of the survivors allowed, was to his mind irrational. He would at least see such absurdities weren't practiced on him. In his case, a special provision had to be made, because he was one of a group of members of the American Neurological Association who had joined in an agreement to leave their brains to Harvard Medical School. His brain, then, was to be removed and duly forwarded; the rest of him was to be incinerated.

Jotting a note, for later translation into legal language, my young Uncle Theodore may have said: "How about you, Kay?"

I doubt if my mother gave serious thought to an event that could occur only in the distant future. It would have been like her to make a small joke about nobody wanting *her* brain; and to add, laughing: "Yes; why not? I'll be cremated too."

Given my father's regard for the rational, and my mother's cheerful disregard of far-off morbid matters, the decision would be emotionless. Settled in a moment, the grown-up mind dismissed it. Though, as I've said, I saw myself at fifteen as pretty well grown up — if, admittedly not an adult; at least, not a little boy — the thinking of fifteen has seldom wholly discarded concepts natural to every child; among them, the pathetic fallacy. A moldering in a well-made grave was one thing. The vacated body, sleeping the sabbath of the tomb's sleep, might never feel its gentle, gradual dissolution. But could it, could any flesh, rest in the furnace of fire; not know the flames raged? With the funeral soon to end, I had to consider where the casket under the flowers was to be taken. On the conscious level I could do and say nothing; since on that level I couldn't so much as know what lively horror hid in me; but if nothing could be done *by* me, something could notwithstanding be done *for* me. The subconscious, sick with its own fear, holding its own arbitrary ideas of "protection," made accustomed moves. I would later find that, as far as I was able to remember, the funeral had no end.

*

Remembered by me or not, the end of the funeral must have come shortly after four o'clock. Neighbors of ours named Parmelee, who lived in a big house, had undertaken to offer tea to those mourners known as "close personal friends of the family." There were a lot of them. Despite the size of the house, I found myself in a continuing press of people; though with the difference that, instead of being formed in silent ranks, everybody now moved around and talked. A blurred picture results; perhaps because of repeated flushes of embarrassment I can recall. A number of my elders, to whom I suppose I looked forlorn and confused, decided they ought to say something to me; and did. Under any circumstances I would hardly have known what to answer; but, as it happened, I had developed for myself a new disquiet; and it was one that proffers of sympathy or comfort could only intensify.

Boys who suffer the tragic, the sudden, the surely desolating loss of beloved mothers must, by terms of definition, be inconsolable. That they should look and be confused and forlorn is only right. Those fears, those startings, those puzzled bodings of mine had done a good job in bringing me moments of desolation that might equal grief. My occasion of disquiet was that, even in those moments, an uneasy awareness was growing that if I didn't concentrate on feeling sorrow I might, in appalling fact, forget to feel it. That first shock of props knocked out, that falling and falling while I walked with Aunt Dorothy at the station, must in the nature of things, being severe, be short. I don't know just how soon, yet presently, my mind picked itself up; slow and fearful, felt itself over. The impossible truth (*ten masts at each make not the altitude*) became indubitable truth. Nothing was broken. I spoke. I stood. I was sound.

Here in the Parmelees' house I surveyed the dressed-up yet everyday people thronging the big rooms of the downstairs floor. In polite circulation, they grouped to speak together in sober yet ordinary voices. The tea from the cup I held tasted in my mouth as tea always tasted. I was conscious of wanting to go to the bathroom; but not in any way that couldn't wait until we left and went home. The Parmelees had made lavish provision for their company. Dozens of silver plates, platters and bowls heaped with good things to eat were arrayed under the light of pink-shaded silver candlesticks on the heavy damask cloth that covered a very long oval dining-room table. There was no doubt about the fact that my mouth watered.

But can the inconsolable be hungry? Can things to eat look good to them? Don't they have to be coaxed to eat? Cousin Lois's fair hair and fair skin breathed their scent of violets. Her china-blue eyes softened in concern to see me with nothing but a cup of tea. She said I must eat. She put a hand on my arm and moved me to join the guests around the table who were helping themselves and each other to this or that. Self-conscious, only too aware of that good appetite I ought not to have, I let Cousin Lois select my food. I had hardly accepted the well-filled plate when I saw with consternation that our hostess, Mrs. Parmelee (did she think I was making a pig of myself?), was looking with sharp attention from a smaller table where she and another woman were pouring the tea. Of course, what everyone looked at was Cousin Lois; but since she stayed beside me to see I did eat, those who looked couldn't help seeing me too. Hungry though I was, I had almost as much trouble swallowing as, guiltily, I felt I should. I was glad when my Uncle George came up. No doubt he had Cousin Lois's idea; for, noting my plate, he said: "Good. Good—" To have a clergyman in clericals beside me seemed to make forking up the food less reprehensible so I soon emptied my plate. Uncle George then told me that, if I'd finished, my father wanted to speak to me.

My father was with Uncle Dwight and Aunt Sarah. I learned that I was to go over to our house with Uncle Dwight and show him where the telephone was. (The telephone was in a closet under the front stairs, with a light you could put on.)

My Uncle Dwight was saying: "I said that if it were in any way possible I would call around five o'clock. We appreciate very much your readiness to have us stay over, Charles; but there are matters pending which I can't leave to anyone else; so it may be necessary for us to take tonight's train. . . ."

I got my coat and Uncle Dwight got his hat and coat; and my father said I needn't go to thank Mrs. Parmelee, he would thank her for me. Uncle Dwight and I came out together on the extensive veranda which ran most of the way around the house. It was clear, quite cold, and almost dark. Through big bare branches of trees along the street, a full moon, low, large and pale, could be seen. After some moments of silence while our heels hit sharp together on the flagstone sidewalk, Uncle Dwight cleared his throat and said: "When do you go back to school, Richard?"

I said: "Tomorrow, sir."

Though I took this for the kind of "made" conversation that older people were apt to engage me in, I think it wasn't impossible that Uncle Dwight, a methodical man, meant to check on my father's story about why the funeral had been held with so little delay.

Uncle Dwight said: "Do you like it there?"

I said: "Yes, sir."

He said: "Your mother was a wonderful woman. Of course you know that. I hope remembering her will always help you—" His precise voice seemed to fail; at loss, for once, for words; and one of those unexpected intimations of mine came to me. Uncle Dwight, who seemed so determinedly detached from everything, had been, perhaps in a carry-over of some youthful feeling, silently and you could be sure undemonstratively attached to his sister. He said: "Er—that is; you'll live the kind of life, be the kind of man, she'd have wanted you to be—would have been proud of. You'll try, won't you?"

I said: "Yes, sir."

At our house, Emma, the maid, had lights on. I showed Uncle Dwight the telephone; and went upstairs to the bathroom.

*

I hardly need say that developments in Boston *had* developed to call Uncle Dwight back at once. My father and the others were home before he finished getting a connection, and talking. He came out to announce his news to us with a frown. In fact, he would be bound to find flimflammery of this kind not at all to his liking. His pride or, if you wished, self-regard, which made him so much of a prig, would also make repellent anything that amounted to deceit. Moreover, there was some risk of this particular deceit's being read to mean his position was somehow subordinate, that he had to come when called, that he saw people at their convenience, not (as was, I'm sure, the actual case) only at his own. Still, he probably thought that risk worth running; and since bankers are supposed to be reticent about the affairs of their business, absence of further explanation was only to be expected. My father got a taxi to take him and Aunt Sarah to the ferry; and formal regrets were expressed all around. Uncle Dwight went so far as to give Cousin Eben his hand to shake. My Aunt Sarah's expression, even while kissing me good-by, was tight-lipped; which may have meant Uncle Dwight was going to hear from her about making "difficulties" as soon as the cab door closed.

With Uncle Dwight and Aunt Sarah out of the house, everyone

seemed easier; and I might then have observed (though I don't think I did) that I wasn't alone in the seeming want of feeling which, even on a funeral day, forgets to remember the dead. Thus the evening progressed, not with sad looks and mournful silences, but with constant talk while we waited for supper — which was to be late because of the tea at the Parmelees' — and while we ate. Bereaved though he might be, my father showed himself capable of taking a definite interest in this school of Cousin Eben's; and Cousin Eben seemed gratified by the chance to talk about it. Uncle George, presumably because he was in the religion business himself, seemed interested in getting some firsthand facts about that extinct community whose buildings the school used, about that "sect" which "Aunt Margaret" had been, my Aunt Dorothy thought, so romantic in joining.

Aunt Dorothy, on the other hand, plainly felt the curiosity, in women often consuming, which goes to personalities, to named people, to the stuff of gossip. What she wanted to know was a lot more about Cousin Eben and Cousin Lois, about their children, about their home and their way of life. Particulars of the organization and work of the Boyd School for Exceptional Children couldn't be to her purpose; and neither were Uncle George's restrained inquiries into the doctrine and discipline of the disciples of that Theophilus Pell who, according to my father, might make an interesting study in aberration. When she could, without seeming too openly to ignore the men, Aunt Dorothy applied herself to Cousin Lois on those matters of so much greater interest.

I was again largely left out; but now I wasn't discontented in the way I had been when the letters and telegrams were opened. At the time, most young people were still being taught to be seen, not heard; and to speak only when spoken to. Free to listen or not listen as I chose, I even learned a few things of moderate interest. For instance, from what my father had said, it was plain to me that an "exceptional child" was no more nor less than a child I would have bluntly termed a half-wit. At present, Cousin Eben told my father, they had forty-three of them; and the idea of an all-half-wit school seemed to me fantastic — though not in that way that caused me consternation; just in a comfortable funny way.

I then learned that twelve of the half-wits were girls; and Cousin Eben went into this at length. He explained to my father, who kept nodding, that they were part of what he, half laughing, called the "therapy." The school worked on habits of behavior. (My father, I remembered, had suggested something of the kind to Aunt Dorothy; so I could see why he was nodding.) The girls were most useful. Half laughing again, Cousin Eben said they were for the boys to be polite to. These children, just as my father's *Journal of Abnormal Psychology* article proposed, were apt to prove even more suggestible than normal children. Here the suggestion, through fairly formal etiquette, was that the girls were ladies. Along with the effect on the boys, there was of course a complementing effect on the girls; the effective suggestion that they must *act* like ladies. The girls had a building of their own in charge of "Martha." (I was indebted to Aunt Dorothy's interest for the information that this was Martha Jay, Mrs. Jay; a sister of "Edward.") Several afternoons a week the girls were at home to the boys, who came to tea as guests. Callous, my imagination presented me with a picture, hilariously funny, of the idiot boys bowing and scraping, the idiot girls with grimace and chatter playing lady and pouring tea. I managed not to laugh out loud; but, barely.

Meanwhile (though, as indicated, keeping track of what the men were saying) Aunt Dorothy was learning a few things on her own. Cousin Lois said they had three children; a boy, named Victor; and two girls, named Jessica and Muriel.

"Victor's fifteen," she said. Seeing that I was listening, she gave me a friendly side glance and said: "Just your age, Dick."

Aunt Dorothy said: "How old are the girls?"

Cousin Lois said: "Jessica's fourteen; and Muriel's thirteen."

Though ready and simple enough, the answer certainly took me aback. Her tone showed that Cousin Lois saw nothing out of the way in this; but what I saw was that Cousin Lois and Cousin Eben when first married had so conducted themselves that three children were generated in three years. I quite realized that I, an only child, would be and was an exception in these matters; but, going by the families of my friends, or my parents' friends, production at a rate like that was absolutely unheard-of. As far as I knew, it could only happen among the very poor and very ignorant, who night be expected to do vulgar and indecent things as a matter of course.

In this embarrassment I quickly shifted my attention to Cousin Eben, who was saying to my Uncle George: "Our Joseph's unusual in some ways. For one thing, he's a Turk. The story's curious. For a short time in the eighteen-eighties the Mount Zion conventicle sent missionaries abroad. Some of the Brethren would get what was called a Direction. I don't think Father really approved; but there'd been the split with Noyes, and the exodus, as they said, from Oneida; and Father may have thought that if he didn't want another split he'd better countenance it, at least for the moment. At any rate, those who went out went in pairs, a man and a woman. The Direction of one pair was to Phrygia—the geography was always biblical. Of course, proselytizing among Moslems was never the safest thing in the world. That may have been an incentive—a supposed possibility of martyrdom."

Uncle George looked uncomfortable. His cloth was token of distinctively Anglican tolerance; or better, absence of bigotry; which comes not so much from any broad-mindedness in admitting there may be more truths than one, as from regard for manners. While not scrupling to state or show (time and place being appropriate) his own beliefs, no gentleman argues about them; and he really can't urge them on others. Uncle George might also be thinking that here, in this man and woman with their persuasion that God directed them to convert the Turk, was all too typical an example of what followed departures, whether papist or evangelical, from the Episcopal Church's faith and order.

This view I shared. Though it was true that I had recently constituted myself atheist, I could still feel that good form in religion mattered. Surely you did not have to have "conventicles" and call yourselves Brethren. You did not have to get Directions to go to Phrygia; or to split with whoever Noyes was; or to undertake exoduses from Oneida, whatever that was. I'd never heard of anything so crazy; which was to say, I knew nothing of the vagaries of religious enthusiasm in an era just past.

American history courses at school had taught me that William Penn was a Quaker. Quakers did not believe in war; but in spite of that, and of some original quaintnesses of speech and dress, they were to be respected for their gentle manners and high principles. I could check this for myself; since I'd known some Quakers, or the children of some; and there wasn't anything wrong with them. Then, a little had been taught me about Mormons. I could identify Joseph Smith and Brigham Young. I knew about the migration to Utah, and of the "practice of polygamy," which my history text assured me had been given up. I knew too that also still extant were certain ludicrous pentacostal sects called Holy Rollers; and that there was a publicity-seeking (and getting) evangelist named Billy Sunday, regarded by all real and proper clergymen (like Uncle George or Doctor Canfield) as a vulgar mountebank whose antics would only be effective with common and uneducated people.

But of Mother Ann Lee and the Shaker communities I had never heard. I had never heard of Perfectionists or Bible Communists; of Brook Farm or the Battle Axe group; of the advent of Swedenborgianism or of the thirty or forty sects of the Baptist schisms; of Fourierism, or of Robert Owen's New Harmony; of Millerites or Rappites; of Zoarites or Ebenesers. Never having heard of John Humphrey Noyes and the Oneida community, it went without saying I would never before have heard of Theophilus Pell, or the Mount Zion Brethren, the Pellites. Now I did hear of him and them, I could in my ignorance suppose them unique in craziness. I'm afraid that, again, I just barely managed not to laugh.

Cousin Eben said: "As a matter of fact, martyrdom was exactly what it may have come to. Things appear to have gone on all right for a while. I suppose, at first, they didn't make many, or even any, converts. Then, amazingly enough, they began to make them. Probably only a few; but enough to stir up popular resentment; because serious rioting broke out in the town where they'd established themselves; and after that nothing was heard of them. Joseph was one of the converts—that is, I imagine what happened was that his parents were converted. He couldn't have been more than sixteen or seventeen. However, he seems to have been no ordinary boy, even then. It was said that three months after he'd heard English for the first time, he was able to speak it, read it, and write it just as if it were his native language. I think this must have been true, or almost true. It would explain why they picked Joseph to go to Mount Zion with some report or message. While he was gone, whatever happened, happened. So Joseph stayed at Mount Zion with Father; never went back."

This was more in Aunt Dorothy's line. She said: "I think I remember Joseph. I think he came to Newport with Mr. Pell once. A stocky dark man. I forget what they came about."

Cousin Eben said: "Yes. That would be Joseph. As long as Father was able to get around, Joseph went everywhere with him. The odd thing is; if you remember Joseph then, you'd know him now. He doesn't change at all. He can't be less than sixty-five—but that's what he still is; a stocky dark man."

My father said: "What they came about was a difficulty over money of Aunt Margaret's—your mother's. The family was making legal efforts to keep Mr. Pell from getting it, claiming coercion, undue influence; though they had no evidence that stood up."

Cousin Eben said: "Well, if it was money, Joseph would certainly have been there. He handled all Father's financial affairs— only too well, from the standpoint of Joseph's own advantage; Edward and Martha think. For instance, a lot of money went into a trust. The purpose was to collect, edit, and finally publish a history of the Brethren, running into a good many volumes. Joseph began working on it even before Father's death. The trust of course pays the expenses; so, as trustee, Joseph in effect pays himself. Not that anyone suggests he wasn't and isn't perfectly honest; or that the arrangements didn't reflect Father's wishes, weren't arrangements Father wanted. But Edward's probably right about Joseph's influence being what made Father want them. He feels, and I'm afraid I feel myself, that the work's a great waste of money."

Among things I then took little interest in were money matters, "financial affairs." They must have interested Aunt Dorothy however; for she was all attention, her conversation with Cousin Lois suspended. This meant Cousin Lois was now left out too. Her evident natural amiability made her give me a smile. She set herself to talk to me. At one point she asked me what sports I liked. When I told her I liked swimming, she said with warmth: "Oh, you must come to Mount Zion next summer, Dick. There's a wonderful beach. The children would love having you."

Mention of the children, forcing me to remember the unseemly rate of their production, fussed me again; but Cousin Lois may have thought my constraint, if she noticed it, was simple shyness. Gently animated, she went on about the children. It seemed that Victor was always collecting sea shells, and had a wonderful collection. The girls, it seemed, liked swimming too; and were wonderful swimmers. Perhaps because I was fussed, I was unthinking. At least, for no reason I can think of, I asked if they went to the Boyd school. Cousin Lois said: "Oh, dear, no! They go to Country Day on the mainland." She explained that Mount Zion was an island, at least at high tide; but there was a causeway you could drive across any time. "We don't see the Boyd school children," she said. "They live in some of what were the conventicle houses. We live in the Great House."

I thought it a queer term to use in speaking of your home. I had been half or more won by Cousin Lois's pleasant manner which seemed to show convincing liking, or, even, regard for me; but everything considered (meaning: my attitude conditioned as usual by concern about what "fellows at school" might think or say), I couldn't see this Mount Zion as the kind of place I'd want to have it known I went to. Next summer I certainly wouldn't be there if I could help it; no matter how much the shell-collecting Victor and those wonderful swimmers (but girls) Jessica and Muriel might love having me.

Meanwhile Cousin Eben, probably answering questions of Uncle George's about that history they spoke of, seemed to be explaining a few historical points. He was saying: "I know, in Father's version, Noyes brought about the break, departing from the faith. Certainly Joseph will write it that way. What seems to have happened is that Noyes let Father know that he had suddenly, as they put it, been taught of God, that stirpiculture and complex marriage — which, of course, made stirpiculture feasible — must be abandoned. Noyes himself had said, or written: 'All things are lawful for me; but all things are not expedient; all things are lawful for me; but all things edify not.' "

Since I saw my private decision on Mount Zion as final, Cousin Lois's continuing cordial account of what they did — they had clambakes; they had sailing parties — and of the good times I could look forward to with Victor and Jessica and Muriel made me awkward. I knew it was not polite of me; but, defensive, I tried, by looks at him, to indicate that I was again listening to Cousin Eben; and, in fact, I began to. I couldn't imagine what "stirpiculture" was; but, seeing this too was a "religion" I was quick to guess that "complex marriage" would be something on the order of that Mormon "practice of polygamy" — a guess that Uncle George's expression, still interested but a little strained, might pretty well confirm.

Cousin Eben said: "Father seems to have felt that what was expedient and what edified kept looking more and more like hard cash — that is, the prosperity of the community; their trade, and so on, was becoming too important. I think what Noyes felt was that public opinion must, after all, be considered, if the community was to continue — in short; nothing was expedient that endangered his Oneida." He laughed. "Perhaps there's some irony there. As things fell out, Mount Zion, which Father and the others set up when they thought Noyes was too much interested in money, took in, through various donations and business transactions, a great deal more money than Oneida ever had. Father was a rich man when he died. Of course, what came to them never belonged to the Brethren — it was always Father's."

Uncle George said: "But the others? Did they disband?"

He was probably noting with some regret that, though he granted the right to a wrong religion when sincerely believed in, a religious leader, said to have been taught of God, who ended up with all the money must seem something of a confidence man.

Cousin Eben said: "Mount Zion was virtually disbanded before nineteen-hundred. When I was a child, a group of the older people were still living the community life. But no more laying on of hands; so, no more Brethren. A sign was given Father that the new generation was unacceptable. Grace was deprived; and without grace, perfectibility was impossible." He smiled. "I know the language. The conventicles at Flemington, New Jersey, where they profitably raised and preserved peaches; and at Barre, Vermont, where they quarried, also profitably, marble, continued for a few years. But they're long gone now. Some of the people who work for us at the school and on the farms are Brethren; but there aren't any religious observances. Except of course that Edward and I don't shave. We had to promise Father we never would."

Uncle George said: "That had to do, I suppose, with the Old Testament prescription?"

Cousin Eben said: "Yes. 'Neither shalt thou mar the corners of thy beard.' But I know Father didn't think of it as just an arbitrary prescription. He was convinced that shaving the beard impaired virility or potency in some way; and that was why the Jews forbade it."

Uncle George was again looking most uncomfortable. There had been the, to him sacrilegious, idea of a Theophilus Pell presuming to lay on hands, and getting signs, blasphemously claimed to be from God. There had been those marital usages at least technically immoral; and now there was this direct reference to the sexual powers, the prowess of the male. Somewhat weakly, he said: "Very interesting indeed."

Given sudden great light on that baffling mystery of Cousin Eben's magnificent beard, I was startled into forgetting I should be seen and not heard. I surprised myself by saying: "But, Cousin Eben, if Mr. Pell was your father, and Mr. Boyd's father, why do you have different names?"

I suppose I surprised everybody else, too. My father said: "Don't interrupt, Dick. You're being impertinent."

Cousin Eben, giving the beard a stroke, said with all good humor: "On the contrary. I think your question's very natural, Dick. That was the custom of the community. They felt a woman had a right to keep her own name, not be just Mrs. So-and-So. Her children, as hers, took her name."

I said: "You mean, like —" I caught myself in time.

Smiling, Cousin Eben said: "Yes. Like bastards. And of course in the law's eyes that's what I am. A bastard."

I was shocked. The word was one of our "dirty" words at school. We used it freely among ourselves; but we knew it was never to be used in the presence of adults; who, if they were people of any breeding, couldn't be imagined using it.

Cousin Lois, rather faint-sounding, said: "Oh, Eben! to say that in front of people . . ."

"Why not speak the truth?" Cousin Eben said with composure. "The Brethren considered their form of wedlock as holy as any other — more so, really; since it didn't involve the sin of selfishness. But, outside the community, the view that children of complex marriage were bastards was certainly the usual one." He smiled. "I don't doubt your relative, Mr. Brownell, for example, is of this opinion."

Aunt Dorothy, speaking with an abruptness and vehemence quite unlike her, said: "He's no relative of *mine*. I always thought him a nasty little man."

By his work my father must long ago have been prepared to have nothing shock him; and to feel little or no surprise at anything anyone said. I could see him, his air reflective, gazing at Cousin Eben with what I recognized even then as professional interest. He might be pondering, in terms of behavior symptoms, the significance of what Cousin Eben had said — why Cousin Eben, "in front of people," wished to assert his bastardy; whether, in fact, Cousin Eben had always felt the hurt of that "truth" he spoke; and so must bluff it out with a smile of unconcern; whether some other emotional need of his was met by, in a small way, shocking people.

Clearing his throat, Uncle George said: "I've never been able to see reason or justice in stigmatizing a child for something with which he himself had nothing whatever to do."

Cousin Lois said: "Eben, will you please not say any more about it?"

"Gladly, my dear," Cousin Eben said. "There's nothing more to say."

*

I had an early train to catch in the morning, so I was sent to bed about ten. I was tired, ready for bed; yet I had trouble getting to sleep. I was in the dressing room; where I had been moved the night before when it was thought we would have a full house; and though the cot set up for me was comfortable enough, it wasn't a bed, or a room, I was accustomed to sleep in.

Moreover, the eventful day had left me with my nerves strung high. The many strong impressions made on me, the swings of feeling that had exercised me, kept my mind tense, making me go over them, anxiously searching through them, reliving, in no order and at random, this or that moment. I knelt reluctant and embarrassed on Doctor Canfield's study rug for our morning prayer; I heard Uncle Dwight's whispers of incensement coming from the library. In the gloom of gothic vaults and stained glass I saw amazed the mass meeting of strangers, the strange people who silently packed the church. Confined by the same stone vaults, that tremendous voice of the singing woman in the chancel burst on my unprepared ears.

Cousin Lois, with crisp of black silk, her person scented, her motions somehow lithe, somehow plastic, somehow pliable, came close to me in the throng at the Parmelees', the china-blue eyes softening with concern while she pressed me to eat good things. Her fair hair shone under the light of our dining room's bead-fringed chandelier while she then pressed me to come, for good times with Victor, Jessica, and Muriel, to the seaside at Mount Zion. I saw Cousin Eben's smile in church, made secret by that full surprising beard in the end to be so surprisingly explained to me. He could not shave it off because he had promised Theophilus Pell (I found the name's fall of syllables queer and haunting), whose *bastard* Cousin Eben smiled to say he was, that he would not. Remembering other things Cousin Eben said, I repictured, with a soundless giggle but more agitated now than amused, what my

imagination had made of those reported tea parties at the Boyd
school for little idiots.

So I was restless; now dozing, now waking to see with a start
squares of bright moonlight on the strange floor. Brought to
realize, dazed, where I was, I lay drowsy in a vague further review,
wondering and uncertain, of these last few astounding days — the
new things I had been told; a confusion of things heard I had never
heard before, of things seen that showed me mysteries and then left
them unresolved; of people and their lives, partly indicated or
outlined for me, but never explained in full and telling me no more
than that the extent of the untold was infinite, a trackless and
boundless tangle of the unseen, the undiscovered, through which I
was going to have to pick a guideless way. I did not know what to
do. Fearful, and trying to think, I would then fall asleep for a while.

When they came up from downstairs, I suppose really not long
after, I happened to be awake. I was seeing that great hazed
early-evening moon behind our street's bare trees while I listened
to Uncle Dwight's neat heels on flagstone and to that stumbling
voice of feeling, so remarkable in his small severe mouth. Though
what he had spoken of was my mother, strangely or not I had no
thoughts of her. All of them must have come up together. I could
hear some exchanges, though not what was said, at the far end of
the hall — Uncle George and Aunt Dorothy going into their room.
The sounds now moved down to this end. I heard my father
saying: "That's your bathroom. Have you everything . . ."

Cousin Lois said: "Oh, Cousin Charles, how I hope you
sleep. . . ."

An electric switch snapped on; the hall door went shut; and,
turning my head, I saw under the dressing room's closed door to
that room, light shining in a thin line.

*

I must have slept again. What wakened me was a voice; and in
my start from sleep, that moment's not knowing where I was, I
couldn't imagine who had spoken. The voice was being kept low,
but a note like that of alarm seemed to sharpen it, letting me hear. I

realized it was a woman speaking; so then I realized it must be Cousin Lois in the next room. She was whispering earnestly: "Eben . . . now; Eben . . ."

I saw the thin line of light still coming under the door. I could hear a murmuring. Then quite clear, Cousin Lois said: "Oh, but just after a funeral . . . someone else's house . . . oh, you must be out of your mind. . . ."

There was extended, renewed murmuring. Cousin Lois interrupted. She said: "But, Lover, I don't have things . . . I . . ."

The perplexity, in part, daze of sleep, with which I heard her first, left me. I was shocked wide awake; while my heart began a slow hammering. I understood what proposition was being put to Cousin Lois; though I could, in fact, hardly believe I heard right. These were grownups; in my eyes, even old people. Why, at home there was that Victor of my age; and two girls, too. Their rapid begetting I couldn't but think indecent; yet it was no more than mild indecency palliated by its having happened so long ago. But what could possibly be thought or said in palliation of present immediate indecency; the indecency, enormous and appalling, of a here and now fresh knowing of Cousin Lois; of a new uncovering of what the Bible called her nakedness that was almost a forcing; of a disregard of time, place, and what was right at their age that required her willy-nilly to lie with him today, tonight?

I pictured Cousin Eben, towering and dignified in the ornate silk hat and old-fashioned coat of fine cloth. I heard his cordial grave voice making conversation, if often extraordinary in substance, in manner ordinary—*our Joseph's unusual in some ways. For one thing, he's a Turk.* . . . That Cousin Eben couldn't, he really couldn't, be imagined as the low murmurer in there, perhaps wearing pajamas, perhaps with no clothes, by whom a lady reluctant, a woman unwilling, was being importuned to permit him to climb on top of her and have them do it together. Then I thought, I had to, of Cousin Lois's fair skin and fair hair, of the lithe motions, the pliable form, the scent of violets. I thought of Cousin Eben's swelling bush of black beard, of that "virility" or "potency" kept unimpaired by the "bastard" of Theophilus Pell. With horror of helplessness I had to feel (. . . *just after a funeral*) the stir, slow but strong, of my own response.

Cousin Lois, a sort of despair in her voice, said: "Oh, it's not right. It couldn't be. . . . Oh, suppose they hear us. . . ."

Cousin Eben's voice, thick in a way that made me tremble; yet for the first time intelligible in its note of question, was saying: "Dear Heart? Dear Heart?"

There was a pause; silence. I heard nothing but the pound of blood in my ears. The pause prolonged itself; and my stirred feeling checked, faltered, in a kind of fright that might presently be terror. Had nonexistent God struck those two dead? I was almost sure God had, when I heard movements resume. There were rustlings of cloth; perhaps garments thrown down; perhaps a counterpane taken off, or pillows shifted. Then came steps, maybe of bare feet; a switch snapped, and the glow under the door was gone. Immediately followed recognizable noises from a bed; sounds I could take to be first, lightly, she; then, heavier, he; lying down together. These bed noises became now continual; faint creakings; steady slight squeaking of springs; and soon an added sound, for an instant unnerving, was heard. It was Cousin Lois again. She had begun a moaning low, but not dolorous; a gentle groaning, but of gratification. To hear her was to know that what was done to her was triumphing over her, reducing her to some extremity where speech failed. Fair-haired, fair-skinned Cousin Lois, now lady unreluctant, now woman willing, could manage only syllables of what seemed to be direction: "Ah, do . . . ah, do . . ."

My first concept of indecency enormous, monstrous; my horror to discover then my own responsiveness; and my succeeding chill of fright while the long pause lasted, were all in some ways still with me. They joined to make me still recoil (like Cousin Lois; but with even more fervency) from any such horrid last-hour profanation of the solemn day. I was held back a little. In despair (like Cousin Lois's) I tried to pray myself forbearance. I willed myself to close my ears and shut my mind. However, I had reason to know such measures, even when taken against no more than unaided mere fancying, seldom availed. They were not going to avail now. Here, from the next room the explicit sounds kept reaching me. Here, listening had been made as good as looking; and, here, the heated mind, looking its fill at perfumed Cousin Lois, laid bare, put down supine, spread-eagled for enjoyment, must press me to enjoy her too.

Shaking all over, all out of breath, I also, in extremis, had to give way; and, to that groaning ah, do, ah, do ditty's quickening accompaniment, proceed with procuring (*O my offence is rank!*) my own undoing. At this stage, I made short work of it. In no time, I had done my sharing in Cousin Lois; and on this fine accomplishment's very heels, in the qualmish expense of spirit, in the grievous waste of shame, I could feel, despairing or not, undone or not, the blessed pall of sleepiness decending. Simple oblivion was ready to comfort me, ready to forgive me my trespasses. All passion spent, the past days' task, the new aquist of true incredible experience, could be seen completed. After fitful fever, that child in me, deceased (like "Mother" the child had known; like the Kay Maitland he had never known), would now sleep well.